THE
CRUSADE

Also by Colin Smith:

Carlos: Portrait of a Terrorist
Cut-out

COLIN SMITH

THE LAST CRUSADE

SINCLAIR-STEVENSON

First published in Great Britain 1991
by Sinclair-Stevenson
an imprint of Reed Consumer Books Ltd
Michelin House, 81 Fulham Road, London SW3 6RB
and Auckland, Melbourne, Singapore and Toronto

This paperback edition published 1994

A CIP catalogue record for this book
is available at the British Library
ISBN 1 85619 475 2

Printed and bound in Great Britain
by Cox & Wyman Ltd, Reading, Berkshire

*F*or Sylvia and in memory of the men of the Warwickshire and Worcestershire Yeomanry regiments who fought in Palestine, especially Private Harry Cromie of Newry. Private Cromie was the last living survivor and probably the only Irishman to take part in the Yeomanry's charge at Huj, which was mainly made by Englishmen from the shires. Also with fond memories of the late Mr Horatio Vester, proprietor of the American Colony Hotel in East Jerusalem, a great raconteur who, as a child, watched the Turks march out of Jerusalem for the last time.

AUTHOR'S NOTE

This is a novel about the British campaign in Palestine in 1917, which ended five hundred years of Turkish occupation and led to the creation of the Jewish state. Readers may be puzzled why a book set in Palestine does not mention the Palestinians as such. This is because, before the collapse of the Ottoman Empire and the initial division of the spoils between Britain and France, most of the Arabic-speaking inhabitants of the territory between the Mediterranean, the Euphrates, the Taurus and the Arabian Desert called themselves Syrians. Thus a popular Victorian hymn refers to the Galilee as 'the Syrian sea'. Some of the historical characters who pass through my story are well known. Others, such as the Aaronsohns, Bertha Vester and Richard Meinertzhagen, usually only make footnotes in the better known chronicles of those times, although their accomplishments and suffering cry out for recognition. I have tried, in word and deed, to be faithful to all of them.

C.S.

'. . . Allenby knew with certainty from his Intelligence of all the preparations and all the movements of his enemy. All the cards of his enemy were revealed to him and so he could play his own hand with complete confidence. Under these conditions victory was certain before we ever began.'

Assessment of Intelligence contribution to General Allenby's victory in Palestine by Lt-General G. G. MacDonough, head of Military Intelligence at the War Office from 1916 to 1919.

'The projected offensive was, for secrecy's sake, to be known by the name "Yilderim" – that is to say, "lightning". In view of the rate at which preparations and moves were normally carried out in Turkey the name was unduly optimistic; nor did it secure secrecy, for the plan came to the knowledge of the Intelligence Services of the Entente at a very early stage.'

Colonel Archibald Wavell MC, from his book The Palestine Campaign.

'Some Iscariotical bastard is betraying us!'

Colonel Kress von Kressenstein, commander of the Turkish Eighth Army Corps.

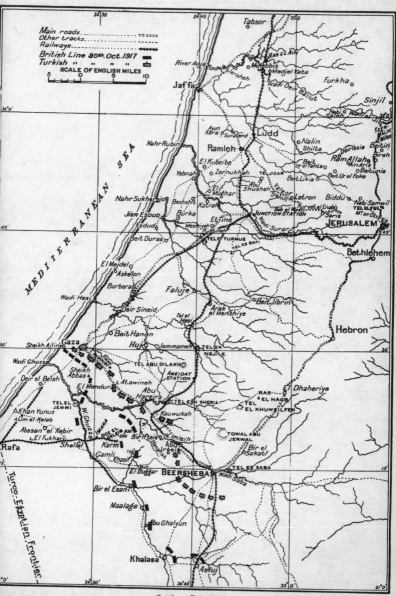

Southern Palestine.

PROLOGUE

Huj, 8 November 1917: about 2.30 p.m.

There were dead men and dead horses, but at first it was mostly dead horses.

Meinertzhagen and Ponting arrived with the cleaners, human and otherwise. The birds circled in the low thermals above the ambulances and stretcher parties, especially over the far ridge where the Turkish dead were thickly clustered.

'Buzzards,' said Meinertzhagen, pushing up the peak of the solar topee and holding a hand over his eyes. 'Long-legged buzzards and a few Booted Eagles by the look of 'em.'

Ponting shuddered. 'They disgust me.'

'But why? It's their nature.'

The officers rode on in silence for a while after that, each apparently lost in his own thoughts. They were freshly horsed on the tough little Australian remounts that were known in that campaign as Walers because they were bred in New South Wales. Now they walked their Walers down the ridge behind which the Warwicks and Worcesters had assembled before making their sudden appearance on the skyline to start their half-mile gallop towards the Austrian seventy-fives.

The guns were hidden in a hollow in the enemy-held ridge, so that as the English cavalry crossed the flat of the little valley they had ridden into dead ground, where the gunners could no longer fire at them over open sights and had to rely on air bursts – those and the protection of German machine-gunners and Turkish infantry, who were dug in higher up behind them and could see the Yeomanry coming all the way.

As they got nearer the Austrian battery Meinertzhagen and Ponting saw bundles of khaki huddled together by the dead horses. Great clouds of flies rose off human and animal cadavers alike, settling down again once they were past.

They did not go down to the Skoda guns in the hollow right away but rode to the left of them, up to the crest of the ridge where the nationalities were intertwined. Further down the far slope the dead were exclusively Turkish, for it was here that the English had run them through with their long swords as they ran away.

Close to a Turkish corpse with a gaping back wound was an open, red-covered book, also lying with its spine uppermost. It was such an incongruous sight that Ponting dismounted and picked it up, half-expecting it to be a Koran, which would have made a nice keepsake. But it turned out to be in English. *The Complete Letter-Writer for Ladies and Gentlemen*, he read, and he could see by flicking through the chapter headings that it gave advice on how to conduct all kinds of correspondence: business, social, family – even amorous. On the title page was an inscription written in black ink in the large and precise style Ponting always thought of as Working-Class Copperplate: 'To our dearest son Walter, in the hope that he might learn these lessons well and keep us informed of all his adventures. May God keep you safe and sound until you return to us. Your loving parents, Mr and Mrs Albert Calderwell.'

Ponting wondered what sort of self-improving Tommy Atkins would take such a volume into battle with him. Written in pencil in the inside front cover of the book was 'Private W. Calderwell, Warwickshire Yeomanry'. Underneath, inscribed in block capitals in a different, darker pencil lead were the words 'B Squadron', which indicated to Ponting, who had a deductive mind, that the man was probably one of a recent draft of reinforcements who had not known which squadron of his regiment he would be allotted to until he arrived in Egypt. It didn't look as if the poor boy had lasted long.

'Interesting?' asked Meinertzhagen.

'It's from one of ours,' said Ponting, slipping the book into a tunic pocket and remounting.

They turned around and went back to the top of the ridge where, on the English side, the slaughter had only been exceeded by that which had occurred around the Austrian artillery itself. The farriers were busy putting down those horses that could not be persuaded to stand. A single bullet wound, even several, was not always reason

2

enough to kill a horse. Mules were even tougher, but mules didn't make charges.

A soldier with hair the colour of corn was crouched with his rifle beside a brown horse lying on its side with its neck outstretched on the ground. Every so often the head and neck would come up, the mane shake enough to dislodge the flies, and then shudder down again. Above the horse stood a farrier corporal holding what Ponting at first mistook for some sort of outsize pistol and then realised was one of those captive bolt devices they had started to use in abattoirs shortly before the start of the war.

'She'll come round. I know she will,' the corn-haired boy was saying. Ponting saw that he was one of the very young ones, nineteen at the most.

'C'mon, son, it don't always work first time with a rifle,' said the corporal farrier, who had a blacksmith's forearms.

'Fuck off or I might shoot you,' the youth said quietly, although not quietly enough for Ponting not to overhear him.

He thought for a moment that Meinertzhagen would see the youth as another dreadful example of the callowness of these New Army civilian volunteers, and have him awarded field punishment for insolence to a non-commissioned officer.

But Meinertzhagen did not appear to have heard. He was looking beyond them towards a lorry parked on a dirt track about four hundred yards from the Skoda guns. Next to the lorry, which was of German manufacture, was a horse-drawn British field ambulance. A man was being loaded into the back of the ambulance on a stretcher, watched by a British officer and a woman.

It was, of course, the woman who had attracted Meinertzhagen's attention. After the war, when he had polished it to one of those anecdotes that neither bored nor gave away too much, Ponting used to say that he would have been less surprised to see a Clapham omnibus than a female at Huj.

From that distance she appeared to be European. She was quite tall and dark-looking and was wearing a grubby white dress and a large straw hat. They rode towards her. As they got closer they could see that most of the grubbiness on the woman's dress was blood – and fresh blood at that, because the heat quickly dried it brown. Ponting wondered why nobody was assisting her. Then he realised that the blood was probably not her own.

PART 1
*Even
In
Our
Time*

1

A prisoner was sobbing softly in one of the deeper cells.

The Moudir, the head of the Turkish gendarmerie in Caesarea, was on the way out of the building with a little sack of grain in his hands when he heard it. He paused for a moment to listen, but could not make out whether the weeping came from the Christian Syrian boy whom he suspected of being a deserter from one of the regiments at the Gaza front, or the wasted and, to his mind, obviously syphilitic Armenian whore caught stealing from soldiers who had declined her services. He shrugged. It could wait. He had his friends to attend to.

Convict labour had refurbished the dungeons and built the pigeon loft for him years ago amidst the overgrown ruins of King Louis IX's coastal fortress at Caesarea. It should have been a pleasant place, its palms fanned by sea breezes and in summer full of the restful cool that only large stone blocks and marble-tiled floors can bring. But on the whole men had never been happy there for long.

Even by Crusader standards it had had an anguished history. Before Louis there had been King Baldwin I of Jerusalem, Gautier of Avense and Jean de Brieme. Sometimes the knights barely held it a year before it was back in Muslim hands. Louis had lasted for fifteen, which was longer than any of them.

His luck ran out in 1265, when it was successfully stormed by Sultan Baybars. Perhaps Baybars sensed that the fortress was cursed, because he had it pulled asunder in a manner that foreshadowed high explosive and ordered that it should never be inhabited again. For this reason the Moudir made sure he never spent a night there, though he was dismissive of the tales of wailing djinns and spirits he heard

7

from his Kurdish guards. As a young man he had chased Kurdish bandits and he sometimes suspected that these mountain people clung to beliefs that predated Islam and that comforted them when the snow blocked their high passes and wolf packs roamed the ridge lines.

He was a fat man, this Moudir, and he moved slowly towards the jetty, the jellabea he always wore for his siesta flapping at his ankles, his podgy feet squeezed into sandals which slapped along the flagged path. The Crusaders had built the jetty too; for some reason Baybars had not destroyed it, although it might have made a landing-stage for a Frankish sortie from Acre or Cyprus. Perhaps he knew they had had enough. Nor had he destroyed the dungeons, though the Moudir had required his chain gangs to fit bars and doors and the kind of wall shackles the Armenian woman was now attached to.

The Moudir scattered his grain, as he always did, at the seawards end of the jetty. He did this because it amused him to see the first birds down fly off to their wooden loft at the other end, only to make a weary return a few minutes later, unable to miss out on a feed.

On the horizon the sun was going down in a blaze of copper-coloured clouds. Before it he could make out the dark silhouette of a steamship sailing north and guessed it was one of the British or French warships that were enforcing the Entente's blockade of the Levantine coast all the way from Latakia to Khan Yunis. A few gulls cried and wheeled, but there was as yet no sign of his birds.

This was always an anxious moment. He had never lost his sense of wonder at their navigation. One day, he was convinced, the magic would fail. Something would go wrong with that compass in their heads and the poor little dears would be unable to find their way home to him. The very idea made his throat dry and his eyes warm with tears.

He looked along the narrow silver highway the setting sun had laid from the jetty to the Mediterranean horizon, shutting his left eye completely and blinkering his other with his right hand. For a guilty moment he wondered whether he should get some of those darkened spectacles the Germans sometimes wore, as if Allah had not given them eyes strong enough to face the day. But then, being infidels, perhaps He had not.

There was a shadow in the sun, and what was at first barely a smudge, not much harder in outline than the puffs of smoke from the passing ship, slowly became his flapping flock. As usual, they circled high above him, the white ones in the lead, as if they needed to fix various landmarks before committing themselves – in much the same way as the German airmen flew around the country. After

8

a couple of circuits they began to descend in slow spirals which took them out over the sea again until the white-feathered leaders dropped down onto the jetty and began bobbing away at their feed.

The Moudir threw some more grain into their midst and then crouched among them, holding it in his hands, so that they pecked at his palm and then grew bolder and flew up onto his forearms where he could feel the strength of their talons as they sought a grip. 'Come on my pretties,' he said. 'Come on.'

The lead pigeons flew to the loft and then swooped almost immediately back again, just as they always did. There were names for the favourites. 'Come on, Nur, come on, Fatima, you greedy little thing.'

The birds fluttered around him until all the grain was gone. Once night began to close in, they retreated into their loft from which emerged the sound of contented cooing.

Back in the ruins of the old keep, where the dungeons were, the prisoner was still weeping. If it was the Armenian, he thought, it was unnecessary because they would not have touched her yet. His Kurds did not like beating women who were not related to them, not even whores. It offended their dignity as men. He had had trouble before trying to get them to soften up some female suspect with a touch of the bastinado. Perhaps she was not crying for herself, but for others. He had heard reports that thousands of Armenians had perished when they were driven out of the border areas with Russia along the Caucasian front. And quite right too. They were a menace these Christians, always willing to start trouble if the price was right.

The Jews were no better either, at least not the Zionists, who even offended their religious brethren with their strange notions of settling and farming the land as if it was some virgin wilderness for the taking. On the surface they were grateful and loyal citizens of the Ottoman Empire. But when you visited their settlements, took a little bakshish from them in order to make some minor matter to their liking, you could sense the superiority, even contempt, behind the smiles and effusive thanks. Didn't they consider themselves the Chosen Race? And wasn't this Palestine their promised land? They even had their own flag. He had seen it. It was blue with a star of David, and below that a Hebrew word meaning 'Zion'. There were plenty of arms in those settlements too: Martini-Henrys, Winchesters, even the odd Mauser which they should have given up at the start of the war but which they claimed they needed to protect them from Arab brigands.

They were not without a certain influence, these Zionists, there was no doubt about that. They had the ear of the Germans for a start – of the Kaiser himself, some said. So many came from the

9

German-speaking countries that it had become the first language of the race. The Moudir had witnessed the riots between the Jews in Haifa just before the war when some of them wanted to open a school in which instruction would be in German, while others thought it should be in French or even Hebrew – the dead tongue of their faith, which some of the more fanatical were trying to bring back to life. The Jews would use the Germans to grab as much as they could in Palestine, he was sure of that.

And yet there were reports that some of the Zionists were dealing with the English, because the English held Egypt and were the greatest Christian power in the area. And the English would promise them anything because they needed Jewish gold to feed their war machine. There was supposed to be a lot of Jewish gold in the United States and those foolish Americans had just declared war against Germany. Well let them! And let the English continue to hammer on the gates of Palestine, and the Turks to pull them back by their ears and slaughter them like sheep.

A month ago he would not have been so sure. Baghdad had fallen at last to the English general Maude, and although he had never been there the Moudir felt its loss badly. After Mecca and Jerusalem it was the third great city of the Empire, and thanks to that unspeakable traitor Hussein, who had been appointed Sheriff of Mecca by the Sultan himself, they had lost the Holy City the summer before.

Now things were looking up. Twice they had thrown the English back at Gaza even though the enemy had given the land its first taste of poison gas and sent those landships they called tanks crawling at them like some monstrous bug from your worst nightmare. Nor were many of their best troops in Palestine, though Jemal Pasha was doing his best to get the Arab regiments replaced by proper Turkish soldiers. At the moment most of the iron regiments were fighting the Russians in the Caucasus – fighting the Germans' battles for them, if the truth be known.

Like most of his compatriots, the Moudir felt uneasy about the Germans. In fact, he would have been hard pressed to find anybody who had much liking for them. Respect, yes. For Christians they were brave enough, and there was no doubt that they were clever. Their equipment was probably the best in the world, unless you believed these stories that every American soldier had a machine-gun as well as a horsehair mattress and a gramophone.

But they were Christians and their allies – which made the Sultan's declaration that this was a Jihad, a holy war against the infidel English and the French, rather confusing. Here, after all, was the world's most powerful Muslim nation, led by a sultan who was also the Caliph, the spiritual leader of all Muslims, not only allied to Christians but at war with other Muslims, such as some of the Indian mercenaries the English employed – and even the traitor Hussein's goat-fucking Bedu, the so-called Hejaz army, the very people of the Prophet, blessed be His name. The Moudir sometimes found himself wondering what Allah, the Merciful and Compassionate, made of it all.

When it was all over they would probably have to deal with the Bedu in the same way they dealt with the white kaffirs. There was no room in the Empire for kaffir riff-raff. They were there on tolerance, especially those wretched Christian priests in Jerusalem always squabbling over which bit of stone the Blessed Jesus had been born or died on. A Muslim family even had to keep the keys of the Holy Sepulchre – otherwise the Christians would have long since pulled the place to pieces with their feuds. He tried to imagine what it would be like if a Christian guarded the holy places in Mecca, and found such blasphemy unimaginable. Better that the traitor Hussein should have temporary control than the English army. Which was only further proof, if any were needed, of the rightness of the true religion. Here were all these Christian nations with their new learning and free thinking and Jewish gold and none of them, not even the Germans, would dare to take the keys of the Holy Sepulchre from a Muslim.

No, there should be none of this equal rights nonsense for Christians and Jews and madmen like those Bahai devil-worshippers from Persia who had their so-called temple up on Mount Carmel. It might be different if you could rely on their loyalty, but you could not. When they got out of hand they had to be dealt with firmly – the way the Armenians had been dealt with, by all accounts.

Thinking these stern, dutiful thoughts, the Moudir went to the small room above the cells that he liked to call his office and picked up a riding-crop that was lying across the desk next to a field telephone handset. He was still uncertain which prisoner was sobbing. Perhaps he would give them both something to cry about, have them singing through the soles of their feet. He called for a couple of Kurdish jailers and went down to the cells. As he approached the prisoners could hear the slap of his sandals on the stairs.

His Majesty's Ship *Monegam*, the monitor the Moudir had watched steaming north, was now a mile or so off the coast and almost

11

stationary. They were opposte the little fishing port of Athlit, just south of Haifa.

Once the engines had been set to slow the swell caught the ship's shallow draught, and it began to rock gently from side to side as well as up and down. The sailors were hardly aware of it, but on the bridge Major Ponting found it harder to ignore the first queasy prelude to his seasickness.

'It's all clear,' said the captain of the vessel. A lieutenant-commander, he stood alongside Ponting and peered through binoculars at a shoreline that was darkening fast with dusk. 'They're coming out.'

'Where's the signal?' asked the major.

'You see the tower on the end of the promontory?'

Ponting nodded. He would have had to be blind not to see it. It was more like a miniature castle than a tower. There were several of these Crusader fortifications dotted up and down the coast. In some of them the Turks had placed permanent garrisons. Others were simply visited by passing patrols, who might stay a night or two. The tower of Athlit was one of these.

'Go to about ten o'clock behind it and you'll see a small wooden house. Looks like it might be a farm house. It's got wooden stairs leading to a balcony that stretches along the entire length of its first floor. If you look closely at that balcony you'll see a white sheet has been draped over it.'

Ponting reluctantly raised his own field glasses and tried to focus. Aboard ship he rated trying to use binoculars as one better than attempting to read fine print while eating a bacon sandwich. The bridge refused to keep still. One moment he was thrust against the squat roundness of the Crusader tower and the next he was peering into the white top of a breaker. He felt his stomach rise to his throat and swallowed hard. He was tempted to take the naval officer's word for it, or even pretend that he had seen the signal; but he kept searching, although his insides had begun to churn.

'Can't you see it?' The lieutenant-commander sounded impatient. They had a lot to do, and every second they spent at that speed made them a better target for a U-boat.

Ponting ignored him. A flash of white in the lens vanished when the vessel rolled again and he found himself looking at what appeared to be a stone wall on a terraced slope. He took another deep breath, put his legs slightly further apart, and jammed his knees against the bulkhead of the open bridge. He found the tower again and went to ten, no, eleven o'clock. He managed to steady the glasses on it this time. Behind the sheet were the three windows of the wood house's upper storey, and beyond its sloping roof a bunch of tall conifers.

Ponting let his field glasses hang on the short strap around his neck and took another large gulp of air. He felt the nausea rise from his innards. It was going to happen.

'Can you get any closer?' he asked. 'It will save time.'

'A bit – but we have to be careful of mines. They're difficult to spot in this light.'

Ponting grunted. He had become quite well acquainted with the Royal Navy during the last six months, and was not all that impressed. They were always being careful about something. He sometimes had the feeling Nelson wouldn't recognise the service.

Nevertheless, HMS *Monegam* turned towards the shore and a couple of sailors went on her bow with a plumb line to test the depth. Gun crews turned their pieces towards the medieval stonework on the promontory while teenaged boy sailors took eight-inch shells off the hoists that came up from the magazine.

Now that Ponting no longer had to look through the binoculars he felt a little better. He extracted one of the Egyptian cigarettes he had become fond of lately. Suddenly the cigarette got to him and he stumbled down to his cabin with his hand over his mouth, hating the sailors he bumped into for not being sharp enough about giving him gangway.

By the time he was back on the bridge the ship was steadier and they were closer to the shore. Although it was almost dark by now he could distinctly make out feathery-leaved tamarisks on the beach, and beyond them a few scraggy-looking palms.

'Boat to starboard,' called a lookout.

Ponting, determined to redeem himself, spotted it before the lieutenant-commander. It was an Arab fishing boat with a high bow and a small triangular sail, a design basically unchanged since the Phoenicians. The sailcloth appeared to be brown or blue, he could not tell which in the dying light. He guessed that they had chosen it so that they would be less visible to a casual watcher from the shore although he was willing to bet there were nets and lines on board in case they were challenged.

The little boat tacked expertly towards them, taking advantage of every scrap of wind. 'He knows his business,' murmured the lieutenant-commander. 'And a good thing too. We don't want to be hanging about.'

It was the naval officer's first involvement with cloak and dagger stuff. From what he could see it was all cloak and no dagger. This particular job involved Ponting collecting and sending messages via the courier who then returned to shore. He assumed it was difficult to equip these spies with the kind of wireless telegraphy equipment that would be easy to operate and, in any case, wireless messages were almost invariably intercepted by the enemy. As long as weather conditions didn't make the rendezvous difficult, the whole operation wasn't supposed to take more than ten minutes. Even so, it was very hard on the nerves. The captain was sure he would rather be in a pitched battle between cruiser squadrons than endure all this creeping about an enemy coast with the army breathing down your neck and making it plain that they thought you an absolute pansy if you weren't over-keen about risking your ship.

He was pleased that Ponting had been sick, because it should make him as anxious to get away as he was. The trouble with the army, he mused, was that officers like the good major had no idea what it was like to be in charge of thousands of pounds of equipment. All they knew was what it was like to be in charge of thousands of men – and they didn't appear to come so expensive, if the way they spent them was anything to go by. It seemed one had to lose an awful lot of soldiers before anybody began to wonder whether you had been careless. It was not at all like that with a ship.

The fishing boat was almost alongside now. There were three occupants. Two of them appeared to be Syrian fishermen for they wore the local chequered headdress known as the keffiyeh. The third, who was seated in the stern alongside the man on the tiller, wore a straw hat held in place with a scarf that was tied under the chin. It occurred to the lieutenant-commander that it was the kind of thing that a woman might wear back home for a motoring trip on a summer's day.

The *Monegam's* engines were already on slow. The captain now ordered the port screw to be set in reverse. This made the monitor revolve slowly in the water, able to spring away at the first whiff of danger from the enemy coast.

A Jacob's ladder was put over the side and a couple of sailors with boat-hooks pulled the fishing boat towards them. The captain looked over his bridge to see how things were coming along just as the figure in the stern of the boat stood up. My God, it *was* a woman! A young, European-looking woman, quite pretty too if you like them a bit on the plump side. She was wearing a light blue, high-collared dress which ended just above her ankles. As she stepped onto the Jacob's ladder one of the sailors, who seized her firmly by the arm, noted with interest that she did not appear to be wearing stockings.

The lieutenant-commander turned to say something to Ponting but he was no longer there. He looked down again and saw that the major was down by the rail helping her aboard with all the proprietary airs of some jumped-up mill owner receiving guests aboard his gin palace during Cowes Week.

'Good evening,' the captain heard him say. 'I do hope we weren't late. Any news of Daniel?'

He spoke to her in French.

2

As he approached the front entrance of Fast's Hotel Maeltzer saw that Magnus was at his ranting again.

Today he was wearing a crown of thorns on his long blond hair and carrying a pole with a short cross-piece at about chest height – so that apart from forming the insignia of his faith it also made a handy staff. Magnus was a tall man – it was rare to find a Syrian or Turk who could meet the level of his mad blue eyes – and the pole was well over five feet long. His full beard was as wild and ragged as an Orthodox priest's. This made it difficult to guess his age, which could have been anything between twenty-five and forty.

Sometimes Magnus preached in his native Swedish, sometimes in heavily accented English or a kind of German. Very often, when the Lord was pleased to bless him with gift of tongues, he spoke in what sounded to most poor sinners like an incoherent babble. This morning he had been so blessed.

'Whaboosh, doidy krakoo cervantees eek,' he boomed at the stone-faced Turkish sentries standing with bayonets fixed either side of the hotel's main door. 'Doidy-dee-doi-dee-doi,' he chanted. 'God bellum abca ravi Inglesi napoo Christos rei.'

Suddenly he switched to English. 'For the Lord hath given and the Lord hath taken away,' he told the soldiers, primitive Anatolians who believed that the afflicted were blessed by Allah. 'And they clothed him with the purple and plotted a thorn crown and be putting it on his head,' lectured Magnus, waving his cross dangerously near the nose of one of the gentlemen from Asia Minor.

16

'Ah Easter!' thought Maeltzer. 'Of course, crown of thorns equals Easter. Forgotten all about it this year. Must be the war.'

It occurred to him that Magnus was overdoing it a bit, waving his stick about like that. You could never tell with the Turks. One moment they were all docility and the next they'd shove a bayonet through you. He wondered for a moment whether he should intervene, but decided against it. Magnus would only feel obliged to give him one of his lectures. He went up the steps quickly, a big man in a panama hat and a tan tropical suit, chosen because it never looked as dirty as it was.

Just inside the lobby with its wood panelling and high vaulted ceiling stood a monocled German colonel wearing a boat-shaped Astrakhan hat and about to take his leave of some junior officers. This was Kress von Kressenstein, a Bavarian aristocrat who, as chief of staff to the Turkish Eighth Army Corps, had just been responsible for giving the British their latest bloody nose at Gaza. Maeltzer thought he looked pleased with himself, as well he might.

'Ah, Herr Maeltzer,' said Kressenstein, catching sight of him. 'You have heard the news?'

'Of the battle? Of course . . . I . . .'

'No, no. Not that,' said the Bavarian impatiently. 'I know you know that. A poor newspaperman you'd be if you had not already informed Zürich of that. No, I mean about the British prisoners?'

'Prisoners?'

'Yes, three hundred of them. English and Australians. Our Turkish friends are showing them round the holy sights at this very moment.'

'Showing them the sights?' Maeltzer often greeted von Kressenstein's announcements with an air of astonishment even if, as was now the case, they were already the gossip of the souk. It was one of the reasons the colonel enjoyed telling him things.

'Yes, I mean it. Giving them a tour of the Holy Sepulchre, St Anne's, the Dome of the Rock, el Aksa mosque, the Jews' wailing place, everything. Real chivalry, eh? The world has not seen such a thing since Saladin sent Richard Coeur de Lion fruit for his fever.'

Maeltzer had noticed that most of the Austro-German officer corps were obsessed with the Crusades. The trouble was that, as the allies of the Turks, they were on the wrong side. The English talked of the 'Last Crusade' and ending six hundred years of Muslim domination.

'There was France on Christmas Day '14, sir,' interrupted a young Oberleutnant with an empty left sleeve. 'When we had a truce with the Tommies and beat them at football. Their own sport!'

'And now you beat them at your sport,' said Maeltzer whose admiration for German military skills was apparently boundless.

17

They liked that. Even two Turkish officers attached to the staff for mainly cosmetic reasons joined in the laughter. It was the kind of remark which renewed the Swiss journalist's popularity among his German contacts. That and his unashamedly pro-German despatches – his loyalty to the father tongue, as it were. The only one who did not join in the laughter was a tall cadaverous-looking major, whose yellow skin was stretched tight over high cheek-bones. This was Erwin Krag, the senior German intelligence officer on the staff; people would have been surprised if he had.

Kressenstein finished saying his goodbyes to the Corset Staves, as the Germans liked to call themselves – on the grounds that they put some stiffening into the Ottoman forces. Maeltzer guessed that he was off to Damascus to give Djemal Pasha a first-hand account of the way they had twice rebuffed a greatly superior British army. Liman von Sanders, the head of the German mission to the Turkish army, would also be there and eager to know how it had been done. Unlike many of his compatriots, von Kressenstein knew how to handle the Turks, how not to damage their precious *amour propre*. To Djemal Pasha he would praise, and quite rightly so, the fighting qualities of *mehmedjik*, the ordinary Turkish soldier, and understate the part German staff officers and Austrian 75mm Skoda gun batteries had played in the proceedings.

Before he left, the Bavarian turned to Maeltzer again. 'Get your friend Oberleutnant Weidinger to show you the British prisoners,' he said. 'I'm sure they'll make an excellent article for you.'

Maeltzer allowed himself to be steered into the main foyer area by Weidinger, the one-armed Oberleutnant. One of the amazing things about Fast's was although all its bedrooms had been taken over by the military, it continued to attempt to function as an ordinary hotel as far as its public rooms were concerned. Once they were seated on a sofa, a barefoot waiter – who wore a fez with a matching cummerbund around his baggy trousers – padded up to them and asked if they wanted coffee. Both ordered medium-sweet cups.

'Do you think we can see them?' Maeltzer asked.

'Who?'

'The British prisoners.'

'Of course: those are my instructions,' said Weidinger, who smiled to show that this was an order he was happy to comply with. He was pleased that Kress should have noted and obviously approved of his growing friendship with Karl Maeltzer.

The journalist was almost twice Weidinger's twenty-three years. He was well over six foot, and his height diminished the belly he had

18

acquired through years of good living in the capitals of Europe. His jackets almost invariably seemed too tight for his powerful shoulders. Weidinger always thought of him as 'bearlike'.

He had pepper-and-salt moustache and hair, and a large, almost macrocephalic head that the Oberleutnant was convinced had grown that way in order to accomodate its owner's extra brain power. Few people who had known him for long were fooled by Maeltzer's air of perpetual bewilderment. His eyes betrayed him first. Weidinger sometimes found them a little disconcerting. They were so dark brown as to be almost black, and could project the kind of cruel intelligence found in a bird of prey. Sometimes Weidinger had seen Bedouin with similar eyes.

The coffee arrived on a copper tray. Fast's, which had opened a few years before the war, was undoubtedly the best hotel in Jerusalem. Though only a few minutes' walk from the Jaffa Gate, it was well outside the walls and the stench of what was becoming known as the Old City – where the bulk of the population lived in the awful hovels that, over the centuries, had accreted like coral reef around the various mosques, churches and synagogues to become the Muslim, Christian and Jewish quarters.

The hotel's healthier location, plus the fact that it was German-owned and managed, made it the obvious choice when von Kressenstein was looking for billets for officers on his staff. In summer when, even at Jerusalem's altitude, the heat could become unpleasant, its rooms were cooled by electric propeller fans. The power came from the hotel's own petrol-driven generator, which also provided electric light in the public rooms and on the first floor, the bedrooms of which had now become the headquarters of the Eighth Army Corps.

When they had sipped their coffee and lit up faintly scented Turkish cigarettes, Weidinger said, 'Of course, you know why my master was so anxious that you should see the British prisoners?'

'Now let me think,' said Maeltzer, scratching his massive head and drawing deeply on his cigarette. 'Well, apart from the obvious one – to have the German ambassador in Switzerland report that the Zürich press is full of Kressenstein's famous victory – I'd say "Kut".'

'Exactly. Kress wishes to see an esteemed and highly neutral organ such as yours present our gallant Turkish allies as the honourable fellows they are, chivalrous to a fault, the reincarnation of Saladin. Especially now that Baghdad has fallen and every citizen who has remained behind will be bending Tommy's ear about how awful the terrible Turk was to the Kut prisoners.'

Two years before, after a brilliant start to the Mesopotamia

19

campaign against demoralised Arab levies, General Townshend had collided with the Turkish army proper. His Anglo-Indian force had ended up being besieged at Kut on the Euphrates, where they had surrendered after several attempts to relieve them had failed.

Maeltzer nodded. 'Quite so,' he said. 'Well, if the British had made more of what happened to their men after Townshend had surrendered that might be difficult. The neutral consuls who saw British and Indian soldiers being whipped through the streets of Baghdad by those Kurdish and Arab regiments were most upset about it. Especially the Americans. Half-starved men trying to march with bits of bloody puttee cloth wrapped around their feet because their guards had stolen their boots. Terrible business.'

'I know,' said Weidinger. 'I was talking to Major Krag about it, the other day. He's seen the report of a medical officer who saw the prisoners come into Baghdad. Almost all of them had dysentery. They were dropping like flies. It must have been terrible seeing a pack of Arabs treating Europeans like that and not being able to do anything about it.'

Weidinger paused to take another sip of coffee. 'There was something else in that report too,' he said. 'I'll tell you, but you'll have to promise me that it will go no further.'

'That's always a difficult promise for a newspaperman to make,' said Maeltzer solemnly. He knew that the young Berliner could rarely resist passing on some morsel of gossip, the more scandalous the better.

'Oh, but it's not the kind of stuff you could get into a newspaper, at least not into a respectable newspaper like yours. Do I have your word that you won't repeat it to anyone?'

The journalist gave an almost imperceptible nod.

Weidinger dropped his voice to a whisper for, apart from security considerations, there were women present at some of the other tables. 'It is a known fact,' he said, 'that some of the prisoners were raped on that death march. The doctor whom Krag spoke to knew this because he personally treated two of them for their, hmm, injuries.'

'My God!' said Maeltzer, genuinely impressed.

'Yes,' said Weidinger. 'A fate worse than death.' He giggled nervously, not quite certain whether this was the kind of joke a German officer should make, let alone to a foreign civilian, however friendly. 'I agree with you,' he said, suddenly serious. 'It's surprising the English did not make more of it.'

'Perhaps they didn't want to make a fuss because of their line on Turkey.'

'What do you mean?'

'Well, they've always taken the position that the Turkish people have merely been misled by the government, which is the dupe of the Central Powers. With the Germans it's different. You're the new Huns, spiking Belgian babies on your bayonets.'

'What nonsense,' said Weidinger. 'If the Turks are our puppets then the puppet-master ought to be shot. Look at Mustapha Kemal, the hero of Gallipoli. Even von Sanders can't handle him.'

'True,' said Maeltzer. 'I'm simply saying that this is what the English believe – not that it's a fact. It has always seemed to me that the English are a nation with a great capacity for self-delusion.'

The foyer was filling up. A fat, sweating Austrian prelate called Liebermann, who acted as chaplain to the German-speaking Catholics among the Jerusalem military, and for whom the journalist bore what he admitted was an irrational dislike, was speaking to a nursing sister. The nurse, who was no older than Weidinger, was carrying a bundle of mail and looked anxious to get away.

Maeltzer noticed that there were now quite a few women present – some of them ladies and some of them definitely not. A couple of German aviators, one of whom had draped a knee-length leather jerkin over a chair, were in deep conversation with a pair of Levantine beauties in western clothes who were just a touch over-dressed for the time of day.

Seated a little apart from the rest were a rather plump young woman with her hair parted down the middle and flicked back at the sides, and a stocky, broad-shouldered male of about the same age wearing a brown tweed suit and an improbable monocle. Maeltzer recognised the woman as a Rumanian Jewess called Sarah Aaronsohn, who came from Zichron Jacob, a Zionist settlement on the slopes of Mount Carmel, near the northern port of Haifa. She was the younger sister of the famous agronomist Aaron Aaronsohn, a man admired by Djemal Pasha, who had put him in charge of Palestine's locust control programme. Now with Enver and Talaat, one of Constantinople's ruling triumvirate, Djemal was Governor and Commander-in-Chief of the Ottoman forces throughout Syria – and must, Maeltzer thought, look back on the locust wars with some nostalgia.

In any case, Aaronsohn was no longer in the country, and there were confused reports about his whereabouts. He had sailed for the United States almost a year before, having persuaded the authorities that he needed to do some research there on a project to extract oil from sesame seeds. Some said that his ship had been intercepted by a British destroyer, and that a boarding party had seized Aaronsohn as an enemy alien. Others claimed that Aaronsohn had in fact

21

reached New York, but was unable to return now that the United States was at war with Germany.

Maeltzer wondered what Sarah Aaronsohn and her man friend were doing down here such a long way from home and how large a bribe they had paid for their travel documents. Written permission was needed to cross from one *vilyat* to another – a great source of income for threadbare railway clerks and gendarmerie moudirs.

He watched as the Aaronsohn woman gave a little wave to a passing major, who answered it with a broad smile and walked over to where they were sitting. The young man got to his feet and shook hands. Maeltzer thought he looked a bit sullen.

Weidinger followed the journalist's gaze. 'Ah, Major Tiller,' he said. 'A lucky fellow.'

'How so?'

'He was in command of the town garrison in Gaza and nobody remembered to tell him we were winning. He was almost out of ammunition, had blown up his wireless and was about to surrender when the British attack stopped and they started to retreat.'

'So it was that close?' said Maeltzer.

'It couldn't have been closer. If they weren't such incompetents the British would be here by now. It's well known they outnumber us in men and guns. You know they even used gas and tanks? A real Western Front-type assault and we still beat them! Shook them off like a dog getting rid of his fleas. Of course, well led the Turk is one of the best defensive fighters in the world – no doubt about that.'

Like most of his colleagues Weidinger positively glowed with this latest proof of what good German staff work could do with unpromising material. Maeltzer guessed that von Kressenstein had set the tone when it came to a pat on the back for the 'well led Turk'. Most of the time his officers found their allies exasperatingly indolent. By comparison, they said, the Austro-Hungarians were military paragons. Nor was the journalist altogether surprised at British incompetence. Seventeen years before he had watched the Boers make fools of Tommy Atkins because they were better led, better armed and better motivated – at least at the beginning. Mind you, as he often used to tell his German friends, when it came to the Empire on which the sun never set, he had to admit to a certain prejudice. Maeltzer had spent six months in a British PoW camp on Ceylon before his newspaper got him out. Luckily, he had managed to get rid of the Mauser he was carrying before he was captured – otherwise he might have been shot.

'Well, the Syrians have never doubted that the British would fail,' said Maeltzer now. 'You know their prophecy? "When the waters of the Nile come to Palestine then shall Jerusalem be taken from the Turks."'

'We should be safe then,' observed Weidinger. 'As long as there are a few Germans around to watch the waters that is. Ah, I see Major Tiller is closing on the spoils of war.'

The journalist saw that Sarah Aaronsohn was now deep in conversation with the major. Every now and then she would respond to something he had said with a coquettish little laugh. The young man at her side looked increasingly sulky and ill at ease.

A tall man, tanned like a peasant, with a drooping gingerish moustache, walked into the hotel. His whipcord breeches were tucked into lace-up riding boots which were covered in dust, as was his clothing. His broad-brimmed hat reminded Maeltzer of the Transvaal. He removed it to reveal hair of deeper ginger than his moustache, and then looked around the foyer until his eyes alighted on the Swiss journalist. This was Doctor Jacob Rosenblum, a German Jew of some influence among the Zionists who came from a settlement along the River Jordan near the northern shore of the Sea of Galilee.

'Good morning, Herr Maeltzer,' he boomed. 'Nothing but good news to report, eh?'

Rosenblum represented a distinctly pro-German stratum among the Zionists. His affection for the Fatherland had, if anything, grown in his years of living away. Forgotten now were the slights, the remorseless prejudice whose tiny darts could spoil a perfect day. Rosenblum was one of those who had opposed the decision of the Zionist Congress to move its headquarters from Berlin to neutral Copenhagen for the duration.

Maeltzer introduced the Zionist to Weidinger, and motioned him to sit down.

'Just for a moment,' he said, sinking into an armchair opposite their couch and laying his hat on his knees. 'I have business with Fraulein Aaronsohn over there.'

'And are you going to ask the whereabouts of her brother, by any chance?' murmured Maeltzer.

'Among other things. A brilliant man, of course, but it is possible that he may have been misguided. I have often found that the scientific intellect does not mix readily with politics. There is – what shall I say? – a chemical reaction that can spell disaster.'

'You would put Dr Weizmann, the chemist, in the same category?' inquired Maeltzer innocently.

'Indeed I would, sir.'

'What chemist is this?' Weidinger wanted to know.

'Weizmann is one of the leaders of the Jews in England,' Maeltzer explained. 'I think he was born in Russia.'

'Poland actually,' said Rosenblum. 'Near Pinsk. I believe he is working for the British navy now.'

'A Jewish sailor?' said Weidinger. 'With respect, Herr Doktor, I didn't think that a love of sea was among the many accomplishments of your race.'

'No, he isn't a sailor, Herr Oberleutnant,' said Rosenblum. 'He is, as Herr Maeltzer said, a chemist. He is probably working on explosives. One day the British may well give the fruits of his labours to the Russians and the next time they feel like having a pogrom they will use it to kill more Jews. I can tell you, gentlemen, it makes me sick. It makes me quite sick to think about it. In this war the English have become our enemies by becoming the friends of our enemies. Any Jew who thinks otherwise is a traitor to his race.'

No one could doubt Rosenblum's sincerity. His eyes were blazing, his face set. Weidinger felt flattered. It was always a pleasure to meet a Jew who was quite unequivocal about where his true interests lay. 'Talking of Russia, Dr Rosenblum,' he said, 'what do you make of recent events in Petrograd?'

'I think it's excellent news. They can't stand up to your soldiers and face revolution at home. The Russian army will crumble. You mark my words, it'll collapse. They're a bunch of half-starved, highly superstitious, illiterate peasants. I know them. Now they won't be sure whether they should be fighting or looting their officers' homes and ravishing their Dresden china ladies.'

'What about this Kerensky fellow? He's promised the English and the French that he'll fight on.'

'He may have promised, but has he asked the Russian soldiers? Taking away the Czar is like taking away their church. They'll be running around like headless chickens. And all the time the workers' militias will be getting stronger and the real lunatics, the Bolsheviks, will be gnawing away at their innards.'

'Aren't some of these Bolsheviks of your religion?' asked Weidinger.

'I believe they might be,' said Rosenblum and he gave a tight little self-satisfied smile, as if to indicate that this was all part of a grand conspiracy in which he himself was a leading player.

Then, rather in the manner of a man who has no more time for tittle-tattle, he bade them good-day and walked over to Sarah Aaronsohn, who was now sitting alone with her monocled companion. They did not look all that pleased to see him.

'Do you think many Jews feel like he does?' asked Weidinger, staring thoughtfully at Rosenblum's departing back. 'Do they really think the English are their enemy?'

'I think some of them do,' said Maeltzer, 'for the simple reason that their enemy's enemy is their friend. And as far as the Jews are concerned the Russians are their enemy. You know that thousands of them starved to death when they expelled the Jews from that part of the Pale along the frontier in '14. It was almost as bad as the Turks with the Armenians. They did it for the same reason too. Said they were a security risk.'

'That was after Tannenburg,' said Weidinger. 'We thrashed them. What was his name – their general who killed himself?'

'Samsanov.'

'That's right. Samsanov.'

'Nowhere in the world is there as much hatred against the Jews as there is in Russia,' Maeltzer went on. 'From what I've heard of the pogroms that happened there in the Eighties and the Nineties they were probably the worst the race had faced anywhere. And then when it comes to the Rosenblums of this world you have to remember that German Jews are very assimilated – far more than the French since Dreyfus. They do tend to feel very German, that's my experience anyway.'

'You're right enough there,' agreed Weidinger. 'More German than the Kaiser. It's embarrassing at times. Nature didn't intend them to be Germans and they never will be. They're not very popular at home, especially among the working people. They're respected sometimes, but not popular. Especially the kind who try and hide their Jewishness.'

Weidinger started gnawing at his remaining wrist. Strangers found it an alarming habit, but he was merely using his teeth to pull the stud that held down the leather flap on the face of his wristwatch – a device popular among infantry officers, which prevented a sun-flash off the glass from heliographing their position to a sniper.

Maeltzer had once asked him why, now that he was in a staff job in Palestine, he didn't remove the cover and Weidinger had replied, rather curtly, that apart from the fact that he frequently visited the front lines it helped keep the dust out. The journalist realised then that, for Weidinger, the watch cover was the next best thing to the Iron Cross, an award that was almost *de rigueur* for an officer so grievously mutilated for the Fatherland yet was strangely absent from Weidinger's chest. In the six months he had known the young cavalry officer Maeltzer had often wanted to ask him how he got his wound but somehow, even when they got a bit drunk together, it was never the right moment.

Weidinger nuzzled the leather flap back with his chin and squinted down at the face of the watch. 'I think we'd better go if you want to see those prisoners,' he said.

On their way out they both paused to acknowledge briefly various acquaintances. An apple-cheeked Austrian artillery lieutenant called Pichler gave Weidinger a mock salute.

'Greetings, Oh Master of the Cannon,' said Weidinger. 'I hear you've slain the iron tortoise.'

Pichler's battery had knocked out one of the British tanks at Gaza.

'I've known harder shooting,' said Pichler. 'Ducks, for instance. Does the esteemed Horse Soldier know what the staff have in store for us next? Elephants perhaps.'

'We were wondering if you would like a trip around the Pyramids,' announced Weidinger grandly.

'Haven't you heard?' sighed Pichler. 'It's been done. What's his name? Little short-arsed fellow. Corsican. When he found the old Sphinx looking a bit down in the mouth he gave him a cannon ball on the nose to get a smile on his face.'

'Never heard of him,' snorted Weidinger. 'You'll be telling me next he was too short to get on a horse.'

'Not true. He just knew they were going out of fashion.'

'He was wrong. Tanks are already out of fashion.'

Maeltzer smiled. Some cavalrymen he had met had managed to come to terms with the fact that their main role nowadays, indeed some people argued their *only* role, was that of mounted infantrymen. The machine-gun had relegated charges to the story books. Dismount and use your rifle was the order of the day. That was something the Boers had taught the world.

Weidinger would have none of it. Around headquarters he was well known for his unshakeable belief that opportunities could still be created for mounted men armed with sabres and lances to wreak havoc. Even in the kind of Uhlan lancer regiment he came from, this view was diminishing after three years bogged down in Flanders and never being sent to places like Palestine where they might do some good. Officer talent was drifting to the air force.

Yet it was still less than fifty years since the greatest cavalry battle Europe had ever seen had been fought on the plateau of Mars-La-Tour. There, on a sweltering August afternoon, the Prussians had blocked the retreat to Paris of a French army five times their size.

As a boy Weidinger had often ridden with von Bredow's brigade in *Der Todtenritt*, the terrible 'Death Ride' which bought the breathing space that spelt the French defeat. Sometimes he was an Altmark Uhlan thrusting with his lance until a cowardly bullet from a

Chassepot rifle delivered him to glory; on other occasions a Magdeburg cuirassier, bruised and bleeding, hacking his way through the French with a berserker's fury. In the space of forty minutes less than five hundred German horsemen had changed the course of history!

Now the field of honour had been turned into an insane competition in open mining – which was why Weidinger was delighted to get to Palestine, where both sides made some use of cavalry. He relished every example he discovered of malfunctioning machinery. He could be almost as jubilant about his own side's disasters in this sphere as he was about the vulnerability of such awful science fiction as the crawling blockhouses Pichler had dealt with.

Outside, the glare of the spring sunshine against the stones made them screw up their eyes until they got used to it again. Magnus had apparently tired of taunting the guards. He was now sitting cross-legged on the ground, his cross planted in the earth like a lance, and engrossed in cleaning his toenails with a matchstick. He still wore his crown of thorns, which had nicked his forehead, so that a trickle of blood flowed into his left eyebrow.

Maeltzer thought that Magnus had not noticed them until the Swede suddenly looked up from his pedicure and yelled in English, 'Now go and smite the Amalek and utterly destroy all that they have and spare them not!'

'He wants us to destroy the Amalek,' explained Maeltzer who had first acquired some English during his incarceration in Ceylon, and then polished it by working in London and New York.

'Where shall we find them – the Amalek?' asked Weidinger.

'Somewhere around the Book of Samuel. I think they're enemies of the Children of Israel.'

'I see. Why doesn't that fellow have the courtesy to rave in German? It would be so much more convenient.'

'He does sometimes. And Swedish. And the many languages of God.'

'I don't know why the Turks tolerate these headcases, why they don't just send them home.'

'He was in a bit of trouble once, during one of those Turkish roundups of miscreants. They threw them into some dungeon in the Citadel and hauled them out one at a time for a public flogging with a kourbash. I think it was one of Djemal Pasha's whims. Krag got to hear that a European was involved and got him out.'

'Well, I'm not suggesting he should be at the wrong end of a

27

kourbash' – Weidinger gave an involuntary shudder at the very thought of the hippopotamus-hide whip, which was said to open backs up like shrapnel – 'but half the country is starving, and he's another mouth to feed.'

'He doesn't do any harm.'

'I disagree, Herr Maeltzer. He eats and by eating he harms as much as any other locust. Come to think of it, how does he eat? The man doesn't look as if he starves.'

'No doubt those Swedes of Mrs Vester's at the American Colony give him something. And, of course, he begs.'

'Begs – a European?' A mild antipathy on Weidinger's part was beginning to turn to full-blown contempt. 'Do you ever give him anything?'

'Sometimes.'

'My God, you're a strange one, Maeltzer.'

The journalist laughed. 'I do it for luck,' he said.

3

S econd Lieutenant Anthony Buchan had, quite unconsciously, adopted the languid position sometimes assumed by opening bats in the school first eleven's annual team photograph.

In fact, poor co-ordination and a secret terror of fast bowlers had left Buchan with miserable memories of schoolboy cricket; he had never made the first eleven, let alone opening bat. Nevertheless, now he lay bareheaded on a dusty patch of grass with his long legs crossed at the ankles, his long shorts flapping about his bandaged knees, his left elbow on his discarded pith helmet and his chin cupped in his left hand. If anybody had told Buchan that he was, even now, aping those exalted beings he had so envied in adolescence he would have become quite indignant.

How did one act when His Majesty's enemies, having just given you a Cook's tour of the local antiquities, wished to take your photograph? Under the circumstances, glaring defiance seemed churlish. Nevertheless, a chap could hardly sit there saying 'cheese' as if he was at the end of some seaside pier. It certainly wouldn't do to look as if one really was on a Cook's tour. After all, unless you were ordered to surrender, like the people at Kut, a certain stigma did attach itself to unwounded prisoners, especially officers.

Not that Buchan was without pain. His knees hurt abominably. They had become infected from the cuts he had received when obliged to dive into one of those ghastly cactus hedges around Gaza after the Turkish machine-guns had pinned them down. And hundreds of the shrub's little yellow thorns were bristling from his face and hands. The more he extracted the more he found, and the puffier the flesh around them became. But although these poisonous darts hurt like hell they hardly counted as an honourable wound.

He envied the captain, who had taken up a rather similar bookend position at the other side of the officers' group – there were five of them altogether, with most of the other ranks clustered in a semi-circle behind them. Somehow it was quite obvious that the bandage around this officer's head could not possibly be connected with an unfriendly bush.

Choosing the right pose was not easy. It had to be made quite clear that one had had a hard time of it without looking like a whipped cur. At the same time Buchan felt it would be rank bad manners to offend captors who had turned out to be so remarkably sporting. It was all quite amazing, especially after the stories about the fate of some of the Kut garrison that were buzzing around Cairo.

The photographer was a wiry man with reddish hair, who had been introduced to the officers as a Mr Eric Matson of Sweden. It seemed that Mr Matson had been living in Jerusalem for some years and before the war had done some work on behalf of the Palestine Exploration Fund. Matson had a Syrian assistant who wore an old-fashioned black frock-coat and a fez, the flowerpot headdress of the Ottoman Empire that British troops tended to associate with organ grinders' monkeys. The assistant was taking an interminable time to prepare the equipment, which stood on a tripod before them – including a black hood, which he occasionally draped over his head and shoulders to make some arcane adjustment.

'Why are we waiting?' sang one of the non-commissioned ranks softly. Buchan thought it sounded like an Australian. Some of the others began to join in. 'Why are we way-tin? Oh why eye are we wait –'

'Steady, lads,' commanded the captain with the head wound, without looking round or in any way altering his position.

The singing subsided almost immediately, far more quickly than under normal circumstances. They're unsure of themselves as well, thought Buchan. He turned and smiled at them and was relieved to see that some of them smiled back.

He felt desperately sorry for the men, especially those of his own platoon. Sorry and not a little ashamed. He was destined for an officers' PoW camp where he would not be required to work. Other ranks were employed as slave labour. In Cairo it was common knowledge that British prisoners were digging the debris away from the tunnels being blasted through the Taurus and Amanus mountains to accommodate the new wide-gauge railway which German engineers were laying to Mesopotamia and Palestine.

Buchan had always suspected that he was quite unworthy of his men. Apart from some regular NCOs they were all volunteers who had answered Kitchener's call, a mixture of East Anglian ploughboys and bored clerks and shop assistants from the new dormitory towns that were springing up in Essex. More often than not, their patriotism had been spurred by an understandable desire to break the monotony of their lives before they were trapped by marriage. It was a well-known fact that French girls were fast, and few of them had dreamed that they would campaign outside Europe. In the villages around Ipswich people sometimes thought they could hear the artillery thunder from Flanders just one hundred miles across the North Sea.

To Buchan it had always seemed quite unfair to both parties that a mere accident of birth should put him in charge of them. He remembered how at school he had derived almost exactly the same satisfaction from their Officer Training Corps parades and field exercises as from the drama lessons he so enjoyed. All that dressing up, choreographed movement and bellowing your lungs out. Now he felt he was once again playing a part, made no more or less a real leader of men by the addition of a Sam Browne belt over his khaki than a laurel wreath and a bed sheet had made him Augustus Caesar.

A Turkish officer with a waxed moustache and a furled umbrella over one arm appeared. Buchan assumed the umbrella must be against the sun, for there would be no more rain in Jerusalem before next November.

'Strewth! It's Charlie Chaplin.' This time the voice was unmistakably Australian. The Turk took up position with some other Turkish and German officers who were standing to the right of Buchan.

'*Oh the moon shines bright on Charlie Chaplin*,' a *sotto voce* chorus from the other ranks' lines began. '*His boots need blackin', his kit needs packin', And his old baggy trousis they want mendin'.*'

The voices had grown stronger now. 'Pipe down,' said the captain with the head bandage. Buchan noticed that he wore the broken spur insignia of the 74th Division, the dismounted Yeomanry.

The song became a barely audible whisper: '*Before they send 'im. To the Dardanelles.*'

The Turkish officer showed no sign of having heard any of this. His only reaction was to nod politely to the British officers and run an affectionate finger under his moustache. Matson decided that the picture was now complete. He slipped under the hood and worked the shutter, while the assistant held up a smoking flash.

Buchan fished in his top-left tunic pocket for his silver cigarette case, a recent twenty-first birthday present from his parents. His mother had instructed him to wear it over his heart because she had read of lives being saved this way. Small armour-plated New Testaments were becoming popular among the ranks, but were regarded as a bit vulgar by the officer class. Buchan counted himself lucky to be still in possession of his birthday present. It had been about to disappear into the pockets of the first Turkish private who searched him when an officer had given the man a tremendous back-hander along the side of his head and ordered its return.

The subaltern lit his cigarette, and was about to return the case to his pocket when he saw the blurred reflection of his stubbled chin. It had now been four days since he last shaved and he was fascinated by this. It was, after all, the nearest thing he had had to a beard. He shined the case with his sleeve and looked again, running the fingers of his right hand over the bristles as he did so.

He was engaged in this minor narcissism when the reflection suddenly darkened and he was aware that somebody was standing over him. He looked up and found a pair of coal-black eyes boring into him.

'Good afternoon,' said Maeltzer in English, touching the brim of his panama in a kind of salute. It had in fact only just turned noon but the journalist liked to be punctilious about these things. 'My name is Karl Maeltzer. I'm the correspondent here for the *Zürcher Zeitung*.' He held out his hand.

Buchan got to his feet, not without difficulty. It was extremely painful to bend his knees. He returned the handshake and rather reluctantly introduced himself. First a photograph and now the neutral press: it was all a bit much. Behind the journalist stood a smug-looking German officer of about his own age with the left sleeve pinned neatly to the front of his tunic; he was wearing the flat mortarboard hat, the Polish *schapska*, of one of the Uhlan lancer regiments. Buchan glanced around to see if any of the other officers might come to his rescue — preferably the incisive captain with the head wound. It seemed that none of them had noticed this latest turn in events. This was hardly surprising, the entire morning had been so bizarre that he did not suppose that any of them would have batted an eyelid if the Sultan himself had turned up complete with his harem.

'Are you a Swiss citizen?' he asked, for it had occurred to him that a correspondent for a neutral publication was not necessarily himself a neutral.

'Of course,' said Maeltzer. 'Do you wish to see my papers?'

'It won't be necessary,' said Buchan, who had already made up his mind that the man could prove he was the Pope for all the useful information that he was going to get out of him. 'It just occurred to me that you might be able to get word back to my people that I'm all right, in good health, that sort of thing?'

'Your people?' Maeltzer looked genuinely perplexed.

'My parents.'

'I can't see why not.'

Maeltzer produced a notebook and pencil and, after a couple of false starts, got down the Englishman's name and home address. While he did this Weidinger, who hardly spoke any English, wandered off for a chat with Pichler, who had just turned up in a Mercedes-Benz driven by one of the aviators from Fast's.

'I should say then that you have been well treated?' inquired Maeltzer. There was a cautious tone to his inquiry.

'So far, yes, you could say,' agreed Buchan.

'And how did you enjoy your visit to the Holy Sepulchre and the other holy sights this morning?'

'Most interesting. Of course, one would have liked to have visited them under different circumstances.'

There was a short pause while Maeltzer wrote this down. Suddenly Buchan had a flash of inspiration. 'But if you're going to stay on here I think you'll be seeing a lot more of the British army.'

'Do you mean that soon we will capture the entire Egyptian Expeditionary Force?' demanded a new voice. 'How are we going to feed you all?' It was Krag, the intelligence officer, brushing the dust off the sleeves of his white summer uniform.

'I meant no such thing,' said Buchan, the colour rising to his cheeks. He could not remember being put down so neatly since he left school.

'My apologies, er, Lieutenant,' said Krag, taking in the prisoner's badges of rank. 'I must have misunderstood you.' As he spoke he took out a packet of oval-shaped Turkish cigarettes and screwed one into an amber-coloured holder.

'Ah, Major Krag,' said Maeltzer. 'Are you feeling better? I was told you were unwell.' He continued to speak English. He did not wish to remind Buchan that he was more at home in the language of the enemy.

'A touch of malaria, that's all,' said Krag, who also continued to speak in an English that Maeltzer found surprisingly good. 'God's curse on both armies is it not, Lieutenant? But now I suppose you'll tell me that your side has never heard of it, eh?'

I would if I had thought of it, thought Buchan.

'But please excuse me. I must not interrupt your work, Herr Maeltzer.' This time Krag spoke in German. He bent forward slightly from the waist, made a slight clicking movement with his heels and moved off.

'*Auf Wiedersehn, Herr Major.*'

'Who was that?' asked Buchan.

'Major Krag, an intelligence officer. He's the one you have to watch.'

'And not you, Herr Smaltzer? I don't have to watch you?'

'Maeltzer,' corrected the journalist softly. For the first time he appeared to notice the young Englishman's bandaged knees. 'But you are wounded,' he said with what sounded like genuine concern. Like most journalists, spies and prostitutes, Maeltzer never hesitated to dissemble in the pursuit of his vocation.

'Not really. I fell into a cactus hedge, that's all.'

'You must get them looked at,' urged Maeltzer. 'If the thorns aren't removed and the flesh becomes infected it can be very serious. How did it happen?'

How did it happen? Buchan was not really certain how it had happened, and even if he had been he was not at all sure it was something he wanted to discuss with a foreign journalist living in the enemy camp.

He was trying to formulate a suitable reply when a voice at his side said, 'It 'appened because the bleedin' staff had their maps arse about face. That's what 'appened.'

The speaker was a small man wearing an Australian's digger hat. To Buchan's ears his accent sounded like a hybrid of Cockney and that awful twang from which not even some Australian officers were entirely immune.

'Arse about what?' asked Maeltzer politely. He knew all the words. The problem was his English wasn't quite up to hearing them linked up like this.

'They made a fuckin' Fred Karno's army of it, that's what they did,' said the little man. 'They got –'

'Look,' interrupted Buchan. 'Some of the men have had a hard time of it. I don't think it's fair –'

But the little man would not be silenced, and Buchan shied away from giving him a direct order to shut up. Unlike his own fellows, who might rag you a bit when the sergeant's back was turned but generally knew where to draw the line, you could never tell with these colonial troops. For the most part they lived up to the reputation they had first acquired against the Boers: excellent horsemen, fine shots, splendid physiques – though this fellow seemed to be an exception to the rule in that area. They were also famous for a lack of discipline that sometimes made them less reliable than English troops. Certainly there was no automatic respect for His Majesty's commission, for orders delivered in a certain accent.

'They got us stuck in that bleedin' cactus didn't they. Rear fuckin' guard, that's what we were.'

34

Buchan guessed that he must have been among a detachment of Australian Light Horse who had been sent in to cover their retreat from the slopes of Ali Muntar Ridge. 'Then the Royal fuckin' Navy starts shelling' us, our own bleedin' ships start blowin' us to fuckin' glory.'

Maeltzer was nodding sympathetically and scribbling away in his notebook. Buchan walked stiffly away. His knees were hurting, and he wanted to find a place where he could sit down quietly for a few minutes. The Australian continued his diatribe, 'If I ever get my hands on one of those bleedin' matlows,' he was saying. 'I'll guard his fuckin' rear for him.'

Buchan sat down with his back against the Crusader stones that made up the lower part of the city's wall, stubbed his cigarette out and almost immediately lit up another one. His knees were hurting like hell; he suddenly felt very tired and depressed, almost near to tears.

Of course, the Digger was right. It *had* been the most frightful shambles, he realised that now. At first he had not felt qualified to form an opinion, for the simple reason that he had never been in a battle before. He had expected noise, smoke, dust and a certain amount of confusion. But there were other things he had not been prepared for.

He had never imagined, for instance, just how terrifying the zizz of a single rifle bullet fired by an enemy could be, even when its course was probably several feet above your head. Or how easy it was for a new officer to make a fool of himself in front of his men by jumping and flinching at the sound of your own artillery. Or that it was possible to get as tired in battle as he did in that first week when his brigade took the place they called Green Hill, using bayonets and Mills bombs to winkle the Turks out of the holes they had dug themselves behind the cactus hedges. Not, thank God, that he had done much winkling himself, although he had followed the other platoon commander's example and carried a rifle in addition to his revolver so that snipers would not immediately spot his rank. He had thrown a couple of grenades and later fallen into a hole and shot a dead man who had the temerity to stare. The Turkish defence was in depth and there were other lines to bomb and stab their way through. When they had done so they were ordered to withdraw, because elsewhere on the front things had gone wrong and they had become a long finger exposed to attack on three sides. After they had rested for a week they were ordered to take it back again.

35

He had expected to have to hide his fear among men who were braver and more experienced than he was. Some of his fellow-subalterns seemed to have iced water running in their veins, and exuded an air of enjoying the whole business. He had hoped that their courage would prove contagious, and to a certain extent this had happened.

What he had not expected was for the oldest member of his platoon, a corporal who had turned down a soft billet with a home service battalion, to start sobbing like a child when they were being shelled. He had been crouched in a shallow Turkish trench with his arm around the weeping man's shoulder when a runner, a hero if ever there was one, had arrived from company HQ with a message that the fire was coming from two Royal Navy monitors and a French cruiser offshore, and was intended to cover their withdrawal.

The next shell had killed the runner on his way back. When the barrage did slacken it was only because it had shifted slightly further south, cutting off their line of retreat as effectively as a steel curtain.

When they tried to get out the Turks added to their misery by bringing up their machine-guns. Buchan had hardly noticed the cactus thorns when he and his men flopped onto their bellies and the lead stitched neat little holes in the wicked vegetation around them.

Somebody must have told the ships they were firing too far south for, once again, the gun crews altered their elevation – but not enough. Their next salvo had fallen directly onto the forward British positions.

Buchan recalled how the blast from the first eight-inch shell had tugged at his clothing like some flirtatious spirit while the second had sucked the breath out of him. After that he had lost count: he had pressed his chin, chest, stomach, tiny detumesced genitals, thighs and knees against an earth which rocked and cracked and whined, while one hand squeezed the stock of his rifle and the other pulled and pinched at the thin flesh of his chest. Three of his men had been killed outright, and of the eleven wounded another three would later die of their injuries.

Leaning against the ancient stones, absently patting his bandaged knees, Buchan looked up to see that one of his Essex men was talking to Maeltzer, who was nodding and smiling in an encouraging manner. '. . . one moment I'm layin' on the ground sayin' my prayers then it all goes quiet and the next thing I know old Johnny Turkeycock is standin' there. "Ello Tommy," he says . . .'

Not for the first time Buchan marvelled at his men's marvellous capacity to make a joke of the most horrendous things. His own capture had proved almost as terrifying as the naval bombardment.

There had been a sudden and inexplicable silence, so that he could almost hear the drumming of his heart. For a few seconds he had lain there quite motionless, savouring the fact that he was still alive, feeling the heat of the sun through his tunic. Then the drumming had become more insistent; there were occasional shots, though they sounded far off. After a minute or so he had realised what the drumming was.

He had raised his head a couple of inches from the ground. At first he could see nothing but swirling clouds of dust. Then he had made them out, coming through the dust fog like ghosts: figures on horseback carrying long poles, walking their mounts through the cactus scrub because there was no longer any room to canter. Turkish lancers.

Somewhere nearby one of his wounded had began to moan loudly, and he had hated him for drawing attention to themselves. He had got to his knees and watched the poles come closer, utterly transfixed. He recalled how once at his prep school a retired Indian Army officer on the staff had enthralled him with his tales of the Raj, until it came to the noble sport of pig-sticking. 'Nothing as dangerous as a wounded boar in a thicket,' the old sportsman had declared, but try as he would the twelve-year-old Buchan had been unable to shed his sympathy for the pig at bay.

Now he was the pig – but unwounded, undangerous, and petrified by the notion that he was about to be impaled on one of those long lances. He had five rounds left in his rifle and the full six in his holstered revolver. He had picked up his Lee-Enfield, but even as he did so he resolved that he would only fire if they looked eager for skewering practice.

Some men on foot had appeared around the horses. To his amazement he had realised that they were his own men and that they had their hands up in surrender, except for the sad cameo of a wounded soldier with his arms draped around the shoulders of two of his mates. This isn't right, he had thought. I didn't order them to give up. He had wanted to shout something, but couldn't think what to say.

Turkish infantry with bayonets fixed had appeared on the scene. Buchan had dropped his rifle and stood with his arms by his side. It had seemed absurdly theatrical to put them over his head until one of the infantry approached him and he saw that the bayonet was the serrated, saw-edge type banned by the Geneva Convention. At this point he had put his hands up to shoulder level and tried to smile, the Turk, a powerful-looking man who needed a shave, had grunted something.

As it turned out his captor, who was wearing a kind of pointed leather slipper rather than boots, was more interested in loot than murder. Within a second he had jerked Buchan's revolver from its holster and, holding his rifle near the muzzle, used his bayonet to cut through the lanyard that ran under the right epaulette to the ring on the butt of the pistol. Then he had expertly run his hands through Buchan's pockets and found the cigarette case.

The soldier had been busy with the strap of Buchan's wristwatch when a Turkish officer had come up silently behind him and delivered a sickening backhander to the side of his head. The soldier had stood rigidly to attention while the officer continued to berate him, all the time punctuating his remarks with slaps across the face. When he had finished and the cigarette case had been returned, the Turkish officer had saluted Buchan and walked off.

Thus commenced the first five days of captivity, which had culminated in a silent prayer for his wellbeing at the altar of the Holy Sepulchre and a photographic session near the Jaffa Gate. Buchan thought that if his knees were not hurting so much he might have seen the funny side of it.

The captain with the head wound came up to the men clustered around Maeltzer and shooed them away. The journalist did not mind. He had more than enough for a decent despatch.

4

After interviewing the prisoners Maeltzer accepted an invitation to join Weidinger, a couple of other junior staff officers, the artilleryman Pichler and his aviator friend for a late lunch at Fast's.

His hosts, none of whom had yet reached thirty, were in a relaxed mood, buoyed up by the sight of the prisoners. On the whole they had thought them dignified enough, but – with the possible exception of the Australians – poor physical material compared to German infantry. Maeltzer decided it was best not to point out that the British had not sent a single Guards battalion to Palestine.

Had he wished, the journalist could easily have lingered with them over coffee and cigars for another half hour or so. But he excused himself, explaining that he wanted to write his despatch in time to give it to an officer who was going home on convalescent leave the next day. Depending on the state of the railways, he should take no more than five days to reach Vienna. He had promised to see that the despatch was delivered to his newspaper's bureau there, and they would cable it to Zürich.

Pichler asked him why he did not telegraph it directly from Jerusalem, and Maeltzer told him that his newspaper was so mean they would think it excessive if he telegraphed an account of the battle of Armageddon. This was only a slight exaggeration. He had sent a short telegram setting out the bare facts of the Gaza battle: his editors believed that readers anxious for further details would not have their appetites blunted by a week's delay.

France, Russia, the American factor and unrestricted submarine warfare were still the centres of attention, Maeltzer had reminded them. Palestine, he regretted to say, was regarded as a sideshow, along with Mesopotamia, Salonika, Italy, Rumania, East Africa,

Japanese assaults on German naval bases in China, air raids in London and all the other minor mayhem of a world at war. After the young men around the table had digested this proposition, he added, 'But personally I find these sideshows, these forgotten fields, can be more fun.'

They all drank to that, toasting each other in a local red wine from a monastery at Latrun. Weidinger noticed that Maeltzer drank sparingly, his mind obviously on his work.

'Tell me, Herr Maeltzer,' asked Pichler as the journalist rose to leave. 'Do our noble allies subject your despatches to censorship?'

'They used to. It was called the postal service. One simply dropped something in this end – and it was never seen again.'

Pichler and Weidinger both laughed at this. Good old Herr Professor Maeltzer! It was a title they sometimes honoured him with, for he aroused the kind of affection in them – but particularly in Weidinger – that seventeen-year-olds will bestow on a favourite schoolmaster. Besides, jokes about the inefficiency, sloth and sexual desperation of the Turks, however weak, were always welcome. Maeltzer knew full well that the postal service was one of the better things about the Ottoman Empire. Before the war all the major powers had been allowed to maintain their own post offices in Jerusalem. The Austro-Hungarians and the Germans still had theirs, but military demands on the rail network meant that there was a backlog of everything civilian, including mail.

Maeltzer stayed at the Grand New Hotel, which had been eclipsed by Fast's long before the outbreak of hostilities and was now neither grand nor new. It was an imposing enough building; its three storeys were built around a central courtyard, while its railed flat roof provided a good all-round view of the Jerusalem skyline. Its architect – an Italian, Maeltzer suspected – had attempted the requisite neo-classical look, but Maeltzer thought the effect was more Egyptian than Greek.

Whereas Fast's was outside the walls, the Grand New was part of the noise, stench, filth and summer diseases that flourished behind them. The hotel was just inside the Jaffa Gate, near the gap in the ramparts that had been made for the Kaiser's entrance in '98 so that he could enter the Holy City on a caparisoned charger without upsetting Ottoman protocol by riding under one of its ancient portals. Opposite the hotel was the Citadel, the fortress within a fortress with its own moat and drawbridge, where the Turkish garrison had its headquarters. Its battlements were frequently adorned with tripod gallows where the condemned dangled in their ankle-length shrouds. On several mornings Maeltzer had been greeted by the sight of a dangling man with his head on his chest. He had taken to opening his curtains a few inches at a time, hurriedly drawing them again if a preliminary reconnaissance seemed to confirm his worse fears. He could watch burial parties clean up a day-old battlefield and eat a hearty meal afterwards, but the very thought of those gallows left him trembling.

The Grand New was the best a neutral civilian could do, and it was only a few minutes' walk from Fast's, which saved the exhausting business of haggling with Syrian cabmen who still started by demanding outrageous fares even though their ribs were often getting as easy to count as those of their horses. He walked there now, relieved to see that Magnus was no longer about. Go and slaughter the Amalek indeed!

It was a pleasant afternoon. Elsewhere in the land, in the cactus scrub around the port of Gaza for instance, the heat could be oppressive for uniformed Europeans. In Jerusalem the altitude made all the difference. On a spring day like this the climate was almost perfect, the air faintly scented with pine and purple bougainvillaea.

A cab insisted on following him, the horse's hooves clip-clopping on the baked earth road. He had given all the drivers outside Fast's a firm 'no', but one of them was always desperate enough to persist, however ludicrous the distance. The trick was to avoid all eye contact. The difficult moment came when the cabbie tired of the game and overtook, at the same time making a strange hissing sound in a last attempt to make a stubborn pedestrian stare hunger in the face.

Maeltzer's lunch had made him sleepy, and he was annoyed he had to work. He felt like seeking out some warm spot where he could snooze for a while, stretching occasionally like some contented cat.

He paused to yawn, tapping his mouth with his hand as he did so. This was a mistake because the driver came up and hissed at him, and he caught a glimpse of an anguished old man's face as he waved him away. Overhead a biplane was flying in the direction of the Mount of Olives. This too was soporific. The monotony of its engine reminded Maeltzer of the kind of sewing-machine used in factories that produced cheap garments, the sort that was operated by a treadle. He wondered whether the aircraft was piloted by a German or a Turk. There were said to be at least a dozen Turkish pilots in the country now. There was little chance that he was English. He had heard that the British had more aircraft in Palestine then the Germans, but most of them were very old and the Germans were always shooting them down. It would be a very brave Royal Flying Corps pilot indeed who risked a solo sortie over Jerusalem.

The plane flew off in a north-westerly direction, towards the coast and Jaffa and the dipping sun. Definitely not English.

Thinking about the English reminded Maeltzer that he had promised to inform Buchan's parents of his capture. He got out his notebook and looked again at their address: *Mr and Mrs Horatio Buchan, The Gables, Cowden-in-the-Marsh, near Brentwood, Essex.* He tried to imagined what The Gables was like. Possibly a thatched roof. Bay windows, leaded lights, a gravel drive. Perhaps a tennis court at the back, not much used now. He had never visited Brentwood but he knew England quite well. He had spent two years in his newspaper's London office, partly because a genial editor had wished to cure him of what he considered excessive Anglophobia.

Maeltzer had told Weidinger that this had not been a success. He had, he assured him, found the British strangely unwholesome at every level. Quite apart from their irritating assumption that they were the only Europeans fit to run an Empire, their upper classes had only confirmed his belief that they were either bone-headed sportsmen or effete dilettantes. The urban masses, he said, tended to be undernourished, stunted creatures with pungent body odour.

Like Weidinger and his friends, Maeltzer had found Buchan and the other British prisoners unimpressive. What was one supposed to think of a young officer discovered staring at his reflection like some tortured schoolgirl? It was true that the British had better soldiers in France and perhaps he *should* have reminded Weidinger that they did not have a single Guards battalion in Egypt; but it was hard to imagine them beating a people as courageous and efficient as the Germans, the technically most advanced nation in Europe. The English could be brave enough at times but their generals were abysmal, accustomed to using maxim guns on spear-chuckers. That's why the Boers had led them such a dance.

Despite greatly superior numbers, they had succeeded in getting their troops caught up like a flock of sheep on the cactus hedges around Gaza. Over lunch he had been told that the British general, Sir Archibald Murray, had tried to direct the battle from a railway carriage that was barely out of Cairo. Lunacy! No, that was too grand a word for it. Stupidity was more like it. Stupidity born out of ignorance and sloth, plus a gentleman's reluctance to get too involved.

Maeltzer paused for a moment to let the thought sink in, and the cab driver was instantly alongside.

'Tired, effendi?' he asked in Arabic. It was a dignified inquiry. He was starving but he was not begging; he was offering a service.

'I wish to walk,' said Maeltzer whose Arabic was quite good. He fished in the pockets of his jacket and emerged with a handful of piastres. The sadness of the man appalled him.

'Here,' he said. 'Take this.' The driver hesitated. 'In case I need you later.'

'Thank you, effendi.' He gave a toothless smile and leant down from his perch to take the money. As he did so he suddenly grabbed Maeltzer's hand and kissed it.

'For God's sake,' said the journalist and pulled it away. At the same time he realised that an aircraft was overhead again. Its engine was much louder this time, as if it was directly above them.

Both Maeltzer and the cabbie looked up, the journalist putting one hand to the brim of his panama.

The biplane was in a shallow dive, not much higher it seemed than the dome of the el Aksa mosque, heading back towards the Mount of Olives. Almost simultaneously he heard the explosions, though it was not until he saw the black puffs of smoke around the plane that he realised they were anti-aircraft fire.

'Inglisi, effendi?'

The aircraft appeared to dip down into the Kidron Valley and had disappeared from sight by the time they heard the machine-gun fire and two much louder explosions, which Maeltzer rightly guessed were bombs.

'Yes,' he said. 'Inglisi.' So some British flier had been brave enough to pay Jerusalem a visit after all. He searched the sky for German planes in pursuit, but could not see any. After a minute or so the aircraft briefly reappeared, flying south-west in the direction of Beersheba.

Back in his hotel room, Maeltzer scribbled a note for Weidinger asking him around for a drink that evening and tipped one of the bell boys a small amount to take it around to Fast's. Waiting for the boy to return made it difficult to concentrate on the long article he wanted to write on the Gaza battle, plus a separate account of the demoralised English and Australian prisoners he had interviewed.

His desk was by a window overlooking the ramparts of the Citadel. Sometimes he would find himself pacing the room, and yet have no memory of drawing back his chair and leaving his desk. That afternoon he was worse than ever. He would write a few lines and then pace up and down, leaving one of the little cheroots his sister had sent him to extinguish itself in the ashtray.

The air raid was the first noteworthy event in Jerusalem since six twisting and jerking Syrian deserters had appeared on the Citadel's gibbets after the authorities had felt the need to set a firm example in the face of the enemy build-up before Gaza. Maeltzer wanted to know what the air raid had achieved – and, more importantly, why the German squadrons had made no attempt to intercept this solitary raider.

In the suite of rooms below, the Widow Shemsi listened to Maeltzer pacing up and down, frowned and then went back to the task of pinning up her hair in preparation for a visit from Major Krag. Her hair was black, but henna had given it a distinct auburn tint, almost copper in strong sunlight. Not that it saw much sun, for the Widow Shemsi was famous for the kind of large hats that required hair pads and pins like duelling foils – the sort of headgear that had become unfashionably frivolous in Europe. She was a Syrian, born into a prosperous Greek Catholic trading family in Beirut: Nadia's father had sold out his share in the family business to his brothers and become a doctor. It was the kind of background that nurtured the Levantine fluency in languages. French was spoken at home except to the servants, who were addressed in Arabic. There had been private tuition in English. Her German was coming along well, just as she had learned passable Turkish in order to please her late husband.

Major Shemsi had succumbed to a combination of arak and malaria in the September of 1915, when he had been part of the Jericho garrison. He had been heavily in debt at the time of his death, largely because his passion for backgammon almost equalled his love of hard liquor. To the astonishment of his brother-officers, his feelings for both were exceeded by the love he bore his new wife, who was a little over twenty years his junior.

After spending the greater part of his career campaigning in the Yemen, Shemsi had met Nadia Haddad in Beirut while on civil administration duties there. At first Dr Haddad had been no more than amused when the major he brought home for cards and backgammon so obviously played court to his eldest daughter. But then his only son was among a group of students arrested as subversives, accused of being prominent members of the student wing of a secret society preaching Arab nationalism and total separation from the Sublime Porte. Suddenly the major's admiration for Nadia was no longer a joke, but a means by which her baby brother might be freed. Despite the religious differences, her parents, and especially her mother, persuaded her to take his attention seriously.

The major realised exactly what was required. As a result of the match charges were dropped, and baby brother was allowed to emigrate to the United States. Her parents salved any twinges of conscience they might have felt about the matter by telling themselves that Nadia had not done too badly. She was already in her late twenties, well past her prime. There had been a suitable young man once whose interest had pleased both them and her, but he had gone first to Egypt and then, like her brother, to California. From there his careful letters, with their involved salutes to her parents and accounts of homesickness brought on by the scent of a citrus grove, had become gradually less frequent and then ceased. Later she had heard, through a member of his family in Beirut, that he had married an Irish woman.

On the night before her wedding to Shemsi, which was now almost ten years ago, a tearful younger sister had asked her, in so many words, if she was not about to go through a fate worse than death, and she had replied that there were worse things. And she had been right. Shemsi had his weaknesses, but in his way he proved a loving husband.

It had never occurred to her that if Shemsi died she might be left destitute. But the war killed off the family business, for Beirut was under blockade and there were no longer the fruits of Brummagem to supply to a greedy Arab hinterland. Her father died treating an outbreak of typhus and his death revealed that he too owed large gambling debts. Her mother had gone to live with one of Nadia's married sisters. After Shemsi died there were siblings in and around Beirut who would have dutifully taken her in, but she did not want to live on sufferance, a widow of a certain age, unlikely to remarry. Instead, she intended to join her brother in San Francisco. However, he was not in a position to help her with her boat fare so it was necessary to save enough money for that, plus the bribes that would enable her to travel to some neutral port now that America was in the war. Meanwhile, her affair with Krag was hardly discreet. She had probably become the best-known mistress in the autonomous Sanjak of Jerusalem.

Maeltzer continued to pace her ceiling, his footfalls regularly punctuated by the creaking of single floorboard. Shemsi thought this must be when he turned round. For several weeks now she had intended to raise the matter of his marathon perambulations, but somehow she could never bring herself to do it. There was a quality of authority about the journalist, which would make even the lightest reproach seem like a gross impertinence. Not that he was anything but civil to her. Most of Krag's brother-officers cut her dead, whether out of prudery or jealousy she couldn't tell. Maeltzer invariably wished her the time of day, opened doors and raised his hat when appropriate, without ever making the slightest suggestion that he might wish to be on more intimate terms with her. She sometimes imagined she detected a hint of defiance in his manner, the devil-may-care attitude of a man who was answerable to no one but himself.

This was a lot more than she could say for the gentleman she was expecting. She sighed again, more a kind of impatience with herself than self-pity, and examined her face in the cheval glass. She was not pleased with what she saw. In the last few months she had aged, she knew that. What men called 'the bloom' was gone. For some reason, although her diet was perfectly adequate, she was beginning to lose weight. She had always been too slimly built to achieve the contemporary notion of beauty, but now she fancied that her cheeks were stretched and sallow-looking. And one of her front teeth had begun to darken. She practised a crooked smile which almost hid it. Well, it would have to do. It would certainly do for Major Krag.

5

A couple of hours after the air raid Magnus's sandalled feet picked their way carefully along the striated Byzantine flagstones that paved Christian Quarter Street.

Russian pilgrims once came there to buy their funeral shrouds, but the pilgrim trade had died along with the peace when Turkey found itself at war with most of Christendom. For the first time since the Byzantine emperors the Eastern Church did not dominate the Christian establishment of the city. Most of the Russian and Greek Orthodox had fled along with French and Italian Catholics and all the Anglican schism.

While the war lasted, the Lutherans were meant to be looking after the interests of their departed co-religionists. Their showpiece was the Church of the Saviour with its great square belltower. The church had been completed in time to celebrate Kaiser Wilhelm's arrival in Jerusalem almost twenty years before on the tour that had done much to revive the notion of pilgrimage in fashionable Europe.

Along the Christian Quarter Street a few of the shops that specialised in selling *objets de piété* and other religious bric-a-brac were still open. Their proprietors believed in miracles. They believed that those recently arrived members of the Austrian and German contingents whose kitbags were not already bulging with olive wood crucifixes, rosary beads, nativity sets, Noah's arks, heads of John the Baptist and splinters of the true cross would certainly pass by sooner or later. As an act of faith it was impressive; as is often the case, its rewards were mostly intangible. In order to feed their families some shopkeepers had begun to offer the soldiery real bargains. Men who had once amassed fortunes out of the pilgrim trade were now reduced to selling their wives' jewellery at olive-wood prices.

As he walked Magnus tapped the pavement with his cross, his blazing eyes looking everywhere and nowhere at once. He was one of the few relatively young civilian men to be walking the streets of the Old City that afternoon. Male citizens of Jerusalem who had not already been conscripted into one of the Arab regiments presently confronting the British along the Gaza-Beersheba line rarely ventured out in case they met up with an army patrol anxious that they should share their fortune.

There were, in addition, estimated to be another three thousand actual deserters hiding out within the walls. And even those who by virtue of their sex or age were obviously non-combatant tended to conserve their strength by staying at home as much as possible given the shortage of food. During the last two years the land had not only suffered the casual depredations of warfare, with cavalry grazing their horses in hard-grown barley fields and treasured olive groves being chopped down for fuel, but harvests had also been destroyed by a plague of locusts that would have satisfied any Old Testament prophet's longing for divine retribution.

Such locals as were out mostly regarded Magnus without much curiosity. Before the war there had been many like him around – men who had allowed their conceit to blow them across that blurred frontier which divides genuine grace from plain lunacy. The only people who paused to give him a second look were occasional groups of soldiers, Turkish and European. Some were tempted to tease him, but there was something about the evident madness of Magnus's gaze from the cosy nest of his full beard, that made them resist.

Weidinger was in one of the shops. He had just concluded a most satisfactory deal over a gold bracelet for a younger sister when he spotted Magnus outside. The shopkeeper, a lugubrious Greek Catholic Syrian whose roots in the country went back a couple of thousand years or so, paused in his mournful wrapping of the gift and followed the officer's stare. 'Blessed by God,' he said. He spoke German. He also spoke Arabic, Turkish, French, English, Yiddish and a smattering of Syriac. He was, after all, a Levantine trader.

'You think so?' said Weidinger, watching the Swedish messiah loping down the street.

'Also by man. There's always meat on that fellows' plate.'

'So I've noticed,' said Weidinger, recalling his conversation with Maeltzer. He was not all that interested.

'Yes,' said the Syrian. 'People think he is like this' – and he screwed a bent left forefinger into his temple – 'but he has money.'

'Yes, I know,' said Weidinger. 'He begs for it.'

Had he not been in such a good mood over the bracelet he might have told the fellow that he had better things to do than gossip about passing lunatics.

'Do beggars get these?' In his hand the shopkeeper held a gold sovereign stamped with the avuncular, bearded head of Edward VII, monarch of Great Britain and Ireland, Emperor of India. Weidinger picked it up and saw that it had been minted in 1905. 'The Swedish Christ changed this last week,' the Syrian, said. 'He was afraid that somebody might steal it, and wanted small coins for it.'

'Did he?' said Weidinger, making the coin turn little somersaults in the palm of his hand.

There was nothing unusual in itself about a man owning an English sovereign, as long as it had not been minted after the outbreak of hostilities. Germany may have long outpaced Britain in steel production and be pushing ahead in the new chemical and electrical industries, but sterling remained the strongest currency on earth and much sought after. Thousands of the Czar's kopecks were still in circulation in Jerusalem, as were Austrian Maria Theresas, French francs, United States dollars and German marks. Indeed, the citizens of the Ottoman Empire preferred almost anything to its own frequently devalued lire.

All the same Weidinger was intrigued to know how a man as crazy as the Swede, with no visible means of support, could have possessed such a coin. There could, of course, be several perfectly innocent explanations. He might be a remittance man, supported by some wealthy family who preferred that he remained as far away as possible rather than embarrass them on the streets of Stockholm. Or the coin could have belonged to an ever-diminishing nest egg. He may even have sold something recently – a watch, his mother's wedding-ring – though as the price of the bracelet only went to show, jewellery tended to lose its value in hungry cities.

Then again, Magnus could have obtained it by committing some crime: he could have bludgeoned some wretch to death with that ridiculous staff he carried, or sneaked a purse or wallet from somewhere like Fast's Hotel. He was always hanging about there.

And then, thought Weidinger, he could have earned it for some service or some favour. But what? Had he persuaded some gullible young private that he really did have the ear of the Almighty and that his prayers would deflect bullets? Or had he run an errand for some blackmarket swindle, masterminded by the Jews perhaps?

Finally there was the possibility of espionage. European neutrals were obviously the most sought-after agents, but surely the English would not be desperate enough to use a madman like Magnus – unless, of course, he was not as mad as he made out to be? If that was the case, he was a very good actor: but what was a spy if he wasn't an actor?

Weidinger wondered whether Krag bothered to keep a file on the Swede. He was said to have them on other neutrals remaining in Jerusalem, even on Maeltzer. Perhaps he should have a word with him about it. But it might be worth probing a little deeper before he told anybody else. One of the most efficient Turkish creations was their system of informers – as long as one remembered it was a circular affair, whereby informer informed on informer. It would cost a pittance to have Magnus followed for twenty-four hours a day. If there was anything in it, Kress should know that he was the one who uncovered it. God only knew, the war owed him a little luck.

———————

Magnus strode on, past the Lutheran church with its tall steeple, and into David Street. Here he turned left and went down to the bazaar area on the edge of the Muslim quarter, before turning right into the Jewish neighbourhood.

A rat almost collided with his feet but if he was aware of this the Swede did not show it. Magnus was tired. Magnus was hungry, but food and rest must wait. Magnus had work to do. Wise were the ways of the Lord.

6

'Oh Lord build! Oh Lord build!' cried the white-bearded Jew, 'build thy house speedily.'

Tears coursed the old man's cheeks. His voice broke and quavered like that of a boy reaching adolescence.

'In haste! In haste!' chanted the women standing at their section of the wall a few feet to his left: 'even in our days.'

Then together they all chorused: 'Build thy house speedily. In haste! In haste!

'Even in our days,' finished the patriarch.

They were all weeping now, old and young, men and women. They were mourning a two thousand-year-old defeat, the destruction of King Herod's Temple by the Roman legions of the Emperor Titus in 70 AD.

When their Muslim Syrian guide had showed them earlier in the day what he called 'the Jews' wailing place', most of the British prisoners, Buchan included, had been shocked at what they saw. If they had given the matter any thought at all they had always regarded the Jews as near-as-damn-it Europeans, sometimes stinking rich bankers or merchants, but most miserly usurers or dirt-poor half-blind tailors who lived in slums where their women either worked in sweatshops or prostituted themselves. They had never imagined them behaving so demonstrably, 'like a bunch of bleedin' 'eathens', as one private put it.

For a start, there was the bizarre costume of these Orthodox Jews – basically seventeenth-century Polish dress, consisting of a kaftan, knee breeches, buckled shoes and – despite the heat – huge round fur hats with flat tops, from below which dangled long corkscrew side-curls. The women were more conventionally attired, though all of them wore tightly wrapped head-scarves. The Syrian had smirked and told the British prisoners that underneath the women were as bald as eggs because they had shaved their hair off so as not to be attractive to other men. Some of the better-off, he had added, sometimes wore a wig over their shaved scalps, because even their husbands thought them ugly.

Buchan found it difficult to believe that they could inspire much lust among their menfolk even with their hair. Both sexes were painfully thin and undernourished-looking, with none of the robustness of Zionists like Sarah Aaronsohn – whose attempts to rebuild the Jewish nation before the restoration of the Temple they considered an appalling blasphemy. Only the Lord could decide when He would redeem Zion for his Chosen People. Meanwhile, there was no harm in praying that it might be in their time.

When they were not praying the men were studying the Torah or debating its more arcane teachings with various sages, so that they rarely saw the sun and their skins never lost the pallor of the European ghettos. This was often combined with myopia, and, in quite a few cases, the eyes which stared from behind thick-lensed spectacles bulged hugely, the result of a genetical hyperthyroid condition caused by inbreeding.

The old man was one of these. He was also desperately poor, having spent his meagre resources on bringing with him from the Russian Pale sixteen members of the family so that he should not be lonely while waiting for death in King David's city. Every day he prayed before the stones that had formed the western wall of Herod's Temple, singing out the penitential psalms while at the same time swaying back and forth from the waist up with the sudden, jerky energy of a clockwork toy.

During his prayers he would occasionally go up to the wall and touch the stones themselves, caressing the crevices where worshippers like himself sometimes tucked the tiny scrolls of prayerful petition they called *kvitals*. When he touched the stones he felt that he was in contact with a living thing. They seemed electric; it was as if the whole earth was vibrating through them. Sometimes his fingers brushed a scroll and he would feel the blood rush around his body, so that afterwards he was almost ashamed of such arousal.

The feeling of renewal he acquired from these daily devotions usually lasted him until he got home – four rooms in the Jewish quarter, which was easily the poorest, most squalid and most pestilential area of the city. Heaps of garbage littered its unswept alleys, the Muslim and Christian communities claimed that the Jews' rats had grown so big even the dogs fled in terror of them.

Before the war rich Jewish benefactors had come from abroad to help their brethren and, perhaps, to atone somehow for their own success among the *goyim*. The Montefiores, the Sassoons, the Rothschilds had all built new almshouses outside the city walls, hoping to tempt the Jews out of their hovels. Montefiore had even put up a windmill for grinding corn. Unfortunately, it was in the wrong position and its sails obstinately refused to turn on a regular enough basis to make its operation worthwhile. In the end, all these benefactors despaired of ever prising the Orthodox away from their stinking poverty, and took heart instead at the achievements of the 'new Jews' in the Zionist settlements. There was the proof that the wind sometimes did blow in the right direction.

Now very little money came into the Jewish quarter. That month yet another source of aid had dried up, since the United States' entry into the war had effectively stopped the flow of dollars from New York. Only a few lucky families still received aid from beyond the walls.

When they had finished their prayers the patriarch and his flock trudged home, careful to exert themselves as little as possible so as not to bring on hunger pangs that they could never fully assuage. And yet a careful observer might have noticed that this particular Orthodox family were not quite as thin as many of the others and that, although their demeanour was just as careworn, their eyes were a little brighter than many of their neighbours'. Some of their young women were even sufficiently nourished to be capable of menstruation.

It was one of these, absent from prayers because she was unclean, who greeted her grandfather with a grubby white envelope from which he extracted some coins and a small roll of paper about as big as a *kvital*. The old Jew looked anxious, as he always did on these occasions – much to the surprise of his family, who simply delighted that this particular miracle should have repeated itself. He asked his grand-daughter if anybody had observed the arrival of the person who had brought these things and she replied, as she always did, that she thought not. They were probably the only family in their immediate neighbourhood, perhaps in the entire Jewish quarter, who still had a benefactor. It was a secret. The old man never tired of emphasising that. It was a secret, and they must never tell a living soul. His eyes bulged even larger when he said this, and the whole family gathered round to assure him of their discretion.

7

*I*t was not until shortly after seven that Weidinger knocked on the door of Maeltzer's room – by which time, despite an open window, the room was fogged from the cigarettes the journalist always preferred to cigars when he was under pressure.

'Come in, come in,' he said, beaming his pleasure. 'Like some schnapps?'

Maeltzer dived into a wardrobe for a bottle and a couple of glasses. Unlike many of his calling, he was only occasionally more than a social drinker.

'I'm afraid I can't stay long,' said Weidinger as he waited for his glass to be filled. 'We have a mess-night this evening to honour one of our gallant allies – Mustafa Kemal, no less.'

'Wouldn't do to be late for him,' agreed Maeltzer. 'Not the hero of Gallipoli. *Prosit!*'

'*Prosit!*' said Weidinger, emptying the glass in a couple of gulps, and making no objection when Maeltzer refilled it. He was seriously tempted to tell him how he had just arranged for a tail, one of the headquarters' messengers, to be put on Magnus. He resisted it. He knew Maeltzer. He would only put a damper on it, dream up some logical explanation for the sovereign. It would be marvellous to see his face if his poor mad Swede turned out to have something more on his mind than saving the world from sin. Meanwhile, he stuck to more familiar ground.

'Kemal wants our guns but thinks he can do without our brains,' he said. 'He's already complained to von Sanders that there are too many Germans on his staff. Personally, I think the man is getting too big for his boots, and I'm not the only one. There is a feeling that we might all be happier if he went back to the Caucasus. This is strictly between ourselves, of course.'

'My lips are glued,' promised Maeltzer. 'But I was hoping you could tell me something about the air raid this afternoon before I sent my despatch. The English have never dared to do anything like that before. I thought it quite astonishing.'

'So did the Turkish supply wagons he attacked on the Bethany road,' said Weidinger.

'Was it bad?'

'A couple of dead mules and some very frightened drivers, I believe.'

'A famous victory,' said Maeltzer.

'Well, it shook up our own intrepid birdmen – and not before time.'

As a rule, Weidinger disliked all pilots regardless of nationality. He had barely tolerated Pichler's friend at lunch. Quite apart from his suspicion of anyone who had come to terms with machinery more advanced than the magazine-loading rifle, his dislike of airmen had been exacerbated recently when he heard one brag that he had machine-gunned some cavalry. Weidinger was, in his way, a religious young man who felt that to fool around in the heavens was unnatural enough without adding to the blasphemy of slaughtering men and horses with complete impunity.

'How did he get through?' Maeltzer asked. 'Was it just luck – God looks after drunks and fools, as the English say? I suppose everybody believed that a lone aircraft buzzing about Jerusalem couldn't possibly be anything else but one of yours?'

'Well, that explains why the anti-aircraft was so slow to get started, but I don't think it was luck. There's a bit of a flap going on about it.' Weidinger looked conspiratorial. 'I shouldn't be telling you this, but you're bound to hear it sooner or later. The British shot three of our planes down today. You can't send that to your newspaper, of course. The censor would never allow it. But I think you should be aware of it, because it's going to make things even more difficult for us.'

Maeltzer nodded. 'What happened?'

'Apparently they've got a new aircraft called the Bristol Fighter. They sent some of their older ones over Hebron; we went up to chase them away, and these new machines were waiting to pounce. Then later they sent in the one you saw over Jerusalem with a couple of small bombs, but the Albatross boys thought it was another trap and wouldn't go up. We've just sent a cable to Kress in Damascus telling him what's happened. I shouldn't be at all surprised if he's putting pressure on von Sanders to squeeze some Fokkers out of Berlin right now.

'Some people are very excited about it — you ought to hear Krag. I can't think why. He could have done a lot more damage — he could have bombed Djemal Pasha's headquarters on the Mount of Olives, which would have impressed the locals more than a pair of mules.'

Once Weidinger had left, Maeltzer went back to his work, scratching the words in fountain pen on lined paper because he preferred the authority of ink to pencil. During his last visit home he had noticed that some of the younger reporters at head office had taken to using typewriters, but if a man had an educated hand he could not see the point. Between each paragraph he left a line.

When he had finished his despatch he turned to the diary he was keeping in an exercise book with a bright green cover. One day he intended to turn this diary into a book about the Palestine campaign, just as he had done on South Africa.* In the diary he wrote the number of German aeroplanes shot down.

Dusk fell. There were gas lights in the room but no gas in the hotel. Maeltzer lit three oil lamps made out of sardine tins in which two holes had been pierced, one for the wick and the other for the fuel.

One lamp would have been enough. As it was, Maeltzer's window on the top floor was the brightest in the hotel. Weidinger had once remarked on this and the journalist had told him that he needed the extra lamps because his eyes were getting dim — though he rarely bothered to use his reading spectacles.

Outside a tall figure in the full dress uniform of a German officer was striding out from the Grand New Hotel towards Fast's in order to be in time for the dinner with Mustafa Kemal. It was Major Krag, departing from his tryst with the Widow Shemsi.

* *England und die Volkslied Krieg* von Carl Maeltzer

8

Others did not move so easily in the night. Buchan had escaped. At first it had been ridiculously easy.

After the photograph, the Turks had brought up a line of mules bearing steaming dixies of stew. It was made from a mixture of captured cans of British bully beef and some other meat which the Australians informed the English was horse in the hope that they would leave the eating of it to them. The strategy failed. Everybody was famished. Some had not eaten more than hard tack biscuits and a little fruit since the day before they were captured – almost five days ago. Those who had lost their spoons used their hands. When the food had gone they lay around smoking the last of their tobacco with an abandon they would soon regret.

The officers sat a little apart from the men. The senior man was the captain with the head wound from the dismounted Yeomanry, the rest all lieutenants or second-lieutenants. Buchan was enjoying his second post-prandial cigarette while the Yeomanry captain spoke about the need to ensure the men kept their boots by them at all times – otherwise the guards would steal them – when he was suddenly gripped by an appalling bout of intestinal cramps. He grabbed his stomach with both hands almost as if he had been shot and thrust his head between his knees.

'Something wrong, old chap?' the captain inquired.

Buchan managed to bring his head up. His face had gone quite pale and his eyes were watery. 'Cramps,' he explained. 'Stomach cramps. Must have been that stew.'

'Well, it wasn't the Ritz,' said the captain. 'Doesn't seem to have hurt the rest of us though. Then perhaps you're not a horse-lover?'

'More like dog,' gasped Buchan. He got up and walked away with about as much dignity as a man can muster cradling his belly, hating his body's treachery even more than their laughter.

The truth was that he had always been prone to stomach upsets. During his first month in Egypt he was still gazing at the canvas sides of the officer's latrines six times a day long after the other fresh subalterns had restored their bowels to normal working order. He might have ended up in a dysentery ward had his unit not had a Scots medical officer who put great faith in the cementing properties of yoghurt. 'You've got to get some of the local bacteria inside you, laddie.'

He walked past the sentry in charge of guarding the officers in search of some dark corner. If the Turk – who was not a Turk at all, but a Syrian conscript from Aleppo – saw him passing, the effendi's reasons were so obvious it would have seemed an impertinence to intervene. Besides, the Ottoman rank-and-file were just as bemused by their superiors' behaviour towards these captives as the British were themselves. Were they guests or were they prisoners?

Buchan's stumbling gait took him down into a wadi carpeted with tin cans, sheep bones and other refuse, where even when walking upright, or nearly upright, he was hidden from the view of the rest.

He squatted there for some time. When at last he rose he saw, to his alarm at first, that people were in the process of leaving. All the prisoners were on their feet, and he could hear one of the English sergeants making parade-ground noises. 'All right, lads, let's 'ave you. Bags of swank now. Show 'em we're not beaten.'

The officers were standing in a knot at the head of the men, listening to a Turkish officer in a fez who appeared to be explaining something to them. The guards were forming up either side of the column with rifles slung.

My God! they're leaving without me, thought Buchan. He began to clamber hastily out of the wadi, his boots clattering the abandoned cans aside. Then, for the first time, it occurred to him that the Turks had not noticed his absence. An almost sensual shiver that came from both excitement and fear ran through him, and he dropped out of sight to consider his position.

The other officers, he assumed, must by now have concluded that his stomach cramps were no more than a ruse to slip by the guards. The way they were grouped so attentively around that Turkish officer might indicate a wish to distract. For the moment, anyway, he had escaped. Being a very serious young man, Buchan began to wonder if this was the right thing to do. He was not much given to shows of initiative, and on the rare occasions he had displayed this quality in the past it had often led to disaster.

It was, he knew, a soldier's duty to escape, but he was an officer and it was also his duty to look after his men. There were, it was true, four other officers, and in any case they would soon be separated from the men in a different PoW camp. But what if his escape caused trouble for the others? What if there were reprisals? Perhaps he should have asked the Yeomanry captain for permission? No, that was absurd. A chance had occurred and he had taken it. After all, there had never been any question of their being on parole. The memory of the Yeomanry officer's joke at his expense still rankled too. Who was he anyway? Some fox-fixated squire. No doubt his peacetime motives for enlisting had something to do with fattening up his hunters for the season on free War Office oats at summer camp.

Buchan decided to stay where he was. He unbuckled his belt again and dropped his shorts. If the Turks came he would not be an escaper but simply a man suffering a prolonged attack of diarrhoea. If they did not come . . . well, he would see what happened.

After a few minutes, this fatalism evaporated. The more Buchan realised that he might succeed in escaping, the more he wanted to. It occurred to him how ghastly captivity would be if he spent years looking back on these moments thinking how differently he should have done it.

He pulled up his shorts and set off along the wadi in a shambling crouch, painful because he had to bend his bandaged knees. The wadi still had a thin trickle of water from the winter rains running down its centre. After about twenty yards he came to a hole in the bank. He squeezed into this niche and waited for the commotion that would ensue once they realised he was missing.

Buchan tried to remember when the Turks had last counted them. They had been counted before they were put aboard some freight wagons at Deir Sineid, the railhead a few miles north of Gaza, and then again when they emerged at Jerusalem, when they were handed over to a new set of guards. The officers were always mixed in with the men, so there was a good chance that, at NCO level at least, the Turks might not be aware how many officer prisoners they had. They had all been struck by how slack the Turks were away from the scene of battle.

Buchan's luck might have run out if the prisoners had not started singing. The English started it with 'Pack all your Troubles', and the Australians joined in with 'Goodbye Dolly Gray'. By the time they had got into the second verse the Turks were furious. Perhaps they were tired of German and Austrian contingents strutting about the countryside bellowing out songs about comrades and the Fatherland, but they were determined that this particular lot of Christian visitors should behave with a little decorum.

The Yeomanry captain heard the Turkish major scream something, but assumed he was addressing his own troops. It was not until the Turk drew his revolver and fired a shot in the air that he realised what was amiss. By then the guards were pointing fixed bayonets at them and the situation looked very ugly indeed. The singing did not come to a ragged halt but stopped like a gramophone going off. He managed to defuse the situation further by bellowing a quite unnecessary order at the men to keep quiet, but not until the major had wagged a finger at him and said in the only language he had in common with the British officers: 'Vous êtes prisonniers maintenant! Vous êtes prisonniers!' It was definitely the end of the Cook's tour.

Crouched in his niche in the wadi Buchan heard all and saw nothing. For the first time since his capture he knew real fear. He could only imagine that someone had been shot while trying to escape, perhaps thinking that the singing had put the Turks off their guard; that a roll call would be made; that it would be discovered that another prisoner was missing; that a search would be mounted.

The captain knew, of course, that Buchan was missing and had decided that it was better to assume he had escaped rather than that his stomach cramps had turned out to be a burst appendix and that he was lying near to death not far away. He had to admit that the lanky young subaltern would have probably been the last on his list of potential escapers, but now he took his hat off to him. The whole charade had been brilliantly done. Like Buchan, his main concern now was that the Turks would take it into their heads to count them.

But the Turkish major was much too angry to think straight. Shepherded by their sullen-looking guards, the prisoners were marched off towards the Citadel where they were to be kept until transport could be arranged to take them north.

After they had gone Buchan was so overwhelmed by the loneliness of his situation that he almost wished he had been caught. He was desperately ill-equipped for an escape attempt. He had no food or water, map or compass. The infection in his knees was becoming worse and walking would become an increasingly painful business. Running was almost out of the question. And he was immediately identifiable as a British soldier because he was wearing shorts, a garment the enemy considered unbecoming on grown men.

Buchan decided to stay put until dark. It seemed like an interminable wait, lightened only by the fact that he discovered in a shirt pocket an almost full packet of cigarettes. He transferred all but one

60

to his case and then lit up, cupping the lighted end like an old sweat on sentry go.

The cramps returned and he gripped his stomach with both hands as if he had been shot. A couple of times he heard movements of some kind but whether they were made by man or beast he could not tell. When this happened he shrunk into his niche and held his breath, his body tense for a yell of triumph and the probing bayonet.

The dusk slid slowly in. Buchan looked over the rim of his wadi, and the nearest living thing he could see beyond some stunted olive trees was a bullock cart creaking towards the Jaffa Gate. He decided he would try to make his way towards the right flank of the British line which, the last he heard, was somewhere south of Beersheba. This was about fifty miles away as the crow flies, but it was closer than Gaza, and as his route lay mostly over scrubland and desert it was the least populated part of the front. He imagined he might encounter some Bedouin, and persuade them to escort him to safety in exchange for a large reward. There was a risk, of course, that they would hand him over to the Turks. No doubt it depended on whose gold they most believed in.

Once he had a plan, however nebulous, his spirits rose. He tried to recall the big Palestine Exploration Fund maps he used to study from time to time. Bethlehem was shown south-east of Jerusalem; then Hebron; and then, a long way below it, Beersheba. He remembered seeing a wooden signpost near the Jaffa Gate pointing towards Bethlehem, and finding it oddly blasphemous to see the familiar name used in a strictly functional way, as if the place was as secular as Colchester or Hornchurch.

He climbed out of the wadi and began to walk towards the road. When he got to where they had had their meal his feet caught on something. He looked down, and saw that someone had forgotten a blanket. He picked it up. It was good quality, Australian he guessed. A lot of their equipment, especially when it came to comforts, was better than theirs. So was their pay and tobacco allowance. The men were always grumbling about it.

Buchan draped the blanket around his shoulders. It almost reached his boots. The important thing was that it covered his shorts. From a distance, in silhouette, he might pass as a Syrian peasant – though this might not afford any protection if the Turks imposed a night curfew outside the city limits.

He walked in the scrubland alongside the Bethlehem road, trying to keep at least one hundred yards away from it. Three times he dived for cover in case he was seen from passing vehicles. The first was a lorry with blazing headlights and a crowd of Austrians or

Germans in the back belting out a drinking song, the second a donkey cart with a couple of Turkish soldiers on the front seat, while the third was what Buchan had been brought up to call a governess cart, the kind of thing he had gone to nursery school in, and was pulled by a horse so emaciated it took an eternity to pass.

Not that he minded too much. His knees made walking difficult, and each step sent pains shooting up his thighs. In order to move his infected joints as little as possible he began to develop a peculiar, stiff-legged, sliding gait, almost as if he was wearing snow-shoes. After a while, this became very painful too, and he found himself sitting on his blanket without being aware that he had decided to rest.

He was leaning against a large rock. It had become quite cold and he was shivering slightly. He thought this might be because he was becoming feverish.

At first the darkness held no sound, but then a symphony orchestra started to tune up. From behind blades of grass and in the overhang of pebbles the cicadas began to vibrate their abdominal organs until they produced their famous high-pitched drone; the movement was taken up by a whole castanet chorus line of grasshoppers; a larger species moving among the tufts of grass between the rocks made a sound akin to the shuffle of brushes on a drum skin, and Buchan drew his feet inside his blanket as he added snakes to his list of woes. There was the low whistle of night birds, and then the whistle of a steam locomotive.

Buchan wondered if he was dreaming at first. Then he distinctly made out the rattle of slow-moving rolling-stock and realised that he could not be far from Jerusalem railway station. It was there that his rail journey from Gaza had ended, and it was from there that Turkish soldiers set off to the western sector of their line against the British.

It had now become quite obvious to Buchan that he was in no fit state to walk as far as Bethlehem, let alone Hebron. But if he could somehow smuggle himself onto a train, he could get down at Deir Sineid railhead, only a few miles from his own front line.

He remembered seeing dozens of ragged-arsed civilians hanging about Jerusalem station. Surely as long as he kept his shorts covered and hid his boots — perhaps he could tie them to the back of his belt — he would not stand out?

The more he thought about his plan, the more feasible it became, and in his mercurial state of mind Buchan's spirits suddenly soared again. He put his head against the rock and drew the blanket closer about him. He didn't feel so cold now. Nearby there was a brief flurry of agitated rustling and then quiet again. He ignored it. A night bird whistled. He closed his eyes. The bird sounded quite tuneful. The grasshoppers and cicadas continued their counterpoint. Buchan did not hear them. He was asleep.

9

*I*t was a splendid-looking locomotive. It had been made in America to a design that had the Great Plains in mind, the cow-catcher on the front useful for nudging stray camels and sheep off the track. Like most steam engines, it was intended to run on coal. But thanks to the Entente's blockade, coal was at a premium in the Levant, so it was run on a cocktail of olive branches, cotton seed, liquorice, vines and camel dung instead. In the circumstances, it worked quite well.

Its main drawback was that a considerable amount of this fuel was needed to build up a decent head of steam, so the locomotive had two tenders instead of one to carry it all. It also meant that nowadays the morning train, the one that ran from Jerusalem station down the western escarpment of the Judaean hills to Junction Station and then on to Ramleh, Lod, and other points north, was invariably late in starting. Very often the olive wood had not been cut to the right length, and the Syrian stoker had to set to work with a bow saw and hachet before he could throw it into the firebox.

At the rear of the train were some Turkish soldiers travelling in freight cars, which would be unhitched at Junction Station and attached to another train heading south to Gaza. They crowded around the open sliding doors of their transport, reluctant to step back into its gloomy interior where only a few cracks and holes in the wooden sides allowed weak shafts of light to illuminate a jumble of kitbags and rifles.

Unlike the common soldiery, officers and civilian passengers travelling in the three carriages behind the tender were not required to stay on board by bad-tempered NCOs tired of counting heads. Most of them, their luggage safely stowed, were chatting on the platform, determined not to take their seats until the very last moment. Nobody faced a journey of less than three hours.

Among this crowd was Sarah Aaronsohn, whose journey back to Haifa and from there to the Zionist settlement of Zichron Jacob would take the best part of twenty-four hours. She was clearly agitated. Her eyes kept darting from the iron gate through which prospective travellers emerged onto the platform and then back to the locomotive, which had begun to send a promising amount of exhaust steam hissing down its blast pipe.

She was wondering what had delayed Joseph Lishansky, the young man with the monocle who had been sitting with her at Fast's Hotel. She wished he would hurry up: she was the only unaccompanied woman on the platform, and a group of young Turkish cavalry officers were becoming increasingly bold in their stares.

Maeltzer was there too, saying goodbye to a gaunt Austrian artillery officer who was off to Vienna on convalescent leave. In the same envelope as his despatch was a note to Mr and Mrs Horatio Buchan informing them that their son was a prisoner-of-war and in good health. Maeltzer had hesitated before adding the last bit, recalling those awful cactus thorns in the boy's knees, and then decided that the young mend fast and there was no need to cause undue distress. If he had been asked why a man who displayed such a *Gott Strafe England* mentality was going to this trouble, he would probably have murmured something about the pleasure of moral superiority. Those who refused to be fooled by this would insist that Maeltzer was the kind who liked to keep his word.

Like his despatch, the letter would be sent by his newspaper's Vienna bureau to his editors in Zürich. Maeltzer had asked them to forward it to the British embassy in Geneva. He would have been hard put to find a faster way of getting information to England from an enemy-held city.

One of the Lancer officers took another hard look in Sarah Aaronsohn's direction and then turned away and said something to his fellows, who let out great guffaws of laughter, slapping their thighs and fiddling around with cigarettes and holders. She walked a little away from them towards Maeltzer, conscious of the tapping noise her heels made on the wooden platform and that the officers were almost certainly watching the way her body moved under her clothes. She was beginning to feel angry as well as anxious. Having nothing better to do, she retied the knot of the chiffon scarf she wore over her straw hat in the manner motor-car slipstreams had made fashionable.

Lishansky had gone to pray at the Wailing Wall. This would have amazed most of his acquaintences for he scarcely seemed to observe his religion in any other way; yet he always did this on his last day in Jerusalem. Sarah never went with him, but she hoped he might pray for them both.

The hissing from the blast pipe grew louder and a cloud of steam temporarily obscured the people standing at one end of the platform. A guard wearing a fez, with a green flag in one hand a whistle on a string around his neck walked up to the cab of the locomotive and started chatting with the driver and his fireman. Some of the passengers began to open the doors of their carriages. The guard left the engine crew and walked towards the rear of the train, taking his time, aware of his central role.

Sarah was wondering whether she should go without Joseph or wait for the next train. She partly blamed herself for his absence. She should have insisted on his coming to the station directly from the Zion Gate, the nearest exit from the Wailing Wall. Joseph had almost certainly decided to hire a dog-cart from the Jaffa Gate so that he could browse through what remained of the souk. He was such a country boy. Jerusalem, half starved and in rags though it might be, was still the bright lights. He had come to Palestine with his parents when he was very young, and had rarely left their Galilee settlement. He had grown into manhood with the youth of the local Druse village, who had taught him how to ride and shoot and be prickly about slights to his honour. Sarah had shown him how to wear a suit, knot a cravat and open doors for ladies. The monocle had been his own idea.

By now she was one of the few passengers still on the platform. Maeltzer was standing next to her saying goodbye to his Austrian friend, who was leaning out of the window.

'Give my regards to Secher's major,' he was saying. 'And all the pretty widows.'

Suddenly he turned to Sarah. 'You will miss your train, Fräulein. Why don't you get aboard?'

'I'm waiting for a friend.'

'He can always get the next one.'

'Yes,' said Sarah. She was thinking that Joseph might have been delayed for reasons beyond his control. The guard blew his whistle and there was a general slamming of doors.

'Come on, I'll help you. Is this your carriage? Is your luggage in?'

His voice was full of concern and at the same time he had the door open and was almost pushing her up the steps into the compartment.

At that moment there was a commotion by the iron gate and Lishansky appeared on the platform. He was obviously in some disarray: breathless, beads of sweat breaking from his forehead, holding onto his hat, his monocle bouncing uselessly by its black silk ribbon against his waistcoat. In his right hand he held a half-closed leather grip from which jutted what looked like a wooden doll with a round head and a black painted moustache.

'Just in time, young man,' reprimanded Maeltzer, holding the door open for him.

Joseph gave him a blank look, trying to take in the words. He had some Yiddish, but his German was not very good. Polish was his native language and although they sometimes experimented in Hebrew he spoke French to Sarah Aaronsohn most of the time. 'Wretched horse,' he muttered. 'It would have been quicker to eat it and walk here.'

The train began moving, Maeltzer slammed the door.

'Au revoir,' he said, lifting his hat slightly.

'Au revoir, monsieur,' said Sarah.

There was nobody else in the compartment and they were able to talk freely.

'For God's sake,' she said. 'Where were you? I was beginning to think you had been arrested. I was going to leave without you.'

'I told you, the driver's horse was the thinnest in Jerusalem. It was all I could get.'

'And where did you get it?'

'Jaffa Gate,' he said, after a moment's hesitation.

'Why? Why didn't you go to the Zion Gate? There are horse cabs there.'

'Not always. Besides, I had business to do.'

He stared out of the window, his face set. The train was slipping past stony terraces where a few black-haired goats grazed under the shade of the last remaining olive trees. Whole groves had been cut down for the hungry locomotives and many of the survivors had been grotesquely pollarded.

'What business?' She was not going to let him get away with it.

Lishansky continued to look out of the window. Here and there groups of Syrian goatherds were visible, boys and their grandfathers squatting close to their animals and armed with slingshots and staves against civilian predators. Against the military kind they were helpless.

'What business?' she repeated. 'Some worthless trinket from the souk, I suppose?' And she tapped her foot against the bag from which

67

the protruding doll's head was plainly visible. 'What, may I ask, have you got in there?'

He sighed a caught-out boy's sigh and brought the doll out of the grip. Except it was not a doll exactly. It was a wooden model of two acrobats or high-wire artistes, Latin daredevils judging by the pencil moustaches and large eyes with lustrous lashes. The main figure stood about a foot high and his feet disappeared into the kind of base normally associated with a lampshade or candlestick holder. In the upturned forehead, just below a cone-shaped hat with a white bobble on the end, was a hole into which Joseph now screwed an object about four inches long shaped like a child's spinning-top. He went back to the bag and produced a second figure, smaller than the first, which was holding through its cylinder-shaped hands a balancing pole bent in the form of an inverted 'U', with two balls about the size of small apples at each end.

The train was moving quite fast now, picking up speed down the gradient. The vibration made it impossible for Joseph to get his acrobats to perform their trick until it came to a halt at the little plateau of el-Burkeih, where it took on some more soldiers from a tented camp there.

The smaller figure had a central peg-leg. Joseph held it by the pom-pom on its hat and placed its leg on the flat top of the spinning-top device sprouting from the other acrobat's head. For a moment the smaller acrobat lurched backwards and teetered on one edge of its peg-leg, rocking from side to side at such a crazy angle that it seemed a matter of seconds before it fell to the floor. Gradually the rocking began to subside, and a for a few seconds, although it was still in motion, it was obvious that equilibrium had been achieved.

'You see, he's like me,' said Joseph. 'You think he is going to fall but he doesn't. He keeps his balance. He stays up.'

Just then the guard released his brake and the train moved forward again with a jerk that almost threw them off their seats. The tiny acrobat flew off his perch but was saved from falling further when his balancing pole became entangled around the arms of the large figure.

'Now you see,' said Joseph triumphantly.

'Yes,' said Sarah. 'You're the little daring one who takes too many chances, I'm the big steady one, and I've just saved you as usual.'

She smiled, revealing the deep laugh lines she was due to get around her eyes when she got older. He smiled back and shrugged, relieved – as he always was – that the row was over.

He put the toy back into the bag. 'It's for one of my brothers,' he said.

She nodded. In Joseph's case a brother could as easily mean a Druse as a Jew. 'And apart from your shopping – did everything else go all right?'

'Yes – no problem.'

'Can I have it?'

He took out of the breast pocket of his suit a small roll of paper and handed it to her. She gave it a brief glance and then took off her left shoe and placed it between the sole and a bit of the leather lining that was coming away.

The train gathered speed and was going quite fast down the Vale of Ajalaon. Sarah remembered how, as a fourteen-year-old girl, she had travelled up this slope on a train hauled by a steam engine so under-powered that it rarely exceeded walking pace. She had been accompanying her brother Aaron, who had persuaded their parents to let him show her Jerusalem for the first time.

When they got to where the gradient was steepest, Aaron had announced: 'I think you should have a bouquet, young lady.' He had then opened the carriage door, stepped out – it was moving so slowly he barely had to break his stride – and run off into the meadows and started plucking wild flowers. As he picked, the train slowly began to gather speed. Had Sarah been a bit younger, or even a little older, she might have yelled and screamed and stamped her foot and demanded that he come back that instant. As it was, she was at that age when she would have died rather than draw attention to herself, so she just stood there, biting her bottom lip, watching her brother's leisurely progress from one splash of colour to another. Of course, he knew how to gauge it so that it looked as though he had left it too late before breaking into a sprint and bounding back into the carriage. When Aaron presented his bouquet she had burst into tears and he had laughed and teased her until she felt foolish enough to join the laughter. But he had not played any more tricks on her that trip.

Sarah could never recall feeling so abandoned again until today, when she had allowed the large man she had glimpsed talking to the one-armed German officer at Fast's the day before to put her so firmly onto the train. She supposed she had allowed him to make up her mind for her because she knew that it was the right thing to do. Even so, Sarah was surprised she had permitted herself to be dominated the way she had. It was true the man's size and greying moustache lent him a certain air of authority, but she was not normally influenced by this sort of thing. She remembered the urgency in his voice: 'He can always get the next one.'

And there was that 'he'. The certainty that she was travelling with the person he had seen her with at Fast's the day before. Was that simply intuition? She wondered what he did, this German out of uniform. Could he be one of them, a member of the Yishuv? There were many kinds of Jews in the Zionist community. And she had seen that fool Rosenblum talking to him before he came over to lecture Joseph and herself. But his clothes and his mannerisms were wrong for a Zionist settler. He lacked that strutting, devil-may-care manner Joseph and even people like her brother had. His poise came from a deeper confidence. His looks could be Jewish – the nose was prominent and slightly aquiline – but the same could be said for many people who were not. What then? A preacher? No. Certainly not. Her German was good enough to have caught that farewell remark about the pretty widows. A doctor? A surgeon? Yes, that might be it. That would account for the air of authority.

Joseph dozed. He had a knack of being able to sleep any time, whereas her own racing mind sometimes found it difficult enough in bed. The train was moving well now. There was a brief glimpse of Syrian labourers digging trenches and gun pits under the direction of Turkish officers. Once she nudged Joseph awake to point out a fair-haired German in a white tunic supervising the erection of some barbed wire entanglements. 'Look. They know the English are coming despite their little victory.'

Joseph yawned. 'I wish they'd hurry up.'

By nightfall they had reached Lod, where the train rested while the locomotive was refuelled and rewatered. Sarah and Joseph slept fitfully. Sometimes Turkish officers would peer in but when they saw she was accompanied by a male they went on their way again.

They came through Hadera just as dawn was breaking. By the time they got to Caesarea, where the fat Moudir would sleep for another two hours, the sun was a bowler hat of molten metal on the horizon.

The train did not stop at Zichron Jacob nor at Athlit and as usual they had to put up with the frustration of travelling the extra twenty miles north to Haifa from where they would have to hire a gig to the settlement. Just before Haifa they looked out at the Mediterranean and saw first a smudge of smoke and then the quite distinct silhouette of a British monitor.

10

After he left the station Maeltzer headed back towards the Old City in the same dilapidated hansom that had brought Joseph there. The young Zionist had been quite truthful about the state of his transport. The horse had suppurating sores on its rump and every time it took a step its ribs stretched so tightly that the journalist thought they were going to burst through its skin.

The sun was climbing rapidly but the heat was by no means unpleasant and the air was scented with wild flowers and conifers. Maeltzer sniffed at the fragrance and smiled and allowed himself to lean back in the upholstery and stretch out his legs and close his eyes. It was always such a relief to get his despatches off. Of course, there was still much that could go wrong between Jerusalem station and their arrival at the proper place. But that was a matter now out of his control and it was not his habit to worry much about things he could do nothing about.

For a while he thought about the Aaronsohn girl. Thank God she had got on the train! It was ridiculous for her to linger around Jerusalem a moment longer than necessary when there was so much conjecture about the whereabouts of her brother, and every Turkish officer was trying to look down her blouse.

Maeltzer was contemplating this, his hands clasped loosely beneath his paunch, when he realised that the horse had stopped moving altogether. He opened his eyes, prepared to find it dead between the traces, but it was still upright, flies buzzing around its twitching ears. A Turkish soldier was holding the horse by its bridle while another, a sergeant, was talking to the driver. Maeltzer asked the NCO in Turkish what was going on.

'An English officer has escaped, effendi,' the sergeant replied in a

71

mixture of Turkish and Arabic. Maeltzer guessed that the man was probably a Kurd.

'One of the prisoners you took at Gaza?'

'Yes, effendi. One of those we treated like brothers and showed the holy sights and the Christian places.'

Spoken like a true fanatic, thought Maeltzer. He decided that the man was probably an eastern Kurd, possibly from somewhere around Kirkuk where the Germans were rumoured to be prospecting for oil. He could see that he was tired and irritable and had obviously been up half the night searching for this ingrate Inglisi.

Tired though he was, the Kurd could not resist going through the charade of inspecting the effendi's papers. Maeltzer watched him closely. He had yet to meet an ordinary Turkish solider who could read.

The journalist's *laissez-passer* was a unique document, wheedled out of a major on Mustafa Kemal's staff whom he had rewarded with a handsome ivory-handled Colt revolver. The pass had two large red wax seals and three lengthy sentences in copperplate classical Arabic, the gist of which was that by the Grace of Allah and his Prophet Mohammed, blessed be His name, the bearer enjoyed the protection of the Sublime Porte and woe unto those who hindered him in the pursuit of his lawful duties in military areas.

The soldier furrowed his brow and moved his lips – only partly bluffing for he could understand the familiar Koranic phrases in the document and, being an intelligent man, it infuriated him that he could not understand more.

'Tell me,' said Maeltzer, beginning to get impatient. 'What does this Inglisi look like?'

'He is a young man, tall and thin with bandages on his legs. He has hair the colour of dirty straw.'

'Has he a moustache?' asked Maeltzer, tugging at his own.

'No,' said the soldier, hardly glancing up. He had just worked out Sublime Porte and was beginning to feel rather pleased with himself.

Maeltzer thrust his large head at the Kurd and patted his belly. 'And do you think I'm keeping him in here then?'

The Kurd handed the document back without a word and then waved them on with an abrupt toss of his hand. Once again the horse defied veterinary science and the wheels of the hansom began to turn at quite a respectable rate. Maeltzer glanced back to see the Kurd staring after them. Now that, he smiled to himself, is a very angry man.

He tried to resume his former position, but the road had become too bumpy to lie back in comfort. He sat up and surveyed the surrounding countryside.

To the left the land started out flat and rocky, with a few wizened olives, before slanting down to the south-west as the Judaean range crumbled onto the plain. There was not much on it. A few black-haired goats, and beyond them an old man who might have been their shepherd walking slowly in the direction of the station. Not much cover there. If the young English officer was around they would soon flush him out.

Maeltzer had no doubt that the escapee must be the same Second Lieutenant Anthony Buchan whose parents would shortly be receiving his note informing them that their son was alive. He could not recall any other English officers with 'hair the colour of straw' and bandages around his legs. Where did he expect to run to, especially with those knees of his?

Maeltzer watched the goatherd take a few stiff-legged, old man's steps before collapsing into the shade of a carob. After he had repeated his erratic progress once again, Maeltzer realised whom he was watching. It was obvious that Buchan's legs were not going to take him much further.

'Walk, you idle bastard,' Buchan said out loud. 'Go on. Walk.'

But first he had to get up. He sat leaning back on his hands with his legs outstretched on the ground. A mixture of blood and pus was seeping through the bandage on his left knee. Things were not going well, but Buchan told himself he had been brought up to play to the final whistle. He had slept in fits and starts through a long night. More than once he had debated whether he should take advantage of the night and get going, and on each occasion he had been swayed by the argument that sentries would be on the look-out for Arab pilferers and therefore more alert. Eventually he started walking as the dawn came up. He had collapsed and dragged himself to his feet again a dozen times before Maeltzer marked his erratic progress.

Now he was in the process of a debate, or rather he was the audience of a debate in which he would be required to make the casting vote. He was familiar with both speakers. In fact, they had moved into his head at the onset of pubescence – about the time he had first started reading the novels of Rider Haggard and G. A. Henty – and never stayed away for very long.

Speaker Number One's argument was short and to the point, and what it lacked in wit it made up with the passion of its convictions. 'Of course, you can do it,' this speaker was saying. 'Naturally, it's difficult. If it wasn't difficult it wouldn't be worth doing. My dear fellow, I *know* your knees feel like a colony of maggots have taken up residence, but you're not going to let something as trivial as that upset you, are you? Surely you've got more backbone than that?'

The other speaker was more eloquent, teasing. 'Why don't you just stop this nonsense?' he demanded. 'Just walk off the pitch. Tell them you don't want to play any more. You don't *have* to play, you know. It really is about time you realised that life isn't a game, and that you're an adult not a schoolboy.

'The trouble is with you is that you're so damn anxious to please, to impress. You worry far too much about what others think. You're never your own man and it gets you into trouble. Look at you now. You're not exactly a born soldier and you're lucky to have survived a battle. And yet you're throwing away the chance to spend the rest of the war honourably tucked up in a PoW camp.

'Do you think they'll say, "What a gallant fellow Buchan was!" Of course they won't! Heroes don't have bowel movements. Certainly don't have diarrhoea. When did Mr Henty ever have a hero with the squitters? Think of *With Buller in Natal* or *With Moore at Corunna* or *On the Irrawaddy* or *At Aboukir and Acre* or *With Cochrane the Dauntless*. You can see them on your shelf at home now, can't you? That's what they're going to remember most about you. Can't you hear that Yeomanry captain talking about it when it's all over?

'"Poor fool, must have got lost," he'll say, puffing on his cigar. "Had an attack of the stomach cramps, if you follow my meaning. Went off into the wadis to relieve himself and just never came back. Poor show really. We were practically on parole not to escape at the time you know. Good man, Johnny Turk. Shown us around Jerusalem – the Holy Sepulchre and all the other sights. They just let him walk right past them."

'Why don't you save yourself a lot of trouble and give yourself up to the first Turkish transport that passes? You could tell them that you got lost, fainted, touch-of-the-sun, anything. They'll probably want to believe it. After all, it's very embarrassing for them, your just walking off like that. And what if they do say you were on parole?'

Here Speaker Number Two, who had been doing pretty well up to then, over-stepped the mark. 'Dammit,' said Buchan. 'There was no question of parole.' He was quite certain in his own mind that he had never made any promise that he would not attempt to escape. How could he? He had hardly exchanged two words with a Turkish officer since he was captured.

He decided he would not make a decision until he had given the matter some more thought. He might even give both speakers a final say. 'Damn fool,' cried Speaker Number Two, who thought he was home and dry. 'Life isn't a game of football. You'll regret it, mark my words.'

'Perhaps,' muttered Buchan, pushing himself first into a crouch and then a position that was almost upright. He paused for a moment in the hope that he might hear a few words of encouragement, even praise, from Speaker Number One. But none came. Alone, he moved on.

About a kilometre further down the road Maeltzer was stopped by another road block, under the command of Major Krag.

The intelligence officer's servant had brought him the news of the Englishman's escape with his morning coffee. The batman, in civilian life an innkeeper from Coblenz, had long since become inured to the eccentricities of officers. In France he had once served at a very jolly little dugout Sunday lunch party which, as soon as they had consumed the last of the cognac, had sprinted across no-man's-land and returned with an astonished Frenchman. But even he was amazed when Krag at once announced that they would be joining in the hunt for Buchan. A couple of Austrian clerks, who felt that they were above such capers, had been roped in as well and now stood with their unaccustomed rifles and ammunition pouches near a group of scratching Turkish infantry. Krag too had equipped himself with a Mauser '98 which he carried crooked under one arm as if he was going on a Black Forest boar shoot.

Maeltzer was aware that Krag, by nature misanthropic, had developed a certain antipathy towards him. As far as he knew this dislike was not founded on anything tangible. The journalist had concluded that it was probably the result of vague stirrings of irritation caused by his easy familiarity with von Kressenstein, and by Krag's own inability to feel anything other than self-conscious and awkward in the presence of the aristocracy, becoming quite tongue-tied and even more clipped than usual in his speech. He had studied Krag, and knew he was capable of demonstrating a kind of policeman's bloody-mindedness. This bothered him, for the German had it within his powers to make things difficult for him, to limit his access, to remind his superiors subtly that there were frontiers of knowledge which neutral journalists, however sympathetic, should not be permitted to cross. In this respect he knew that Krag's strength was the very thing the German probably loathed most about himself:

he was not what the English would call a gentleman. Nor, it seemed, was he capable of sniffing out the breed, recognising the signals and behaving accordingly. Sometimes Maeltzer felt that it was not that he saw through people, but that he didn't see them at all.

Now he said: 'Good morning, Herr Maeltzer. I see that you are about your business early. You may have heard we are looking for an escaped prisoner, an English officer. I don't suppose you can help us in this matter?'

'Indeed I can,' said Maeltzer.

It was not a difficult decision for him to make. After all, since the boy was so obviously done for he was probably doing him another favour — and he did need to keep the right side of Krag.

It took Buchan some time to realise that the Turks were closing in.

His first indication was when he began to notice a series of mirror-like flashes coming from the direction of the main road to his left. It soon became apparent that these flashes came from the long bayonets attached to a line of Turkish rifles that were advancing in extended order.

They looked about half a mile away. For a few minutes Buchan continued towards the station, convinced that if he could only get beyond the end of the line quickly enough the sweep of their search would miss him. For the space of two hundred yards he even achieved something like normal walking pace until the pain in his knees became unbearable and he had to stop and hang onto a friendly carob tree.

While he tried to recover himself another line of troops seemed to grow from the very ground in front of him as they emerged from the dip or wadi that had hidden them. They were about four hundred yards away, close enough to see the serrated edges on their terrible saw bayonets.

He looked towards the Turks coming from the road and could now discern among them a couple of pith-helmeted figures in the field-grey uniform of the Germany army. As they got closer, he saw that one of them was carrying his weapon in the crook of his arm the way a gamekeeper would carry a shotgun.

Even if he could run there was nowhere left to run to. He had lost. Buchan stood rock still and for the first time realised how thirsty he was.

Then there was a shot. The bullet was close enough to the lieutenant's head for him to catch the zizz of it. 'Swine,' he said out loud.

'Quite unnecessary.' Despite his indignation, Buchan raised his hands as far as he could stretch them. The shot seemed to have come from the line advancing from the road. He saw the gamekeeper figure was waving his free hand about in an agitated manner.

Buchan looked at the other line, for these were the Turks that would be the first to reach him. He was astonished to see that half of them had disappeared again. Then, even as he watched, the missing men got to their feet, and he realised that the shot must have been fired at an angle that had taken it as close to their heads as his own. Buchan found this very amusing and the only reason he did not laugh out loud was that he no longer had the strength to do so.

Krag was finding it heavy going across the scrubland in his high cavalry boots. Even if he hadn't been, he was reluctant to get ahead of the line in case another of the boneheads became over excited. Apart from the Austrian and German clerks he had donated, most of his group were Syrian conscripts. The Kurdish sergeant who had stopped Maeltzer earlier was with the other line. He was well into the lead, despite the fact that he had been among those who went to ground when the shot was fired – an event which had stoked the fury started by Maeltzer's jibe to the point where he was very angry indeed. The Kurd promised himself that when he found the idiot responsible for that shot – and he would wager a week's pay it was one of those Christians from the Galilee they had started conscripting – he would have very warm feet indeed. Meanwhile, there was this Englishman to deal with. He could see him quite clearly now standing with his hands up and a stupid grin on his face, as if he was playing some silly child's game.

Buchan was near to collapse again. It was as if the shot had drained away his last reserves of strength. Slowly, his arms came down to shoulder level. The morning sun was getting high, and the way it flashed off the bayonet of the nearest Turk reminded him of a heliograph. Buchan had always been fascinated by heliographs, ever since he first saw them in action on a combined public schools Officers' Training Corps exercise on Salisbury Plain in the summer of 1914, his last at school.

Then there had been days when there was not enough sun, and the instruments would not transmit properly. Of course, this climate was ideal for them, it was marvellous to watch them working. *Flash – flash – flash.* Just before they went in at Gaza they were going all the time. *Send reinforcements we're going to advance. No, send three-and-fourpence we're going to a dance. Flash – flash – flash.* Marvellous stuff. All done by mirrors. Much better than semaphore.

During the course of this reverie Buchan had, without really being aware of it, sunk to the ground. He sat there with his right arm raised while his left hand caressed the filthy bandage round his swollen left knee, which he now felt to be disgustingly luscious.

After all he had been through that morning, the sight of the Englishman sitting there greatly offended the Kurd. Who was he to sit, this Christian? He placed the tip of his awful bayonet firmly above the third button of Buchan's tunic, the area of the diaphragm, and yelled at him in Arabic to get to his feet.

Buchan looked up, hardly comprehending. Then it dawned. The fellow wanted him to get up. Well, I'll need a little assistance there, old chum. He stretched out his left hand.

The Kurd, incensed by this insolence, barked something and jabbed at him with his bayonet. It drew a little blood. Buchan was not exactly aware of this but he did feel the prick, like squeezing a holly leaf. It had the desired effect. It concentrated his mind. He began to lever himself to his feet while the Kurd brought his rifle up like an angler raising his catch.

Buchan's legs were almost straight when his knees collapsed on him for the last time. He fell forward and slightly to the left, gutting himself on the bayonet on the way down before the Kurd had a chance to get it out of his way.

Anthony Buchan did not cry out immediately. He gave a kind of deep gasp, and shortly afterwards he began to haemorrhage from the mouth. He managed a little scream when the bayonet was extracted but by then there was blood in his lungs as well as his mouth. Face down in the dirt, Buchan started coughing and spitting away the blood in his mouth, which filled almost as soon as he got rid of it. At the same time his hands searched his tunic until they found the warm, sticky places.

The Kurd was almost in a state of shock. Despite his rank and background, this was the first time in his life that he had done serious harm to anyone with cold steel, and it was an accident. At the same time he was surprised how easy it had been, how the sound and feel of it was so similar to that first butcher's incision into the belly of a sheep.

He did not know what to do next. Had it been in battle he might have finished the Englishman off with a bullet or another thrust. But these were entirely different circumstances, so he just stood there, holding his rifle with its bloody bayonet with both hands and watching Buchan coughing and drawing his legs up and gently squeezing his scrotum in an effort to make the pain go away.

This was how Krag found them. At first he thought Buchan had merely fainted and asked one of the Austrian clerks to pass him a water-bottle. But as he unscrewed the top he noticed the blood on the ground for the first time and the awful gore on the Kurd's bayonet. Krag grew angry then and pushed the Kurd aside.

Once his servant had helped him to turn the Englishman over, Krag saw immediately that he was dying. Buchan had gone a terrible grey colour. His hands were on his stomach trying to push his insides back in and every few seconds he would make a little choked scream which brought bubbles of blood to his lips. It occurred to Krag that the proper thing to do was to put the boy out of his misery. He got as far as undoing the flap on his holster and then hesitated. Was it proper to hasten the end of a mortally wounded officer escapee in front of witnesses? It might be misinterpreted. He could imagine Kress taking a very dim view of it. While Krag pondered the pros and cons of the matter Buchan had another fit of coughing, and then neatly solved Krag's dilemma by drowning in his own blood.

Next to his body lay the silver cigarette case, which had fallen out of his top pocket when they turned him over. Krag picked it up. A corner of it was sticky to the touch.

11

Maeltzer had drawn the shutters of his room in the Grand New Hotel and was asleep fully clothed on his bed. The room smelt of vomit.

Outside, the shadows around the old stones of the Jaffa Gate began to lengthen. Syrians and Jews, often listless with hunger, watched the ammunition limbers clatter by and then ox-carts bearing parts of aeroplanes, creaking wagons that had already taken almost the entire morning to come up from Jerusalem station. The parts were bound for the aerodromes around Beersheba where the *Luftstreitkrafte* had based its forward reconnaissance squadrons, on the left flank of the Turkish line.

In the commandeered English school, now a Turkish army barracks, the afternoon session of corporal punishment was taking place. An abject line of soldiers and conscript labour, some of the younger ones already finding it hard to fight back their tears, were waiting their turn. Each man was already bare-footed, clutching his boots or sandals, toes flexing nervously in the dust. At the head of the line was the conscript who had fired at Buchan. As the Kurd had suspected, he was a Christian Arab from Nazareth, an excitable youth who shot out of sheer exuberance for the chase. Now he was promising himself he would desert at the first opportunity.

Two sergeants, both built like wrestlers, threw the Nazarene to the ground and tied around his ankles a rope attached to a stick which ended up tight against his insteps. Each Turk held one end of this stick, then lifted his feet to about the height of their waists, and began to beat his soles with short, springy lengths of bamboo.

The Nazarene's offence was regarded as serious enough for sixty strokes. The Kurdish sergeant who had killed Buchan could hear the screams from the nearby cells where, at Krag's insistence, he had been placed awaiting court martial. Nobody believed that the Englishman had fallen onto his bayonet, not even his own officer who had given him cigarettes and told him that he would soon have him out.

A bucket of water was available to revive those who fainted whilst undergoing the bastinado, but the Nazarene was too young and fit for his body to grant him even that brief respite. Each stroke was like the touch of a red-hot poker, and every nerve in his body seemed to be jangling like a thousand toothaches.

His screams were such that even old sweats waiting for their ten or fifteen strokes began to look nervous. A young Turkish officer stepped out of the school building to draw deeply on a cigarette and wonder at the majesty of Ottoman justice. The Nazarene's cries were truly awe-inspiring, exciting his floggers to greater effort. They seemed almost loud enough to be heard at the Grand New Hotel, where Maeltzer's large, troubled head occasionally jerked from side to side as he slept. A glass and an empty bottle of schnapps lay on the floor beside him.

Maeltzer was having a nightmare. He was back in Zürich talking to an editor across his desk. There was something strange about the man, something peculiar, even grotesque. For some time his face was a blur, as if it was lying under water. Then he came sharply into focus, and to his horror Maeltzer saw what was troubling him. The man had two heads. One was normally formed, although flat and round; the other was a parody of the live head, a bloodless dead-looking thing that existed alongside it, with the same nose but half-formed eyes and mouth. It reminded him of an aborted foetus a doctor friend used to keep pickled in a jar.

It was revolting. Nonetheless, common courtesy dictated he disguise his revulsion. After all, the poor fellow must be accustomed to stares and whispers and people pulling faces. Yet even as they spoke the other head came alive with eyes and teeth, and then detached itself from its partner. It grew an identically clothed body but had abnormally large hands which it waved in Maeltzer's face, as if to demonstrate their power, before slipping behind the chair on which he was sitting and out of sight. The editor was now grinning at him, a malevolent, hateful grin, and Maeltzer realised too late that this was a truly evil hydra, that something terrible was about to happen to him. Even as he became aware of his danger he heard the heavy breathing of the man's ghastly *doppelganger* behind him. He was paralysed, quite incapable of turning round in his chair and confronting the monster. Maeltzer distinctly felt those huge, remorseless strangler's hands brush his throat but lay there – somehow he was no longer sitting – helpless as a school-girl as he began to choke.

The journalist awoke with the sound of his own tormented breathing still in his ears, pulled his collar and tie loose and then groped his way towards the window, knocking over the empty schnapps bottle in the process. He tugged at the shutters like a drowning man, screwing up his eyes against the daylight and gulping down the clean air. He could still feel those hands about his throat: gentle, almost a caress, a taste of dying.

Maeltzer wondered by what convoluted chemistry his brain should have conjured up a silly two-headed monster instead of the clean young Englishman for whose death he held himself to be at least partly culpable. Though God knows why he should torment himself about the fate of one Englishman. He recalled the tales the Boer prisoners had told him in Ceylon about the camps in which Kitchener had concentrated their wives and children so that the commandos would find it harder to live off the land, and the lack of sanitation and proper medical care when the inevitable typhus and cholera came.

After he had told Krag what he had seen, Maeltzer had lingered by the road block instead of going on into the city. He had no pressing business, and was curious to find out whether he was right in thinking his weary goatherd was Buchan. He had watched Krag lead a file of men off without the least foreboding.

He had watched the soldiers return, and when they got closer he saw that they were carrying a makeshift stretcher made out of rifles and blankets. At three hundred metres Maeltzer began to have doubts; at one hundred and fifty he could see that Buchan's face was covered.

'What happened?' Krag had snapped back when he asked. 'What happened? The scum bayoneted him, that's what happened.'

'Why?' said Maeltzer, aware even as he mouthed the word that the question was ridiculous as well as redundant. At the same time he was quite taken aback by the vehemence of Krag's own response.

'Why?' Krag had roared, apparently delighted to discover this unsuspected vein of naivety in the Swiss. 'Why? Because they needed the practice, I suppose.'

'There was a shot. I heard a shot.' There had to be a better explanation. He could not have set something like this in train.

'Correct, Herr Maeltzer. You did indeed hear a shot. One of the fools almost killed one of his own. They're much better with cold steel, you know. They don't have to suffer this tedious business of co-ordinating the eye and the trigger finger.'

After that Maeltzer had fled for the city and the security of his room at the Grand New Hotel, wiping the smile of greeting off the face of the Widow Shemsi as he rushed past her on the stairs.

At first it had been his intention to send a cable – nothing less would do – to Zürich to be sent on to Buchan's parents, which would at least relay the terrible news before their hopes were buoyed by his earlier message. But even as he began to write Maeltzer realised that any such telegram would be subject to military censorship, and the authorities were hardly likely to release the information before their own inquiry. And they might well take a dim view of his acting as a go-between for a captured British officer. It would be days, perhaps weeks, before he found somebody who was going back to Vienna or Berlin and willing to take mail. Not only had he been responsible for the boy's death, but he had increased the anguish of his parents a hundredfold.

In his own anguish, slumped on his desk, Maeltzer had demanded out loud, 'My God! What can I do?' And the desk with the half-written telegram lying next to the sardine-tin lamps, and the bed and the matching water jug and bowl, and the trunk he had covered with an embroidered bedouin saddle bag, and the stern looking wardrobe all answered: nothing, you can do nothing. What is done is done.

For a man unaccustomed to heavy drinking it had taken the journalist some time to get drunk. The schnapps bottle, the one he had opened in Weidinger's honour, was two-thirds full and he had almost finished it before he had dulled the pain to the point where he could distance his own involvement in recent events.

But when he switched from drinking to pacing the room, mumbling to himself, sometimes pausing to stare unseeing out of the window before he at last closed the shutters and lay on the bed, he almost immediately felt nauseous. Twice he had to get to his wash-bowl and be sick until his stomach would allow him to sleep. And then his brain continued to conjure up new monsters, so that Maeltzer's large head tossed on the pillow and the feathery fingers came to his throat.

He gazed at the city below, neither hungover or entirely sober. He caught the vomit stench coming up from his wash bowl, and decided that he had better do something about it. There was a lavatory in the corridor of the floor below – quite a modern affair, with a flushing water closet that worked as long as the head porter could be chivvied into organising a daily bucket chain to fill the tank on the roof that fed the cistern.

Maeltzer was returning from the lavatory when he met Shemsi for the second time that day. Fearing another snub, she contrived to look distracted, staring down at her feet in order to avoid catching his eye. His pacing had been particularly heavy that morning.

Maeltzer recalled the hurt expression on Shemsi's face as he ran past her on the stairs a few hours earlier. 'Good morning,' he said, disorientated by his sleep. 'I mean, good afternoon.'

'Oh Herr Maeltzer,' she said, as if she had had difficulty in placing him at first. 'How are you?'

'I am –' he began. 'I am most distressed, madam. An awful thing happened this morning. A young English officer who had tried to escape was killed. Bayoneted. A lieutenant. No more than twenty, I would guess.'

'How awful,' she said although her tone implied, 'how odd'. How odd that one death, an enemy death when all was said and done, should move this man during a war when thousands were dying all over the world every day.

'I grieve because I bear some responsibility,' said Maeltzer who sensed her perplexity.

'Responsibility. By why?' She was genuinely intrigued.

'I –' But the journalist suddenly became conscious how odd he must seem standing in this corridor with his china wash bowl in one hand and his detachable collar askew, reeking of drink and stale sweat and God knows what else. He gave a curt nod and was on the second step of the stairs back to his floor before Shemsi was aware that the conversation had ended.

It was the longest chat she had ever had with him, and she was a little hurt that it should have ended in her second rebuff of the day. She resolved that the next time she saw Maeltzer she would pretend that she had not and then became annoyed with herself for becoming concerned with such trivialities. She was acting like an adolescent. Perhaps it was those coal-black eyes of his, so unusual for a European.

That night Maeltzer paced the floor of his room until well after midnight. Shemsi lay awake next to the slumbering Krag wondering whether this latest bout of insomnia was solely the fault of the dead Englishman.

Krag, who rarely seemed to sleep much himself, was suddenly awake beside her. 'What's that?' he said.

'Herr Maeltzer. I've told you. He paces.'

The intelligence officer lay with his hands clasped behind his head for a few seconds, listening. 'A troubled man,' he said.

'He told me he is responsible for the death of an English soldier. A young officer. Is he responsible?'

Krag considered this for a moment. 'In a way he is,' he said. 'He spotted him trying to get away and told us where he was.'

'And you? Were you involved?'

'I was involved in a hunt for an escaped prisoner. When we caught him something happened and he died.'

'It was an accident? Herr Maeltzer said he was bayoneted.'

'Of course it wasn't an accident,' he snorted. 'The swine murdered him. I have the man responsible in jail now. With luck he may face a firing squad.'

His anger startled her. 'You too? Why do you care so much about an English officer?'

'I care very little about an English officer,' sighed Krag who was not accustomed to explaining how he felt about things. 'But I do care about the good name of Germany and German officers. And I happen to think that our gallant ally should behave in a manner which does not disgrace our cause.'

Shemsi had never known Krag like this. He was sitting up in bed, his eyes bright. A livid scar just below his left collar bone seemed to pulsate purple.

'You really hate the Turks, don't you? You think they're sub-humans?' It had never occurred to her before, the man's innate sense of racial superiority. She wondered how far down his scale she would be even if she was still a seventeen-year-old virgin.

'Do you know when I first came to the East?' he asked.

'The East?' She looked confused. To Shemsi the East was China.

'To Turkey? Do you know when I first came to Turkey? I'll tell you. It was in the spring of '96. Do you remember what happened in Constantinople a few months later, that August?'

She shook her head. Why should she? She would have been ten years old at the time, in the stone house in her father's village in the Chouf they went up to every summer to escape the heat of Beirut.

'I'll tell you,' he said. 'I'll tell you what happened. One moment.'

She watched as he got out of bed, walked naked to the chair on which he had carefully draped his tunic and extracted Buchan's cigarette case from the top pocket together with a box of matches. He was very thin and almost without bodily hair. The late Major Shemsi had had a belly on him, and the matt on his chest had extended around his shoulders like a cape. She imagined Maeltzer, who continued to pace, might look the same.

'Would you like one?' He proffered the open cigarette case.

'No,' she said, after a moment's hesitation. There were occasions when she smoked, but never in public of course. A woman in her position had to be doubly sure to maintain all the outward respectabilities. It gave her a perverse satisfaction to deny Krag the intimacy of seeing her do it. God knows he wanted enough else.

'They're English,' he said, lighting up. 'It was his case – the young officer who was bayoneted.'

'So what happened?' She had never seen Krag in such a forthcoming mood. She was fearful he would lapse back into one of his long silences or merely fall asleep. 'What happened in '96?'

'There were massacres of Armenians. Not the first and almost certainly not the last. They had started the summer before but these were in Constantinople itself. Some terrorists took over the Ottoman Bank and made various demands. While they pretended to negotiate the Palace encouraged the mob to take reprisals. They killed until they were tired of killing. It went on for three days and for months after that in the provinces. The Armenians were slaughtered. They ravished nine-year-olds before they dashed their brains out.'

Krag paused to look for an ashtray. Seeing none, he used the inside of the cigarette case. 'I was twenty. Newly commissioned and seconded to our military mission because I had passed out near the top in the artillery school. They wanted to teach them how to use our guns, you see. It was supposed to be a great honour, but I had wanted to go to South West Africa and fight the Herero. Unblooded young soldiers always like to fight you know – at least they would like to know what it's like to fight.

'So there I was, going to our mission overlooking the Bosphorus every day, an aide to a colonel whose task it was to try and teach some supercilious Turkish aristocrats masquerading as officers how to make proper use of all the good things provided by Herr Krupp. At least twice a week there would be some official reception to attend. They were often held at the homes of other foreign missions – the British and the French among others. These were not the most light-hearted affairs. Everybody was on his guard, anxious not to give anything away. You can imagine what a relief it was to be invited to the homes of the Greeks and the Armenians, who were always anxious to cultivate the resident foreigners. These could be truly enjoyable occasions. One could relax.'

'I suppose they felt more secure having you around.' Shemsi knew how it felt to be a besieged Christian rock in a Muslim sea. She had grown up on the tale of how the Druse of the Chouf had treated the Maronite Catholics. It was why she was born a Protestant.

'I suppose they did, poor fools. We didn't do very much to stop it. I think we "expressed our concern", but most of the shouting was done by the British and the French. The American newspapers made more fuss than we did.'

'So a lot of your Armenian friends were killed?'

'Not a lot. I didn't have a lot of Armenian friends. But, yes, there was one family I knew well who were already in mourning. They were beaten to death in their own homes.'

'And ever since then you've hated the Turks?'

'Not hated exactly. Despised sometimes.'

'Strange,' she said. 'I've hated and loved them but never despised them.'

'I said sometimes,' he said. Krag's tone did not invite further discussion, and shortly afterwards he slipped quietly out of her suite and returned to his own quarters – as he usually did.

For some time after he had gone Shemsi lay awake listening to the steady tread above. She wondered at an anguish that kept Maeltzer's mind whirring on like this, denying the body sleep. It was strange, she thought, that two men with so little in common should be so affected by the death of a young Englishman who was practically unknown to them. '*I do care about the honour of Germany and German officers.*'

She noticed that Krag had left Buchan's cigarette case on her bedside table and wondered whether it was meant to be a gift. She picked it up and caught her reflection in the polished silver. It felt heavy, valuable. She held it at arm's length and tried to study her face in it but the light or the angle at which she was holding it must have been wrong for it seemed to give her a crooked nose and thick lips. '*Despised sometimes.*' She wondered how much he despised her – or she him for that matter.

The Widow Shemsi was about to put the cigarette case down when she noticed the dark brown stain on one of its corners. She gave a little shudder, for it was quite obvious what it was, and resolved to give it back to Krag at the next opportunity. In the morning she could not remember whether Maeltzer had stopped pacing before she fell asleep or not.

12

*I*t is forbidden in Islam for a fresh corpse to remain unburied for more than a day, but Buchan's body was kept in a hospital mortuary for almost four because nobody got around to making the arrangements.

For the first forty-eight hours it was surrounded by blocks of ice with one particularly large block resting on the gaping abdominal wound as a final barricade against the flies. By the morning of the third day the ice had melted and the Syrian in charge of the arrangements was too lazy to replace it. Eventually a stick grenade accident on a crowded troop train brought an Austrian doctor along to inspect the accommodation. He became highly indignant about the smell and got in touch with a friend at Kress's headquarters. Buchan was buried the next day.

The funeral took place at one of the city's small Catholic cemeteries although Buchan was Church of England, as a proper examination of his dog tags would have shown. Nonetheless, the Germans put on a good show. There was a firing party for the coffin, which was draped with a Union flag, and a sweating Father Liebermann to remind everyone of the promise of resurrection. As the senior British officer among the prisoners the Yeomanry captain was allowed to attend. Buchan would have been surprised to see how obviously moved he was by the occasion.

Krag had organised it. He put Weidinger in command of the firing party, the same collection of clerks and signallers whom the intelligence officer had pressganged into the hunt for the British escapee. After the priest had finished, they delivered a volley while Syrian workmen took the strain on the ropes and the box was lowered into the flinty earth. Some Turkish officers were quite thrilled by it all. It had that chevalier touch they so admired; burying the English officer was even better than showing him around the holy places.

Among the few civilians present was Maeltzer, who had come to punish himself and found to his surprise that he must have expiated his sin for it was not the mental scourging he had expected. He wondered if this had anything to do with the fact that Liebermann was officiating.

Another was Mrs Vester, the pious Chicago woman who ran the American Colony and its increasingly popular soup kitchen. Maeltzer was glad to see that Doctor Vester had done the right thing and decided to stay away. Although Mrs Vester's husband was a German, he was ostracised by the rest of the community because he had publicly stated his opposition to the Kaiser's war. And his position was even more difficult now that his wife's country had entered hostilities on the Entente's side – though they had not got around to declaring war on Turkey, and were unlikely to do so.

Also present, at least in body, was Magnus, who was seated with his back against the head of an old tombstone, his right leg cocked over his left knee and his great staff lying on the ground beside him. When the rifles went off he had given a little jump and put his hands over his ears. Weidinger, at attention with his sabre inches from his nose, caught the movement out of the corner of his eye.

After the firing party had been dismissed and the gravediggers began to cover Buchan with the small mound of Palestine that had been displaced for him, people began to drift away. The Yeomanry captain spoke briefly to both the priest and Mrs Vester before he was led back to the Citadel.

Weidinger looked around for Maeltzer. The journalist was crouched alongside the Swedish Messiah who was waving a finger in his face. The Oberleutnant returned his sabre to his scabbard and walked over to them. 'Magnus wonders where you're going to bury the rest of the Egyptian Expeditionary Force,' said Maeltzer. 'He thinks this cemetery is too small.'

'We'll leave them for the crows,' said Weidinger. He was thinking about the English sovereign. Perhaps he should confront Magnus with it now, in front of Maeltzer?

Magnus continued to stare at the ground, and for the first time Weidinger became aware of how much the Swedish Messiah stank. He had obviously not washed for weeks. How could the journalist even bear to acknowledge the stupid swine?

Maeltzer stood up, banging some dust from his tan suit with his panama. 'I thought it went very well,' he said.

'Thank you.'

'He maketh the wars to cease unto the end of the earth,' said Magnus in English. 'He breaketh the bow and cutteth the spear in sunder; he burneth –'

'Now come along, Magnus.'

It was Mrs Vester. Weidinger saluted. Maeltzer raised his hat. Magnus hauled himself to his feet by his staff and towered above them all, looking huge and mad. He reminded Weidinger of an illustration of John the Baptist which he used to stare at in his children's Bible.

'He raiseth the poor out of the dust and lifteth the needy out of the dunghill,' responded the Swede as he followed her out, one pace behind. Mrs Vester did not look back to see if he was there.

'Thank God for that,' sighed Maeltzer. 'It's a long book, Psalms.'

'He has a good memory,' said Weidinger. 'Very retentive.'

'It's part of his madness.'

Magnus was walking alongside Mrs Vester now, talking to her. Weidinger noticed that Krag was staring after the Swede while pretending to listen to one of the garrulous Turkish officers.

Magnus took his usual route down David Street, punting himself along by landing his great staff exactly in the cracks in the flagstones. He had eaten well at the American Colony – two bowls of soup and half a loaf – and he walked with the energy of a man who was trying to aid his digestion. In any case, there was only about an hour to go before curfew and most other people were hurrying. The only time people slowed up was to give as wide a berth as possible to the litters on which the typhoid and smallpox cases were being taken to die in the pesthouse. As summer approached the epidemics got worse.

Behind the Swede trudged one of those gaunt men typical of Jerusalem in this third year of war. His jellaba contrived to open at the chest, providing glimpses of an emaciated torso and prominent collar bones. When it rose above his bare feet it revealed twig-like legs. As he walked his eyes rarely left the ground, presumably in the hope that some poor fool had dropped a crust. Only occasionally did he look up to make sure that Magnus's blond mane was still ten feet ahead.

As they reached the claustrophobic covered passageways of the old souk, a litter came by and everybody but Magnus, who showed not the slightest regard for such things, flattened themselves against the walls. In the wake of the litter came a wailing female, careless of her veil. She was a large women, wide-hipped, and her grief made her sway from side to side. Weidinger's Syrian had difficulty in getting past her, and for a moment he thought he had lost Magnus.

He pivoted almost a full circle on one heel, his eyes darting in all directions. It was the staff that led him back to the Swede. He could hear it clonking away on the flagstones. He turned again and saw Magnus going down a dark passageway that took him into the Jewish corner. He almost ran after him. Almost.

Krag looked again at the report, one-and-a-half-written pages of dates, times and places. Even when added together it produced nothing damning. So what if Swedish maniac with sovereigns to spare visited an old Jew from time to time? Nobody could make anything out of that. The Turks could, of course. The Turks could probably make the Pope confess to being a Bolshevik with Calvinistic tendencies, but the Turks weren't going to get the chance if he had anything to do with it. 'Either something is missing or he's innocent,' he told Weidinger, who tried not to look as crestfallen as he felt. He had been hoping for a better reaction than this.

'However, you're right to have drawn the matter to my attention,' Krag went on. 'I just wish you'd done it earlier. For all I know your man may be quite good, but having him followed about like that is risky. He could have spotted him and if he *is* working for somebody other than God he will have stopped what he is doing. I have people who are very good at watching without being seen – years of experience working for the Turks. So call your dog off and I'll put my own on the scent. Understood?'

'Yes, sir.'

'Good. Please don't misunderstand me, Oberleutnant. I am extremely grateful that you should have taken time off to do this. It shows great initiative and I commend you for it. I shall make sure others hear of it too.'

'Thank you, sir,' said Weidinger.

'In the meantime – discretion please! Mention it to nobody. You know how everyone loves to gossip in this city.' There may have been the slightest hint of irony in Krag's voice.

When Weidinger had gone Krag looked down at the report again. The Oberleutnant's investigations had not thrown any light as to where the Swede's money was coming from and Weidinger had felt duty-bound to mention the fact that he was known to beg: he had even cited Maeltzer as an example of the kind of person who donated.

Ah Maeltzer! Good old Maeltzer. Kress's favourite newspaperman. Now there was a thought.

PART 2
The Waters of the Nile

13

*F*locks of panic-stricken sparrows stampeded up and down the Nile, their wings flattening against their bodies every third beat as they raced to find a perch for the night in palms silhouetted by a dying sun.

Ponting watched the birds from his office in the Savoy Hotel and thought such frenetic activity was quite in keeping with the present mood of the place. The city was abuzz with rumours, the anticipation of being swept up in great events. Those who had been with the Egyptian Expeditionary Force since the beginning declared there had not been such electricity in the air since December 1914 when, for a moment, it seemed the Turks might breach the defences along the canal and spark an insurrection among the felaheen in the name of the Caliph.

It was like the heavy energy in the air before a storm breaks. Ponting could feel it gathering around the marble-topped tables in those cafés where the Egyptian intelligentsia showed their distaste for most things British by breaking loudly into French over their interminable coffees and sticky cakes, thwacking away flies with rolled copies of *Images* and *al-Muqattam*. It was particularly notice-able among the officers gossiping in the bar at Shepheard's and on the trim lawns of the river island of Gezira where the senior adminis-trators of the Protectorate asked each other when the army was ever going to put its house in order?

Everybody knew that Sir Archibald Murray's days as Com-mander-in-Chief of the Egyptian Expeditionary Force were num-bered. Twice he had failed to break through at Gaza despite the

EEF's numerical superiority. Now it was not a question of whether he would be relieved of his command but when and by whom.

At GHQ some people thought the job should go to General Sir Stanley Maude, the man who had avenged Townshend's defeat at Kut by capturing Baghdad. Maude was a bit of a plodder – his staff called him 'Systematic Jo' – but he had justified his reputation for getting there in the end. Yet it was Ponting's opinion that this would not be the case.

Just over a month before General Erich von Falkenhayn had been given what was virtually command of all the Turkish forces in the theatre. Von Falkenhayn had been sacked as commander-in-chief on the Western Front the previous August after his costly failure to break through against the French at Verdun. Since then he had redeemed himself somewhat by driving the Kaiser's enemies out of Rumania, using a hotch-potch of Bulgarians, Turks and Austro-Hungarians. Ponting found von Falkenhayn a very worrying prospect indeed. Here was a hungry Prussian, still in his fifties, seeking the kind of success that would restore him to what he surely regarded as his rightful position in the main fray – the Western Front.

For the life of him Ponting could not see the War Office matching von Falkenhayn with Systematic Jo – especially with a prime minister in office who saw quick morale-boosting victories in other theatres as the best way around the European stalemate. It would have to be someone with a bit of flair, not a meatgrinder. The trouble was most of the talent remained convinced that with so much blood and treasure invested in Flanders, the breakthrough had to come on the Western Front. And when it happened they wanted to be there, not stuck in some sandpit while old friends mopped up the glory or, almost as bad, the Americans did it for them.

Meanwhile, as the EEF licked its wounds and waited to hear who its new boss would be, Ponting's unit was under pressure to produce. Signals had been sent out to all their agents urging them to be on the look-out for the kind of build-up in men and materials that might herald an offensive. So far, the only indication of anything untoward was a report from a spy in Constantinople that the Germans were removing some of the heavy guns from the cruisers *Breslau* and *Goeben*, which had been trapped there since the beginning of the war.

Ponting watched as the sparrows continued with their terrified dash against the waning light and, once they got to the trees, brawled with each other over the most suitable accommodation. Below them a troop of cavalry in newish-looking tropical-weight khaki came into view, walking their horses down the street which ran along the bank towards the Kasr el-Nil barracks. Ponting guessed that they were recently-arrived reinforcements for some of the Yeomanry regiments brought into Cairo in order to help out with internal security while they were getting acclimatised.

There was need for a show of force in the city at the moment. Last month there had been serious riots; property had been burned and the ringleaders shot dead in the streets before order had been restored. The reason was the growing discontent about recruitment into the Egyptian Labour Corps. Officially Egypt was a self-governing 'Protectorate of the Crown'. As far as the war effort was concerned, all that was required of its citizens was that they should not befriend His Majesty's enemies.

The campaign that had evolved east of the canal in the Sinai desert and then up to Gaza, as the British slowly pushed the Turks back, had changed all that. More and more men were required to build railroads or lay the pipe line that was slowly bringing the waters of the Nile to Palestine. In Upper Egypt village headmen were paid well for maintaining a steady flow of 'volunteers' to the Labour Corps. Ponting and every British soldier in Egypt had heard the favourite Arabic song of these pressed men. 'I miss my home,' they sang. 'I want to go home.' Over and over again.

Ponting noticed that the Yeomanry had sword scabbards as well as rifle-buckets attached to their saddles. All right for keeping the wogs in order, he thought, but bloody useless when old Johnny Turk was smiling at you down the sights of his '98. He had started his career in the Rifle Brigade, and his natural prejudice against horse soldiers had been reinforced by present trends.

All the same, he was heartened to see that there was no nonsense about not reinforcing defeat. New men were pouring in despite the setbacks at Gaza. There was certainly something reassuring about that. Of course, it was common knowledge that the prime minister himself had declared that the EEF must be strengthened. Personally, Ponting had never had much time for David Lloyd George. For a start he had been a Boer-lover, and then there had been his fiscal polices, his so-called 'People's Budget' in '09 which was downright Bolshevism and had been promptly nipped in the bud by the Lords. Lloyd George as a war leader, in what he believed was a *casus belli*, was a different kettle of fish. He had hit on this idea of what he called 'knocking the props away', going for Germany's allies. And it was hard not to warm to a man who was a convinced 'Easterner', whatever his motives.

The 60th Division, Cockney Territorials under General Shea who had started the war in France, had begun to arrive from Salonika

97

where they had been resting after an ill-advised mountain offensive against the Bulgars. At one point the enemy had responded by loosening little avalanches against them. The Italians and French had sent token contingents in order to reinforce their claim to some of the spoils that would surely follow the disintegration of the Ottoman Empire. The French wanted territory – Damascus and the northern coastal lands around Mount Lebanon; the Italians claimed long-term ecclesiastical interests in Jerusalem, the latest round in the old quarrel between Byzantium and Rome. They had sent a unit of Bersaglieri who wore the feathers of black fighting cocks in their solar topees and were constantly getting into fights with Australians or Tommies who wished to transfer them to their own headgear.

Ponting went back to his desk, eased the heel of his right boot off with the toe of his left, and then decided that he could not be caught sitting in his socks and stomped it back into place. Despite the heat he wore long brown riding-boots with a batman's shine still discernible under the dust that always covered everything in Cairo. All the British military intelligence officers working in the Savoy Hotel wore similar footwear except for some of the odd-balls from the Arab Bureau like Newcombe and Lawrence.

The major thought little Lawrence was becoming an appalling exhibitionist, always tricked out in his night-shirt and sandals even for his increasingly rare visits to Cairo. According to his latest despatch, he was poised to take Akaba, the Turks' remaining port on the Red Sea coast. Ponting was not alone in thinking that this was unlikely even if Faisal's Bedouin rebels did outnumber the garrison five-to-one. Irregulars rarely brought off a frontal attack. Nor did it matter all that much since the Gulf of Akaba was blockaded by British and French warships which regularly sailed up to the port and shelled it. As far as Ponting could see, the only conceivable point in capturing the place would be to relieve this flotilla for duties elsewhere. He supposed that Lawrence was doing some good making a thorough nuisance of himself, mining the Hejaz railway, that sort of thing. He had to admit that sometimes gifted amateurs could be an asset – as long as they were properly controlled.

Take the man whose report he was dealing with at that moment – Aaron Aaronsohn. It was an attempt by the Jewish agronomist to persuade the British High Command that they could augment the water they were piping across the Sinai by drilling for the vast natural cisterns beneath the sand. 'The rocks indicate it and Josephus Flavius corroborates it,' Aaronsohn argued in his scholarly way.

If the enemy was still unaware of the defection of Sarah Aaron-sohn's elder brother then their spies in Cairo were blind men with cracked ear trumpets, and Ponting happened to know that this was not the case. It was just over a year ago that Aaronsohn had persuaded Djemal Pasha that he needed to leave Palestine to consult with various experts in Sweden and America about a process to extract oil from sesame seeds. When they were off the Orkneys their ship had been intercepted by a Royal Navy destroyer, and Aaronsohn and his companions had been taken off by a boarding-party.

In London Aaronsohn had seen Lord Rothschild, Weizmann, and sympathetic people like Churchill; and within the month he was in Cairo lunching with Ponting at Shepheard's.

'Do you not think that your presence here might endanger your sister?' Ponting had asked him.

'There's always a danger,' Aaronsohn had replied. 'But the Turks will pay less attention to a woman. They're too contemptuous of them. It's not their way to see how dangerous the weaker sex can be.'

Ponting had let the matter drop – there was no choice. His department – Field Intelligence Levant or FIL – had wanted the Jew to stay in place. After all, it wasn't every day you ran an agent with an ear to one of Turkey's ruling triumvirate. Even the spy Daniel, FIL's other star performer, wasn't that well placed. But Aaronsohn had insisted that his relationship with Djemal Pasha was deteriorating and that he would be more use outside, where he could analyse and interpret reports from the Nili group, the network he had set up.

The major suspected that his real reason was that Weizmann had asked him to do his best to get the British moving before the Turks did to the Yishuv what they had already done to the Armenians. For the moment the Germans were holding them off. The future of the Zionist settlers seemed to depend on how much the Kaiser still rated Jewish influence now that American Jewry had not prevented the United States coming in on the same side as the Cossack rapists. If Wilhelm withdrew his protection and the EEF did not succeed in occupying Palestine immediately, they might be in a lot of trouble.

'Please tell me, Major Ponting,' Aaronsohn had inquired shortly after that first meeting, 'is it an irrefutable law of military science that a big army is always a slow army? I think even an elephant can charge.'

And Ponting had tried to explain to this impertinent civilian that vast armies were not nomadic tribes to be moved overnight. But in a way he was right. The EEF was not the lean machine that had started out in 1915, and if it had never known outright defeat it had never known a victory either.

He found Aaronsohn's solution to the water supply problem an interesting one. God only knew, it was one of their biggest headaches. The animals and men of the EEF were estimated to consume 400,000 gallons of water a day. They had just bought some twelve-inch piping from the Standard Oil Company of America to join a network that stretched hundreds of miles from the Sweet Water Canal to the rail-head at Rafah where it was transferred to camels. Each beast carried on its flanks two small tanks known as fanatis. They were supposed to hold twelve-and-a-half gallons each, but often it was much less by the time they had sloshed up to the forward positions.

Ponting set to work on a précis of Aaronsohn's account of the natural water resources they could tap. He did go on a bit – Joseph Flavius indeed! The major wrote in a large clear hand he had developed especially for the male typists who worked in cubbyholes down the corridor with the dedication of men who knew there were worse ways to spend a war.

When he had finished he rang a bell on his desk, and a private soldier came to bear his message to the lance-corporals and a corporal crouched over their Underwoods.

'Tell them three copies,' he said. 'Two up to Colonel Meinertzhagen and one back to me.'

'Yessir.'

Richard Meinertzhagen was Ponting's new boss. He was already somewhat in awe of him. He had arrived in Cairo some three weeks before, a little later than scheduled because his ship had been torpedoed off the Italian coast. The colonel claimed to have spent five hours in the water fighting off some panic-stricken horses with the African knobkerrie he habitually carried with him, and consuming two bottles of brandy he had had the foresight to remove from the officers' wardroom before abandoning ship.

One of the drowning chargers had winded him with a flailing hoof before he was rescued by a Jap destroyer which scooped the survivors up in a net. He told Ponting that as soon as he had recovered he had written a report pointing out that troops on sinking ships should not be permitted to sing ragtime songs since it impeded the carrying out of orders necessary for their survival. Over two hundred had died, some of them singing. He had been surprised at the number of non-swimmers.

Despite this unfortunate start Meinertzhagen had thrown himself into his new post with considerable enthusiasm, and was obviously more than sympathetic to the Zionist aspirations of Aaron Aaronsohn's Jewish network. At first Ponting had wondered whether Meinertzhagen's enthusiasm might be explained by the fact that he was that extraordinary thing, a regular British army officer and a

Jew. But an officer who had known Meinertzhagen in Africa before the war had explained to Ponting that his superior came from a family of Danish descent who had made their considerable fortune as merchant bankers in London. As an old Africa hand Meinertzhagen had spent most of his war in East Africa trying to pin down the Lilliputian forces of General Paul von Lettow-Vorbeck, who had turned out to be one of the most nimble-footed tacticians the world conflict had produced.

Meinertzhagen had emerged from his campaign with a great respect for the enemy and an abiding contempt for almost everybody on his own side except for the askaris of the King's African Rifles and white Rhodesians. He was particularly fond of the Africans, whose martial ferocity apparently twanged some atavistic Viking chord. Otherwise he considered Kitchener's volunteer battalions to be no more than a collection of callow, undisciplined youths and Smuts's South Africans a bunch of badly officered snipers reluctant to press home an attack. But his real contempt was reserved for Indian troops. Apart from the Kashmiris and Gurkhas, he thought them awful cowards and had put it about that he shot one dead for refusing to obey his orders.

Since his arrival in Cairo he had begun to transfer his Indian phobia to the Arabs despite the assurances of some of his colleagues that one simply could not compare the Cairenes with Faisal's Bedu. Ponting remained neutral. He had often found the fierce paternalism of officers serving with native troops amusing; forever arguing the merits of their Punjabis or their Gurkhas. Ponting had been brought up to believe that in most cases soldiers were as good as their officers, and that was the end of the matter.

The messenger had gone upstairs bearing Aaronsohn's solution to the water problem and Ponting went back to his in-tray. He had one more matter to clear up before he called it a day and that concerned a report from their agent Daniel in Jerusalem.

It was a good message. Nothing sensational but a lot of juicy tit-bits. There was confirmation of the RFC's claim of several kills following their first dogfight with the Hun in their new Bristol Fighters and some suggested targets for future raids. There was the tantalising information that the German in charge of the Gaza garrison, one Major Tiller, was so convinced that he was beaten during the April offensive that he had blown up his wireless station while waiting to surrender. That would be enough for GHQ to restart the post-mortems into the April offensive.

There was a suggestion that Mustafa Kemal was becoming increasingly unco-operative with the German Military Mission, particularly now that Falkenhayn had more or less taken over the show and elbowed aside poor old Liman von Sanders who remained in Damascus. Apparently Kemal had been particularly tricky during some official dinner held at Fast's Hotel – which was one of the suggested targets for the RFC, along with the Turks' civil administration headquarters at the Augusta Victoria Stiftung on the Mount of Olives. There was some more stuff on the Kut prisoners that was so horrible it really made Ponting's blood boil.

Daniel was undoubtedly their best, most sensitively placed spy in Jerusalem, yet it had taken over a month for his report to get back to Cairo. Meinertzhagen wanted to know why.

Ponting explained the reasons for the delay in a slightly less legible hand than the one he had previously used. In theory the clerks were cleared to handle all grades of classified material, but this would not be going through them. The gist of what he had to say was this:

Urgent messages were sometimes entrusted to Bedouin couriers, who knew their way through the Turkish frontline. But this was an extremely risky business. Even if the courier was not intercepted there was always a good chance that he was a double agent bearing a despatch that had been skilfully laced with disinformation.

An agent who had a contact in a neutral country might try to pass a message through the mail, perhaps by making an invisible ink and writing between the lines of some legitimate correspondence. But this too was fraught with risk. All mail was liable to be censored and tests might be made to see if the paper had been tampered with. Most invisible inks, for instance, respond to heat.

Having explained why Daniel had not entrusted his message to either a Bedouin or invisible ink, Ponting went on to give the reasons for the delay. The agent had sent his information through Aaron Aaronsohn's network even though they were quite unaware of Daniel's existence as such – a healthy arrangement. In the past this had always been regarded as the safest way to get information back. But there had been a disaster.

The *Monegam*'s sister ship, the gunboat which shared its pick-up duties off the Levantine coast, had been torpedoed before it even reached the little fishing-port with its round Crusader tower. A lieutenant from FIL was missing, either drowned or captured. Then spring storms had delayed the *Monegam* from making the pick-up. Now experiments were being conducted to install a more powerful wireless transmitter on the monitor to enable it to send material back to Cairo almost as soon as the pick-up was made. To facilitate reception, Signals had set up an aerial on the summit of the Great Pyramid itself – much to the consternation of some of the locals, who feared the English had added witchcraft to their war effort.

'However,' wrote Ponting, 'we face the usual problems with wire-less telegraphy. One is that even with the assistance of the Great Pyramid atmospherics might sometimes make it impossible to get a clear message back to Cairo. Another is that whether we receive the message or not German operators based on the coast almost certainly would, and even if they were unable to decode our morse cypher the transmission would alert the enemy to the vessel's presence. Knowing the Navy's caution in these matters, a prudent captain might well insist on maintaining wireless silence until he was practically back in Alexandria harbour.'

Ponting paused here and asked himself if he wasn't going a bit far? After all, they had just lost a ship. He looked at it again. Dammit! He was damned if he was going to rewrite the whole page, and it was just the sort of thing the Navy would come up with. So what if they had just lost a ship? They weren't excused casualties. The sooner Meinertzhagen realised what they had to put up with from the Senior Service the better.

Now he needed something to conclude his memorandum – prefer-ably a suggestion. One thing he had learned about his new boss was that he was a man who expected his subordinates to come up with solutions as well as problems.

He got up and walked over to the window again and looked down at the Nile. The sun had not quite set. Some late sparrows were still in headlong flight. In the distance he could make out the triangular silhouette of a felucca's sails.

Nearer the bank was a high-bowed skiff with a small boy in a dingy jellaba struggling with a massive pair of crudely-cut oars shaped like chop-sticks and twisting his young shoulders against the current. Another flock of sparrows flew above the skiff. It came to him then, watching the birds: pigeons. Why don't they use carrier pigeons?

He went back to his desk and started a fresh paragraph, pointing out that pigeons had been well used, admittedly over a much shorter distance, by Belgian agents on the Western Front. He added that some Signals units were already using birds in the Sinai. All they had to do was acquire some Egyptian homing pigeons and deliver them to Sarah Aaronsohn.

Ponting was certain Meinertzhagen would like the idea. In fact, he would probably kick himself for not thinking of it first. For although Meinertzhagen took almost as much delight in killing all feathered and furry things as he did in disposing of His Majesty's enemies, he was also a passionate ornithologist. His notes and sketches on the subject already filled several exercise books. He was, of course, particularly fond of birds of prey, the result of being allowed to keep a pet eagle at school.

When he had finished he took it up to Meinertzhagen personally, since it was his custom to see his superior before he left for the night in case any urgent business had cropped up. Ponting's slightly dilettante manner was thin camouflage for a very conscientious soul.

The colonel's office was one of the Savoy's finest suites. It was across the gable end of the building and approached down a long corridor.

'Enter,' boomed Meinertzhagen to Ponting's short knock and turn of the brass door knob. He was sitting behind a large desk and was just about to return a telephone to its cradle. Ponting noticed that his knobkerrie had been placed neatly along the edge of the desk. The business end of the club was darker than the rest of the wood, as if it had been marinaded in blood for a century.

Meinertzhagen glanced at the first couple of lines of the report on Daniel's communication problem and then put it down again. 'Allenby,' he said.

'I beg your pardon, sir?' said Ponting, his mind on migratory birds.

'Lieutenant-General Edmund Henry Hynman Allenby to be precise – the new Commander-in-Chief of His Majesty's Egyptian Expeditionary Force.'

For the first time Ponting noticed that an open copy of the Army List lay on the desk. 'Old chum of mine at GHQ just called to tell me. Been looking him up. Cavalryman. Skin.* Started in France commanding the Cavalry Division. Last job was commanding Third Army Corps at Arras.'

'Ah yes,' said Ponting. He remembered the name now. Allenby had been charge of the Canadians when they took Vimy Ridge. That had been last April when the EEF was making a mess of things at Gaza and Meinertzhagen was still in East Africa running around in circles after von Lettow-Vorbeck. A breath of cheer from the mud plot. Early in the war Ponting had served in that sector himself until a bad chest wound left him unfit for regimental duties and he transferred to Intelligence. He would not be overseas now had a Medical Board not allowed him to persuade them that Egypt's dry heat would be good for his damaged lungs.

'Ever met him?' inquired Meinertzhagen.

'General Allenby? Can't think that I have, sir.'

* Nickname for Royal Inniskilling Dragoon Guards – a cavalry regiment recruited in Ireland.

'I'll tell you something – I once got him out of bed at sword-point!'

'Good heavens!' Despite the fact that he knew this was going to lead to a long anecdote, and he badly wanted to tell him about his carrier pigeon idea and then get off and have a bath and some dinner, Ponting's curiosity was genuinely aroused. Meinertzhagen was a good story-teller, uninhibited by false modesty. There was, for instance, the matter of that knobkerrie, which he insisted he had wrestled off a German officer in the dark and then used to bash the man's brains out.

'Quite true,' said Meinertzhagen who was loading his pipe from a zebra-skin pouch. 'Before I came into the army properly I was in the Hampshire Yeomanry. That would be about '97 or '98. We had an exercise against the Aldershot Cavalry Brigade under French. Allenby was on his staff. I don't know whether you know the area – Farley Down? Anyway, one night four of us were sent out on an officers' patrol to try and locate the "enemy"! We found French's headquarters bivouacked at a spot called Beacon Hill. I suppose we should have slipped quietly away to tell our side.

'But I was about eighteen at the time, a very new second-lieutenant just down from Harrow and not all that *au fait* with military etiquette. As soon as I realised they didn't have any pickets out I drew my sword, started yelling like a Red Indian and we charged. I suppose we were all pretty young fellows. You can imagine what it was like. All that top brass tucked up in their flea bags and us crashing right through them, whooping our heads off, swords flashing. They had hobbled their horses but that didn't prevent them tottering off in all directions as fast as the ropes would let them.

'Of course, the next day the exercise had to be cancelled while everybody helped to round them up. I expected to get a real dressing-down from French, but he and Allenby and some of the others were quite tickled about it. Cavalrymen like a good raid, y'know.'

Meinertzhagen paused to puff at his pipe, obviously pleased with his reckless youth.

'Do you think he's going to be the right man for the job, sir?' asked Ponting. It had suddenly occurred to him that if Allenby harboured a deep, consuming desire to use cavalry they might be getting the kind of general who would tilt at cactus hedges.

'There's no reason why this shouldn't develop into the right sort of campaign for a cavalryman,' said Meinertzhagen, as if he had read his deputy's thoughts. Like Ponting he was an infantryman; his horse soldiering had stopped with the Yeomanry, although all infantry officers in the pre-war army rode. In any case, he had been detached from regimental duties for too long to allow corps prejudices to cloud his innovative mind. 'The terrain's right for it until you get to the Judaean foothills. If we could punch the right sort of hole in the Turkish line and pour the cavalry through they would have a field day.'

'Providing we can find the right sort of water for their horses,' reminded Ponting, who often felt all cavalry should suffer the fate of the dismounted 74th Yeomanry division.

'Ah, the water problem. Our friend Aaronsohn could be on the right track there. Just a matter of knowing where the wells are and digging for it, eh?'

'As long as the geology hasn't changed in the last two thousand years. It might not be as simple as Professor Aaronsohn would have us believe, sir,' cautioned Ponting, who was beginning to wish he had added this codicil to his report. Meinertzhagen's enthusiasms could be worrying.

'No, I don't suppose it will – but I've heard of madder schemes working and it has the genius of the race. I'm going to send it to GHQ with my blessing. The way I remember it two thousand years is about two minutes as far as geology is concerned. If Allenby wants to use his cavalry properly he'll need all the water he can get.'

Meinertzhagen began to leaf through the document Ponting had placed on his desk. 'Ah pigeons,' he beamed. 'Now there's an interesting thought.'

14

Walter Calderwell sauntered back to his tent from the armourers with his new sword, which he held under the hilt by the scabbard. He was one of the new draft to the Yeomanry – reinforcements sent out to replace casualties and the men felled by malaria and the waterborne sickness bilharzia, which the Tommies called Billy Harry. All had arrived in Egypt equipped with gleaming *armes blanches*. And all had been told by their respective sergeants that if they wished to ride with his troop they would kindly go and get their toy soldier cutlery replaced by a proper weapon with a dulled bowl guard and scabbard which would not catch the rays of a rising sun and heliograph the presence of a dawn patrol to a Hun airman out to commit murder before breakfast.

Private Calderwell fancied himself as a bit of a card, as is often the way of very young men barely out of adolescence. Suddenly his sword transmogrified into a cane, his knees bent and he did his Charlie Chaplin walk. But he stopped after a few paces when he somehow placed the weapon between his legs and seemed to come perilously close to snapping it in two. A cavalry sword was really too long to be a proper substitute for the little fellow's chief prop. He recalled his introduction to the weapon during basic training which, coming after a morning of gas mask instruction, had caused a fellow-recruit to remark: 'From Jules Verne to the Three Musketeers in one ruddy day.'

The man's imagery had undoubtedly been inspired by their middle-aged Cockney sergeant instructor, a regular from the Life Guards and as fiercely moustached as any Dumas chevalier.

107

'Now this is known as the ho-hate, basket 'ilted cavalry sword,' he had screeched, holding the aforesaid between two outstretched hands above his head. 'And its blade is exactly thirty-six inches long, which the clever ones among you will know is three feet. It is called the ho hate sword because it was designed in the year nineteen hundred and hate by a committee of distinguished cavalrymen presided over by none other than Colonel Baden-Powell, with whom I had the honour to serve during the late unpleasantness in South Africa. Those of you who can read and write might 'ave heard of that distinguished officer. I dare say some of you 'ave even been little boy scouters and know all about tyin' knots and 'elpin old ladies across the road. Now listen carefully. This is a sword. I repeat – a sword. I 'ave heard some ignorant people around this depot talk about sabres. It is not a sabre. Sabres are what old-fashioned cavalrymen use for slashin' at the enemy. Nowadays we do not slash. We stick. We lean out of the saddle with our arms outstretched and we puncture the enemy like a sausage. A German sausage. Any questions?'

The words came back to Calderwell as he reached a crossroads in the pattern of bell tents. He made a savage, sausage-puncturing lunge, his left arm curved above his head like a musketeer.

'Steady Yeoman!' A portly officer coming from Calderwell's left escaped a severe denting with a sheathed blade only by sucking in his belly. 'Trying to arrange a bit more sick leave for me, are you?'

Captain Rudolph Valintine, Calderwell's squadron commander, had recently returned from England where he had been convalescing from wounds received the previous spring. It was common knowledge he had turned down a desk job in Cairo in order to be back with his regiment, the Warwickshire Yeomanry.

'Sorry, sir,' said Calderwell, snapping to attention and transferring the sword to his left hand with credible dexterity so that he could salute.

'What exactly were you doing?' asked Valintine, returning the salute.

'Practising, sir.'

'Practising? Practising for what – the ballet? Calderwell, isn't it – one of the new draft?'

'Yessir.'

'Well, I'll tell you something, Calderwell: to quote one of our more successful generals, you might not frighten the enemy but by God you frighten me! If you want to play with cold steel I'm sure I can make arrangements for you to attack something in the kitchen. The cooks are always looking for volunteers.'

'Yessir.'

'Now take your sword to your tent and don't wave it about again until you see some Turks in front of you. Understood?'

'Yessir,' said Calderwell, blushing madly. He who was no longer a card, just a crestfallen teenager.

Valintine walked off a couple of paces and then he stopped. 'Calderwell,' he said.

'Sir?'

'We mostly shoot 'em.'

When the private got back to the bell tent he shared with seven others the only other occupant was Isaiah Mace, who was lying on his palliasse with a fag going, contrary to standing orders which forbade smoking under canvas. In camp almost everybody smoked continuously for as long as they had tobacco. The maintenance of a constant smoke-screen seemed to be the only way to keep the number of flies at a tolerable level. Calderwell had neglected to drape a piece of mosquito curtain over his helmet. While eating a jam sandwich in the transit camp in Alexandria, he had been stung on the tongue by a wasp and unable to take anything but liquids for two days.

He nodded to Mace who said by way of greeting, 'Don't forget your kit's being inspected tomorrow,' and walked out.

Mace was basically a friendly soul but Calderwell was too new for a man who'd got his knees brown to spend too much time with. The sergeants were looking at all the new men's kit which meant an awful lot of work because, unlike the infantry, it was not just two pairs of boots that had to be polished. There was also a saddle, bridle, head-collar, rifle-bucket and the cases which the spare horse-shoes were carried in, one fore and one hind. There were no irons available for pressing, but clothing had to be clean and folded in the regimental manner. And some sergeants took a delight in opening up every piece of kit, however small, including that item known to the War Office as the 'housewife', a cloth pouch which was supposed to contain a specific number of needles, spare buttons, cottons and bootlaces.

As it happened Calderwell was already well ahead with his kit. He had always derived a certain satisfaction from the application of polish and saddlesoap. So once he had placed his sword behind the chain around the tent pole which ran through the trigger guards of their rifles, he went to his haversack and extracted the only book it contained. He flicked through its pages until he came to letter number 186, entitled 'From a gentleman to his sweetheart.' It was quite promising.

'. . . for if you anticipate pleasure in the company of your husband,' the private read, 'I assure you I sincerely return you the compliment. I expect much in your society – much that will dispel one's troubles.'

He paused to savour the words 'if you anticipate pleasure in the company of your husband'. Now *that* could only mean one thing. It was amazing what you could find in *The Complete Letter-Writer for Ladies and Gentlemen* if you knew where to look – which was even more amazing when he considered that the book had been a parting gift from his chapel-going Ma, who had obviously not vetted its contents.

Calderwell's greatest disappointment since arriving in Egypt had been to find himself confined to barracks during the three days the reinforcements spent in Alexandria. All the way out on the troop ship there had been sailors and old sweats among the infantry reinforcements on board who had told them of the whores' parlours to be found there and in Cairo, where a man would think he was in paradise for the price of a packet of Woodbines. Sweet-smelling olive-skinned bints, dressed in yashmaks and baggy silk trousers, who would let you do anything with them.

The regulars' tales had been confirmed by an unlikely source – a colonel from the Indian Army Medical Corps, a stout man with thin mutton-chop whiskers and the flushed nose and cheeks of a drinker. The colonel had had them paraded on the boat deck to hear about what he called, 'the full price of nights of shame'. The younger Yeomen had been enthralled, hanging on every word.

'Those of you who are even contemplating indulging in sins of the flesh,' this learned physician had begun, 'should remember that syphilis contracted by Europeans from Asiatic women is much more severe than the sort you get in England. It is a long, lingering death of which the sufferer is only too aware.

'First great handfuls of his hair fall out. Then his flesh begins to rot, eaten away by slow cancerous and stinking ulcerations. Afterwards, his nose falls in at the bridge and then rots and falls off; his sight gradually fails and he eventually becomes blind; his voice first becomes husky, and then fades to a hoarse whisper as his throat is eaten away by ulcerations as big as shillings which cause his breath to stink.

'I have met these people,' the MO had thundered, his cheeks bursting into flame. 'I have met them on morning sick parades, I have met them in the pox wards and I have met them on the mortician's slab after they had slashed their wrists because they could no longer live with the pain and infamy. Your last days are spent in agony and

110

often as an outcast. And all for what? A few minutes' pleasure. Ask a man without a nose if he thought it was worth it?'

When they had been dismissed a lanky, jug-eared boy in the Worcesters, who parted his hair down the middle, said that he knew for a fact that most of the regulars stuck their main members where he wouldn't put the point of his sword. Almost all the reinforcements draft on board had been brought up to believe that the ranks of the regular peacetime army were filled by the sweepings of the gutter. Yet Calderwell was not the only one present who had never met a man without a nose, and in any case he believed he was just as immune to syphilis as he was to bullets. In the right circumstances he might confront the chance of disease with the same recklessness that he intended to face the powder.

When they got to the transit camp the reinforcements discovered men there from other units who swore that all the regulars' tales of olive-skinned bints who would do it for the price of a beer were true. Apparently there was an Armenian refugee camp nearby where the women were red-hot. But to their fury the draft were not allowed out of the camp and were hardly off the ship before they moved to Cairo, where the wogs were getting stroppy and the authorities wanted a show of force. Calderwell had been one of those Yeomanry whom Ponting had spotted from his window at the Savoy.

Private Calderwell was bitterly disappointed. He told himself not to think about it but he thought of little else. Furtive assignations with what the old sweats called the 'five-fingered widow' – difficult when you were sharing a tent with seven others – were followed by shame and remorse. Sometimes he wondered what was worse – going blind, or risking your nose and your hair? Here he was, nineteen years of age and a trained soldier, and he might as well be a monk for all he knew of women.

'Look at this,' said Private Isaiah Mace. 'Bare arse bare back.'

Calderwell was still too unsure of himself to risk appearing standoffish with an old hand. Reluctantly, he put aside his copy of *The Complete Letter-Writer*, and went to the entrance of the tent which was flapping gently in the sea breeze.

The farrier corporal and two of his men were fooling around in the surf with one of Captain Valintine's hunters they had just shoed in readiness for the next day's race meeting with the Australians. The horse was a big grey mare and the men were as naked as she was. Two of them were on her back while the farrier, stripped to the waist with his trousers rolled tight above his knees, led the animal by its bridle through the foam. Suddenly, he gave the mare a great slap on her rump and she cantered off down the beach, her riders cheering wildly until the rear man contrived to fall off onto the wet sand.

'Strewth,' said Calderwell. 'On the ship out here they used to put you on a charge if you went up on deck without your hat on.'

'Oh ah, they used to 'ere,' said Mace. 'Now they don't bother – not off duty any road. It was the colonials what started it. One of the first things we noticed was how they were always running around their bivouacs without their 'ats or shirts on most of the time and nobody was dying of sunstroke. At first they said it was because they were brought up to it like, but then after a while people began to realise that half them bloody Diggers were born and raised in England or Ireland and the other half only a grandad away.'

They watched the man who had fallen off knock the sand from his body. Calderwell had already recognised him from the crop of angry red spots on his back – which for the first time he saw extended to his buttocks – as a former blacksmith's apprentice called Perkins. Almost everybody who had been in the country for more than a month was continually scratching flea and mosquito bites, but Perkins had one of those fair, greasy skins that was particularly prone to erupt into the pus-filled bumps some time after adolescence had given way to young manhood. Even more so when it had been denied the benefits of a wash and a clean shirt for weeks at a stretch. Now all the men were being encouraged to take a daily dip while they were in the rest area. There were even classes organised for the non-swimmers like Calderwell. There were plenty of these, for most of these Midlands men had got their first glimpse of the sea when the troop train rolled into Portsmouth.

'That sea water might be all right for Perkins' spotty botty,' said Mace, 'but you can bet me it ain't going to be much good for the bloody 'orse. They'll be combing the salt out of her coat for days.'

'It'll be good for any cuts she's got,' said Calderwell, who pretended to know more about horses than he did, though he happened to be right on this occasion. At least half the regiment had never felt a horse between their legs until they enlisted. Calderwell had distinguished himself during basic training by keeping his seat when his nag bolted on him in the grounds of Warwick Castle, the regimental depot. He counted himself lucky to have been given a sweet-natured chestnut mare from among the latest batch of Waler remounts. He called her Villa after Aston Villa, the Birmingham team which had won the Football Association Cup more times than any other.

Both he and Mace spoke with the flat Midlands' nasal whine most of the rest of the country simply regarded as Brummy. They said 'dowin' for 'doing'; 'yow' for 'you' and pronounced 'combing' as 'cowmin' and 'going' as 'gooin' and like as 'loike'. The Fifth Mounted Brigade was one of the most English units in the entire Egyptian Expeditionary Force. It was made up of three territorial regiments whose rank and file were mainly recruited from the land's most central, most Saxon shires. Calderwell and Mace wore the black diamond flash of the Warwicks on their solar topees. Brigaded alongside them were the Worcestershire and Gloucestershire Yeomanry. The brigade was part of Major-General Sir Harry Hodgson's Australian Mounted Division and was its only genuine cavalry arm because the Australians were not equipped with swords. The colonials were merely mounted infantry intended for fast deployment and then dismounting and peppering the enemy with rapid rifle fire.

The farrier section led the mare back to their piled uniforms. Now they were all out of water Calderwell found their nakedness made him feel uncomfortable: those marble loins with the indistinct meat in the bush. It brought back memories of a picture that had terrified him as a child. It showed stern-looking angels rousing the unclothed dead from their graves on the Day of Judgment, and it had hung in the home of a Methodist minister he had visited with his mother when he was enrolled for Sunday School. To hide his embarrassment he asked Mace, 'What do you think her chances are tomorrow?'

'Good. And I'll tell you why they're good. It's because our Val 'as decided he still ain't fit enough to race 'er.'

'Is he no good then – at riding, I mean?' asked Calderwell. In his short time in the Yeomanry Calderwell had never met an officer who had not been hunting since he was a child and rode like a demon.

'Oh 'e's got a good enough seat,' said Mace. 'But she'll do better with somebody lighter up. Our Val ain't built for speed. He's 'ad too much bloody puddin', 'e 'as. That's always been 'is trouble.'

'Did you know him before the war, then?' asked Calderwell. Although he lacked any stripes on his arm Mace had quickly established his position as a pre-war territorial among the new men, one of the original 'Saturday afternoon butterfly shooters.'

'Oh 'ar, I knew him all right,' said Mace, sucking on his pipe. 'Val's from Snittersfield and I'm from 'enley-in-Arden.'

'You're almost neighbours, then,' said Calderwell who was from Coventry and knew both places as part of a rural playground entered down narrow lanes which meandered through oak woods and miles of rolling fields divided by ancient hedges. He and his pals from the Humber car works had cycled much further afield than Henley in search of girls and good ale before Lord Derby's recruiting drive had made them feel awkward to be almost nineteen years old and still out of uniform. It was even worse if you stumbled onto a place where

113

several of the young married men had already been persuaded to go – not that some of them needed much persuading.

Until then they would think nothing of taking a spin down through Kenilworth and Warwick – where the Yeomanry had its headquarters in the Norman castle – to Stratford for bread and cheese and beer somewhere on the river, with a little of their bread cast on the limpid waters so they could watch the perch play. Then it might be back through the Roman fortress town of Alcester, where in the spring they would linger in Oversley Woods in the hope of meeting factory girls picking bluebells, although nothing much ever came of it even if they did. After that they would take the winding short cut that led through places named by the people who burned the Roman Britons out and didn't know how to live in towns: Great Alne and Little Alne and Wootton Wawen. Then into Henley by the main Solihull road before they turned off into the green tunnels again, crossing the Avon at Lawsonford and the Grand Union Canal just before Shrewsley, and home with the light fading via Yew Green and Leek Wootton. Or perhaps they would only go as far as Stratford and then follow the river along a bit to, say, Hampton Lucy before turning round and going back through the Welcombe Hills, which they all thought were spelt 'welcome'. Once they made the top they would freewheel down into Snittersfield before they pushed up to Norton Lindsey with legs like lead.

'Neighbours?' said Mace. 'Well, in a manner of speakin' I suppose we were. 'E was magistrate was Val and a church warden, dare say 'e still is. Between that and is 'untin' and shootin' and 'is polo and the Yeomanry I'm buggered if I know how he ever found the time to farm.'

'A magistrate!' said Calderwell, who was genuinely surprised that anybody so venerable should do something so banal as go to war.

'Yes,' said Mace. 'A good 'un too. A very fair man is our Val. That's how I ended up in the Yeomanry. Me and a couple of mates used to go poachin' pheasants. Nestin' hens mostly. We used to try and lure them into a quiet spot with an aniseed trail and then use Daisy air guns so the gamekeepers wouldn't hear us. It was pure devilment really. We didn't need to do it although I suppose we made a couple of bob from those that fancy a bite from the gentry's larder and didn't ask no questions. Of course, in a place as small as ours we were bound to get caught sooner or later. So there we were up before the Bench when old Val was on and he gave us a choice. Being as we were first offenders loike he said we could either have a birchin' from the police sergeant – big bugger 'e was, built like the fuckin' pyramids – or be bound over to keep the peace and join the Yeomanry. Well, I think all of us had already had a right laruppin' from our fathers and we didn't fancy any more of it so we signed up. Of course, the captain knew our families. I had an uncle who was with him in the Yeomanry in South Africa and my mate's father was there.'

'Are your mates over here now?'

'No. One's a bloody sergeant instructor at Warwick now so he's no mate of mine. Nice cushy number. 'E was always full of bullshit, talk the leg off an iron pot. The other one never really could get on with 'orses. When he weren't fallin' off 'em they were bitin' him, poor bastard. He just seemed to have a talent for rilin' them one way or the other. When the war started he saw 'is chance and transferred to the infantry. South Staffs. Last I 'eard he was in France.'

'Well, rather him than me,' said Calderwell. 'Too much bloody mud in France. This must be a much better pitch for cavalry work.'

'You think so? You should have been with us at Katia,' said Mace in his flat, matter-of-fact way.

'Why? What happened?'

'We got beat, that's what 'appened. We got our arses kicked. The officers didn't know whether they were comin' or goin'. They didn't know whether it was April or December.'

'Including Valintine?'

'Everybody.'

'I thought the only thing our officers are frightened of is fartin' in the parlour, sorry the drawing-room?' said Calderwell.

'Oh they're brave enough all right. Too bloody brave some of the younger ones, about as much sense as their bloody horses half the time. That's the trouble. You get the impression that old Kress and the other Fritzes they've got in charge over there take it more seriously. Professionals versus amateurs. Sometimes, our lot seem to be playing at it. They think it's just another bloody 'unt. There's Johnny Turk. Tally-ho! After 'im! Do you know there's a captain in the Worcesters, Toby Albright his name is, who goes into action with a bloody huntin' 'orn? I 'eard 'im blowin' the fuckin' thing at Katia.'

Calderwell was shocked by this. Here was someone, whom he had to accept as a more or less reliable source, suggesting that British officers were in some ways inferior to their German counterparts. Yet for three years now the newspapers had told him that the war would have been won long ago had it not been for the unreliability of one's allies, the terrain, the weather – somehow it had rained more in France and Belgium since the start of the war – and, above all, the downright beastliness and treachery of the Hun. For although it was generally acknowledged that the enemy were a bunch of posturing militarists who had been playing war games since they first strutted around their kindergartens, it must in no way be concluded that such dedication produced better soldiers. Maeltzer would have found Calderwell a touching product of the British genius for self-deception. But, pressed, he might have conceded that myths could be useful if people believed in them enough.

15

'*I*'ve got some good news for you,' she said, 'You'll be going home soon.'

Sarah Aaronsohn held the pigeon to her chest while she stroked it and made little cooing noises. After a few seconds the bird started cooing back in the way that a cat will sometimes answer a non-feline miaow. She held it tighter and could feel the bird's heart throbbing madly, so much faster than her own. It seemed so vulnerable, she thought, almost as if the pulsating life it contained was in danger of exploding its fragile frame. How could such endurance belong to anything so delicate!

They kept the pigeons in a loft hidden among the conifers behind the two-storey wooden house with its sloping roof and first-floor balcony that was both Aaron's living quarters and the laboratory for his agricultural experimental station. Ever since her return from Cairo with the pigeons she had been trying to think of a better place for them. She had asked George but he had made some vague excuses; Sarah had guessed that he thought the birds might attract too much attention, and had not liked to press him. Christian Arab fishing clans were another minority the Turks were becoming wary about. The fishermen took enough risks on their behalf ferrying them out to the British monitors.

It had been George who had taken her out last time in his boat with the rust-red sail. And it had been George who had placed the white sheet for all clear on the balcony that overlooked the broad sweep of the bay when the monitor had reappeared ten days later

117

flying a purple pennant among its signal flags to show that there was a passenger on board who wished to land.

Arabs and Jews united against the Turk! Exactly as it should be. If only people like Vladimir Jabotinsky, who was said to be in London raising a corps of Jewish volunteers to fight in Palestine, could meet people like George. Sarah was sure that if he did he would not continue to talk about Arabs, at least not all Arabs, like a Cossack.

She paused to imagine a meeting between the two men. George would put on his Western suit for the occasion. But he would not wear a fez because it would no longer be necessary to don the headgear the Ottoman authorities demanded of all male citizens in Western clothing to demonstrate their fealty towards the Sublime Porte. Monsieur Jabotinsky would be wearing ... well, she was not quite sure what the Russian Jew would be wearing, although she did dimly recall newspaper photographs of an aristocratic-looking gentleman wearing long riding-boots.

They would talk and George would occasionally pause and play with his amber worry beads in that dignified way of his. Jabotinsky was undoubtedly a cultured man. Was he not engaged in translating the works of Edgar Allen Poe into the new Hebrew of Ben Yehuda né Perleman? He would soon see that they could live side by side with people who had also suffered the indignities of Turkish rule. One meeting with George, she was sure, would be enough to disabuse him of these crazy notions that a reborn Jewish nation, a proper Zionist entity, could only maintain its integrity by becoming a warrior state, in a constant state of siege with its neighbours.

But, of course, George was a Christian, and therefore more receptive to European ideas like Zionism. Sarah knew hardly any Muslim Syrian Arabs. Certainly, she knew none of them as well as George, whom she almost counted as a comrade.

Sarah put the pigeon back with its five companions in the loft Joseph had constructed out of a few struts of wood and some wire netting. It had been Ponting, white-faced with seasickness as usual, who had helped her board the monitor and suggested that she might concoct some story to explain her absence from Zichron Jacob and spend a few days in Cairo. 'Somebody wants to talk to you,' he had said, and the thought of seeing Aaron again had made up her mind for her.

Making up a story to explain her absence had not been very difficult, for even before Aaron left she had established a pattern of spending weeks away from the settlement at the experimental station. Nevertheless, to cover herself in case anybody called she had sent a note to her father explaining that she might be going to Petah Tikvah,

118

which was not all that far from the battle front at Gaza, to see a relative of her husband. She knew that this would quickly get around Zichron Jacob and this, she had thought, was no bad thing.

The allusion to her husband, public acknowledgement of his existence on her part, was a good opportunity to silence tongues wagging about the exact nature of her relationship with Joseph Lishansky. She had married Chaim Abraham, a Constantinople Jew of Bulgarian extraction, shortly before the outbreak of war. Soon after they settled into their new home in Constantinople it became evident to both of them that the marriage was a grave mistake.

At first the age difference (he was some fifteen years older) had not worried her. He was not an unobtrusive man, dark and slim with chiselled features, and the marriage would not have foundered on the physical side of it had been more watertight in other compartments. The fact that he was from a more observant background than Sarah and that she was, for instance, required to supervise a kosher kitchen with separate dishes for meat and dairy could be irritating but she could have lived with it, even laughed about it. What she found intolerable was the discovery of his intolerance of the creed she had been brought up on: the establishment of a Jewish state in Palestine.

When they had met while he was on a business trip to Haifa she had thought he was malleable, ripe for conversion to Zionism. Instead, she found that he had merely indulged her convictions for the period of the courtship and was as violently opposed to the ideas of Dr Theodore Herzl as any of the assimilated Jews of Western Europe. How could you compare, he would argue, the half-baked utopian theories of some distracted Viennese scribbler with so tangible a thing as the Young Turks' emancipation of the Jews along with every other minority in the Ottoman Empire?

'But the Jews were emancipated in Western Europe after the French revolution and still there's anti-Semitism and persecution.'

'There's no persecution here.'

'And what about the Armenians?'

'What about them,' this worthy merchant would reply. 'They're treacherous scum. They're in league with the Czar! Since when does a Jew worry about friends of Moscow? The Turks are realistic. They allow people to settle in Palestine as long as there's no foolish talk about setting up their own state. Herzl and his kind are power-hungry madmen. Every one of them secretly wants to be King of the Jews. Don't you see that? If it was not Palestine he was willing to settle for a bit of Argentina. Even Uganda! He didn't care what godforsaken plot the Jews were given as long as he was in charge.'

And Sarah would sigh and think what her brother Aaron would say to hear the late literary editor of the *Neue Freie Presse* dismissed with such vehemence.

Aaron had been there to welcome her when the monitor came alongside the mole at Alexandria although Ponting had not allowed her to walk down the gangway to the waiting car until he had arranged a screen of four large sailors to proceed crabwise either side of her. 'Young ladies don't normally emerge from His Majesty's warships, and ports tend to be watched,' he had explained.

Sarah thought this unnecessary, likely to attract even more attention not less. The English always seemed to think that the Turks were much better than they were. And even if they were suspicious, the Germans were too worried about Jewish influence at home to permit any reprisals. At first she had not recognised her brother, one among several English officers waiting by the dusty staff car with its goggled chauffeur. Aaron in uniform! She could hardly suppress her giggles. But there he was, his blond hair crushed under a flat cap and even giving Ponting a kind of salute. Aaron the soldier! Incredible!

'Shalom,' he had said, which was almost the limit of his demotic Hebrew, despite his sympathy with the aspirations of the grammarian Ben Yehuda.

'Nili,' she grinned. Nili was an acronym for the biblical Hebrew of a line to be found in the Book of Samuel, chapter fifteen, verse twenty-nine: 'And all the glory of Israel will not lie.' It had been Aaron's idea to use it as their password. After these greetings they spoke to each other in French.

'Why are you wearing your scarf like that?'

Ponting had persuaded her to wrap her scarf around her face like a touareg.

'The major didn't want anybody to recognise me. He thinks Alexandria is full of Turkish spies.'

'If there were they'd think you were an admiral's daughter.' He had been going to say mistress but she was his little sister.

They had gone to the villa he had been given on Gezira, where a Nubian servant served them iced lemon tea on the veranda. 'Has it been interesting here?'

'Certainly, very interesting.'

Sarah had waited for him to tell her more but her brother just smiled and sipped his tea and deposited the ash of his oval Turkish cigarette into a saucer with maddening precision.

'Aaron, don't play games. What have you been doing?'

'Trying to teach the British about Joseph Flavius, among other things.'

'The wells? Do they believe you?'

'I think so. Up to a point. They rarely show what their true opinion of anything is. You must have noticed that with Ponting. It can be very irritating. At first you think they're not taking you seriously so you start to talk too much. Sometimes I stand back and listen to myself and hear this jabbering bazaar merchant. Then one day you suddenly realise that they've been thinking quite hard about what you've been telling them.'

'You've always found everyone slow.'

'Compared to the Turks the English have minds like lightning. Ponting's boss is good, Meinertzhagen. Very open-minded for a soldier.' He waved away some cigarette smoke with an impatient backhand flap. 'And for water they also have their pipeline of course.'

'Pipeline?'

'Yes. It goes from the Nile to the Great Bitter Lake and on up to the front line before Gaza. They were gangs of felaheen laying the pipes but I don't think they'll be able to bring it up fast enough once their offensive begins.'

My God! Such confidence, she thought. The British would start an offensive and they would advance. As simple as that. No question about it. They used tanks and gas last time, and still the Turks beat them back. She remembered those prisoners being shown around Jerusalem.

'So this time they're going to win?'

'Yes, they are. Look, the British are war weary. I know, I saw them in London. There are food shortages there now and air raids. They badly need a victory. A nice cheap victory without the kind of casualty lists they get from France. This new general, Allenby, is getting thousands of reinforcements for a winter campaign. Not only the English but colonials: Australians, New Zealanders, Indians. They're saying that Allenby has promised Lloyd George that he will give him Jerusualem for Christmas. In the spring some of the reinforcements will go back to France. There is even a battalion of Fusiliers coming out that is mainly recruited from New York and London Jews. Jabotinsky is an officer with them. Jewish soldiers for the first time in two thousand years! What do you think of that? What do you think all those Jews at home are going to say? All those people who thought the words Jewish and soldier were a contradiction in terms?'

'They're not going to believe it. Not until they see them,' Sarah had said. 'And even then some of them will still tell us it's wrong to fight for friends of the Russians.'

She had been thinking of Rosenblum and the last conversation she

121

had with him when he buttonholed her at Fast's. 'Do you think the Americans will come as well now they're in the war?'

'Perhaps. But I should imagine they'll go to France first. It'll probably all be over by the time they get here. You know that Faisal's Arabs have captured Akaba? They were led by a British intelligence officer, a Major Lawrence. He goes around in Arab clothes and apparently the Bedouin worship him.'

'Will Akaba make any difference?'

'Of course it will. A port will enable the British to give Bedouin rebels more supplies. Guns, even armoured cars. Their Hejaz army will be nipping away at the Turkish right flank and will help take the pressure off Allenby.'

'Long life to Mister Lawrence then,' said Sarah. And they clinked their glasses of lemonade.

At moments like this a casual observer might have thought them lovers rather than siblings – which was exactly what the same Thomas Edward Lawrence surmised when he saw the Jew Aaronsohn talking intently to a busty and not unattractive little woman at a table in Café Groppis in Cairo the next day. Lawrence was in uniform, having had his fun around the Savoy in his Bedouin rig – the best being a wretched army clerk reduced to crimson-faced attention while being lectured on the fighting qualities of the sons of the desert by the diminutive little wog he had just been abusing. Now he had grown weary of making sudden demonstrations of the King's English to the xenophobic soldiery. He had with him several back copies of *The Times* and some mail, including archaeological papers from Oxford concerning the Syrian dig at Carchemish he had been working on just before the war. He was rather hoping that Aaronsohn was sufficiently engaged to pretend not to have seen him, but the Jew had called him over.

'Major Lawrence. I would like you to meet my sister, Miss Sarah Aaronsohn.'

Afterwards she had asked her brother why he had introduced her as an unmarried woman and he could not or would not tell her. All he had said was, 'Perhaps I have difficulty thinking of you as married.'

He did not apologise. Aaron rarely apologised for anything. Not that Sarah had really minded, since she could not conceive ever living with her husband again. It had just been curious that Aaron should have done that. He never mentioned Joseph who had spent several weeks in Cairo earlier in the year after being discovered by an Australian patrol, wounded and half-mad, wandering in the Sinai after being ambushed by Bedouin. He had been trying to reach British lines with Absolom Feinberg, a poet who was the romantic soul of Nili and betrothed to Sarah's younger sister, Rivka. Feinberg had been killed. After that they had started the boat pick-ups at Athlit.

Looking back, Sarah thought her first meeting with Lawrence had not been particularly noteworthy apart from a disconcerting way the Englishman had of gazing steadfastly into people's eyes so that you were either obliged to enter into some childish outstaring game with him or look the other way. When this happened even Aaron, Sarah had noticed, became fascinated with the contents of his coffee cup.

At first Lawrence had brought his papers to their table and talked in a fairly desultory way. He had paid her, she thought, only polite attention and not really come alive at all until Aaron, at considerable expense to his own ego, asked him about the capture of Akaba. The little blond Englishman brightened up then and told them how his Bedouin troops had slowly tightened their grip around the port: crawling over boiling rocks to wear down the outlying posts with their sniping, needling the Turks to waste ammunition on phantoms lost in the heat haze. As he spoke Lawrence raised his hands above the table and mimed a man squeezing off a rifle shot – almost as if, or so it seemed to Sarah, they had never seen a weapon! To her added annoyance she had seen that her brother was looking at him with an expression that she could only describe as solemn respect – even grateful for this impromptu demonstration of weapons handling. She had found herself staring resolutely at the table top. But if he was aware of her irritation Lawrence did not show it.

'Then we had this camel charge, you see.'

Sarah looked up. Sure enough Lawrence was jigging up and down in his chair waving his right hand in the air. A scimitar? A lasso? A polo stick? She had tried to keep a straight face.

'I was in the lead, firing from the saddle with my revolver.'

(Ah, not a scimitar then.)

'Suddenly my beast went down. Pole-axed. Shot from under me. It was as if I had hit an invisible fence. I thought every bone in my body was broken. Do you know what had happened?'

To her fury she had found herself shaking her head like a little girl.

'The bullet came from my own pistol. I had shot my favourite racing camel in the back of the head!'

The sound of her high-pitched laughter had echoed around the café. It was only when Sarah saw that he was laughing just as much as she was that she began to revise her opinion of Major Lawrence.

'There I was, curled up on the ground while the others broke around me like waves around a rock. All I could hear was the pounding of their hooves. I though it was the end.'

At this, they all laughed again as if what had happened was of no more consequence than a custard pie in the face. Sarah noticed that Lawrence looked at her again but this time it was different. He was avoiding eye contact. It was a sly look of appraisal. 'He knows,' she had thought. 'He knows all about me. He knows what I do.'

As a matter of fact Lawrence knew no such thing at the time. He discovered it the next day when he mentioned that he had met Aaronsohn's sister to Meinertzhagen, who had recently returned to Cairo from the forward intelligence headquarters they had set up just south of Gaza.

'Plucky little thing,' the intelligence officer had said.

'From Palestine?' Lawrence had asked, beginning to catch on.

'Lives up around Haifa somewhere. Runs the network there now that her brother has left. We brought her out by ship to see her brother for a few days – that and other things. Where did you meet her?'

After Lawrence told him Meinertzhagen flew into one of his dark rages. 'Bloody pair of fools – both of them.'

The Oxford scholar had smiled faintly at the tautology and this made Meinertzhagen angrier. 'I don't know what you're smiling at. This city is full of spies and there's her own brother parading her about café society as if she's a ruddy debutante. It's a wonder he didn't stick a notice of her arrival in the Egyptian Gazette. As if we haven't already let things slide far enough with him wandering about dressed up like a dog's dinner. And as if she hasn't got enough problems. What do they think they're at? Where do they think they are? At the end of Brighton pier, I suppose.'

'Well, that's the trouble with us amateurs,' Lawrence had said, pretending to be offended. 'No sense of occasion.'

Meinertzhagen had not been a bit abashed. 'My dear fellow, some amateurs are more amateur than others. I think we're going to have to keep that young lady safely amused for all our sakes.'

So the twenty-nine-year-old archaeologist, research fellow of All Souls, an officer of the Arab Bureau on temporary attachment to the Hejaz Expeditionary Force, the retiring, the self-publicist, the heroic, the sadomasochist, the noble dreamer, the unmitigated liar was privy to Meinertzhagen's schedule for Sarah Aaronsohn from the start. And he took full advantage of it.

Yet it had not occured to Sarah that she was seeing Thomas Edward rather more than mere coincidence permitted until the last day of his almost week-long stay in Cairo. By that time she had sat

124

by his side at a dinner-party in another of Gezira island's secluded and well-guarded villas, not far from the one Aaron was staying in.

That evening the talk at table had mostly been gloomy. On the Western Front another French attack in the Champagne region had failed. The latest reports from Petrograd seemed to indicate that the Russian offensive was running out of steam and the Germans were rallying under Bruchmuller, the great artillery general. Ponting had attempted to cheer everybody up by proposing a toast to the Hejaz army and to Lawrence, who had turned up in Bedouin robes and headdress and drank lemonade throughout; but when the others had all dutifully sipped, in some cases drained, the glasses of very decent claret Ponting had manage to acquire, they seemed no more cheerful. To Sarah's amazement they hardly spoke about their own war. It had seemed that not even Lawrence could bring himself to believe that the capture of a Red Sea port was worth half a mile of those blood-soaked vineyards or the Russian marchlands.

Meinertzhagen had been the only one to sound a positive note, and then it was on a comparatively minor matter.

'I'll you what. The Hun is worried about those new Bristol Fighters the RFC is getting. I've been up twice in one of 'em on a recce and we never saw one of their kites.'

Sarah's English was not quite up to this and Aaron, who was sitting on the other side of her from Lawrence, translated into French.

'Not a hair of them,' Meinertzhagen had gone on. 'We caught one of their cavalry patrols on the hop. Gave 'em a couple of squirts and they were off like the Grand National.' He had taken a spoonful of his soup before adding, 'Those that could still run, that is.'

Sarah had understood the gist of this without translation and she had not liked it very much. She had realised that she was in the presence of someone to whom war was just a rougher kind of sport. But when she had looked around the table it did not seem to have bothered anybody else. Perhaps Lawrence, who had caught her eye, wore an expression that might have been halfway between admiration and horror. At any rate, he had changed the subject by suddenly posing a question. 'Mr Aaronsohn,' the little man had asked in his Oxford drawl, 'do you really believe that when the Turks have gone – and I've no doubt that they will go, for they are a tired old empire – enough Jews will want to come to Palestine to start this homeland you yearn for?

'Please don't misunderstand me. Before the war I visited some of your settlements, particularly the ones around Tiberius, and saw the way they had enriched the land. I think Zionism and Arab nationalism could exist very happily together. Apart from the scientific help people like yourself can offer I suppose there is also the prospect of financial assistance from your richer brethren. People like Faisal have no money and it will be years before they can exploit the Mesopotamian oil. Perhaps Jewish banking could provide funds, but will they have reason to? Surely people like you and your family are the exception? Palestine is a hard country full of malarial swamps and brigands. Jews are a clever people – no doubt about that. But they are mainly city dwellers. Why on earth should they want to undergo these hardships?'

Sarah and Aaron smiled at each other. It was a question they had heard before.

'Tell me, Major Lawrence,' said Aaron, wiping the corner of his mouth with a napkin. 'Have you ever been to Poland or Western Russia? From time to time they are the same place, of course. Anyway, Galicia?'

'Regrettably not.' For Lawrence it was always a genuine matter of regret if he had not been somewhere.

'I thought as much. Look, you English see us Jews all wrong because you have a very limited experience of us. In Berlin, Vienna or Paris our race is more embourgeoised: there are Jewish doctors, lawyers, and the better kind of journalists – Herzl for example. Respectable people with some standing in the host community – unless things go wrong. You gentlemen may not be aware that the nastiest thing the Paris mob could think to call Dreyfus was Jew. In England you have extremes. There is either the old Anglo-Jewish aristocracy, the Mocattas, Sebags, Montefiores, Sassoons etcetera, some of them descendants of the Spanish Jews Cromwell let back in. They intermarried with some wealthy Ashkenazim who arrived from Germany and Holland shortly afterwards, the Rothschilds, Samuels and Montagues, and now you can't tell them apart. In most cases they are more English than the English. In fact, they consider themselves Englishmen first and Jews second.' Aaron had paused to sniff and let the corners of his mouth go down at this point, as if to indicate the error of his co-religionists' ways. 'Then there are your poor Jews. The jobbing tailors in the Whitechapel sweatshops sewing on twelve pockets an hour with Mr Singer's wondrous invention and sleeping on the floor between the machines at night. These are the people who have been flooding into the East End of London since the Russian pogroms of the 1880s. A lot of them thought they were going on to America. Instead they were tricked out of their fares by crooked shipping agents. But who are these people? Where did they come from? I'll tell you what a lot of them were. They were poor farmers, peasants, driven off the land on the Russian Pale by what they call the Czar's May Laws. They were required to give written proof of ownership that the authorities knew they didn't have. But that's what they are – farmers. Strong men and women who were accustomed to rise at dawn and work outdoors until dusk. In Whitechapel and Bethnal Green their sons and daughters may have become myopic tailors, but the stock is there.

'What I'm trying to say is that what you are looking at, gentlemen, your *conception* of the Jew, is the minority of European Jewry. Most of the descendants of twelve tribes in Europe continue to live on poor farms or in the ghettos. These are not your soft-handed bankers. For them life is hard, as hard as it is for the Syrian peasants in Palestine.'

'It's true enough,' Meinertzhagen had said. 'Before the war I happened to be visiting Odessa when there was a pogrom. Terrible business. I rescued one poor fellow from the Cossacks myself – murderous swines.'

'Your allies now,' the male Aaronsohn had said.

'Yours as well, for the moment,' Lawrence had responded softly and smiled at Sarah who, after a moment's hesitation, smiled back.

The next day there was a picnic trip down the river, the same khamsin wind that made Cairo so unpleasantly dusty filling the sail of their felucca and pushing them along at a fair lick. There were four of them on board: Sarah, Lawrence, Ponting and Meinertzhagen, making another of his rare social appearances. Aaron had declined to come on the grounds that he had seen enough of boats of all sizes to last him a lifetime. The smell of that Royal Navy destroyer still filled his nostrils.

Ponting brought along a newly arrived Fortnum and Mason's hamper crammed with tinned delicacies and bars of light and dark chocolate that melted as soon as the silver paper was removed. Sarah was amazed. Much of it was stuff she had never seen even in peacetime. For drink Ponting and Meinertzhagen had beer which they attempted to cool, once they had berthed under a clump of palms on the bank for lunch, by dunking it over the side in a canvas bucket, but since they were thirsty they drank most of it warm. Lawrence and Sarah sipped lemonade from a thermos. 'I'm too long among the Musselmen for strong drink,' the hero of Akaba had explained.

Ponting, in one of his self-effacing moods, had kept apologising for his failure to arrange a tub of ice for the drinks, and Meinertzhagen had responded by teasing him about the brand-new silk puttees he was wearing with shoes instead of the usual riding boots and jodhpurs. The tropical puttees were from the main officers' outfitters

127

in Cairo, part of an extensively advertised shipment that had just been received from England.

'I suppose we *never* wear anything but silk next to our skin,' accused Meinertzhagen.

'Only my hat, sir,' Ponting had replied. His hair had thinned dramatically over the last year.

Sarah had sat up front with her back to the bow, feeling quite the lady as she twirled the white parasol Aaron had found for her.

The boatman, lean and old at forty with grey stubble on his chin, graciously declined an offer of tinned pâté, preferring for some round, flat bread and goat's cheese and a raw onion he had wrapped in a grubby rag. When he had finished he leaned back against the stern panel and lit up a large, sweet-smelling and loosely rolled cigarette. Very soon he was asleep, his mouth open to reveal the rotting stumps of his teeth.

The conversation of his passengers had ceased while they paused to stare at him. Lawrence broke the silence.

'Opium.'

'Not a pretty sight,' said Ponting.

'Opium? Really?' said Meinertzhagen, who had only ever encountered the drug in Sherlock Holmes mysteries. 'Does it normally put people out as quickly as that?'

'At this time of the day, in this heat – certainly it can,' said Lawrence. 'Especially if you want it to.'

'Do the Bedouin use it?'

'Not much. Some would if they could but mostly it is regarded as a city Arab, Levantine habit. Also it's dangerous. Some blood enemy might enter your dreams with a dagger and finish them for you. The Turks use it although they're flogged in the army if they're caught.'

'Are they now?' said Meinertzhagen, who had lit up his pipe and was puffing thoughtfully away. After a while he seemed to become bored and started tapping at the boatman's bare and hugely calloused feet with his knobkerrie, gently at first and then with increasing violence. 'You'd need a howitzer to enter this fellow's dreams.'

The Egyptian had woken slowly, stung into consciousness by the bastinado pains creeping up his legs, glared at his tormentor and then started fumbling with the knot of the rope that linked them to a palm. In the bow Lawrence and Sarah started to giggle, and as she caught his eye she realised the way he was looking at her and started to blush.

A week later, back in Zichron Jacob, Sarah remembered that when she got over the shock she began to wonder if he would pursue the matter and what she would do if he did? She was beginning to find him not unattractive, although it was a pity about the height.

The rest of that stifling afternoon passed in a dream of exchanged glances, of increasingly unlikely collisions of knees and hands as the slightest shift in position in the confines of the boat suddenly took on the most sensuous possibilities. Sarah had become filled with a delicious sense of anticipation. She could feel the melting starting between her legs. Once she had caught something in his look that she found really disturbing. Could it have been admiration? Not even Joseph looked at her like that.

They had parted in front of the others normally enough.

'A pleasant trip, Major. I enjoyed it.'

'Yes, one of the better days of my war' – accompanied by a wan smile which only Sarah had known was meant to illustrate that this was a mountainous understatement.

She did not see him again. She learned later that he had gone up to Alexandria by train the same evening and boarded a Royal Navy ship bound for Akaba. But the next day a motorcycle despatch-rider had delivered a package to the villa where she was staying with Aaron. Her brother was out at the time and the soldier would not give it to the servant. 'Miss Aaronsohn?' he had asked when she went to the door. 'Would you sign for this please, miss?'

It was no bigger than her hand, scruffily wrapped in an old copy of the *Egyptian Gazette* and well tied with string that had been double-knotted. There was a luggage label tied to the string, on which her name had been misspelt in pencil, 'Miss Sarah Aranson.'

It felt heavy, solid. She had placed it on a table and cut through the string with a kitchen knife. When she had pulled the wrappings apart she found an oily blue kerchief that had itself been knotted. She could feel two things in it: a small box and something flat like a cigarette case, although the gun oil smell from the rag she was now struggling to undo had already alerted her to what it was. On Zichron Jacob they often put their weapons away like this. But it was so small.

It was a nickel-plated Derringer, the nasty little two-shot hideaway pistol originally favoured by Mississippi river-boat gamblers and other low life. It had two large-bore barrels, one over the other, and a double trigger without a guard. A brown luggage label like the one on the package was tied to its pearl-handled butt. On it was written in the same hand that had misspelt her name, 'In case the wrong person steps into your dreams – T.E.L.'

It was quite an old Derringer – its metalwork was scratched and one of the butt plates was chipped at the bottom. There was some Arabic script along the barrel and she guessed that the weapon must

129

have originally belonged to one of Lawrence's Bedouin friends. The cardboard box that came with it contained eight stubby .44–40 Remington rounds, and there were four empty spaces where cartridges had been removed from their packing.

Sarah had extracted one of the rounds. Its copper casing seemed quite tarnished but there was no sign of mildew or corrosion. There was a catch on the side and the Derringer broke open like a shotgun. She had slipped the cartridge in and then walked out onto the veranda in search of a target. She had not had to wait long.

A crow, not the sleek black variety of Europe but one of the desperate grey and black corpse disposers of Asia, had wobbled down and started strutting about what passed for a lawn. Sarah had got to within about five feet of it before she squeezed the trigger with her arm outstretched. It had made a lot of noise for a little gun. What remained of the crow's head was now some distance from his body. Sarah had been impressed.

On the morning before she left Cairo her brother had taken her for a dawn ride around the Pyramids and pointed out the Signals' aerials on top of Cheops.

'That's what they should give us,' Aaron had said. 'A wireless, not pigeons.'

'Major Ponting told me wireless signals can get intercepted.'

'So can pigeons – with a grain of feed.'

Sarah recalled his words as she ran a fingernail along the wire netting of the loft and the birds executed nervous little sidesteps on their perches. It was typical of Aaron to find fault in any idea that was not his own.

'Oh yes, you'll soon be going home,' she said.

16

*S*hortly before reveille there was an unexpected guest. As a result of this Private Calderwell never did get to see the races and how one of the youngest subalterns brought Captain Valintine's grey past the winning-post five lengths ahead of the Australian horse in second place.

The visitor was discovered in a very bedraggled state by one of the cooks, who was scratching and farting and thinking about getting some tea going when he spotted it huddled by the still dew-wet canvas of the C Squadron mess tent. The cook picked the quivering pigeon up – Its feathers were heavy with salt water spray and as he held it he discovered the steel message cylinder attached to the bird's right leg.

The cylinder went to the sergeant cook who took a malicious delight in breaking into the Squadron Sergeant Major's dreams with news of its arrival. Eventually it came to the bell-tent of the adjutant, who was halfway through being shaved by his Egyptian servant. The officer sat on the edge of his camp bed with a towel around his neck, his face half-lathered, staring at the cylinder as if he was the victim of some ill-advised practical joke. The servant, soapy razor still in hand, wore a long green jellaba and a bemused expression.

After he had unrolled the little scroll of paper in the cylinder the adjutant saw that, unless he really was the butt of some elaborate hoax, the message was written in code. Both sides of the thin paper were covered with carefully printed groups of block capitals. Each group contained five letters. The adjutant looked at the sergeant cook who had brought the cylinder to him. The NCO's face was composed, inscrutable.

'And where's our little Mercury now, Sergeant?'

'Beggin' your pardon, sir?'

'The bird, sergeant? The pigeon?'

'He's still in the mess tent, sir.'

'Fat bird?'

'Fair to middlin' sir.'

'Hmm. How about a little roast pigeon for the officers' mess tonight?'

The cook frowned. 'You don't think it's War Office property sir?'

'So is a tin of bully beef, Sergeant. Besides, we must never pass up a chance to live off the land.'

'Yes, sir.'

When the NCO had gone the adjutant wiped the soap off his face and walked over to the regimental headquarters tent from where he called Brigade on the field telephone. It took some time for the clerk there to locate the intelligence officer. When he did come on the line he made, the adjutant thought, some rather fatuous remarks and said, in a not very convincing way, that he would call back. The Yeomanry officer went back to his shave.

About an hour later the intelligence officer was on the line. There was a new note of urgency in his voice. The cylinder should be delivered as soon as possible to a certain Major Ponting, who was to be found in Advance Intelligence Headquarters at Wadi Ghuzze above the railhead at Deir el Belah. Major Ponting also wanted his pigeon back.

———————

Shortly before Wadi Ghuzze the road deteriorated into little more than a goat track and the lorry threw up great clouds of dust behind it. Crouched in the open rear of the vehicle was a strange, sub-human thing, a shapeless hulk with huge bug eyes. This was Calderwell, his body shrouded in a ground-sheet and his eyes protected from the desert grit by a pair of motorcycle goggles which Isaiah Mace had pressed on him.

'You'll need these,' he had said as Calderwell fussed about the bell-tent, buckling on equipment and feeling resentful that a newly promoted lance-corporal had chosen him for the escort job for no better reason than that Calderwell was one of the new draft and he didn't want to upset his old mates.

'Where did you get them from?' Calderwell had asked Mace,

examining his blurred reflection in the back of a mess tin. He had never worn goggles before and he liked the air of dashing flyboy menace they gave him.

'Never you mind,' Mace had said. 'Ask no questions and you'll be told no lies. Just a bit of buckshee that's all.'

Buckshee was one of those Arabic-rooted words, from the beggars' plea for baksheesh, that had been absorbed by Urdu, the lingua franca of the British Indian Army. Mace had never been further east of Suez than Palestine, but anybody who claimed to be an old sweat peppered his speech with the language that was the lingua franca of the Raj. Buckshee meant an item was spare. Items were considered spare when they were not nailed down.

'Good old Macey,' Calderwell thought as they shuddered and bounced from one spine-jarring pothole to another. He would have been half-blind without the goggles. No doubt somewhere in Palestine a motorcycle despatch-rider had had the cost of a new pair of goggles docked from his pay, but he should pay more attention to his kit.

At his feet was the adjutant's picnic hamper, a strong wicker basket from Fortnum and Mason. From it emerged some mournful cooing sounds. The corporal, who was in the cab with the driver, had bought the bird in the souk at Rafa, after the adjutant had discovered that Ponting's pigeon was beyond reprieve.

Calderwell put his hand in the right-hand pocket of his tunic and produced *The Complete Letter-Writer*. As usual he turned to the first part of the book, the section devoted to advice on ladies' correspondence. He flicked through until he came to letter number 161 – 'A Lady Writing to her Lover on Christmas Eve'. It was one of the best. He almost knew it by heart which was as well because it was hard to read with the goggles on and impossible with them off. '. . . I wish, indeed, my dear, I had some better gift to offer you tomorrow. But the will is here, though not the power and you will take that will for the deed . . .'

Calderwell sighed. He tried to imagine some of the girls he knew back in Coventry writing to him like that. In particular he tried to imagine his younger sister's friend Ethel, whom he had kissed behind the bandstand in the park on his embarkation leave, promising him a 'better gift' instead of saying that he was a naughty boy and if there was any more hanky-panky she would have to go home. She had accepted a cigarette fast enough though, and put her head close to his again so he could smell her lavender scent as she cupped her hands around the proffered match.

Come out with her own fags too later on. God knows she could afford them. Ethel had started her working life at fourteen as a live-in housemaid for a family in Lichfield. Now she worked twelve-hour shifts in one of the new munitions factories, machining the belts that held Vickers bullets, and took home almost as much as a working man might have earned to feed a family pre-war. All the factory girls had the reputation for being fast. Calderwell had felt obliged to reprimand his sister when he caught a whiff of gin on her breath.

At the time Ethel had proved a disappointment, not quite fast enough. Now Calderwell felt a certain tenderness about it. After all, she had kissed him and pretended she had not noticed him squeezing her right breast – at least at first she had. Even when he tried the other stuff she had not stopped him right away, though this may have been because it was hard to feel anything under all those clothes. And every young soldier ought to have a sweetheart, or so he thought. To date he had sent her two letters and one Bamforth postcard depicting great-coated soldiers sitting around a camp fire while an angel hovered in the background. 'Will you be my guardian angel?' Calderwell had written. He had not received a reply yet. The last mail from England to be distributed at El Marakes camp had been posted no later than the end of June.

Every now and then the track they were following practically disappeared, but the driver had obviously pinned his faith on the pipeline to their right. Until the railway finished they had not really noticed the twelve-inch circumference pipes, half-buried in places and then glinting dully where some trick of the wind had removed the sand. Once their lorry had slowed alongside a dozen or so soldiers in newish-looking uniforms with Fusilier flashes, and the corporal and driver had called out from the cab, 'Eyes right for the Skinback Fusiliers.' This had been followed by, 'No advance without security.'

They were an advance party from one of the Jewish battalions Jabotinsky had raised in England. These battalions had been designated Fusiliers, for the War Office would not countenance a Jewish regiment as such on the grounds that, before they knew where they were, there would be demands for separate regiments for Catholics and Dissenting Presbyterians etcetera. Most of them were Americans, well-built men whom Calderwell had mistaken at first for Australians.

The corporal and driver had learned their taunts from the Cockneys of 60th Division for, like the majority of the men from the shires, they had never met a Jew and had no real feelings about them one way or the other. Isaiah Mace, for instance, was one of several in the regiment who bore biblical names because of their parents' Nonconformist regard for the Old Testament rather than any Jewishness in their genes. Calderwell looked down and saw an angry-looking Fusilier who pushed his service cap up and yelled at him, 'Why don't you save your lip for the goddam Turks, mister? We're on the same side, you know.'

He had wanted to explain that he had not been responsible for the insults. Indeed, Calderwell had not understood them since he had no knowledge whatsoever of male circumcision rites, any more than he understood the punning allusion to money-lending practices.

Nonetheless, Calderwell was quite shocked when the driver told him later that these muscular-looking, sun-burned men were Jews. His notion of the faith was derived from an uncle who, as a boy, had worked for a Jewish jeweller in Birmingham and swore he was paid only in boiled sweets. ''Ave another sugar fish my son?' Uncle Clarence would always repeat as he got into his tale, and his mother, who knew it by heart, would hold her sides and gasp, 'Oh go on Clal, pull the other one. You're filling the boy's head with rubbish.'

Yet it had been she who had confirmed this Jewish tendency to exploit child labour by reading the Fagin passages from *Oliver Twist* most movingly. Calderwell's mother was proud of her reading voice and rightly so. Jews, then, were hook-nosed, predatory old gentlemen who, like griffins or dragons or unicorns even, were not often to be found in real life. When they did make an appearance they dispensed sugar fish.

For the last hour they had been passing gangs of Egyptian work-men beating back the desert with picks, shovels and camel-drawn heavy rollers. They were almost invariably deracinated fellaheen from Upper Egypt, pressed labour glaring from under fantastic tur-bans which were wound down around the lower half their faces as masks against the dust, so that only a pair of resentful eyes would be showing. Sometimes they would pass a group singing one of their sad, homesick songs and, like most young soldiers, Calderwell would see and hear all this without the slightest comprehension of their misery.

Besides, he had his own problems, for Calderwell and the bird were being thrown this way and that as the lorry's solid tyres bounced from one rut to another. The constant jarring seemed to reduce the bladder's capacity for the brackish water he kept swigging from his canteen. The corporal must have had the same trouble, for every hour or so he called a halt for what he called a 'piss stop'.

'C'mon Caldy, get fell in for short-arm drill,' he would yell as he lurched out of the cab.

During one of these halts they lined up alongside the pipe and pissed their ephemeral little streams into the great desert. When he had finished Calderwell noticed that he had exposed some engraved lettering on the pipe near his right boot. He squatted down beside it and read the words 'Standard Oil Company USA.'

''Ere corp,' he asked. 'Are these pipes taykin' oil up, then?'

'Oil? What the fuck we want oil for?' said the corporal, a worldly man.

'But it says –'

'Aye. I know what it says. We borrowed them pipes from the Yankees for our water. That pipeline is taking water all the way from the fuckin' Nile to Palestine just to give you and me a nice dose of Billy Harry.'

They found Ponting reading a three weeks' old copy of *The Times* and sitting with Meinertzhagen at the sandbagged entrance to a large dugout practically on the beach. Meinertzhagen, who was scribbling in a notebook, was wearing long shorts and puttees and Ponting was in jodhpurs and riding boots. The British front line was about five miles away and every few minutes a series of distant rumbles sounded above the surf.

Calderwell thought the officers looked a little startled when they produced the pigeon from the basket, almost as if they were confronting them with evidence of some shameful deed. And when the corporal handed over the little cylinder containing the coded message Meinertzhagen pocketed it so quickly it was as if it had never existed. Then they were dismissed.

The corporal saluted and turned away, but Calderwell came rigidly to attention. 'Excuse me, sir,' he said to Ponting, 'but can I have the basket back?' The adjutant had made it quite clear that he was responsible for the basket. He wanted it returned, he said, in 'pristine condition'. Calderwell was not quite sure what this meant but he had an idea it had something to do with bird shit.

'The basket?'

'The pigeon's basket, sir. It belongs to our adjutant. It's his picnic basket.'

Meinertzhagen began to beat his left palm with the head of his knobkerrie, like a drummer warming up.

'Oh well, we wouldn't want to deprive him of his picnics, would we?' said Ponting.

'Certainly not,' said Meinertzhagen, speaking for the first time.

'Take the bird to our loft,' ordered Ponting. He pointed towards a couple of palm trees just before the beach where there was a low

136

shed which looked as if it had been made out of old packing cases and driftwood.

As the Yeomanry were about to move off Meinertzhagen rose. 'How long have you been out here, young man?' he said, pointing with his knobkerrie at Calderwell, who had just picked up the basket.

'Two weeks, sir.'

'Well, you'll find that war is no picnic, laddie.'

'Yessir.'

'Just remember that.'

Calderwell started to raise his right arm in a salute, a difficult feat because it involved letting go of one side of the basket and tucking it into his left side. But Colonel Meinertzhagen had not finished with him yet.

'Do you know what this is?' he said, holding his club aloft.

'Not exactly sir.' Of course he knew what it was. It was a bloody old stick but that sort of answer was unlikely to please an officer just as it had never pleased gaffers and schoolmasters and others of that ilk.

'It's an African war club, laddie. It used to belong to a tribal chief who was killed in single combat by a German officer. Now it belongs to me.'

Calderwell tried to look attentive. This was the part of the army he hated most: when some hoity-toity officer treated you like a kid. African war club indeed.

'There is a legend that whoever owns this club shall die from it,' said Meinertzhagen. 'But legend is just another word for fairy story and war isn't a fairy story – is it, corporal?'

The NCO, who had been looking down at the ground with his arms akimbo, uncertain whether to stay or leave, suddenly straightened up. 'No, sir.'

'Seen the enemy yet, corporal?'

'Yessir. I was at Katia and I did a couple of months at Gallipoli before that.'

'How many did you kill?'

'Oh I don't know, sir, a few,' said the NCO, who as a matter of fact had only ever fired a few shots at some distant figures and had no idea what misery, if any, they had caused. Besides, at heart he was a God-fearing man who considered that sort of question indecent.

'Good man,' said Meinertzhagen, rapping one of his cloth bound calves with the knobkerrie. 'See the orderly sergeant about a meal before you go back.'

When the Yeomen had gone Ponting said, 'Extraordinary tale, sir.'

'What?'

'About your club – your knobkerrie.'

'Quite true.'

'And the German officer – how did he die?'

'It was a night action. We bumped into each other in the dark. I wrestled the club off him and brained him with it.'

For a moment Ponting was tempted to ask how he had learned the history of the weapon after such a brief acquaintance with its last owner and, having learned it, why he risked keeping the awful thing. But he thought better of it. Some stories were too good to check. Instead, he went off to see how the cypher clerks were getting on with the message the pigeon had delivered.

Meinertzhagen picked up Ponting's *Times*. There was an account of the latest British offensive in Flanders. The main battle was taking place around a village called Passchendaele, somewhere near Ypres. According to its correspondent there had been an incredible prelude to the attack. Shortly before dawn the British had detonated nineteen mines containing just under one million pounds of high explosive under the Messines ridge. To tunnel under the German lines had taken weeks of nerve-racking labour with muffled picks and shovels. The result had been a series of rose-coloured, mushroom-shaped clouds rising miles in the air and hundreds of dead Germans. Even more incredible – in fact Meinertzhagen could not bring himself to believe it – were reports that the sound of the exploding mines had been clearly audible in London.

The colonel sighed. All the same . . . one million pounds of high explosive . . . that was a very big bang. He closed his eyes and tried to imagine all those Huns and bits of Hun flying around the Belgian countryside. It was a deeply pleasing thought. The knobkerrie warmed to his approval and beat a little tattoo against the side of his leg.

He put the newspaper aside and went back to his notebook. There were several drafts of the work in progress, for he was labouring at his words as diligently as any novelist. Meinertzhagen was trying to write a love letter. His latest attempt was in the explicit style Calderwell had sought in vain among the brisk pages of *The Complete Letter-Writer*. He read it again. 'Dearest Bertie,' it began. 'I miss you so very much. Every night I lie with you but in the morning you are gone. Oh! My Darling Boy. How much longer will . . .'

———

The cypher clerks were housed in a large bell-tent pitched near another dugout. They were good at their job and had almost finished

138

typing out the deciphered signals when Ponting arrived. He looked over the shoulder of the clerk who was handling it. It was from Nili and contained some useful stuff on troop movements, obviously monitored by their agents on the railways. A fresh German machine-gun company had been spotted. Nothing from Daniel.

PART 3
The Book of Daniel

17

'Amateurs talk about tactics,' Marshal Erich von Falkenhayn was saying. 'Professionals talk about logistics.'

Von Falkenhayn emphasised his words with a tight smile, a faint twitching around the left-hand corner of his mouth. In the last year his hair had turned quite white and fatigue was etched into his face like a trench network. As well it might be, thought Krag, who was watching him with the intentness he habitually reserved for the aristocracy. Von Falkenhayn had spent himself against the French anvil at Verdun. Blow after blow until the hammer broke – or at least it would have done had the Kaiser not been persuaded to sack the arm that wielded it.

To an extent he had redeemed himself in Rumania although the opposition there was hardly up to the standard of Petain's *poilus*. It was said that homosexuality was so rife among the Rumanian officer corps that only majors and above were permitted to wear make-up. Now the old warhorse had another easy one. All he had to do was to persuade the British to continue squandering troops in a sideshow. If he succeeded in doing anything else it was a bonus. Von Falkenhayn was a man whose life had been built on winning bonuses.

Almost the entire staff of the Eighth Turkish Army corps were gathered in the Kriegspiel room at Fast's to listen to their new commander. They were standing around several trestle tables pushed together. On them was pinned, section by section, a large-scale map of the Eighth's operational area – more or less everything west of the Jordan from Galilee in the north to the Gaza-Beersheba front line in the south. East of the Jordan was the Seventh Army Corps under the irascible Mustafa Kemal.

Blue, red, green and brown chips represented formations of infantry, cavalry and artillery. There was also a large pair of dice and several steel rulers and protractors, the latter to determine the limits of artillery traverse. The dice were different from ordinary dice in that they did not carry the numbers one to six but had instead an extra three and a four. They were what war gamers call Average Dice and were used to include battlefield imponderables such as the question of fluctuating morale in their equations. Average Dice keep Lady Luck's role down to a realistic level.

But for the moment their war game was forgotten. The marshal was chatting to them with that exaggerated bonhomie sometimes assumed by very senior officers. Everybody seemed entranced. Even Kress, the elegant Bavarian, appeared by no means immune to it.

Permission had been given to smoke and a pall hung over the table. The marshal was telling them about the huge Russian offensive which had been launched by Alexander Kerensky, the War Minister in the Provisional Government that had overthrown the Romanovs. According to communiqués coming out of Berlin, forty-four divisions had been thrown back by German and Austro-Hungarian forces half that size. The marshal believed that one reason for the Russian failure was that Bolshevik agitators had persuaded the railwaymen to go on strike. The Reds had deprived the front of ammunition and rations at a crucial stage. Hence his little homily about the importance of logistics.

The marshal stood at the head of the table with a dapper Uhlan major of medium height called Franz von Papen, his *aide de camp*, on his right and Kress on his left. Behind them was a blackboard. Weidinger had thought at first that the blackboard was blank, but when he got closer he saw that a black cloth had been pinned to it.

As a junior member of the staff Weidinger stood at the end of the table opposite von Falkenhayn while the others had arranged themselves either side of the table, their propinquity to the marshal more or less decided by seniority. There were armed sentries outside the door to the Kriegspiel room, and the more junior officers such as Weidinger had been required to show some proof of identity before they were let in. Von Falkenhayn was not there merely to gossip about the Central Powers' successes on another front, however welcome these might be.

'Good logistics make good tactics,' he continued. 'And logistics need the kind of attention a lady gives her needlework. Which is, of course, why you gentlemen are so important. If the sort of success

144

General Bruchmuller enjoyed against the Russians is to be repeated in this theatre of operations it will be because you people saw to it that the right men with the right equipment were in the right place at the right time.'

It was all terribly patronising stuff, the sort of thing a young officer might expect to hear during his first week at staff college, yet there was Kress apparently drinking in every golden word.

The marshal made a gesture to von Papen who began to unpin the black sheet covering the blackboard. The major did this with great dexterity, a magician's assistant. When he removed a pin he first stored it in his mouth then stabbed it into a neat row on the top of the board.

Once he had finished most of the officers crowded forward to see what the sheet had concealed. Only a small knot of Turkish officers remained aloof, talking among themselves and smoking cigarettes in long holders. When Krag saw what was on the board their indifference seemed justified.

To his astonishment it was no more than a crude map of the greater part of the Ottoman Empire, including some bits that had been in British hands for several months. It stretched from Aleppo, which was practically on the Turkish border, to as far south as Gaza on the Mediterranean coast and eastwards to the Mesopotamian rivers. The cities of Mosul and Baghdad, and the southern port of Basrah, just up the Shatt-el-Arab from the Persian Gulf, were clearly marked.

Two broad arrows told the story. One, more or less crescent-shaped, started just south of Aleppo, swung up to Mosul and then came down the Tigris to Baghdad. The other started a little south of Damascus and swung through the three hundred-mile width of the desert known as the Badiet esh Sham before it bridged the Euphrates and also came to rest against Baghdad. In the bottom left-hand corner of the map, almost as an afterthought, was a broken line of shaded oblongs stretching from Gaza to Beersheba. This was the Eighth Army Corps' front line. Each oblong had a small arrow attached, pointing south at the British lines.

'Gentlemen, we are going to recapture Baghdad,' announced von Falkenhayn in a matter-of-fact voice. He tapped the blackboard with a baton. Where had the baton come from, thought Krag. The magician's assistant? 'There will be two thrusts. Seventh Army Corps under Mustafa Kemal in the north –' here the baton traced the crescent that started at Aleppo – 'and some elements of a reinforced Eighth Army Corps making a surprise attack across the desert in the south.'

Weidinger looked at Kress. He thought the Bavarian looked stunned.

'I have no need to tell you, gentlemen, that the enemy is off balance,' continued von Falkenhayn. 'You did a magnificent job holding his last two attacks on Gaza. Since then he has reinforced, of course, but most of them are ill-trained, third-rate troops and it will be months before they're fit for anything better than guarding a mule train. I understand they even have a regiment of Jews coming.' He paused here for the kind of pitying smile that suggested transvestite Rumanian majors were probably better opposition. 'Now is the time to hit them. When they least expect it.'

The Turkish officers were no longer looking so blasé. Von Falkenhayn looked directly at them. 'Our code word for this operation is Yilderim,' he announced.

The Turks nodded and smiled, flattered to be singled out. The marshal turned towards the Austro-Hungarians and his compatriots. 'Of course, you're all aware that Yilderim is Turkish for lightning,' he said, pausing for one of his tight little smiles. 'It's what the Turks called Napoleon's campaign in Egypt. Yilderim meaning a lightning stroke, a war of lightning speed. We might say *blitzkrieg*.'

Kress spoke. 'Sir, you mentioned a reinforced Eighth Army. Can you tell us what we're getting?'

'Yes, I can,' said von Falkenhayn, letting his eyes wander around the room for a couple of seconds. 'We are expecting at least another three Turkish divisions. In addition, we shall have more German troops. They will not only be support arms, artillery and aircraft and so on. There will also be some small contingents of infantry and cavalry.'

'Incredible!' said Weidinger out loud. German infantry, let alone cavalry, had never been committed to the Ottoman theatre before. All around him other officers were making similar kinds of noises.

Kress was not so easily impressed. He waited for the hubbub to die down. 'These German troops, sir: they will be shared between the Seventh and Eighth armies?'

'Yes.'

'Could you tell me how many and what they will consist of?'

'I believe it is about six thousand, but Major von Papen has the details.'

'Shall I give them, sir?' He already had the piece of paper in his hand. The clever Westphalian.

'Please.'

'There will be three battalions of infantry. There will be three machine-gun companies with six machine-guns each, and three

146

trench mortar sections. There will also be three troops of cavalry. There will be four squadrons of aircraft. There will be some support troops – engineers, signallers and medical units. In all it should total about 6,500 men.'

Weidinger was thinking about the cavalry. Three troops was less than a hundred men. It was no more than a gesture.

Kress turned to von Falkenhayn. 'Sir, according to our latest intelligence reports Allenby has a ration strength of 300,000 men and more are coming. This army corps has about 30,000 combatants and their state of readiness varies enormously. Some parts of the Gaza-Beersheba line are held by men in rags using trench mortars they have made themselves out of captured British cannon.

'In the circumstances, their morale remains amazingly good. But I would not like to take the consequences if the troops along that line were reduced by a single company. If several thousand men were to go it could be disastrous. I could not guarantee that we could hold it. If the British did break through while you were making your thrust on Baghdad it would surely be disastrous. Your lines of communication would be cut. And if the whole of Palestine were lost you might find that you had recaptured Baghdad only to be besieged in it. Three Turkish divisions and 6,500 of our own. That's somewhere in the region of 40,000 – providing the Turkish regiments are up to strength. With respect, it is not enough, sir. We must at least equal the British.'

The room went very quiet. As Weidinger told it afterwards, you could have heard a rank drop. For the first time he realised the strain Kress was under and how well he had done just holding things together. He felt a glow of pride in his commanding officer, the privilege of being one of his team. There were not many colonels who dared inform a field marshal that his grand concept was shit.

Von Falkenhayn managed to look hurt rather than angry. Von Papen merely looked worried. Krag, who also felt a certain reluctant admiration for Kress's outburst, watched the major fold the paper with the details of the fresh German contingents on and put it in the top breast pocket of his tunic.

After what seemed like an eternity von Falkenhayn spoke. 'Perhaps I did not make it clear to you, colonel, that only part of the Eighth Army Corps will be involved in Yilderim,' he said. 'The part will come out of the Turkish and German reinforcements. The northernmost prong of the attack will be made by the Seventh Army under the command of Mustafa Kemal.'

So our troops are to cross 300 miles of desert to make what

147

appears to be a diversionary attack while the Seventh hogs the glory, thought Weidinger. No prizes for guessing which corps most of those fresh faces from the Fatherland will be with. And while we're making it easy for them who's going to be manning the Gaza-Beersheba line? Most of the other officers present were thinking along similar lines. Even Weidinger was no longer mesmerised by the thought of German cavalry.

Kress said no more. He knew he had already said too much. Despite appearances, he did know where to draw the line with field marshals and was conscious that he had already travelled some distance beyond it.

'Thank you, gentlemen,' said von Falkenhayn. There was a certain amount of heel-clicking whilst the man who had once commanded half a million men made his departure. Von Papen held the door open for him. Before he went out Krag thought he caught the *aide de camp* throw Kress a glance and a raised eyebrow as if to say, 'Do you think that was altogether wise, Colonel?' Or could it have been, 'I've got my doubts too.'

After the pair had left, everybody started talking at once. Krag thought the Turkish officers appeared to be having a particularly heated discussion. He wondered what Mustafa Kemal would make of Yilderim. He had already put it about that he had only agreed to accept command of the Seventh Army Corps because he thought there was too much German interference in Turkish affairs and wished to be in a position to put a stop to it.

Von Kressenstein left, still visibly disturbed at what he had just learned.

Krag asked Weidinger what he thought of Yilderim?

'Not enough cavalry.'

'The Turks have cavalry.'

'Their lancers aren't bad,' Weidinger conceded. 'But they're not exactly a Uhlan regiment.'

'True,' said Krag, noting – not for the first time – how the younger man's blue eyes seemed to light up his whole face when he became enthused. He glanced at the neatly pinned sleeve. Where did it end? Above the elbow? Below the elbow? How could he remain the bone-headed Teutonic knight after what he had suffered? 'Yours was a Uhlan regiment wasn't it?'

'Yes. Major von Papen's too.'

'So I noticed. What do you think they will do with three troops of Uhlans?'

'Reconnaissance, I suppose.' For a second Weidinger saw himself at the head of a glorious charge against a bell-tented Tommy camp, the Beau Sabreur, slashing down sentries and carrying away prisoners.

Krag made to leave.

'Sir.'

'Yes?'

'Have you learned anything more about the Swede yet?' Weidinger knew it was not really his place to ask, but it was almost two months since he had first brought the matter to Krag's attention.

'Nothing yet,' said the intelligence officer.

'No more visits to the old Jew?'

'No,' said Krag, shaking his head. He walked out of the room, leaving Weidinger trying to console himself with the thought that at least he must have put the Swede under some sort of surveillance in order to be so emphatic. He couldn't see why Krag simply didn't bring them both in for questioning. Beat the living daylights out of them if necessary. He was damn certain the Turks had hanged people for less. He supposed Krag knew his business, but he was longing to see Maeltzer's face when he learned Magnus was a spy. Then again, perhaps he wasn't a spy. Perhaps he was no more than the lunatic he appeared to be. The Syrian he had hired to follow him about could have invented things to keep the money coming; thrown an old Jew into his concoction to spice the intrigue.

Weidinger wandered over to the Kriegspiel table and studied the map. He imagined making a hole somewhere in the British line and pouring through a couple of divisions of Prussian cavalry that would roll the British up from the rear. The trick would be to do it somewhere unexpected. Gaza was out of the question. The front lines there were as close as the Western Front and there had already been heavy fighting. Somewhere around Beersheba would be more like it. Of course, the terrain would be more difficult there – real desert most of it – and there would be water problems. But if they could get over these – perhaps the Bedouin knew some secret springs? – they could really give Allenby a surprise.

Weidinger picked up a pair of war gamers' Average Dice and rolled them. He got a two and a five. The odds against that happening were quite high.

18

*U*nauthorised civilians were forbidden to walk along the walls of the Old City under a regulation the Turks had introduced shortly after the start of hostilities. Atlhough Maeltzer lacked the proper authorisation he often took a stroll along them for the regulation was, in the main, slackly enforced. If one of the more efficient sentries questioned his presence he produced the ornate *laissez-passer* that had cost him his ivory-handled Colt; if the man persisted, cigarettes or occasionally a cigar would be produced.

In the summer months the journalist liked to tour the walls towards dusk when the heat was out of the day and the colour of things softer. He would walk for a while and then pause at some parapet to gaze at the scene below, to linger, perhaps, near the Jaffa Gate, where the obstinately immobile sails of Sir Moses Montefiore's windmill dominated the view, and stubborn Syrian peasants continued to graze their flocks between the buildings of the Zionists' new Jewish quarter without the walls.

The day after von Falkenhayn's revelations Maeltzer was on the section of the wall immediately above the Damascus Gate when he heard voices. This was something of a puzzle since there was nobody in sight in either direction, not even a sentry. Then he realised that the voices were coming from below him, from beneath the vaulted ceiling of the portal itself.

At first he could not understand why he could hear them so clearly. Then he spotted a narrow slit in the paving-stones of the parapet. He immediately recognised what it was: it had been put there by the seventeenth-century Turkish fortress architects when they heightened the old Crusader walls, and was designed to facilitate the pouring of boiling oil or other obnoxious substances onto the heads of unwelcome callers.

The words rising from below were German — or at least most of them were. One of the speakers was using a foreign word the journalist was unfamiliar with. 'Yilderim,' he was saying. 'Yilderim. I can assure you, major, that during my two years here I have never known the Turks do anything like lightning, and I can't see them changing now. Besides, not only do we lack the men, but we don't have enough rations to feed those we do have.'

'But you must concede, sir, that we are getting reinforcements — some of the best. And besides superior troops we're also going to have the advantage of a certain amount of surprise.'

The first voice, the one raised in what was almost anger, sounded familiar to Maeltzer. He went down on one knee above the machicolation and peered through. At first he could see nothing but two pairs of black cavalry boots, the one immobile and the other circling round like the active partner in a minuet. Then he saw the colonel's rank badges on the epaulettes of a white tunic. Of course, it was Kress.

'Surprise? You talk about surprise!' Kress went on. 'Don't you realise the British are flying more sorties over our lines than ever before? They have sent dozens of their new Bristol Fighters to this front. They know more and more about our movements. And the whole territory is riddled with spies. Every second Syrian here is longing for the British to come and rescue them from the Turkish yoke. And the same can be said for the Jews and the Armenians. Especially the Armenians.

'I can't believe that the High Command really intends to go ahead with this. Nor that somebody of your general's experience cannot see the danger. If the Gaza-Beersheba line was weakened for Yilderim to the point where we could not hold the next British push it would be disastrous. If the British were allowed to advance up that Mediterranean coast to Haifa or even beyond his lines of communication, his logistics would be horribly vulnerable. It could be worse than Verdun.'

'No it wouldn't, Colonel,' said Stationary Boots. 'Nothing could be as bad as that.'

This other voice was quietly spoken so that Maeltzer had to bend his large head closer to the gap in order to catch the words. As he did so his reading spectacles fell out of his top pocket; for a moment they lingered briefly on the edge of the machicolation and then evaded the journalist's desperate fingers to drop neatly through the hole and shatter inches from the gleaming toecaps some fifteen feet below. After a moment's hesitation Maeltzer fled.

Major von Papen picked up the spectacles. As he did so their remaining glass tinkled onto the floor.

Both men looked up at the vaulted roof of the gateway where for the first time they noticed its small slice of sky. 'Extraordinary', said von Kressenstein.

'One of your spies?' said von Papen.

'The only people who are supposed to be up there are the sentries.'

'Eyes have ears,' said the *aide de camp*, waving the shattered spectacles.

'Quite,' said Kress, more than a little irritated. 'Better raise the guard.'

This proved easier said than done, but they eventually found a young private near the Jaffa Gate who had just come on duty. Kress questioned him in his functional Turkish and he stood rigidly to attention and told the Bavarian that he and the other effendi were the first people he had seen since coming on duty.

In the end Kress, with von Papen trailing a couple of paces behind, discovered what they took to be an orderly officer playing backgammon in the Turkish mess in the Citadel. The man, a captain with a livid purple scar down one cheek, was obviously of the same persuasion as Mustafa Kemal when it came to German officers, and in no mood to disguise his feelings. He rose to his feet with obvious reluctance and suggested that the owner of the spectacles was some curious Jew – 'The race are almost always half blind.'

Besides, surely the gentlemen had not been discussing anything of importance out there in the open, by the gate? Kress stomped out in a fury.

Von Papen asked to be excused. He had to join the marshal for dinner. He was almost at the door of Fast's when he realised he was still holding the buckled spectacle frames. For the first time he examined them closely. On one of the arms was the name of a German firm which before the war had supplied hundreds of thousands of frames to opticians throughout Continental Europe.

For some reason, perhaps it was the small amount of gold in the alloy, von Papen was reluctant to throw them away. Once inside he put them in a desk drawer. He thought he might even produce them for von Falkenhayn's amusement at dinner when he recounted the story. Young *aides de camp* were expected to amuse their generals. It was one of the reasons they were selected for the job – that and their ability to sit people in the right order of seniority at dinner, for many a promising ADC had lost his job for seating the wrong man below the salt. And it might be a good way of raising some of the points the colonel had been making. Von Papen had tried not to show it, but Kress had practically won him over as far as Yilderim was concerned.

19

Magnus feared no one save the Lord – except on Thursday. For then it was necessary to mediate with the Fallen One, even do his bidding. Anticipation was a torment. As the appointed hour approached his mouth became dry, his bowels liquefied, his testicles melted away to nothing.

Sometimes atonement was achieved through the medium of a small white rock by a certain olive tree in the Garden of Gethsemane; or beneath a maroon prayer cushion in the white-walled Frankish church of St Anne's; or in a gloomy niche in the collection of competing chapels that comprised the Holy Sepulchre, where his Calvinist core was nauseated by the corrupt smells of old candle wax and incense. He would go to these places, sit there motionless for a while, and then allow his hand to explore the underhang of a stone or beneath the pew cushion, or dart into the time-worn wound in the side of the Chapel of the Invention of the Cross.

When he did these things Magnus could never decide what he wanted the result to be. If nothing was there his relief was always tinged with disappointment. Yet if his hand emerged clutching English sovereigns and a small scroll of tightly-rolled paper he became even more agitated, as nervous as a thief. One sovereign was for him and the rest for the old Christ-killer he hurried the scroll to. Once it had been delivered his euphoria knew no bounds. He would be consumed by the Spirit of the Lord and quite often hear the secret language to which only he knew the proper responses. But until that moment, and especially when he walked the streets with the coins and the scroll on his person, he felt like a drowning man. And although passers-by assumed his eyes blazed with madness, they were also fuelled by fear.

The day after Maeltzer lost his best pair of reading spectacles Magnus sat with pounding heart by the stone in the Garden of Gethsemane. He waited for a while to see that no curious monk or shepherd was watching him and then slipped his hand under the rock. It was there: a plain white envelope containing the money and the scroll, which was always written on yellow paper. He took out one sovereign and put it in the little muslin bag he wore on a shoulder strap beneath his rags. The rest he stuffed in the one serviceable pocket of what had once been a dark blue waistcoat. Then he picked up the staff and strode out south-west along the Kidron Valley, so that he skirted the walls of the city and entered the Jewish quarter through the Zion Gate. Once Magnus looked back, but if anybody was following him they were making a good job of it.

After Magnus had made his delivery the old Jew, whose name was Levi Smolenskin, left the white envelope untouched on the table at which he sat. On the same table were three worn leatherbound volumes of rabbinical debate – two in German and one in Ladino, the language of the aristocratic Sephardic Jews from Spain. He had bartered the books from a neighbour. Smolenskin had always coveted these books, and now they were his for six round loaves, a sack of flour and two litres of olive oil. He could have afforded more but that would have been dangerously ostentatious. Even as they haggled he could see the unspoken question in his neighbour's eyes – 'How is it you have bread to spare for books?'

Smolenskin had been so conscious of that look that he had made up some tale about selling the last of his wife's jewellery – as if she had ever owned a single bauble that would have raised a kopek in that starving city. His children's resentment had been even plainer than his neighbour's. They might eat, but there was never quite enough and the price of flour was going up all the time. Indeed, so obvious was their resentment that he had felt obliged to refer them to the Book of Deuteronomy: 'Man doth not live by bread only.' Did they really expect him to die hungry for the kind of fresh meat he only found in certain books?

He placed a hand on the envelope and moved it around the table a little before opening it. For a second or two, he weighed the coins in the palm of his right hand against the scroll of yellow paper in the other. Then he slipped the sovereigns into a leather purse which he

155

returned to an inside pocket of his kaftan. He picked up the little scroll again and rolled it between his thumb and forefinger for a while, almost as if he was trying to work out what it was made of.

When he had tired of this he placed the scroll on the table and opened it out, keeping his hands on both ends to prevent it from rerolling itself. It was the same as always: line after line of what looked like utter gibberish.

When the Swedish *mishugenner* had first coming knocking at his door, asking in his bad German if he would say a prayer for him at the Wall and pressing the *kvital* and the money into his hands, Smolenskin did not try to discover why he had been chosen. He knew why he had been chosen. It was the answer to prayer. So what if the *goyim* could not lament the loss of a temple that was not theirs. Who cared? He and his children and his grandchildren were hungry, and here was money for bread and a little bit more besides. And what was wanted in return? Prayers – the kind of prayers that only a Jew could utter. What could be more fitting that a man who had devoted his whole life to unravelling the essential mysteries should be rewarded thus? If the Lord had seen fit to pick a well-known lunatic as His chosen instrument then that was His business. That the Almighty should single out Smolenskin for special treatment was, he thought, only a mystery for those who did not have proper knowledge of Levi Smolenskin.

At first he had not opened the *kvitals*. Nor had he thought it all that strange that the Swede should insist that his prayer be lodged between particular stones towards the right-hand side of the Wall. Why not? Madmen were allowed their obsessions. Especially if they paid in gold for them.

Then, about three months after Magnus's first visit, he could not get to that part of the Wall because it was already occupied, so he wedged the Swede's *kvital* into a more central crevice. What did it matter? If the Lord was disposed to accept a *goy's* prayer from the Wall, one stone was surely as good as another. Besides, how would Magnus ever know?

Two days later the Swede was at the front door again. He had opened it himself to find the *mishugenner* standing there, his huge fist gripping his ridiculous staff, glaring at him with those baleful blue eyes that reminded him of the Siamese cats that rich *shiksas* walked around the central park in Odessa. Without waiting to be invited in, Magnus had pushed his way past him and demanded to know where 'the paper' was.

At first Smolenskin was so taken aback he did not understand the question. When he did understand he was terrified. How on earth had this madman found out that he hadn't put it in the usual spot? Surely he had not been able to check it out? In the daylight hours outside curfew there were normally enough Jewish men around to stop a lunatic *goy* getting close to the sacred stones. To his astonishment the Swede demanded that he must go to the Wall immediately, put the *kvital* where it was supposed to be, and never put it anywhere else again. At first Smolenskin had demurred, but Magnus was insistent. The Jew had never known him quite so lucid. 'It is necessary to make this right,' he kept repeating. 'It is necessary.'

In the end, Smolenskin had picked up his *tellith*, the fringed prayer shawl, and the leather *tefillin* boxes containing fragments of the holy writ which he tied by their attached thongs to his arm and around his forehead, and without another word had set off for the Wall. The Swede had followed at a not very discreet distance, so that whenever Smolenskin paused in his stride the tap-tap of Magnus's staff on the flagstones had threatened to catch up with him.

What the old man had dreaded most was that when he got to the Wall he would find that the elder employed to collect spent *kvitals* for burial in an urn (for no holy writ, however humble, could be destroyed) had already removed the Swede's yellow paper. But it was still there and he was able to put it in the required position while Magnus squatted a few metres away nonchalantly scratching at his bug bites.

It was while Magnus was scratching himself that Levi Smolenskin, standing with his bobbing back to him, had opened the scroll for the first time. In fact, it had begun to unravel slightly as it emerged from its niche and his curiosity was sufficiently aroused to want to see what the Swede considered so important. It was utter gibberish, a meaningless jumble of letters in no known language, the madman's ridiculous tongues transposed to paper. Except that on second glance there was a certain rationale about the script, for each 'word', written in tiny capitals using a fine pointed pen and black ink, was exactly five letters long.

It was at that moment, that Smolenskin concluded that he might have become ensnared in a chillingly secular affair. He had, he decided bitterly, wallowed in his so-called blessing with all the stupidity of an animal being fattened for the larder. And yet even now he could not decide whether the papers he had been taking to the Wall at least once a month for the last two years were coded messages or just another indication of the Swede's dementia: a cipher meant for God.

But there was also the matter of money. Since his first visit he had received exactly thirty-seven sovereigns from Magnus. A small fortune! Could it be the Swede's own money? Was he really, as some maintained, the son of a Stockholm lumber king? Or was someone giving him money to ensure that the yellow *kvital* – almost every other *kvital* was written on white paper – was put in the right place, and that for Levi Smolenskin it would be a task worth doing without question any time he was required to?

If that was the case, he reflected, Magnus was an ideal go-between. Who would suspect messages passed from a religious maniac to a half-starved old Jew? Who would suppose they were anything more than part of Magnus's relentless haranguing of the Almighty?

And yet if they were not, what were they?

For Smolenskin this was the most painful question of all, because the answer was very plain: if the *kvitals* were not of Magnus's ravings, then they must be coded communications of a kind somebody did not want to send through the mail or by telegraph. In this case the most likely explanation was that they were messages between British agents, who were using the Wall as a kind of post-box. Smolenskin went cold at the thought of it, and he thought of it often.

Like most of the Orthodox in the city he was apolitical. A world war was far too earthly an occurrence for men who would hardly look up from their books if their beards caught fire. Only when the conflict impinged on himself, his family and his community – the drying up of Hanukka donations from the United States, for instance – did Smolenskin really take an interest.

But if anything he was pro-Turk, for the same reason that Zionists like the red-headed Dr Rosenblum, whose views on everything else he detested, were pro-Turk. Turkey was fighting Russia and Russia was the enemy of all Jewry. Besides, it was Turkey which had allowed him into Palestine and permitted him to stay despite the fact that, technically at least, he was still a Russian citizen and therefore an enemy alien.

For this reason Smolenskin could never be an ingrate like those Zionists who sought salvation through the English, people like that Lithuanian heretic Elizer Perlman who insisted on calling himself Ben Yehuda or 'son of Judaea', and was obsessed with the blasphemy of turning the language of the Prophets into everyday speech. One of the high points of Smolenskin's time in Jerusalem had been his participation in the ceremony at which the black candles were lit, the *shofar* blown thrice and the profane Perlman expelled from the faith! A fanatic! A true fanatic! It was said that his poor children could hardly communicate because they were forbidden to speak any other language but their father's home-grown Hebrew. Well, he was in America now and no loss! Those were the sort of shameless riff-raff who supported the English – heretics, freethinkers, atheists, Zionists like Aaronsohn who thought the Jews could farm the land, men who impudently demanded the redemption of Israel before the return of the Messiah.

But despite his gratitude two things had stopped Smolenskin going to the authorities with his suspicions. One was the capriciousness of the Turks: they were quite likely to thank him for the information and then hang him along with the rest just to be on the safe side. The Germans were almost as bad. They occasionally had members of the Orthodox community brought in for questioning, and it was quite obvious that files were kept on people like himself who had arrived from Russia just before the start of hostilities. His last interrogation by the Germans had been conducted by a tall, thin, sick-looking major who had begun by reciting the names of every one of his children and grandchildren living with him. Smolenskin had found it most disconcerting.

The other reason for not going to the authorities was that, even if they took a sane and lenient view of matters, and after due investigation it turned out that his suspicions were unfounded, it would almost certainly stop the money. Magnus would find another Jew to send his prayers from the Wall. It was, after all, just possible that the Swede did have some rich relative who indulged his maddest whim.

Once Smolenskin had tried to question him about it. 'Where does this money come from?' he had asked.

'From the Fallen One – he sends it to you.'

'The Fallen One? Do you mean Lucifer? The Devil?'

Magnus had nodded.

'But I thought you were on God's side?'

Magnus had nodded again. 'It is a trick,' he said.

Smolenskin, sensing that the conversation was in danger of getting theological, had decided to concentrate on the more practical side. 'And where do you meet him?'

'Many places. Secret places. Sometimes he is under a stone.'

The Swede has worn his usual solemn expression, his right hand carelessly knotting his beard. And Smolenskin had looked into those clear blue eyes and wondered whether it was madness that he saw there or the cunning of a master dissembler.

On a couple of occasions he had lingered around the Wall after depositing his *kvital*, convinced that it would not be long before he saw some other mourner remove the yellow paper. Yet although he never took his eyes from the hands of the men who wept and prayed at that spot he never saw it happen.

Often he had promised that he would come back a few hours later but once home he invariably persuaded himself that the chances of seeing the *kvital* being removed were too slim to be worth the effort. Sometimes it was gone the next day; sometimes it might be there for three or four days before it disappeared. Smolenskin did not like to ask how often the old *kvitals* were removed for fear of drawing attention to his regular contribution.

Besides, there were mysteries that should not be explored. Ignorance could be construed as innocence. Not that they would believe him of course. He looked again at the groups of five letters on the yellow paper. XEIOB YOZBU LTOPQ. He sighed. Did they mean anything at all?

20

*I*n the evenings now there was just the faintest hint that summer might one day end. Instead of the same blanket heat, nightfall brought a welcome cooling that seemed to heighten the chatter of the cicadas like a rumour running through a crowd. The Moudir of Caesarea heard the insects' rattling chorus as he watched the melting sun on the horizon and waited for his flock to return, a bag of feed corn at his feet.

He stood on the jetty, his fat hands clasped behind his back, staring into the sunset for that first telltale shadow that would tell him that his children had almost completed their circuit of land and sea and were coming home. Though cruel the Moudir was a sensitive man, and the poetry of the evening might have moved him if it were not for two smudges of smoke on the horizon some miles apart. The Entente had increased their naval patrols recently, and there were indications that they might be thinking of trying to land troops north of Gaza and cut the line of communications between the front and the railhead at Deir Sineid.

Only a few days earlier sentries down at Wadi Hesi had actually exchanged rifle fire with British sailors rowing about in a whaler not half a mile from the shore line. The boat had been lowered from a monitor and, as they got closer, the sailors were seen to be measuring the shallows with a plumb-line as if they were charting a passage for landing barges. The authorities had taken the event quite seriously and had announced their intention to move Jews and other foreigners away from the coast. They had already begun to confiscate the fire-arms they had been permitted to keep as a protection against bandits.

161

Not a moment too soon, thought the Moudir. Earlier in the month, on the sixth, some British agents had actually managed to blow up the huge ammunition dump at Haida Pasha on the Syrian-Turkish border. Jews or Armenians, almost certainly. The ingrates!

The Moudir bent down and picked up the sack of grain. He had just seen the little shadow in the sun that heralded their arrival and he began to scatter the seeds on the jetty. When he had finished he looked up. They were much closer, the white ones were in the lead as usual. As they came in the Moudir greeted them with more grain, throwing it at some of them a few feet off the ground so that their final approach became unbalanced by greed and they staggered out of the air. Some fed from his palm and the braver, more insolent birds were soon perched on his forearms and shoulders. They cooed and he replied with his traditional endearments. 'Come on my pretties, come on my little beauties, come on you greedy little monsters. Come on Nur, come on Fatima, come on –'

He looked at the bird which had settled on his wrist and was now pecking at the few remaining grains in his palm, once breaking off to give a little trampoline jump and furiously flap its wings to beat off a half-hearted competitor. The rest of the birds appeared to have come to the conclusion that there were richer pickings on the ground and had abandoned the Moudir's person. Indeed, the reason this lone pigeon preferred the flabby palm of their benefactor was that whenever it settled on the ground the rest of the flock, particularly the white leaders, would drive it away.

The Turk saw at once that it was an interloper. It was too fat and too grey apart from some distinctive brown feathers in its right wing shoulder. He noticed all this before he spotted the cylinder attached to its right leg. When he had examined its contents the Moudir went to his office and used the field telephone there.

It took a Turkish staff officer, a clever, indolent fellow skilled at cards and languages, three days to break the code of five-letter groups the pigeon's message was written in. He might have taken longer, but on the second day he happened to see a top secret file codenamed Yilderim lying on a brother officer's desk. He flicked through it, realised its weight and freshness and wondered if the spy's message might have anything to do with it, and as a test he transposed the Arabic Yilderim to the Roman alphabet, using this as his skeleton key to enter the code.

There were in fact two messages in the pigeon's container written

162

in the same hand in block capitals on a single sheet of thin paper. Even before he had finished his work the Turkish officer had discovered that they were written in different languages.

The long one was in French and the short in German. The French message gave an account of recent troop movements, some of it obviously culled from agents in a good position to observe railway traffic. It was signed 'NILI'. The German message told how Falkenhayn had outlined his Yilderim plan and revealed Kressenstein's outspoken objections to it on the grounds that it would denude his front to the point where he would not be able to withstand a fresh British offensive. It was signed 'DANIEL'.

When he had been told about the contents of the Daniel Intercept, as it rapidly became known around Fast's Hotel, Kressenstein called a meeting of all German and Austrian staff officers. Krag was present and so was Weidinger and so, to the great surprise of both, was Major Franz von Papen, whose well deserved reputation for cleverness had saved him from any further exposure to the British creeping barrages around Arras.

Kress's Corset Staves were a bit put out to see von Falkenhayn's nimble magician in attendance. Good regiments kept this sort of thing within the family. But it soon became apparent why the Uhlan officer had been invited.

'Some Iscariotical bastard,' said von Kressenstein in a voice so low it was almost a whisper, 'is betraying us.' The Bavarian was leaning with his back to his desk, legs crossed, hands gripping the desk top. Krag looked to see whether the knuckles were white. They were.

Kress waited for a few seconds to allow them to digest his announcement before he fed them the gist of the deciphered message and the circumstances of its interception. 'We must accept that either here or at the Nazareth headquarters British Intelligence has an agent. Nili watches the trains, but Daniel seems to have eyes and ears in this very building.

'Since I cannot conceive that one of my officers is a traitor I can only conclude that if the information did come from here somebody has been saying too much to the wrong person. In any event, we must get to the bottom of this affair and do it quickly. For this reason it has been agreed that Major von Papen, who has been temporarily detached from his duties with the Herr Marshal, should investigate the matter.'

Another pause. Several officers looked at Krag, trying to gauge his reaction to this news – for, short-handed as they were, it was well-known that his duties combined security with putting together a daily intelligence assessment. If there was going to be a witch hunt he ought to be the man in charge. Even von Papen contrived to look suitably abashed, greatness thrust upon him.

Krag, as usual, was giving nothing away. He just stood there, leaning forward slightly, hands behind his back, thumbs crossed. And because Kress knew what they were all thinking he added: 'This is absolutely no reflection on you, Major Krag. It is simply because I know that certain bonds have grown between us that might tempt us to cover up a comrade's indiscretion. To be certain the job is done properly it is best that it is done by an outsider who will not be vulnerable to the dangers of having sentiment cloud his judgement.'

Weidinger glanced at Krag and tried to imagine anything as malleable as mere sentiment lurking behind that iron mask. He could not. He was sure the man would hang his mistress if duty demanded.

'If one of you remembers mentioning Yilderim to someone who is not in this room today,' Kress went on, 'even if you are certain in your own mind that the person you spoke to is entirely trustworthy, I would consider it an act of courage if that person presented himself to me or Major von Papen.'

For an awful moment Weidinger feared that he was about to respond to the Bavarian's headmasterly request by colouring like a schoolboy. Then the officers were all dismissed – all except Krag and von Papen, whom Kress motioned to stay behind.

As Weidinger filed out he had to fight down the temptation to turn around to see if Kress was looking at him in some special way. Only the day before Maeltzer had asked him in his jovial way, 'What exactly is Yilderim?' His reply, with raised eyebrows, had been. 'Something you shouldn't know about.'

Not that he had not been all that amazed that the journalist had got wind of it, because Fast's *was* a gossipy place and Maeltzer, as one might expect, was good at sweeping up crumbs of information. Too good, sometimes, he thought, absently returning the salute of the sentries as he descended the main steps.

Anyway, Weidinger was damned if he was going to be made to feel guilty about his dealings with Maeltzer. It was well-known that Kress liked to see the journalist fed selective titbits because favourable mention of his sideshow in the neutral press was thought to impress Berlin. And Kress, like most of the professional soldiers here, was forever wondering what effect on his career his prolonged absence from Europe would have once this war was over.

Yes, thought Weidinger, it was easy enough to be forgotten and for one's achievements to be pinned onto some thief's chest. He wondered if the Swedish lunatic and the old Jew had anything to do with the Daniel Intercept. He was not going to risk asking Krag again how his inquiries were going on that score. Krag had made him feel gauche enough the last time he did it. Then it occurred to him that perhaps he should mention the matter to von Papen.

Weidinger would have felt more charitably disposed towards Krag had he been able to hear what he was saying at that moment. For back in the briefing-room at Fast's the intelligence officer was telling Kress and von Papen just what Weidinger had concluded himself: that secrets were hard to keep at this particular headquarters.

'Not only are there Turkish officers at Nazareth aware of the Yilderim plan but there were Turkish officers at the marshal's briefing here,' Krag reminded them. 'And as you know, sir, they tend to be a talkative bunch. Furthermore, most of them do not consider their Syrian servants to be members of the same species. They talk in front of them as if they were dumb animals. Luckily for us the English staff officers in Cairo are almost as bad.'

'Well, perhaps there's some truth in that,' conceded Kress, who much preferred the theory of the eavesdropping servant to that of the Iscariotical bastard. 'But we're going to have to be more careful in future, limit the distribution of documents even more, make sure that only those who need to know do know. We really can't have pigeons dropping in on the Turkish gendarmerie bearing our latest views on military matters. I suppose we should thank the good Lord that the bird had a poor sense of navigation.'

'Yes, sir.'

'Either that or it was one of your double agents.'

Von Papen gave vent to one of the short bursts of sycophantic laughter he reserved for senior officers' jokes. It sounded to Krag like a cat being sick. Nonetheless, the intelligence officer managed one of his attempts at a smile, a faint puckering around the corners of his mouth which his mother, or perhaps Shemsi, might have recognised. 'Not one of mine, sir,' he said.

'Do you think Nili and Daniel exist as individuals?' asked Kress, the levity gone from his voice.

'Difficult to say, sir – at least on the evidence available. They could just as well be codenames for entire networks. On the basis of what has been produced so far I would say that Nili is almost certainly more than one person. I don't believe that an individual could cover that amount of territory. Hard to say about Daniel. Could be one man, could be more.'

'How big do you think the British intelligence operations are in Palestine? Do they have many agents?'

The exact truth of the matter was that Krag did not know, and ordinarily he might have said so – but he was not going to admit it in front of von Papen.

'They laid the groundwork for a good intelligence operation before the war, sir,' he said, and this was accurate enough. 'They have probably set up networks all over the Levant. For instance, this Major Lawrence the Turks want so badly used to come to Syria on archaeological expeditions and stay for months at a time. Then there was an organisation called the Palestine Exploration Fund. They were always in and out of here. Big expeditions, big camps, young archaeologists fresh out of their universities and their Officer Cadet Training Units making maps and taking photographs of everything they saw: bridges, railways, old castles, new castles. Enough gold sovereigns with them to make lasting friendships. I'm sure you can imagine the sort of thing, sir.'

'Why did the Turks allow it?'

'The usual reason. A little baksheesh in the right place. Either that or the British Consulate here or in Beirut or in Damascus would come up with a convincing argument that would produce the necessary paperwork. In my experience, the British can be very persuasive diplomats.'

'So Daniel, network or individual, could have been operating here since the war started?'

'Possibly.'

'Hmm. Well it doesn't seem to have helped them very much. I suppose they call him Daniel because he's in the lion's den, so to speak?'

'Yes, one doesn't exactly get the impression of a great mind at work,' drawled von Papen, who had worked as a military attaché in Washington until his expulsion in '15 and fancied he knew a thing or two about the Great Game.

'He probably didn't choose it himself,' said Krag.

'Quite,' agreed Kress. 'For God's sake don't underestimate your quarry, Major. He's been clever enough so far.'

Krag thought he detected a note of doubt in Kress's voice, as if he had suddenly become aware of von Papen's underlying arrogance and was wondering whether he had got the right man for the job. A point for me, Krag decided. If they had been duelling he would just have opened up one of the cheek bones of the Herr Marshal's clever ADC by a couple of centimetres or so.

'No, I don't underestimate Daniel, sir,' said von Papen, who showed no sign of being hurt. 'I was simply thinking that the people who control him or her are not that clever. I'm not basing this on the codename, although it does to my mind show a depressingly unimaginative mind, but the way they handle his communications. I mean, carrier pigeons. What next? Why don't they try runners with cleft sticks?'

'What would *you* suggest?' asked Krag.

'Wireless,' said von Papen without hesitation. 'If I were British intelligence I would have my spies in Palestine wireless their despatches to a ship and then let that ship relay them by wireless telegraph as soon as Cairo came within range of their transmitter. In fact, they were probably already in range. Marconi was sending telegrams across the Atlantic before the war.'

'But can't such telegrams be intercepted as easily as a pigeon — more easily in fact?' said Kress.

'Yes, but if they are written in a good cypher it doesn't matter. The information is acted upon by the time the enemy has cracked your cypher, which is changed for each message.'

'You have more faith in science than I do, Major.'

Kress seemed to think it was time to change the subject. 'I can't make Nili out,' he said. 'Sounds like it might be an acronym. Do you think the Turks will catch them, Krag?'

'I don't see why not, sir. They're usually very good at police work — they've got the manpower, the informers.'

'You know them well don't you, Krag – the Turks.'

'I've been with the Eastern Military Mission almost nine years, sir – since '09.'

'Yet you don't like them very much, do you?' Kress had a smile on his face which said that he did not find this state of affairs altogether amazing.

'Not very much, sir,' agreed Krag. 'There are perhaps one or two exceptions.'

'The usual reasons, I suppose: lazy, corrupt, degenerate?' Von Papen was looking at him curiously.

'A bit – but I think that is all very exaggerated. You'd be surprised how well they can do things when they really want to. And the discipline of the Turkish army is not entirely based on fear. Properly led they can be very good soilders. Perhaps not as good as us, but a match for the British or the French any day. Nor are they incapable of producing leaders. Look at Mustafa Kemal, our hero of Gallipoli.

No, the thing I dislike about them is their basic xenophobia, their intolerance. It's part of the *jihad* mentality, the fact that they are often so willing to kill men, women and children in the name of religion.'

'You're thinking of the Armenians?'

'Among others.'

'You're right to be concerned. I want to show you something.' From his top pocket Kress drew a folded piece of notepaper and passed it to Krag who opened it out and held it so that von Papen could see it as well, like two men sharing a hymn book.

The notepaper bore the letterhead of the Sonnenaufgang, the German League for the Promotion of Christian Charitable Work in the East. It was a copy of a letter the League had sent to the *Journal de Genève* complaining about the treatment of Armenian refugees in Aleppo. The tone, to say the least, was indignant. 'Out of two thousand or three thousand peasant women brought here in good health,' the letter stated, 'only thirty or forty living skeletons are left.'

'Appalling,' said von Papen. It seemed to be the thing to say.

'The missionaries know how to make themselves unpopular,' was Krag's only comment when he handed the letter back. He assumed that they must have thought a Zurich-based German-language newspaper like Maeltzer's would decline to publish criticism of Germany's allies.

'They are not without influence in Berlin,' said Kress. 'The Foreign Ministry is putting some pressure on the Turks to behave. Some of the language is quite strong, urging them not to allow a repeat of the atrocities, that sort of thing. They're a strange lot our allies,' he sighed. 'One moment they are the supreme chevaliers, inheritors of the Saladin charm – I told you about that business with the British prisoners at Easter didn't I, von Papen?'

The ADC nodded. 'It would not have happened in France.'

'Quite,' said Kress, who always found reminders of the big war going on outside his sandpit irksome. 'Then the next moment they leave you in no doubt that they are direct descendants of the hordes of Genghis Khan. I tell you frankly, gentlemen, I can never make them out.

'Look at this business with the Jews. For years they allow the old and religious to come to King David's city to die. Then they start to get involved with the Zionists, permit them to establish settlements, farm the land. They even turn a blind eye when the rich landlords in Beirut start kicking the Syrian peasants off the land they've farmed for centuries to sell it to the Jews for a huge profit. And if the Syrians, most of them fellow-Muslims, begin to complain they hang a few and tell the rest about the great economic benefits Zionism is going to bring. Then the next thing you know they're upset about this "alien presence" that has been created. The Zionists, of whom at least half must be German-speaking, suddenly all become British spies!'

'Is it true they want to move the Jews away from the coast and disarm them?' asked von Papen.

'I'm afraid that's right,' said Kress. 'Personally, I think it's unwarranted. Perhaps a few do flirt with the Entente, like that fellow Aaronsohn, the agronomist. But Djemal Pasha told me the other day that the Jews were waiting for the English "like a bride".'

'It would only be a few,' agreed Krag, 'and they would have no more than a marriage of convenience in mind.'

Von Papen honoured the intelligence officer with one of his shorter imitations of a cat being sick.

21

Joseph agreed to kill the birds, which they had both grown fond of over the last three months – 'our Egyptian friends,' he liked to call them – and Sarah's sense of duty compelled her to take on the role of assistant executioner. It was almost midnight before they went to the trees where the loft was hidden. The pigeons appeared to be asleep when they arrived.

She got there first and waited for Joseph who had decided to make one last patrol of the grounds to make sure nobody was about. Twice in the last month they had had intruders at the agricultural experimental station. They told each other the most likely culprits were deserters, but they knew that if the station wasn't already under surveillance it soon would be. It was too near the coast, and the Turks were getting jittery.

'Nili?'

Joseph arrived as he often did, each noiseless step a triumph of planning, pleased to startle her with his sudden, gratuitous whispering of their password.

She swung around, hurricane lamp in one hand with the wick turned right down. 'Yes, and also the glory of Israel will not lie, 'she said, surprising herself as well as Joseph with the bitterness she put behind the words.

Yet it was almost certain that what they were about to do was futile. It was coming to an end, she could feel it. Police and soldiers had been hammering up their reward notices for a week now. It seemed that there wasn't a telegraph pole in southern Syria that was not wearing a trilingual poster informing Arabs, Jews and Turks that

170

ten thousand *mejdi* would be paid for information about a person or persons secretly keeping homing pigeons. And there were those around who would persuade themselves that it was their moral duty to inform 'for the good of the Yishuv'.

For the last two days they had been displaying both a white sheet and a red sofa cover over their balcony. But the British monitors had either not spotted their agreed distress signal or would not risk sending a whaler party ashore to investigate it. If it wasn't for the fact that her brother was there Sarah would have believed that Cairo had abandoned them. As it was, she suspected the smoke was from French ships. When it came to Intelligence, the Entente went their separate ways.

It was one of those illuminated Mediterranean nights when an almost full moon and a great dome of stars made the lamp redundant until they got into the conifers. Joseph had built the loft on a platform like a children's tree house. It was positioned between three trunks and reached by the short ladder he was carrying. Joseph went first and then waited at the top while she climbed after him. She heard him snick the first of the bolts he had fixed to the door.

The first bird was easy. One strong hand pinioned its wings to the body and thick fingers briefly stroked its breast before they went up around the neck and twisted. The second bird also suspected nothing and obliged by dying without a fuss. But the third emerged with her wings flapping, obviously aware that something was amiss, and she took longer. The last bird was a cock and it came out fighting. Joseph could not get a firm grip of it and it broke free, clattered madly about the interior and then escaped through the open door. 'Pigeons don't fly at night,' thought Sarah – but this one did.

Joseph had prepared a shallow trench in the vineyard that afternoon and they buried the three dead birds there. It was dark under the vines, which were heavy with grapes. Sarah, who had been fasting that day for Yom Kippur, picked one. It was heavy with juice, slightly sour. She had another and another, swallowing the pips. Aaron wanted to make wine from these vines like the Christian monks did at Carmel. What dreams! What crazy dreams!

'Light,' he said.

'What?'

'I need to see what I'm doing. Light your lamp again.'

The big lucifer match she produced from the box in her sleeve seemed to light up like a flare. She turned up just enough wick to show the broad, powerful shoulders at work, notice the faint sheen of sweat on the thick neck: the thick, vulnerable neck.

'That'll do,' he said, patting the spoil down. 'In the morning I'll

take the loft apart. Get rid of the netting, the feeding-bowls —
everything.'

'And then?'

'And then what?'

'You know very well what,' said Sarah. 'You must go. Hide out
for a while. Wait for the English to come.'

'You don't want to come with me?'

Did she detect a note of relief? Sarah dismissed the idea as
unworthy almost as soon as she thought of it. 'It's impossible, you
know that. If I disappear it will be proof of my guilt. They could
burn the whole settlement down. They might even hang my father.
They're already highly suspicious about Aaron's absence.'

'I thought Ponting was going to arrange to have some mail sent
from America saying that he had got stuck there and was trying to
come back?'

'Yes, it was Meinertzhagen's idea. But it's probably too late. I'm
sure somebody like Krag has dozens of spies in Cairo. The British
have allowed Aaron to become very visible. He's probably been
spotted.'

Sarah preferred to put the blame on their patrons rather than her
brother. She was not going to give Joseph the satisfaction of knowing
that Aaron was almost as big a fool as he was, playing at soldiers in
his khaki and his Sam Browne belt. 'The best thing is for me to stay
where I am,' she told him. 'They sometimes have a certain gallantry
towards women.'

'I wouldn't rely on that.'

Sarah very nearly snapped back, 'You don't have to.' But she held
her tongue. That sort of remark would be the end of the argument.
He would stay.

'Anyway, why must I be the one to go?' he said. She sensed the
stubbornness swelling up, that contrariness that could make him so
damned unpredictable.

'There are good reasons and you know them. There are people at
Zichron Jacob who are not on our side. They resent you. An outsider
making trouble is the way they look at it. Some of them would
probably tell the Turks you were a rebel whether they believed it or
not. Better to inform than to be sorry.'

'I'll see,' he said. 'I'll see how I feel in the morning.'

Sarah knew better than to press him, not now.

They were walking back towards the station house when a sudden
movement froze them both. It sounded like the kind of furtive scurry-
ing made by a small animal or bird being disturbed.

As Sarah turned her lamp off she heard a faint click besides her

172

and saw that Joseph had put down the ladder and cocked the old Colt revolver he liked to carry. He was holding it with his thumb on the hammer and the long barrel pointing upwards. They heard the noise again, a kind of scrabbling high up in the conifers 'It's the last pigeon,' she said. 'It's come back.'

He motioned her to stay where she was and went towards the ladder. Before he climbed it he eased the hammer back on the Colt and returned it to his waistband. Sarah watched him climb into the watchtower and then heard some sharp, definite movements. For a moment she thought it might not be the pigeon and began to hitch up her skirt in case she had to run. Then something dropped out of the door of the tower and landed with a little thud besides her. A breeze twitched the bird's wing feathers and for a moment she thought that Joseph had not done the job properly until he came back down the ladder and picked it up. She could see that the neck was properly broken then, the way she had been told a good hang-man did it.

'I wonder why it came back?' she said. To escape from the condemned cell and then make a voluntary return – what a dreadful thought.

'They mate for life. Perhaps it didn't want to be anywhere else,' said Joseph, who turned away from her and walked towards the trench he had just filled in. As he lifted the spade he added in a low voice, but not so low that she could not catch the words, 'Didn't see the point of running away, did you?'

Yet he was gone the next morning. Sarah checked the loft. He had dismantled it as promised. He could not have had more than three or four hours' sleep. With him had vanished a dun-coloured gelding in much better condition than the mount he had left behind and a well-maintained Mauser '98 pattern rifle belonging to the settlement watch. Once the thefts had been discovered some of the men, including Sarah's father, Ephraim, were outraged and one man wanted to report the matter to the gendarmerie. 'Why get a fellow-Jew into trouble?' begged Sarah. 'In a few days we'll probably have to hand over all our registered weapons to the Turks anyway.'

'And the unregistered ones,' said the man who wanted to go to the gendarmerie. 'I'm not paying the baksheesh to get you off a hanging charge.'

'Swine,' thought Sarah. Not for the first time it occurred to her that she probably had more hatred for some of her own than for any Turk or German.

———————

But when the Turks did come to Zichron Jacob it was, as Sarah knew it would be, not weapons they were after.

They arrived at about noon on the third day after Joseph's departure from Athlit – a squadron of Kurdish cavalry with a hashish addict called Hassan Bey at their head. Riding at his side was the Moudir of Caesarea, who had been invited to accompany them as a reward for his vigilance and had been loaned a particularly boisterous chestnut mare for his ride down from Haifa, which had left him tired and chafed and eager to see somebody in pain.

They headed straight for Aaron's wooden house where Sarah was staying. It was a comfortable place, to the Kurds practically a palace. It was furnished in a style that was a happy marriage of Europe and the Levant so that crammed bookshelves, a gramophone and gateleg tables co-existed with high backed chairs that might have been European except for their Damascene marquetry, and Persian rugs laid on floors of decorated tiles.

An NCO and six men were detailed off to go and get Sarah's father and Joseph Lishansky. They returned with Ephraim but told the Bey that Lishansky was not to be found. The Bey took from his gold case one of the special cigarettes he bought by the gross in Beirut. They contained the best Bekaa valley hashish, bought at half the usual price now that the war had separated the Maronite Christian farmers there from their traditional Egyptian market.

He was a handsome, grey-eyed man with high cheekbones, a waxed moustache and a well pressed and brushed fez, for his servant worshipped the Bey's uniform with the fanaticism of any man with a sane aversion to deserts and shellfire. The servant was carrying the Bey's saddlebags, one with a handle for something sticking out of it, which he placed reverentially in a corner. The Bey waited for his servant to light his cigarette before seating himself in one of the high-backed chairs.

When at last he spoke Hassan Bey chose to do so in French – a language he much preferred to German, which he also spoke tolerably well. 'Perhaps you two will find it difficult,' he said in a conversational tone, 'to remember what became of Monsieur Lishansky? We know he's not at your experimental station because we've searched there and although we found much of interest your friend was not among them. Nor, I suppose, would you much care to

174

discuss things like the migratory habits of the pigeon – a greedy, undiscriminating bird, quite likely to make unannounced calls at the most unsuitable houses if there's a chance of a free meal. Perhaps you feel that this is an unfair assessment?'

Judging by his face the Moudir did. You really couldn't compare a good bird to that misshapen interloper.

'We know nothing of pigeons, your honour,' said Ephraim Aaronsohn in a firm voice. Pigeons? What nonsense was this? He didn't know anything about any pigeons. It was all a dreadful mistake. There was hope.

'Bring that sack in,' said the Bey.

They scattered them over the best rug, filthy and stinking – the birds the Turks had exhumed at Athlit. Sarah remembered the intruders, and guessed that somebody had watched Joseph dig the trench.

Hassan Bey allowed the Moudir to take one by its tail feathers and hold it next to her face so that its decay filled her nostrils. 'You see, Sarah, we know everything.'

She tried to turn away but the Moudir grabbed a hank of hair and pulled her head around so that she had to face the awful thing again.

'Look at it, Sarah,' he whispered. 'Death. How long ago? Two days? Three days? and already rotting. Think of it. An old friend. A loyal friend. A fine bird. Feathers, beak, eyes, heart. Magnificent heart. Why couldn't you be merciful, Sarah? Why didn't you let them fly home to El Arish? Why did you have to murder them? Why Sarah? Why? Do you know what happens to murderers, Sarah? Do you know what happens to murderers, *Jew*?'

The Moudir pushed her away and flung the bird into a corner of the room. For a moment Sarah fiddled with her hair, tried to put it back up into its bun, then gave up and allowed her hands to fall my her side. 'My father knows nothing,' she said.

The Bey muttered something to his servant who went to the corner of the room where he had placed the saddlebags. He opened the one with the cylindrical object protruding and returned with it to his master. The Bey faced Sarah. 'Permit me to introduce you to a friend of mine,' he said. 'Monsieur Kourbash.'

The whip was coiled against the black cylinder of its wooden handle. Sarah thought it looked like a basking snake and began to back away but now there was a Kurd on each arm, pushing her towards the Bey. Still coiled, she felt the hippopotamus hide against her left cheek. The soldiers had twisted her arms up and one was running his free hand around her buttocks and the backs of her upper thighs. She couldn't speak. He scraped the whip down her cheek. She knew that even this small movement had grazed her, possibly drawn blood. It felt like emery paper. 'Please, Sarah,' said the Bey. 'The truth.'

22

Much to his annoyance, Krag learned of Sarah Aaronsohn's arrest from von Papen. The jaunty Westphalian breezed into his office at the Hotel Fast where the intelligence officer was tortured by von Papen's habit of knocking and entering in one fluid movement.

'Well, it seems they've caught our pigeon-fanciers,' his visitor announced. 'Some Jews up around Haifa somewhere. Believe one of 'em is a woman.'

Krag ostentatiously turned over his assessment of what could be deduced from reports of increased British cavalry patrolling on the Beersheba flank.

Von Papen registered this with the ghost of a smile and then went on with his news. 'I heard it from one of Mustafa Kemal's staff this morning,' he said. 'Seems that they're, hmm, interrogating the woman now.'

'Well, of course, after that she'll admit to anything. She'd tell them Kress was Daniel if she thought it would make them stop,' said Krag. 'I wish we'd got hold of her first. Did you get her name?'

He told him and Krag nodded and said, 'It had to happen sooner or later.'

'Well known?'

He told von Papen about the missing big brother, the man who had been so very close to Djemal Pasha.

'And where is this brilliant agronomist now?'

'That's a matter of opinion. Some say he is stuck in America, can't get back. There have also been reports that he has been seen in Cairo in the uniform of a British officer.'

'What do you believe?'

177

'I wouldn't like to have to make a decision on the matter. The agents who report this to me are either Arabs or Egyptians, and both are very unreliable. Some Arabs welcome the Jews because they think they're very rich and clever and that somehow their money and brains are contagious. Others don't think they're worth it at any price. They're the ones who think the Jews are here to steal their land and in a way they're right. They want to get them into trouble. Of course, they don't have to try very hard. In times like these all non-Muslims are enemies of the true believer.'

'I thought the Jews were accepted here, more so than the Arabs?'

'They may be in Constantinople, but not in Palestine. They're a different breed here too. They haven't lived among the Turk long enough. Most of them are Germans or Russians – or at least they would be if language was all that was required.'

'So you're not surprised that they've arrested this Aaronsohn woman? They've just moved against someone they were watching anyway?'

'Perhaps. We shall have to wait and see whether they come up with the kind of proof that has more behind it than Herr Kourbash.'

'According to my informant they've dug up some dead pigeons.'

'I wonder who put them there?' said Krag.

But von Papen could see he was impressed.

'Even if she is involved,' the intelligence officer went on, 'she was probably just a courier, a link in the chain. I doubt if she has any real idea who David or Nili are.'

'Oh do you think so?' von Papen lent forward on Krag's desk, taking his weight on mottled knuckles. 'Surely she's bound to know something, lead somewhere?'

'Not necessarily. As I said, she'll talk; she'll probably talk a lot. But I doubt if much of it will make any sense.'

'Would they really be that bad – to a woman?'

'Yes,' said Krag. 'They will do the things even the worst scum of Europe only ever dream of doing and then wake ashamed.'

'Some people say this city is full of spies. Do you think that's true?' asked von Papen, anxious to change tack. His natural buoyancy could not take the other's certainty of atrocity.

'It's full of citizens who are quite *willing* to be spies,' said Krag. 'Especially now, when people are half starving. The Turks have a tradition of informers.'

'I don't think I've told you about these, have I?' said von Papen. Out of one of his upper tunic pockets he produced Maeltzer's shattered reading spectacles and placed them on the desk.

Krag picked them up and looked at them this way and that while von Papen told him how they had come into his possession.

'Of course,' he concluded. 'They could have been lost days before and it was merely a sentry's boot that sent them skidding along the stone work and down through the machicolation. Even so –'

'Quite. Very disconcerting to have the very walls, at least the ceiling, the roof, grow eyes as it were.' Krag was holding the battered frames up to the light, trying to read the name of the manufacturer. Some of the glass was still in the half-moon frames and he had to be careful not to cut his fingers on these jagged bits.

'But I wouldn't worry about it,' he said. 'That Turkish officer was probably right. It was some curious Jew. They're a myopic bunch, especially the Hasidic Orthodox. It comes from a certain amount of inbreeding and never taking their heads out of some learned work.'

'Well, I'm not suggesting that it was Daniel himself,' said von Papen testily. He was beginning to loathe the patronising tone of this underpromoted pleb ten years his senior. 'I don't suppose he follows Colonel von Kressenstein about listening through keyholes or the slits the Janissaries made for their boiling oil. I just find it disturbing that two German officers cannot hold a conversation after curfew without somebody trying to listen in.'

'As I said, there is a tradition of informers here,' said Krag, slightly uneasy about the speed with which he had got under the other's skin. There was no sense in making too much of an enemy of a von, especially a von who had the ear of other vons. Better that they should be blissfully unaware of his contempt. 'There are scavengers about who will cock an ear at any conversation in the hope that it might lead to a crust. And there's very little trust. They spy on each other. Informers are probably the most informed upon of all. You have to imagine the leaves of an artichoke: layer upon layer.'

'I see,' said von Papen. 'So everybody listens. You make it sound like a kind of national sport.' Fancy somebody like Krag knowing anything at all about artichokes.

'Not a national sport, an Ottoman sport, Major. There are many nationalities here. That's part of the problem.'

A runner – military flattery for an overweight Dusseldorf grocer with flat feet – arrived with a sheaf of telegrams for Krag, and von Papen seized the opportunity to leave. 'I'll keep you informed,' he said at the door.

'Thank you,' said Krag who was busy reading the top message and, despite his misgivings, did not bother to look up as von Papen went out. It was a copy of a signal that had been sent to Kress from the German liaison officer at Hassan Bey's headquarters in Nazareth.

It said that the Jew Sarah Aaronsohn, who was suspected of being the spy codenamed Nili responsible for sending the British coded messages by carrier pigeon, had somehow managed to shoot herself during interrogation. It did not explain how. She was still alive but expected to die. It said nothing about Daniel.

Krag wondered if the liaison man at Haifa really believed the bullet wound was self-inflicted. Whatever their other shortcomings, Turkish soldiers were not usually in the habit of allowing women to grab their rifles.

He made no attempt to call von Papen back. Instead, the intelligence officer studied the document for some time, absently toying with the spectacles his visitor had left on his desk as he did so. After a while he examined the frames again and recalled that he had seen somebody wearing half-moons like these quite recently, but he could not remember who it was.

Krag's instinctive rejection of von Papen's account of how Sarah Aaronsohn got her fatal bullet wound turned out to be quite wrong.

Soon the details would not only come to him but also filter through the entire Yishuv, where the story of Sarah Aaronsohn was passed from settlement to settlement. It was sometimes a little changed in the telling, as sagas tend to be; it was particularly vague about the exact nature of her suffering. But the words of a Turkish officer who was alleged to have witnessed her defiance were invariably quoted: 'She's worth a hundred men.'

Even those Jews who were against her, who were being daily reduced by the new Turkish harshness towards the Zionists, often wept when they heard the tale and took a certain pride in her courage. Pro-German Zionists became neutral, and the neutral became pro-British. Those with no political chasms to leap simply became angry. This last category quoted not only the admiring Turkish officer but a note Sarah is said to have left. 'You are murderers, you are bloodthirsty animals, you are cowards and I, by myself a weak woman – I rose to protect my people so that you will not do to them what you did to the Armenians . . .'

What exactly was done to Sarah Aaronsohn has never been made clear. Some accounts have it that she was first tied to a gate-post and flogged until she was unconscious. This is said to have been followed by rape, the removal of finger nails, burns applied with a heated bayonet, the scalp torn and bloody where hair had been pulled out.

Others would indicate Sarah was not badly hurt if she was hurt

180

at all. In these accounts both sides exhibit a certain chivalry. Sarah confesses that she has been running the Nili group since her brother's departure. In return, the Turks accept her plea that none of the other Jews at Zichron Jacob, including her father, are involved. What is indisputable is that at some point during the second day of interrogation the Bey suddenly announced that she was to be allowed to change her clothes.

His reasons for doing this are again a matter of dispute. Some say it is quite simple: the Bey was a gentleman. The version Krag believed was that he intended to take her to Nazareth or even Damascus for further interrogation and, given the prevalence of German and Austrian staff and liaison officers in those parts, thought it best that she did not appear to have been too ill-used.

Whatever the reason, Sarah was unescorted when she was allowed to use the bathroom, the envy of the settlement with its large enamel bath. The house had already been torn apart and a Winchester carbine removed from its narrow, upright hideyhole, built into the woodwork around a door. They had also found a trapdoor, skilfully set in the tiled floor and covered with a rug, which led through the cellar to a narrow escape tunnel Aaron had built with Syrian raiders in mind.

When they heard the shot the Bey was the first back. Sarah was lying face down on the red tiles in the bathroom, bubbling blood. She was still holding the little Derringer with which she had shot herself through the mouth. There was no sign of where the pistol had been hidden. Later, when they were pressed for explanations, the Turks said they thought it might simply have been placed behind one of the legs of the high bath where a scrap of blue rag soaked in gun oil was found. But Krag was probably the only German officer in Palestine who gave this any credence.

'The Bey gave it to her,' pronounced Kress when the Aaronsohn case came up while, once again, they were going over the Daniel Intercept.

Von Papen agreed. Wasn't it the way the Turks worked? That perverse sense of honour that would enable them first to torture a woman and then to slip her the means to kill herself?

Krag raised an eyebrow at this sudden display of expertise on the Turkish official caste by a newcomer. 'No,' he said. 'They're not like that.'

Some things were apparently indisputable and written in the clear hand of the Jewish doctor — one of several conscripted into the Turkish medical corps at the outbreak of hostilities — who had been summoned from Haifa to attend her. But it did not tell the whole truth. It simply told the Bey as much as he needed to know, as much as the men he had left behind (for he departed almost immediately after Sarah shot herself) might have passed onto him in their layman's fashion.

The Bey had asked for the report yet once he had read it he would have liked to tear it into very small pieces. This, however, was not possible, for Damascus as well as von Kressenstein was interested, so he had to pass it on.

The patient had fired a large-bore .44 bullet into her mouth, the doctor wrote, which had exited through the back of her neck. The round had severed her spinal cord, leaving her a paraplegic. The physician noted that the young woman had other wounds but said that these were not of a life-threatening nature. When he read this Krag shuddered, remembering the way a kourbash could curl round a body like a python.

Certainly, there was much the doctor knew and did not write. He did not write how she had recovered enough voice to plead with the women who were nursing her to finish her off with poison and how, with the Kurds still in attendance, they were too fearful to render this small favour. Only on the fourth day did Sarah Aaronsohn come to terms with the fact that no help was forthcoming and, since it was unscientific to say she willed herself to die, the doctor wrote that it was a haemorrhage that ended it.

The Bey read the report at his headquarters in Nazareth. When he had finished he stood for a while staring out of an open window at the dried up Galilean hills, smoking one of his special cigarettes. Somewhere in the distance he could hear the buzz of an aeroplane engine.

It was his fault, of course; he should not have felt pity for the woman and allowed her to put on fresh clothes. Damascus had already made it plain that they were not pleased with the publicity the Aaronsohn affair had engendered. And the Bey had to agree that it would have been much better had their Christian allies not learned of it until they had found out all there was to find out.

Nili he could not be sure of. But like every other senior Turkish officer aware of the case, right up to Djemal Pasha himself, he was convinced that Daniel was a Turk. Somehow they sensed that here was a man enjoying his revenge. There was about him that sweet smell of treachery they all knew so well.

23

*I*t was much hotter here than in Jerusalem, where every day now the skies promised but never quite delivered the beginning of the winter rain and the first of the migrating storks had been seen heading south down the Jordan Valley towards the Dead Sea.

Here the desert slowed a man's pace, trickled sweat into his eyes and broke up the outlines of distant ridges. In the souk there was camel meat for sale for those who could afford it. Once they had sold their redundant mounts some of the Bedouin stayed to watch the quartermaster's wagons load up at the railway station and note which sentries grew sleepy around noon.

'We have a new trench mortar, Field Marshal,' announced their escorting officer, a Turkish major with a humorous mouth and eyes. 'You must see it.'

Von Falkenhayn motioned him to lead the way, and von Papen and Weidinger came up behind. This was the second and final day of their tour of the Gaza–Beersheba line.

Kress had suggested it casually to von Papen as a means of explaining why he was opposed to Yilderim, and why the better Turkish commanders like Mustafa Kemal, the hero of Gallipoli, shared his views on it. Von Papen was already more than half convinced by Kress's arguments anyway, while von Falkenhayn, like most senior commanders, had a journalist's relish for a quick sniff at the front and jumped at the chance. The *aide de camp* was also glad to get away from the Turko-German sniping and the nasty little social ambushes one could run into at Jerusalem headquarters. He was getting nowhere with the Daniel Affair, and the lugubrious Krag seemed more than content to be in sole charge for a few days.

Weidinger had arrived in Beersheba before any of them and would be staying longer because Kress wanted him to organise some extensive reconnaissance patrols. Kress was increasingly worried about his left flank and wanted reassurance that the desert really did make it impossible for Allenby to push his cavalry from that direction. He was also there to try to gauge how von Falkenhayn felt about the Yilderim plan once he had seen the situation on the ground. Kress liked von Papen, but he wanted to hear from his own man.

The Turkish major picked a careful route through the casual defecations of his troops to a pit about 200 metres behind the unit's most forward entrenchments, where the mortar crew reluctantly extinguished the pipes and cigarettes that were the most effective way of keeping the flies away.

They were Anatolians in grey-green German uniforms whose only concession to the heat was a preference for rope-tied leather sandshoes instead of jackboots. The exception was their commander, a dazzling young Muzalim-i-sani, the Ottoman equivalent of a second lieutenant, who not only wore boots but, against all odds, had somehow managed to wax his moustache.

The machine he was in charge of was even more gleaming, for its barrel was the brass shell-case that had once contained the propellant for a British 18-pounder. This had been set into a carved wooden stock like an outsized rifle butt, and the whole edifice was mounted on a bi-pod that appeared to have been hammered out at a farrier's campaign forge. It reminded Weidinger of those pen-and-ink drawings of medieval siege machinery that used to enliven the pages of his history text books.

'Does it work?' von Falkenhayn wanted to know.

'Certainly, General,' grinned the Muzalim-i-sani. 'It is a good weapon.' He spoke passable German.

'Well, we're waiting,' said the field marshal, ignoring his demotion.

Two of the crew picked up a bomb. It occurred to Weidinger that the machine did not seem to possess any mechanism capable of adjusting the range.

'Hadn't we better step back?' said von Papen. 'It's not exactly Krupp.'

But whether the field marshal might have preferred discretion to a display of confidence at the resourcefulness of the infantry he ultimately commanded the ADC never found out. For at that moment the Muzalim-i-sani yelled fire and the crew dropped the first bomb down the brass spout of their machine. There was an ear-splitting crack, followed by a dull clanging sound as the missile exploded in some low-lying land to the east where the nearest British positions were supposed to be. It was quickly followed by another and then a third.

'If this was France,' thought Weidinger, 'we'd get one back for this.'

'Very good,' said von Falkenhayn.

'How do you adjust the range?' asked Weidinger, anxious to show the field marshal he had taken an intelligent interest in the proceedings.

'Watch,' said waxed moustache. He barked out some fresh orders to his men but they were doing his bidding before he had finished. Two of them placed sandbags beneath the legs of the bi-pods and then lay on their stomachs either side of the mortar holding its legs down onto the bags with both hands. The angle of the barrel was now another ten degrees closer to the vertical.

'Fire!' shouted the Muzalim-i-sani. For the first time Weidinger realised that he said this in German, presumably because he had been trained to use a mortar in that language.

This time the sound of the outgoing crack and the incoming round were almost one and all the Germans, even the field marshal, found that they had sunk to an involuntary crouch. When they got up their ears were ringing, and it must have been a few seconds before they heard the screams.

'What's that?' Weidinger had asked, knowing full well what it was but desperately hoping otherwise.

Smoke drifted from the forward position where the bomb had landed short, and as it cleared some stretcher bearers could be seen running to the scene. The major and the Muzalim-i-sani scrambled out of the pit and headed in the same direction.

'My God!' said the field marshal – and to the amazement of all those present he aimed a kick at the mortar, which collapsed off its sandbags as if shot. 'See to it that this abortion is never used again,' he yelled at no one in particular. As they strode off he turned to von Papen and said, 'Mortars, Franz. Make a note of that. They need proper mortars.'

And von Papen went through the business of extracting his notebook and pencil from the top pocket of his tunic and writing on a fresh page: 'Beersheba – mortars.' After a little while the Turkish major, all the good humour drained from his face, caught up with them and led them tight-lipped to the Mercedes staff car where the chauffeur was waiting to issue them all with goggles against the dust.

Now they stood in the station-master's office at Beersheba while the sleeping-car Djemal Pasha had loaned the marshal – 'like a tart's bedroom,' von Falkenhayn had observed when he first glimpsed its divans and piles of silk cushions – was prepared for the journey back.

The station-master had drawn his blinds against the sun and left his front and back doors open to create a cooling through draught. Nevertheless, it was still stifling in the gloom inside and von Falkenhayn, standing in the yellow bar of light made by the open doors, was constantly dabbing at his forehead with a handkerchief.

Apart from the station-master – a small, worried-looking man with an unctuous manner – coming in to remove an upright chair from a desk in the corner, apologising for the disturbance on entry and departure, they were left to their own devices. When the field marshal's hand went to his forehead both von Papen and Weidinger noticed yellow sweat stains on the armpit of the third white tunic jacket he had changed into since the tour of his southern front had started almost forty-eight hours before.

The unit with the home-made mortar had been one of the better examples of the troops at von Falkenhayn's disposal. There were also some Corset Staves, German and Austrian support troops who were mainly machine-gunners and artillerymen, plus a company of signallers equipped with field telephones and Goertz heliographs. The rest had not been impressive.

Time and again von Falkenhayn and his party had discovered that what the chips on the Yilderim war-game table represented as an entire infantry regiment turned out to be a bunch of sick, demoralised Arabs or Kurds of half that ration strength – when they got rations. There were hardly any reserves, and those that existed were mostly the mutinous recently conscripted who had to be closely watched in case they deserted *en masse*. At the end of that last day in Beersheba von Falkenhayn was stressing the need for barbed wire, minefields, extra trenches – defence-in-depth. Von Papen knew then that Yilderim was over.

Weidinger bid the field marshal and von Papen goodbye on the platform. As he saluted and then warmly shook von Falkenhayn's proffered hand, he felt rather overcome by the gesture. Somehow that awful business with the mortar had brought them all closer together. 'Remember, you're my eyes and ears,' the old soldier said. 'Without you I'm like a blind man with an ear trumpet.'

Von Papen was about to shake hands too when they were all distracted by a commotion at the other end of the platform, where a crowd was gathering.

'What's going on?' said Weidinger.

'Why don't we find out?' said the field marshal.

They walked towards the crowd. On the way they met the unctuous station-master who had disposed of the chair. He looked rather pale.

'What's happening?' asked Weidinger.

'A Bedu is being hanged, your honour,' the official explained.

'What for?'

'He was stealing sugar from one of the quartermaster's wagons. They do it all the time. This one was unlucky.'

They walked into a crowd of Bedouin who stepped reluctantly aside. Von Falkenhayn pretended to be unaware of their hostility; Weidinger and von Papen ostentatiously unclipped the flaps of their holsters. When they had got through the Arabs they came to a semi-circle of Turkish soldiers standing with bayonets fixed around a railway signal arm. A rope with one end made into a noose had been thrown over one of the supporting girders. Beneath it three soldiers were trying to persuade a skinny youth with wild unkempt hair, tears streaking his cheeks and his hands tied behind his back, to step on the station-master's chair.

The boy – Weidinger estimated he was no more than eighteen, and probably younger – was struggling wildly and screaming over and over again in a high-pitched voice, 'Allah, Yah, Allah.' As they struggled their feet ground into the dust the boy's headdress and the black rings which had kept it in place. At one point the soldiers lifted him bodily onto the chair and were about to put the noose around his neck when he managed to jump off and wrap one of his legs around the putteed calf of one of his executioners.

One of the soldiers stabbed the boy with a bayonet in the back and the buttock and soon there were widening red stains on his robe. The boy began to scream even louder, only this time one word was particularly distinct. He was saying, 'Aba, Aba.'

Weidinger, who had picked up a little Arabic, found himself wondering whether the Bedu was calling to a spiritual or earthly father. In any event, he very much wished von Falkenhayn would either intervene or lead them away from the wretched business. Then suddenly a grey-bearded man with blazing eyes came to the front of the crowd and, ignoring a bayonet inches from his chest, yelled something in an angry voice.

The boy stiffened. The old man repeated what he had said in a quieter tone. The boy ceased to struggle and allowed himself to be lifted onto the chair. Ten seconds later he was choking slowly to death over the place where the chair had been. In his agony his knees were drawn up to his chest and his tongue horribly distended. The old man gazed up at him, tears coursing his own cheeks.

'I think he was his father,' Weidinger explained as they walked back to the carriage. 'He was telling him to die like a man and that they would all meet in Paradise.'

The field marshal managed to look quite shocked.

Von Papen said, 'I wonder how many English spies that business made?'

Weidinger shrugged it off. The Turks were always hanging people.

24

Weidinger was nominally leading the patrol, though it was impossible to tell who was in command at first glance because both armies had discovered that cavalry were less vulnerable if they rode abreast in loose, extended lines rather than in column. Horsemen were not so visible from the air this way, their dust being less concentrated. Nor, since they were more spread out, were they likely to take large casualties from a single artillery shell. That was the theory anyway.

They were a troop of twenty-seven Turkish lancers under a Muzalim-i-Sani, their weapons slotted into leather holsters by their right stirrups and the pennanted sharp-ends swaying above them like the masts of a little fishing flotilla. Each man also had a Model 87 Mauser carbine and fifty rounds of ammunition. The lucky ones carried them in the same sort of leather rifle boots the British Yeomanry regiments were equipped with. But at least half the troop had their carbines slung across their backs on bandoliers that chafed their shoulders as they rode.

They had breakfasted shortly before dawn on bread, goat's cheese, coffee and tobacco and had set off with the first grey streaks of daylight coming up behind them as they headed into the no-man's land north-west of Beersheba. Even at that point Weidinger was already beginning to feel a pleasurable little surge of adrenalin at the prospect of the unexpected.

It was, he told himself, only at times like this that he began to feel a whole man again. Certainly, it was better than walking on egg shells around a field marshal. He was looking forward to telling

Maeltzer about it. The journalist had wangled another one of his trips to the front, and a signals officer had passed on a message that von Falkenhayn hoped to be in Beersheba with his escort tomorrow.

Now the German bent to bite the cover off his watch, instinctively tightening his knees on his chestnut mare as he did so. The horse was one of the most sure-footed the lancers had, a Waler captured from the Australians at Gaza last April. Weidinger rode it almost as well with one arm as he would have done with two.

According to his watch it had just turned 9.45. They had been going for over four hours, occasionally breaking the horses from a walk to a brisk trot, but nothing too tiring. Most of the troop were on broken-backed, fistulated mounts that any decent veterinary surgeon would have retired from active service years ago. Weidinger turned to the Muzalim-i-sani who was riding alongside him. 'Shall we look at the map?' he said. He wanted to tell him his plan. There had not been an opportunity before because the Turkish subaltern had been asleep when Weidinger arrived at the lancers' camp late the previous evening.

All the Turk knew was that he was to take this German staff officer on a reconnaissance patrol to the north-west, roughly parallel with the railway track, and that his main task, his squadron commander had emphasised, was to bring their troublesome visitor back in one piece. Or at least with the same number of pieces he had started out with. The missing arm had come as something of a surprise. The subaltern was curious to see whether he would be able to stay on his fine English mount if they had to make a run for it. Still, he was a Uhlan. He had also had the good sense to kit himself out with a field-grey tunic, which he would shortly be sweltering in, instead of those tropical whites some of these Prussians insisted on wearing even at the front.

Once the troop had halted Weidinger offered the Turk his matches and a cigarette because he had watched Kress do this with Turkish officers to whom he was about to make a 'suggestion'. This one was, he thought, a particularly surly specimen: heavy-featured, but with surprisingly blue eyes and a straggly blond moustache.

'Yes, Herr Oberleutnant?' said the Turk, exhaling the words with his smoke.

Weidinger reached for his map case which was hanging by a shoulder strap across his tunic so that it hung under the empty sleeve on his left side. It was folded at the relevant section.

'I think we are about here,' he said, pointing to an area between Wadi Hanafish, which was towards the British line, and Wadi Imleih, which was just behind their own wire. About half an hour before they had left the last of the dunes and were now passing through a flat, cactus-strewn terrain. The place he had pointed to was marked 'Girheir' on the map, but if there had ever been a hamlet of that name it appeared that the Negev had long since swallowed it up.

The Turk scrunched up his eyes, as if the sun was already too strong for them, and stared at the spot where Weidinger held his finger. 'Perhaps,' he said.

'Where do you think we are then?'

'As you say, somewhere between the wadis, but I cannot be exact.' His German instructors had taught him to be exact. Now he was giving them their exactness back.

'Well, I think that's near enough for the moment,' said Weidinger, barely able to conceal his irritation. 'What I want to do is to enter Wadi Hanafish about a quarter of the way along it – that should provide plenty of cover. We go down as far as this fork –' he pointed to an upturned 'V' – 'and then dismount and a small party of us will proceed on foot up the left fork – the one that is going almost due south towards the British lines.'

'And when we have had this walk, what do we do?'

'We wait, we look, we see what we can see. And perhaps before we go we snipe. Leave them our calling card.'

Weidinger offered the last bit because he thought the prospect of a little action might please, but the Turk showed absolutely no emotion unless you counted another deep drag on his cigarette. Then he said: 'There are observation posts. The English have them at Khasif and Goz-el-Geleib.'

Weidinger looked at the map again. The places he had mentioned were hillocks, pimples a couple of hundred feet above the general level of the terrain. 'Can they see into the wadi?'

'Yes.'

'You've been there before?'

'Yes.'

'What happened?'

'Nothing happened. We went as far as the fork. No closer.'

'So at least they can't see us up to there.'

'Perhaps. But there were only three of us. They may have been waiting to see whether more were coming before they used their mortars. The English are cunning like that – unless they're Australians.'

'It's a deep wadi. They probably couldn't see,' said Weidinger with more confidence than he felt.

They moved on and after about ten minutes' ride came across

what might have been a nomads' camel track that appeared to lead down towards the wadi. They were going to descend when the lancer riding scout on the extreme left flank of the patrol, which was now in a loose horn formation, suddenly gave a cry and started pointing.

At first Weidinger could see nothing. Then he made out a moving figure, perhaps a kilometre away on this flat stretch of ground. At that distance it could have been anything from General Allenby to a grazing camel. His field glasses were around his neck on a short strap. When he had focused them he could see that it was a man on a horse riding towards them along the edge of the wadi and on their side. When the man was six or seven hundred metres away he thought it possible that he was wearing the kind of solar topee favoured by the British although he was not positive of that any more than he could be certain, at that range, that the rider was wearing khaki and not field grey. 'What do you think?' he asked the Muzalim-i-sani, who had produced an old-fashioned brass telescope from his saddlebag.

'English,' he said.

'You are sure?'

'Yes. It's the way he rides. Like a statue.'

'Then let's get him.'

Weidinger's Waler had a surprising turn of speed for a small horse. The German and the Muzalim-i-sani, who was on a good-looking grey, were rapidly about three lengths ahead of the rest of the field, who straggled out behind them like some spoilt Derby ruined by bad handicapping.

Ahead of them the lone rider had now taken heed of their presence. For a moment he ceased his leisurely progress and sat rock-still facing them, as if trying to assess the situation; then he turned his horse and, judging by the dust, removed himself at a smart gallop. Almost a length ahead of the Muzalim-i-sani, Weidinger pressed on, intoxicated by the chase. A decent reconnaissance was one thing; a prisoner, God willing even an officer, was gold.

But their quarry was obviously well mounted and it soon became apparent that not even Weidinger had noticeably closed the distance between them. The Muzalim-i-sani caught up with him, his grey foaming at the mouth. 'We must stop,' he said. 'My men are scattered. Besides, he could be leading us into a trap.'

Reluctantly Weidinger reined in, cursing the corruption that meant every horse thief in Syria could sell a broken down nag to the Turkish cavalry if he knew the right procuring officer. The others gradually assembled around them on their winded, wild-eyed, and, in one case, distinctly lame mounts. Weidinger looked ahead. The dust was settling. Surely this Englishman – it must be an Englishman – had not stopped as well? There was no immediate sign of him. Perhaps his horse had gone lame or had snapped a fetlock in some treacherous burrow of a desert rat. Perhaps, thought Weidinger, we haven't finished yet. He was in the act of lifting his field glasses when the first shot rang out.

The bullet zizzed alongside his head and passed through the chest of one of the lancers sitting behind him. The trooper collapsed onto the neck of his horse but managed to hang onto its mane long enough for two of his comrades to dismount and place him gently on the ground. As they did so three more shots came in close succession. One of these drilled the neck of the Muzalim-i-sani's grey, which threw its rider and bolted away in a mad gallop before it suddenly slowed and collapsed about four hundred metres away.

'You swine!' roared Weidinger. He thought he could see him now, crouched behind a clump of cactussy rocks about six hundred metres away. There was no sign of his horse.

Some of the lancers began to return fire from the saddle. Weidinger thought it would be a miracle if they hit him with those old carbines. The 87s were, at best, at the extreme of their range, whereas the British had deliberately designed their Lee-Enfield to be longer than the average carbine and a bit shorter than most European service rifles so that it could double as both an infantry and a cavalry weapon. This put them at a disadvantage sometimes when they came up against the Mauser 98, as they did all the time in Flanders, but made them ideally equipped to refight the South African war or score points in a skirmish in the Palestinian desert.

Somebody near at hand was yelling in Turkish. Weidinger looked down and saw that the Muzalim-i-sani was screaming at a reluctant trooper to hand over his frayed-looking palomino. Weidinger started to yell at the troop in German, 'Form up! Form up!'

Most of them didn't understand, but they were cavalrymen and they guessed his intention. Carbines were slung back over shoulders or rammed into their saddle boots, and right hands began to play with the lances. They formed a rough line, though three or four whose horses were truly spent had difficulty in bringing their mounts up. At the last moment the Muzalim-i-sani came alongside Weidinger on the palomino and started shouting out orders. Walk. Trot. Charge! On the last command the lances went down.

Weidinger's own weapon was a captured Webley .455 revolver Pichler had picked up after Gaza and given him for a bottle of cognac because Weidinger found it impossible to cock his issue '08 Luger automatic with one hand unless his knees were free to hold it. With the Webley he did not even have to bother to thumb the hammer

193

back for the first shot if he didn't want to as long as he had the
strength to pull the trigger.

Once they were at the gallop Weidinger was well in the lead.
For a moment he lost sight of the quarry and then he saw that
the land dipped slightly and that in this dip was the Englishman's
missing horse, a coal-black Arab by the look of it, which he was
now in the process of mounting. There was a crack behind him
and the zizz of a round passing uncomfortably close to his head.
He looked round and saw that the Muzalim-i-sani was firing his
revolver, while immediately behind him were half-a-dozen or so
levelled lances. The rest of the troop were already lagging but,
however badly mounted, everybody was intoxicated by the chase
and yelling like Apaches.

Weidinger saw the Englishman pull himself into the saddle and
rake his animal's flanks with his spurs. He was no more than three
hundred metres away. It was then that the Uhlan officer realised how
truly well-horsed his adversary was, for the black went straight into
a loping gallop and began to increase the distance between them
without any apparent effort. But one thing was for certain – he
wasn't riding like a statue now.

When Weidinger came to the dip where the man had mounted
up he saw that his rifle was lying there. A little further on came
more proof of panic-stricken flight in the form of a haversack
lying across the trail they were following along the steep edge of
the wadi. Then, quite suddenly, Weidinger realised that the dust
had stopped. The pursued had disappeared as neatly as a fox
going to earth. It was as if the ground had swallowed him up.
He slowed his chestnut to a walk for now it was no longer a
chase but some sort of stalking affair and it was necessary to
examine the hoof prints of the horse ahead. The Muzalim-i-sani
caught him up. He was carrying the dropped rifle and haversack.
'He's hurt,' he said. 'Look.'

Weidinger took the Lee-Enfield from him and saw that the butt
and the stock were sticky with blood to which fine grains of sand
had become attached, so that its woodwork felt a bit like emery
paper. Some lucky round had found its mark after all. Amazing!
He handed the weapon back. 'One of your men shot well,' he
said, fighting down the temptation to add that others had not:
firing a revolver from a moving horse when a superior officer is
in front of you was something that should be left to the Bioscope
cowboys. 'Where do you think he's gone? Into the wadi?' Weidinger was looking at the ground to see whether he could spot any
splashes of blood.

'Yes, there must be another track into it up there like the one we were going to take when we spotted him.'

The Turk was right. They soon came to it. The track started after a tall clump of cactus and led into the wadi around a blind corner. They paused and looked down at it, and then they looked at each other.

Weidinger knew that he could not possibly order the man to take his troop down there and that even if he did he would probably refuse. He would be right too. It was one thing to go into the wadi when the British weren't expecting them and quite another when they had been forewarned. Their man could have already reached his forward listening posts and the English would be in the process of preparing a reception for them. They might well send an aircraft up to look for them as well. God only knew they had enough of them nowadays.

'I suppose we'd better go back?' Even now Weidinger was half hoping that the Turk would put common sense aside and want to continue the chase. They had been so close to getting a prisoner.

'Yes,' said the Muzalim-i-sani, trying to keep the relief out of his voice, for he could sense this German would have gone on. Perhaps, he thought, he hadn't been paid in full for that arm? 'They will be waiting for us. He may even have been bait for an ambush. He shot at us when we had stopped. Most people wouldn't do that. It's almost as if he wanted to be followed.'

He's probably not most people, thought Weidinger. He's probably what Maeltzer would call a 'sportin' m'lud'. He's got bone where his brain should be and he thinks he's out on safari. But all he said was 'Possibly,' and turned his horse around.

They went back to where two lancers had remained with the man who had caught the first bullet. His horse had been recaptured and was standing nearby, its ears twitching back. The wounded lancer was lying on the ground with a rolled blanket as a pillow. His eyes kept rolling back so that all the whites showed, and Weidinger knew that he was dying. One of the men was fanning the flies away with his helmet while the other was failing to give him water from a canteen because it kept dribbling back down his chin, so that there was a damp patch on his shirt below the collar immediately above the spreading dark red one.

'Do you read English?' asked the Muzalim-i-sani. He had brought the Englishman's haversack back from the wadi and was busy spreading its contents on the ground. A franked envelope contained a handwritten letter covering both sides of a single sheet of notepaper, and some folded printed paper which turned out to be four large, white five pound notes. The letter was addressed to a Lieutenant-Colonel Bertram Coxhead, General Headquarters, Egyptian Expeditionary Force, Cairo. It started, 'Dearest Bertie,' and was obviously from his wife or sweetheart.

In addition there was a folded canvas-backed map with blue crayon marks on it and a spiral-bound notebook with a plain brown cardboard cover. Jammed through the metal spirals on the top of the notebook was the blue crayon pencil which had presumably made the marks on the map. There were also some slices of bully beef and hard tack biscuits wrapped in greaseproof paper which the Turk threw angrily away as if he suspected them of being poisoned.

Weidinger looked at the notebook first. On the first page was written, 'Wadi Ghuzze, El Buggar, Abu Ghalyun – no water holes visible.' There was little else in it apart from something about camels, and Weidinger concluded that Coxhead had intended to complete his notes when he got back. He continued to flick through its blank pages and then something fell to the ground. He looked down and saw some typewritten pages slowly unfurling at his feet.

There were only two of them, carbon copies on thin tissue paper, and both were marked SECRET at the top. Underneath was written a date – 22. 8. 17. – and 'Report re water availability Beersheba sector. Distribution limited to –' This was followed by various sets of initials starting with GOC and with BC coming towards the end.

Weidinger's understanding of English was very limited. He could probably have got the gist of the main headlines in an English language newspaper but not much more. But when he examined the typewritten pages Weidinger did notice that two words constantly recurred: 'water' and 'cavalry'.

The Muzalim-i-sani gave him a quizzical look.

'You have no English at all?' Weidinger asked.

'No.'

'Pity,' said the German, trying not to look too pleased about it. 'They might be useful.' He jammed the notebook, map and typewritten sheets into the right pocket of his tunic.

'Good,' said the Turk. 'Now I think we'd better go back before their aeroplanes arrive. The men are already too closely bunched together.'

'What about the wounded man?' Weidinger had almost said 'dying' instead of 'wounded'.

'He will come with us, of course.'

'Perhaps we should wait.'

'We can't wait. If the aeroplanes come there will be more than one wounded.'

They both knew that what was needed was a merciful bullet in the back of the head, the way the Bedu were supposed to do it when they knew they could not afford to be slowed down. Neither man had the stomach for it.

The shot man was helped back on his horse, and then the sergeant who had been obliged to give up his palomino to the Muzalim-i-sani got up behind him and rode with his arms around him as if he was a child, while the dying lancer lolled up against the neck of the horse with his chin on his chest. Weidinger was slightly in the lead on his chestnut as they spread out line abreast and went back the way they came. Every so often the German would pause and peer above him, but that blue sky did not even contain a wisp of cloud, let alone an aeroplane – which was strange, he thought. Perhaps they had something better to do.

He hoped Maeltzer would have arrived in Beersheba as promised. Now he was keener to see him than ever, for with his good working knowledge of English the journalist might be able to tell him the value of the captured documents that were burning a hole in his pocket.

Weidinger was pleased with the audacity of his plan. Showing captured enemy documents to a civilian was highly improper under any circumstances, to a neutral civilian was practically treasonable. Yet somehow it was hard to think of Maeltzer as either a civilian or a neutral. Uncle Maeltzer was one of them. He supported them. He wrote good things about them – at least, so he'd been told. He admired the way the Corset Staves did so much with so little. ('You pinch the Turks in the right places,' the journalist once told him.) Besides, he didn't want that miserable bastard Krag getting credit for spotting what he suspected was the worth of those papers, though there was no avoiding the fact that the intelligence officer would have to see them. But, if he could engineer it properly, he wanted to tell Kress about it himself.

They got back to the lancers' camp in the early part of the afternoon unmolested by the Royal Flying Corps. The dying lancer survived a journey which jarred his dressings loose and sent blood oozing down the flanks of the horse, and was taken to a field hospital.

'Another triumph for Anatolian stamina,' commented Weidinger when he was telling Maeltzer about it. They had met at corps headquarters where they arrived within minutes of each other. The journalist was just as grimy as Weidinger, having driven down from Jerusalem as a passenger in an open motor car which had taken the short route through Bethlehem and Hebron. 'The only information I want from you, young man,' he had announced, 'is where can I get a bath?'

25

'*D*o you have them?' said Maeltzer. 'Are they ready for me?'
'Why yes, Herr Doktor,' replied the little Jew behind the counter, one of two opticians who continued to do business in the Holy City.

Maeltzer ignored the Doktor business. It was almost impossible to convince these Yiddish-speakers from the Pale that not all German-speaking professionals merited that title.

He tried on his new reading glasses. The gun-metal frames felt comfortable enough apart from a tendency to pinch the bridge of his nose which could no doubt soon be adjusted. He produced a two-week-old edition of his own newspaper from his overcoat pocket to test them. The lenses seemed excellent. Easily as good as the reserve pair he had been using ever since that unfortunate incident above the Damascus Gate.

The journalist walked quickly back to the Grand New Hotel. He had a long despatch to finish on his recent tour of the front, which he would again be sending to his newspaper's Vienna office by train. This time his pigeon was an Austrian nun, a middle-aged nursing sister who was accompanying a badly burned Albatross pilot.

Maeltzer's arrival at the hotel coincided with that of the Widow Shemsi. She paused, he raised his hat. She smiled – it was obviously one of his better days. They went up the stairs together making small talk in French – he felt it presumptuous to assume she might have acquired a certain fluency in German – about the likelihood of rain and the shortage of fresh fruit. Although the entire citrus crop from the Syrian groves around Jaffa was supposed to go to the military

199

hospitals, Maeltzer said that it was possible to find an early lemon if you knew where to look and were prepared to pay the right price.

To prove his point he produced one from his jacket pocket, spun it in the air and caught it a couple of times like a juggler warming up. Would Madame care for one? He had another. He dived into his other pocket and actually did a little juggle with them, for this was one of his party tricks and what he had been leading up to.

No, Madame wouldn't care for one. He must keep them for himself because Madame could get lemons, couldn't she? Ah, yes, of course, Madame had powerful friends. Yes, but it was nice of you to offer. Not at all, we must all help each other through these difficult times.

Why yes, agreed the Widow Shemsi, and thank God they weren't more difficult. Jerusalem could consider itself lucky that this summer's cholera epidemic had not really been any worse than last year's, could it not? It could indeed, Madame. On this uplifting note they came to her floor and said their goodbyes before Maeltzer strode briskly up the remaining flight in an impressive display of energy for a man of his age and weight.

'You shouldn't tire yourself, Herr Maeltzer,' the Widow Shemsi called after him.

'I have a nun to catch,' he called back when he reached his door, slightly breathless.

'A what?'

'A nursing sister is taking my article to Vienna on tomorrow's train.'

The Widow Shemsi giggled. A nun to catch indeed, whatever next. She would have to tell Erwin that Herr Maeltzer's humour was much improved since his despair at that English boy's death. Major Krag seemed to have an insatiable appetite for gossip about her neighbour. He had even given him a nickname: the Bear in the Attic, he called him. It was the nearest thing to a joke she had ever heard pass his lips.

———————

The burden of Maeltzer's piece was that the beginning of the winter rains were almost upon them, and that the British had still failed to start their offensive against the Gaza–Beersheba line. This was despite the Egyptian Expeditionary Force's undoubted numerical superiority and a new commander since they had made their last disastrous attempt to break through at Gaza six months before.

If the attack did not come soon it had to be assumed that Allenby had decided to postpone it for another year. This was because, even if the British did break through in southern Palestine, they could not hope to exploit their success for long since the tracks that climbed along the Judaean spine towards Jerusalem rapidly became bogs and impassable to wheeled transport. 'And having recently toured the length of the Turks' Gaza–Beersheba line your correspondent considers the prospects for a successful British offensive to be slim.'

He wrote as he always did, scratching away on lined paper with pen and ink and leaving line between each paragraph. As the light began to fade he lit one of his sardine-tin oil lamps and worked steadily on.

This state of affairs, he continued, would undoubtedly persist until the rains stopped the following spring. Maeltzer reminded his readers that Jerusalem received more rain in its five winter months than most Western European capitals did in an entire year. Considering the volume of this winter deluge it was, he wrote, 'a great irony that water, or rather lack of it, should play such an important part in this campaign.'

He paused here. Presumably the British were aware of their lost assessment of the Beersheba water resources – unless the officer who had so carelessly allowed it to fall into enemy hands was keeping quiet in the hope that his haversack had been overlooked. Any despatch from a neutral correspondent based in enemy territory was obviously of interest to either side. Would Weidinger consider it a breach of confidence if he hinted that, after weeks of probes and cavalry manoeuvres in the Beersheba sector, the enemy had decided against switching their main push to this flank because of the lack of water?

Since he had gone on an escorted tour of the front this particular despatch required a censor's stamp before he could give it to his nursing sister who, even if she didn't know about such things, might well be asked if she had been given any papers to carry by somebody who did. It might even pass across the desk of Krag himself, and he didn't want to get Weidinger into trouble. This being the case, he decided to make no hints in his article about any conclusions the English may have reached regarding the Beersheba sector. He consoled himself with the thought that, if it proved correct, nobody would recall his remarkable prescience anyway. Editors and readers only ever remembered mistakes. He would have to content himself with a note in his diary. After the war perhaps – but would anyone care after the war? He could at least postulate that previous British cavalry activity on the Beersheba flank might only be a diversion.

Once the decision was made he got up and cut himself a generous slice of lemon which he squeezed into a small glass of water. He then dropped the segment in for extra flavour, having first run it around the rim of the glass so that his lips instantly met the faint flavour of lemon. He found it very refreshing.

Everybody at Fast's was delighted with Weidinger's work down at Beersheba. Even Krag managed a word of congratulations.

The contents of the captured documents had been telegraphed to Liman von Sanders in Damascus who had wired back a 'very well done' to the officer concerned. And in case there was any doubt that Weidinger's Iron Cross was on the way, Kress had remarked, with a broad grin, that it was a bit unfair that his tunic was so light when others had all this ironmongery to carry around with them.

For Kress the captured papers came as a great relief. In the last two weeks he had become so convinced that the weight of the British offensive would be delivered at Beersheba that he had been trying to persuade both von Falkenhayn and von Sanders that it would be better to withdraw their defence line into the foothills above the town. Von Falkenhayn wouldn't hear of it.

Now it seemed that the field marshal was right. The increased British activity in front of his left flank was a bluff designed to lure troops away from the Gaza sector. That is where Allenby's main thrust would come, just as his predecessor's had. There was no getting around it. And Gaza was as tight as a drum. 'Even if the Beersheba wells were captured intact,' the typewritten pages had noted, 'it is doubtful whether we would be able to draw enough water from them to sustain large-scale cavalry operations.'

And in the notebook were the pencilled jottings of Colonel Coxhead, reporting no sign of any water holes in the no-man's-land of Wadi Ghuzze, El Buggar or Abu Ghalyun that might alleviate the situation for an attacking force. Kress's heart warmed to Weidinger. He thought of him as his dashing Uhlan, the boy who had wangled himself onto his staff when he could easily have settled for pen-pushing in Berlin and strolling down the Unter den Linden with a pretty girl hanging onto his full sleeve. He had done him proud. No doubt about that! Germany had nothing to fear when it possessed young men like these!

Kress tried to imagine the anguish at Allenby's headquarters over those lost papers. He had already noticed that there had been no reports of British cavalry manoeuvres for three days now. The Bavarian wondered whether the loss of those papers had decided

202

them to give up their attempts at a diversion and concentrate on what their forces were going to do opposite Gaza. For it had to be soon now if Allenby was going to beat the rains.

26

*I*t was dusk and the evening breeze brought a faint chill that it would not have carried a week ago. Ponting sat at the entrance to their dugout, watching the Mediterranean caress the beach and trying to keep the insects at bay with cigarette smoke. He found he increasingly preferred cigarettes to pipe tobacco – so much less fuss. He had just poured some water from his canteen into his first whisky of the evening, had stirred it with his finger and was waiting for it to 'settle'. There was an occasional rumble of artillery from the British positions before Gaza. Nothing excessive, and certainly not that sustained grumble of one explosion merging into another, indicating that the softening-up barrage had started and that the attack Lloyd George had sent Allenby to deliver was at last on its way.

Was it possible, mused Ponting, that there would not be an offensive this year? It was getting late and the Egyptian Expeditionary Force were certainly ready enough for it. Allenby set great store by training. There was to be none of your raw Kitchener's battalions lambs-to-the-slaughter stuff in this theatre. But most of them had been ready three months ago when they already outnumbered the enemy three to one. In fact, if Allenby kept them on the leash any longer they would get stale. What on earth could he be waiting for?

Perhaps Meinertzhagen would find out. His superior had been summoned to Cairo by GHQ, and if he knew the reason why he had not divulged it. Ponting recalled he was looking pretty pleased with himself when he left despite what had happened to Nili. If his latest trick had worked this was understandable enough. And if it would

204

work for anybody it would work for Meinertzhagen, who seemed to have the luck of the devil. Earlier that month Ponting had watched him land an aeroplane more or less intact after the pilot had been shot up when they were bumped by a Hun scout during a recce flight over the Turkish lines. He had stepped out of the cockpit looking, just for a moment, like a man who had never expected to walk the earth again. After his last adventure he had been quite different: he had been simply elated.

'Oh me! Oh my!' he had said, diluting two generous tin mug whiskies with their last bottle of warm soda water. 'Lost me pack, lost me rifle – good one too. Let's drink to horse blood.'

'Horse blood?' For a moment Ponting had thought Meinertzhagen must have been practising one of the terrible rites he had learned in the land of the knobkerrie.

'Had to cut me nag. Lovely Arab too. Nothing serious. Little nick in the rump with my pocket knife, squeeze a bit and then smear all the juice over the woodwork of the .303. Might do the trick eh? That and a few things you've seen me scribbling away at from time to time, including a very loving letter from a certain Laura Coxhead which even enclosed the twenty pounds her beloved had requested for some "special shopping" – presents for the spoilt little darling, I shouldn't wonder.

'Of course, Careless Coxhead, his head full of sweet nothings, throws it all into his jolly old field pack along with a copy of a typewritten report on how hopeless the water situation is on the Beersheba flank on which a chum of his at GHQ has scribbled a sharp note begging him to see whether it's all true because he really thinks Allenby a blithering idiot for planning to attack at Gaza again. Then off he goes, doppity, doppity dop, not a care in the world until just beyond Wadi Hanafish he runs slap bang into a patrol of Turkish lancers.

'Now Coxhead is a prize fool – you know the type, GHQ is full of 'em. But somehwere in that dim noddle of his he has retained the basic instincts of self-preservation. He also happens to be mounted on just about the best stallion the Desert Mounted Corps can provide. So he makes a run for it but he soon realises that poor old Johnny Turk is riding dogs meat as usual and doesn't stand a cat in hell's chance of catching up. In fact, the next time he takes a look behind they appear to have stopped to get their breath back.

'Coxhead is the stalkin' sort, bit of a Bisley man in his time, and he decides to show them that nobody chases Bertram Coxhead with impunity. It's probably the family motto. "Chase me not with Impunity". So, he gets behind a handy clump of cactus and rocks, puts his sights up at four hundred and lets them have it. Knocks two of them off their nags before he decides he'd better be off but that's when it all starts to go wrong. He's stirred up a regular wasps' nest. Old Turkeycock has really got his gander up and he's firing away like billy-o with those silly little carbines he has. As luck would have it, just as Bertram's mounting up, one of them managed to hit him in the arm.

'Catastrophe! He's trying to hang onto his rifle but he's bleeding like a stuck pig and the stallion, like all the best, is strung like a violin and not taking too kindly to all this lead flying about. Not to put too fine a point on it, he's beginning to get a bit frisky and Coxhead is having difficulty keeping his seat. After all, they have winged him and it's beginning to hurt. The next time he looks he sees that the Turks are a darn sight closer than they should be. In fact, they're coming at him hard with pig-stickers levelled. This is a bit more than he bargained for. Let's face it, a lot more than he bargained for. Well, to be quite frank, just between you and me, I think Coxhead got into a bit of a funk. Anyway, he uses his spurs on that Arab like a garden rake and comes up at our own pickets so fast he might have been shot if they hadn't been expecting him. But, what with one thing and another, he's dropped his rifle and – oh Lord! – he's dropped his fieldpack with the letter from his missus and the twenty pounds in five pound notes and his bully beef and biscuits wrapped up in greaseproof paper and the report on the water resources ... Oh Careless Coxhead! What do you think?'

'I think Careless Coxhead should be court martialled,' Ponting had said. 'Then given the VC.'

They discussed how long it would be before they knew whether the Turks had swallowed the bait. Meinertzhagen had replied that he hoped Daniel would tell them. Sometime soon he expected to receive a desperate signal from their hero in the lion's den informing them that the Turks now knew from captured documents that Allenby's main thrust was not to be at Beersheba. Ponting had reminded him then that Nili had not got a message through for some time. Next day they heard that there was no hope Daniel could get anything out for the time being because the Nili network had been smashed.

Of course, they had both known something was wrong when the pigeons stopped coming. They had prayed, in Ponting's case literally, that there might be the kind of tame explanation for this that would give them no cause for real concern. Ponting had suggested that perhaps some pigeon influenza had wiped out the entire brood, but Meinertzhagen had merely shaken his head. And soon every story they had ever heard of the birds' unreliability came back to haunt them. The war was full of tales of feathered couriers flying treacherously into enemy air space, although Ponting, with his dogged optimism, had reminded them that the French had awarded one bird a posthumous Croix de Guerre for a heroic crash landing out of Verdun with a message and its shrapnel.

One monitor off Athlit had spotted the red and white distress signal but had been unable to send a party ashore at that moment. The next day, most ominously of all, the shore line refused to speak to them at all: no red sheet, no white sheet. Eventually, one skipper dared to take his vessel in close enough to pick up one of the fishing caiques belonging to George's clan. The fishermen were very nervous that the contact might have been spotted and demanded that some rifle shots be put into their hull as proof that they had not talked to the Royal Navy willingly.

These precautions, they explained, were necessary because the Turks were in savage mood. The Jews were suffering, as were the Bahai at Acre. And Christians like themselves no longer felt safe. One of them wept when he described what had happened to Sarah.

The monitor's news was picked up by the new RN wireless signalling station that had been set up on the coast at Rafah, near the old boundary between British Egypt and Turkish Palestine. Ponting got it the next day because nobody had brought to their attention the existence of an advance intelligence headquarters a few miles up the road, so they relayed it all the way back to Cairo via the aerial on the Cheops pyramid.

Ponting had been rather ashamed to find that his first reaction was one of relief that he was not in Cairo, and that it would not fall to him to tell her brother what had happened. He wondered if Meinertzhagen had encountered Aaron Aaronsohn during his current visit to the Savoy Hotel. And if he had, whether Aaronsohn would blame his sister's death on their desire to speed up the intelligence flow by using pigeons.

Ponting suffered more than usual sadness for the loss of an agent. His abiding memory was of the little figure in a hat coming through the breakers. But there was no guilt on his part, no regrets. Daniel spied on what was essentially a tactical headquarters. What he learned might be out of date within a few days. There could be no doubt that it was essential to receive Daniel's reports by the fastest means possible. Besides, if it came down to it, Aaronsohn's unquenchable flamboyance, his uniformed posturings around Cairo, might have been as much danger to his sister in the long run as any pigeon guilty of navigational error.

Ponting poured himself another whisky, put his tumbler on the sandbagged entrance to the dugout and packed a fresh pipe. A flock of migratory birds was silhouetted by the sunset as they headed south. The birds were another reminder of their most pressing problem: how to renew contact with Daniel?

'Who is Daniel?' Meinertzhagen had asked a few hours before he left for Cairo.

Ponting had looked at him incredulously. 'You mean you don't know either?'

'Search me, old boy. Nobody ever told me.'

'My God! I should have thought they would have told you.'

'No. Not a dicky bird.'

It seemed probable that Daniel had been in place and working for the British before either of them arrived in Egypt. Ponting imagined that he had been recruited in the pre-war years; that he had something to do with those eccentric ex-naval types who inhabited remote Whitehall offices and had been given the purse to concern themselves with things like the growing Turko-German alliance long before the assassination at Sarajevo lit the powder train.

Ponting always imagined that Daniel was a Turkish officer, perhaps from one of the Ottoman minorities with a score to settle against the Anatolian mainstream. He saw him as a dapper man, perhaps a whiff of *eau de cologne* about his cheeks, cigarettes smoked in an amber holder, disdainful but brave enough in his own way. In his more honest moments though he had to admit that, for him, Daniel's courage was tainted by his treachery. Certainly, it was not to be compared with the bravery displayed, even before her capture, by Sarah Aaronsohn, a member of a subject race. Be that as it may, he was the most valuable agent they had in play in Palestine.

'He's worth three divisions to Allenby,' Meinertzhagen had said, 'and now he can't talk to us.'

'Perhaps he doesn't want to talk to us at the moment. Perhaps he intends to go to ground until he's sure that the hounds have lost the scent.'

'This,' Meinertzhagen had muttered, 'is no time to go to ground.'

Ponting picked up his whisky which had gone a strange cloudy colour, the water from the canteen not being as clean as it might be. He took a large sip and told himself that the alcohol would kill off anything in the water. He wondered if Daniel liked whisky. No, arak, he decided. Daniel would be an arak man.

27

Grey-caped Asian crows, slightly smaller than their occidental brethren as well as being two-toned, groaned a last protest at the dying of the day. Magnus skirted the wall the Franciscans had erected around the Garden of Gethsemane and made his way along the track which passed through some of the olive groves that gave the mount its name. Each step was aided by a punt from his great staff. When he got to the Church of the Tomb of the Virgin he did not take the carriageway to the summit, where the Russian hospice had just been commandeered as a billet by newly arrived German reinforcements. Instead, he followed the Bethany road that at this point runs parallel to the Kidron Valley, the fold in the land which lies between the Mount of Olives and the south-eastern walls of the Old City.

Shortly after he had passed the fork that leads down to the Tomb of Abselom, Magnus left the road on its right side and descended into the flinty, terraced land that contains the Jewish cemetery. Here the observant are buried with their faces towards the Holy City to await the return of the Messiah, when those lying nearest to the ancient sones will be the first to be raised and judged at the Resurrection. Here Levi Smolenskin would be buried and had already paid for his plot. And here Magnus sought out a tomb which housed the mortal remains of a Baghdad rabbi.

Hebrew was not among the Swede's tongues, so he had no way of reading the headstone. He had to look out for a grave on which five small stones had been arranged – four light-coloured ones and one dark one placed in the middle. Once he had found these he sat down, with his staff leaning against his leg. He had come directly from a pew in St Anne's church where instead of the usual scroll for Smolenskin he had discovered a note written in German telling him to go to the rabbi's grave at sunset and await instructions. Nothing else, nothing to collect. Just to be there and place the message he had received under the dark stone. He did not know why he had to do this.

It was, Magnus feared, to be a meeting with the Fallen One himself, and he shuddered and scratched angrily at the ground with his staff. Below him the bent figure of a woman in a long brown cloak was hovering over a plot. Otherwise there didn't seem to be anyone else around. Lizards emerged from cracked graves and stalked the evening's insects with their tongues.

Magnus gazed down upon the city whose tortured stones had been awaiting his arrival for so long. It was the city he had dreamed about during the interminable winter nights at home. It was the place he had pined for as a young man while his contemporaries shook their heads and told him that the wheat fields of Minnesota were what a Swedish farm boy should see as God's Own Country. And sometimes they would tease him with tales about what they heard the Irish girls got up to in Chicago.

Well, he had heard the Word and he had never regretted it. Let the others have their Great Plains and their Irish whores.

The sinking sun behind the Temple Mount had set the el Aksa Mosque on fire – a nightly occurrence that for Magnus held a pleasing hint of hellfire. To the right of it he could see the other Islamic shrine, the Dome of the Rock, from where the Muslims believed the Prophet Mohammed had made a short visit to heaven on his winged steed Buyuk. And just visible beyond that were the onion domes of the Holy Sepulchre, which Magnus had vowed that he would one day purge of its Byzantine priests the same way the Lord had once cast the money-lenders out of the temple.

But Magnus loved Jerusalem because and not despite of these abominations. The unclean things were his mission. It had been decreed thus. The city awaited his purifying flame. God was already cleansing the cesspits of Europe with his fire. But this smaller war, which he did not fully understand, had made problems for His chosen agent in Jerusalem. When he first came, the fighting had not started and the authorities were far more lenient than they were now. Once the war became more serious the Turks had become suspicious of prophets and he had been thrown in jail many times.

They would have sent him home too, he knew that, but then Divine Providence had produced the Fallen One who was undoubtedly in the grip of Baal and, if his immortal soul was to be saved, required to pay penitence in gold to Magnus as well as to the old Christ-killer to whom the scrolls were delivered. Of course, he had never told him of this tax on his spiritual welfare. If he did he might not deliver his prayers to Magnus. And if that was the case he would be unable to cleanse them and then the Fallen One's soul would undoubtedly be lost and he, Magnus, would have failed in his duty. Once he had tried to explain all this to Mrs Vester but she had bade him be quiet and drink his broth so he had not tried again.

It was almost night now. The woman in the cloak was no longer to be seen. Beyond where she had been standing Magnus could see the dull glow of the rubbish fires in the Kidron Valley, where generations of Jerusalemites had dumped their garbage. Thin spirals of dirty-coloured smoke rose above the Ottoman walls of the Old City. Something stirred on a stone immediately below him, something quick and crawling – perhaps another lizard. No doubt there were snakes in the cemetery as well. Magnus hated snakes but they did not bite at night, or so he had been told.

Magnus shivered. It was, he thought, typical of the Fallen One to demand a meeting in such a place. In any case, he hated these encounters which, he thanked the Lord, were few and far between. There was a stench, a stench of evil coming off the man like sulphur. Also these meetings were disconcerting because he tried to change his shape although Magnus knew full well who he was and he knew Magnus knew. He scratched his staff in the ground again, irritated with this creature who would keep a prophet waiting. It was getting cold and his clothes were too thin for staying out at night.

So thin that they hardly hindered for a fraction of a second the bayonet which entered his back. It came through low and in an upward direction on his left side, wrecking a kidney, piercing a lung and nicking the liver. A strong hand clamped over his mouth and pulled him down on the blade which was twisted and removed, not without difficulty, and thrust in again and yet again while Magnus summoned all his strength to tear the hand away from his mouth and turn around.

When he did so he saw a figure in the same coloured cloak as the woman who had been tending the grave. The figure stepped back, transformed itself into the Fallen One, and then jabbed him again in the solar plexus. He tried to call on the Lord to strike down this evil-doer. But it was impossible to speak. His mouth was full of blood and his eyes were full of tears, and while he was leaning on his staff sucking at the air the thing came again, this time high up in his left side. Now the creature came close enough for the Swede to smell its sulphurous stink and pushed the steel up to the hilt and left it through him with the tip emerging just below his shoulder blades.

Magnus dropped his great staff and tried to pull the seventeen-inch blade out with both hands. After a few seconds of this, the big man groaned a little, but in an uncomplaining way; it was more of a sigh. Then Magnus sat carefully down again on the edge of the grave and tried once more to pull it out and almost succeeded before he rolled slowly over on one side and twitched a little before at last becoming still.

Hands tugged at the bayonet before their owner changed his mind and left it where it was. 'Poor Magnus,' said a gentle voice in German when it was over. 'Poor stupid thief.'

A hand went to the dark stone and retrieved the scrap of paper Magnus had placed faithfully underneath it.

———————————

Weidinger was the hero of the hour, Kress's darling boy. He had ripped down the curtain and shown there was nothing to fear behind it. The bumps were all being made by grandpa's walking stick. Now plans could be laid to meet the real threat. Weidinger had pulled off the big one. He had been lucky, yes, but the boy deserved a bit of luck, didn't he?

So when the arrests started some of the people around Fast's, including Turks, said that it was typical of Krag to try to steal Weidinger's thunder with some third-rate show involving old Jews and a religious maniac who had disappeared. It was the third person on Krag's list who caused something of a stir.

Maeltzer was arrested a day after Smolenskin, and ten days after he had returned from Beersheba. They came for him shortly after dawn, the decision having been taken the night before. Krag was not one of those present when the Swiss woke into his nightmare – he left the mechanics to the Ottoman soldiery. But he did visit the journalist's room soon after its tenant had been handcuffed and removed to a cell in the Citadel.

The intelligence officer had asked the fat garrison major who organised the arrest to see that Maeltzer's belongings were not tampered with. Indeed, he had stressed the importance of disturbing as little as possible. Yet when the nervous manager opened the door for Krag, apologising profusely for his slowness with the lock, the room looked as if it had been ransacked by a particularly desperate robber band.

Admittedly, some of this had been caused by short-lived resistance on Maeltzer's part before rifle butts brought him to order. The bed on its side, its sheets and blankets draped across the floor, but the rest bore all the trademarks of looting. Krag guessed that his fat major felt it was beneath his dignity to make a personal appearance and that some junior NCO had been in command.

The wardrobe door was open and its contents looked suspiciously meagre. The Bedouin saddle-bag had been pulled off the top of the tin trunk, the lid of which was up. Krag was relieved to find that it still contained several bundles of seemingly undisturbed papers, mostly old letters by the look of it.

Every drawer from the desk facing the window where he had seen Maeltzer working by the flare of his home-made lamps had been removed and emptied onto the floor. The sardine-tin lamps were still on the desk, as was the open spectacle case that had contained Maeltzer's new reading-glasses. But now all the case contained was the optician's receipt. What remained of the spectacles was on the floor where they had been crunched under a boot.

Krag pocketed the receipt and cursed them for their stupidity, for their vandalism, and for the poverty that would drive a man to risk the bastinado if there was as much as an extra waistcoat to be had against the encroaching winter. It appeared that nothing was too trivial to steal, especially if it was edible.

For at first glance he could not see a single lemon in the room. The Widow Shemsi, in her account of Maeltzer's spontaneous juggling display, had drawn his attention to the journalist's regular supply – which had set Maeltzer to thinking that a man could be partial to lemons for all sorts of reasons. For although most intelligence officers knew that a solution made from bird shit was the best and most durable invisible ink, lemon juice was effective enough if the recipient held the page to a candle flame before too many days had elapsed. An agent whose regular means of communication had been cut off might well resort to such tricks.

Eventually he located a broken glass lying under the sheets with a segment of half-chewed lemon at the bottom. Well, it was a lemon. And lemons were difficult to obtain even for a serving officer, let alone a neutral civilian. Not that he really needed any more proof. He already had enough evidence to convince any doubters – he was sure of that but, like the policeman's son he was, he wished to produce everything, however trivial or circumstantial, to show how diligent he had been.

Krag tidied the place up a bit, put the bed back on its four legs and picked up the blankets and sheets, which he noticed could do with changing. After that he went over to the trunk, removed a pile of papers and sat on the bed while he read through them.

They usually turned out to be rather short, hand-written notes from Maeltzer's editor. On a couple of occasions he was asked to keep expenses down and reminded of the ever-increasing cost of newsprint at home. But to Krag's surprise, for it had never occurred to him that Maeltzer might be a man of some standing among his own, the tone was often laudatory, praising him for the perception displayed in his latest article, urging him to look after his health, and generally reassuring.

'Be certain,' said one of the previous year,

> that any criticism that your despatches are too partisan must be balanced, at least for our fairer-minded readers, by the decidedly pro-Allied columns we publish from both Reuter's and some of your colleagues in France. Verdun has excited a lot of admiration for the French and even the English are having to learn how to die (you may have gathered the affair on the Somme did not go well for them) because they are fast running out of agile Frenchmen to fight the Kaiser for them and the Americans still hesitate to enter the fray despite the U-boat sinkings.

Then at the bottom of the trunk, right beneath the pile of letters, Krag saw something different. It was a piece of maroon velvet. He picked it up and thought for a moment there were two pieces of the material before he realised that what he had in his hand was the kind of skullcap worn by observant Jews.

Krag turned it inside out. There was a dirty grey label sewn to its black cotton lining that might once have been white. Somebody, years ago, had inked a name onto this label. Krag walked over to the window and held it up to the light. The name was 'Jacob Gonen'.

It was a very old yarmoulka, the velvet almost bald in places. What did it mean to Maeltzer? The intelligence officer sat there on the bed, running the cap through his fingers as if it were worry beads.

The idea came slowly and he hardly realised it had arrived until he found himself standing up and slapping his outstretched left palm with the hat. It would fit, he thought. It would fit very well. Anybody seeing the look of triumph on Krag's face at that moment might have thought he had just been presented with Allenby's complete order of battle.

A search through the desk drawers revealed a couple of full card-board packets of revolver ammunition; there was no sign of the pistol, and he assumed that it must have been stolen. Maeltzer's possession of a gun did not surprise him. Civilian or not, wartime or peacetime, it was customary for male Europeans to be armed in the Levant. Almost everybody else was. Even so, he pocketed the cartridges which, he noticed, were of American manufacture.

Krag almost overlooked the diary.

The green-covered notebook had been kicked under the desk and he did not spot it until he knelt to replace a drawer and saw it lying there in an age of dust, open and face-down and as beckoning as a ripe fruit. It was open at 14 August 1916:

> I have discovered that the mysterious Widow Shemsi is the mistress of Kress's chief intelligence officer, a certain Major Erwin Krag. The way a woman will exercise her choice in these matters never ceases to amaze me. He is a man of about forty, perhaps older, not very prepossessing to look at being painfully thin, gaunt-featured with permanently yellowed skin stetched over high cheekbones like old parchment. I have met this officer a few times around Fast's and an extremely unpleasant, misanthropic character he appears to be, curt to the point of offensiveness if you greet him. Nor is it that this behaviour is confined to 'neutral civilians'.

Krag paused to light up a cheroot. His face betrayed no emotion. He might have been reading about somebody else.

> My young friend Weidinger informs me that the man is as unpleasant to everyone else he encounters, particularly the rank-and-file Germans and Austrians at headquarters, but sometimes cultivates a most unctuous manner towards Kress and other senior officers. Weidinger puts this down to the man's own lowly social origins which makes him feel the need to constantly demonstrate his authority, behaviour which would be inconceivable in a true Junker.
>
> He has been attached to the German Military Mission to the Turks for almost his entire military career and speaks both Turkish and Arabic. Despite this, or perhaps because of it, he has the reputation of being just as Turkophobe as the rest of the German officers here who often give the impression that they would like to sack the entire Turkish officer corps (with the possible exception of that fellow Mustafa Kemal who is holding the British off at Gallipoli) and replace them all with Prussian NCOs.

Krag allowed himself a faint smile at this. There was a bit about the killing of Lieutenant Buchan.

> *28 April 1917.*
> Utterly distraught. I have no wish to leave this room. I am responsible, albeit unwittingly, for the death of another human being, a young British officer.

Maeltzer went on to describe the circumstances. 'Worst of all,' he concluded, 'I felt that Krag somehow held me personally responsible for it. He acted as if he was my moral superior and this added to my self-disgust, for I felt he was right.'

'Good,' said Krag out loud and then looked around to see if anybody had heard, quite astonished at himself. He continued to flick through more descriptions of people and places evidently intended to provide the raw material for the Maeltzer memoirs.

16 October 1917.

To the station to give the good sister my despatch. Found her easily enough in one of the Red Cross wagons marked for the wounded. Her patient was obviously horribly burned and in great pain although the poor boy seemed stoical enough about it. I suppose the last warriors to bear these sort of wounds were the Crusaders when their foes poured boiling oil over them.

11 October 1917.

Met W. in Beersheba. He was in a great state of excitement having picked up some important enemy papers from an English officer he chased when he went on a reconnaissance patrol with some Turkish lancers. He allowed me to examine them (swearing me to secrecy in his usual fashion) because his English is not very good. The papers appear to show that the English have no intention whatsoever of attacking on the Beersheba flank and that all their demonstrations in this sector are no more than feints and diversions designed to lure units away from the Gaza front, where the main thrust will undoubtedly come. I must say the more I've got to know the English through this campaign the more I have become aware of their reliance on tricks and treachery even when the numbers are very much in their favour. So much for their famous sportsmanship and sense of fair play.

The captured documents were in the haversack of a certain Colonel Bertram Coxhead. (When we were back in Jerusalem W. checked through the British Army list and saw that a Coxhead with that initial had been commissioned into the Royal Engineers in 1899.) They consisted of a letter from his wife containing twenty pounds in notes and two typewritten sheets marked SECRET. These appear to be a report made a few weeks ago by Allenby's staff concluding that the water resources in this sector were dismal and it would be impossible to make any large-scale cavalry manoeuvres. On the top right hand corner of this report was a pencilled note – easy to miss at first – which appeared to come from a friend of Coxhead's, perhaps of senior rank, at the British GHQ. 'Bertie, I don't believe a word of this,' it read, 'but the Bull does and it now appears that it's definitely going to be Gaza again. You know what I think of this. Why don't you take a look.' The signature was illegible.

Whoever he was he must have been disappointed when Bertie got back for the few jottings he had made in his notebook seemed to confirm the report. 'It is difficult to believe that even the camels survive,' he wrote.

Krag was in the room for over an hour. He left it considerably tidier than he found it, having replaced the drawers and most of their contents in the bureau. He took the diary and the optician's receipt with him and left strict instructions with the manager that no one was to be admitted until his men had removed all Herr Maeltzer's belongings to a safe place.

Then he strode up the road to Fast's, brow furrowed in concentration. He was thinking of how best to conduct the interrogation of Maeltzer and how the fat Swiss would react when he saw the weight of the evidence against him. Weidinger was not going to come out of it unscathed either. And all from a man of, what was it? Ah yes. 'Lowly social origins'.

28

REPORT TO COLONEL KRESS VON KRESSENSTEIN,
COMMANDER EIGHTH TURKISH ARMY CORPS.
SUBJECT: THE JOURNALIST KARL MAELTZER AND THE BRITISH
DANIEL NETWORK.
FROM MAJOR ERWIN KRAG. GENERAL STAFF OFFICER
INTELLIGENCE, EIGHTH TURKISH ARMY CORPS. 21 OCTOBER
1917.

There can now be no doubt that the Swiss journalist Karl Maeltzer is the British spy codenamed Daniel whose message was intercepted on the pigeon released by the Jewish agent Sarah Aaronsohn. It appears that one of his main unwitting informants was Oberleutnant Weidinger, who in many ways fell under the spell of this 'neutral civilian' and was not as discreet as he should have been. However, it is possible that Maeltzer had other sources both in Jerusalem headquarters and elsewhere. He is certainly connected with Aaronsohn who used the code name Nili for the group her brother Aaron set up among Zionists disillusioned with Ottoman rule. Attached is a despatch to Maeltzer's newspaper that was to be taken to Vienna by a nursing sister. From there it was to be mailed to Zürich.

It is written on lined paper with an unusual amount of space, three lines in some cases, between each paragraph. When I held page two to a candle flame a message written in 'invisible ink' appeared between paragraphs three and two. It reads: 'SA dead. My last pigeon signal intercepted. Smolenskin arrested. Magnus disappeared. German officer found your assessment BS water resources. Daniel.'

On the 16 October last Maeltzer had submitted this despatch for censorship after he had recently returned from an escorted tour of the

218

Beersheba sector of the line. His article was mostly speculation about the likelihood of an imminent British offensive before the rains and whether the water problem would permit Allenby to push his cavalry through Beersheba instead of Gaza. In my opinion it contained nothing which was detrimental to our cause. On the contrary, as is often the case with Herr Maeltzer's despatches, our enemies could only conclude by reading it that our forces would be able to repulse an attack now as easily as they did a few months ago.

But I was struck (and not for the first time, for I have examined his despatches before) by these odd spaces between paragraphs. Then I recall that an informant had told me that Herr Maeltzer was particularly fond of lemons and would go to some lengths to obtain them despite the shortage. My suspicions were aroused and I decided to intercept the newspaper report at the station and make some tests to discover whether it had been tampered with after it had received the approval of my censor's stamp. It was then that the message quoted above emerged.

Before I saw Maeltzer in the citadel I also ordered the arrest of Smolenskin and Magnus. I had interrogated the Swede once before. He was arrested by the Turks a little over a year ago and would, I think, have been hanged had I not questioned him and concluded that he was, if anything, even madder than he appears. At that time I had asked Mrs Vester of the American Colony to see whether he could be repatriated to Sweden but there does not seem to have been any progress. On this occasion he could not be found in any of his usual haunts and remains missing.

Smolenskin is decidedly not mad. He is, however, very scared and I think he is almost certainly telling the truth when he says that Magnus approached him and offered him money (English sovereigns, but of pre-war mint) to put the prayer scrolls the Jews call *kvitals* into the wall. I must add that I am greatly indebted to Oberleutnant Weidinger, who first drew my attention to the fact that Magnus seemed so amply funded, and thanks to the Oberleutnant's alertness in this matter I was able to have the Swede under surveillance for some time. This established the link between Smolenskin and Magnus although I was quite unable to prove any clandestine contact between Maeltzer and our speaker-of-tongues. This puzzled me and I began to wonder whether I was making a bad mistake.

Then it occurred to me. There was no clandestine contact. There did not need to be. It was well known around this headquarters that Maeltzer was a generous fellow and that when they met on the street he regularly gave Magnus small sums of money and exchanged a few words with him, sometimes I have observed more than a few words. During these 'chance meetings' it was easy for Maeltzer to slip Magnus some of his private prayers; prayers he had sworn him to secrecy about.

Smolenskin said that he thought that Magnus was mad, but in such hard times who was he to question divine providence? He told me that he had sometimes examined 'the gibberish' written on the *kvitals* and this had only confirmed his belief that Magnus was quite insane. He insisted, of course, that it had never occurred to him that this 'gibberish' might possibly be a cypher. Smolenskin is a clever old man and I find this difficult to believe. However, I am willing to accept that he was no more than a go-between for Magnus and the Nili group, for it is my belief that these messages were picked up by the fugitive Joseph Lishansky and passed to Sarah Aaronsohn, since no female could visit that section of the wall without causing a riot. I think in the case of both Smolenskin and Magnus we might try to persuade the Turks to show a little mercy.

When I first saw Maeltzer after his arrest he maintained an indignant attitude and generally acted, I thought, like a well-trained agent who was more than comfortable with the role he had chosen for his camouflage. He made repeated demands to telegraph his newspaper, to see you, to be visited by the Swiss consul. I said it might be better if he answered some questions first.

I did not confront him immediately with the secret message I had discovered in his despatch but rather concentrated on the more circumstantial evidence against him. There was, for instance, the matter of the reading spectacles that had fallen through the machicolation at the Damascus Gate when you were engaged in a conversation with Major von Papen. I showed him the spectacle frames that had been given to me by Major von Papen and asked if they were his? He said they were not. I then produced the receipt (attached) for new reading spectacles I had found in his room and asked him why he had felt it necessary to buy a new pair.

For the first time he began to lose some of his composure. We were sitting at a camp table I had asked to be brought into his cell and he began to mumble and then asked me if he could have some water and something to smoke. I ordered him the water and said that I might be able to find him a cheroot after he had told me what I wanted to know. I put aside, for the moment, the matter of the spectacles and asked him why he had felt it necessary to acquire the Turkish *laissez-passer* I had discovered in his room.

He replied that, as a journalist, such documents were necessary for the pursuit of his craft. He said he had obtained the pass by bribing a Turkish officer with the gift of an American revolver. Ammunition I found in his room would fit a pistol of this type.

Would the document, I asked, enable him to walk along the walls of the Old City, an area forbidden to civilians by the Turkish authorities since the start of hostilities?

'Look,' he replied, 'I admit the spectacles are mine. It was silly of me to lie to you. I supposed I panicked – just as I did when they dropped through the hole. I was out for a walk along the parapet and I heard these voices but couldn't see where they were coming from. You know how that place is at dusk, Major, it's quite ghostly. I was curious to confirm that the voices came from the gate below me, that's all. When the spectacles fell out of my pocket and through the hole I was embarrassed and ran off. Nobody likes to be caught eavesdropping. But if you think I was listening because I am a spy you're crazy. I thought the idea that spies listened in at key holes belonged strictly to Molière.'

This sounded reasonable enough so I permitted him one of my cigarettes and he seemed to relax. I then produced the despatch he had submitted for censorship. He obviously had not expected to see it again and he began to look very alarmed. I turned to the second page and showed him the scorched brown writing that had come through when I held a candle to it.

At this point he became hysterical. He attacked me, tried to tear the despatch to pieces, and had to be restrained by the guards, who manacled him. When I returned, a few hours later, he was calmer. He insisted that the secret message contained in his despatch must have been inserted by somebody with a grudge against him.

However, he admitted that he knew of the captured British documents on the Beersheba water supplies. I asked him who had told him about the documents and whether he had paid for the information? After some prevarication he admitted that the information had come from Oberleutnant Weidinger himself, who showed them to him because his own English was not good enough to gauge their worth. I asked him if Oberleutnant Weidinger had ever told him anything else of military importance. He replied that the Oberleutnant had never informed him of anything that would harm the cause of the Central Powers. When I asked who had told him of Yilderim he said that he had heard the word mentioned when he overheard your conversation with Major von Papen at the Damascus Gate. He said that he had asked Weidinger what Yilderim was about, but this officer refused to discuss it with him.

I then confronted him with the fact that he had gone to great pains to hide the fact that he was a Jew and that he had passed his messages to Sarah Aaronsohn and the Nili group by bribing the lunatic Swede Magnus to carry them to Smolenskin. They were then placed in the crevice in the Jews' Wailing Wall, from where they were collected by the fugitive Joseph Lishansky.

I told him that both Magnus and Smolenskin had confirmed this to me, lying about the Swede to see whether he might give any sort of indication that he knew of his disappearance. He replied that this was impossible, and would have become violent again had it not been for the prompt action of the guards who seized him. I warned him that if there were any more outbursts I would not hesitate to hand him over to the Turks for interrogation and this had the desired effect.

Once he had quietened down Maeltzer declared that he had never denied that he was of Jewish extraction but nobody had ever asked him. I produced a Jewish skullcap with the name 'Jacob Gonen' in the lining, which I had found in the bottom of a trunk in his room at the Grand New Hotel. He said that the cap belonged to his father, a medical doctor, who had married an assimilated Viennese Jewess whose family had changed their name to Maeltzer. At the suggestion of an editor, he had, he said, used his mother's name from the beginning of his career. Maeltzer said he was born in Vienna, but his parents moved to Switzerland when he was a child. When he was a young man he converted to Catholicism although he admitted that he rarely attended Mass. He was very vehement about the fact that he had no sympathy for people like the Aaronsohns because he was, in his own words, 'virulently anti-Zionist'. He said that he thought that assimilation and not a Jewish state was the best solution for the European Jew, and only fools envisaged a Jewish homeland in such a godforsaken spot as Palestine.

I put it to him that he had been a British agent for many years, probably since before the war, and that the secret writing on his despatch was an attempt to get a message out to a British intelligence officer in Switzerland because his usual communications to Cairo had been cut. I suggested that both the German High Command and the Turkish authorities might be tempted to take a more lenient view of his activities if he would co-operate with us. The first thing I had in mind was that he should give us the names of all his informants in Palestine. It might also be of interest to learn the name of his British Secret Service contact in Switzerland, although my guess is that he will simply turn out to be the military attaché or some other official at the embassy there.

There might be an employee at the head office of his newspaper who had been induced to allow an intelligence officer from the British embassy to look over Maeltzer's hand-written text after it had been printed in case it contained any emergency messages. I have in mind that we might get Daniel to pass on the kind of information we would like General Allenby to have at this point.

I reminded Maeltzer that, as he was born in Vienna, according to law he was still an Austro-Hungarian citizen and therefore could be charged with treason. He did not reply to this but it is possible that a rapid court martial and death sentence might concentrate his mind and a deal could be made. But he is a stubborn man and I fear not without courage. He may choose to demonstrate that his loyalty does not always have a price on it.

Colonel Kress von Kressenstein put the report down and dabbed at his brow. Etline was only ten miles from the coast, and after Jerusalem he was unused to the heat. He had moved his advanced headquarters down to the rail junction two days ago so that he would be better placed to meet a blow against the Gaza sector and still be in a good position to look after his left flank if the British should change their minds about Beersheba.

He felt oddly disappointed by Krag's report. All so simple really. A man who is licensed to collect information in the normal course of his work turns out to be a spy. What could be easier? Strangely, all his rage had gone. Instead there was a sense of relief. The Iscariotical bastard was not one of his Turkish officers after all. He was a civilian, a neutral civilian. Admittedly, a man he was acquainted with, had even held in a certain light affection. But by no means one of them.

He wondered why Maeltzer had done it? Commitment? Money? And how long had he been a British agent? Well, the Turks would find all that out before they hanged him, and when at last that moment came Maeltzer would doubtless be glad to feel the rope around his neck. Unless Krag did manage to strike some deal with him – and somehow he doubted whether he would or whether his intelligence officer was all that interested.

Weidinger was finished as well, of course. Krag had made sure of that in his skilful, understated, good policeman way. The boy would be lucky if he avoided a court martial and got away with that medical discharge he had been pulling every possible string to avoid ever since he came out of hospital. He could kiss his Iron Cross goodbye too. Kress wondered at the vanity that could have possessed him to show captured documents to a civilian simply because he was frightened somebody might steal some of his glory.

Come on, old man, he chided himself. You're forgetting what it's like to be hungry, and Weidinger was hungrier than most. His foolishness did not detract from the fact that he had done well to push those Turkish lancers after that English colonel, who had committed the kind of gross foolishness which far outdid Weidinger's blunder. And a colonel would surely be old enough to know better. Showing Maeltzer what he had found was hideously wrong, of course, and as far as his career went Weidinger would pay the ultimate price. In any case he had been on borrowed time, for it had been obvious to Kress for a few months now that Weidinger did not have the head on his shoulders for staff work.

Perhaps, when the ballyhoo had died down, sometime after the next round, he might quietly get that Iron Cross for him – fold it in with the other recommendations that always followed a big show. By that time the boy would be home with his mother and his sisters and his wardrobe full of spare sleeves. For the first time he began to feel a certain repugnance for Maeltzer. Damn the man! Damn and blast him for taking advantage of a generous spirit! It was almost as if one of his daughters had been ravished.

Kress went back to his work which was spread all over his desk in the form of situation reports, and over his adjoining map table in the form of coloured pins. Black pins for his side; red pins for the British, in deference to their old uniform. On the pins were little paper flags indicating whether they were cavalry, infantry or artillery.

The Bavarian stood over the map and stared down it. A forest of red pins was confronted by a straggling line of black ones. And not all the black could be taken too seriously. Desertions, cholera and malaria had reduced his Fifty-fourth Division to about 1,500 rifles, about one-sixth of its official ration strength. Ten to one the British outnumbered him now. His sick little army of Anatolian peasants and Arab malcontents was tying down thirty British Imperial divisions. Berlin, of course, was delighted. The Corset Staves were certainly earning their keep. And yet Allenby continued to give him time. What was keeping him?

Perhaps, he mused, that was the answer. Why wait for Allenby to attack? Why not seize the initiative? Why not strike him a blow that would knock the wind out of him, cause him to delay his offensive until the spring – and who knows what would have occurred by the spring of 1918? The demands of the Western Front might have trimmed this overblown Egyptian Expeditionary Force of theirs back to what the British originally intended it to be: garrison troops protecting the Suez Canal route to India. Allenby would have lost his chance.

He looked at the map again. There was a British salient at a place called Marshrafe. Salients were always risky things, a neck waiting to be chopped. Only commanders with overwhelming superiority could afford to risk them. What if he launched a surprise attack – no artillery softening – and swallowed it up?

He moved a couple of infantry divisions so that they intersected the neck. Then he launched a third in a frontal assault. Why not?

He examined the pin he had just picked up. It was the 54th Division. He shrugged and put it back where he had found it. That's why he had to wait. Kress studied the little red pins again. All that, and Allenby wanted spies as well.

———————

When von Papen burst in to tell Krag that the Swede was dead he found the intelligence officer already reading a report on the matter he had received from the Turkish gendarmerie.

'I suppose he must have offended some Jewish fanatic?' he said.

'Jews don't kill,' said Krag dourly. 'At least Jerusalem Jews don't.

They're too religious. It was more likely some Bedouin tomb-robber.'

'It's a pity,' said von Papen. 'Now you'll never know how closely he was connected with Daniel. How mad he really was.'

'Perhaps,' said Krag, 'but Maeltzer has already told us a lot.'

'Has he confirmed the way his network operated? At the tribunal he was so indignant I almost believed him. In fact, if your evidence had not been so damning I would have believed him. Has he told you any more, or does he try to keep to the same story?'

Krag made a hissing sound. 'Surely you realise we are dealing with a professional here? He neither denies or confirms anything. Even the Turks can't get anything out of him, and they have not been too gentle. He's the sort who will still have a few secrets left when he steps on the gallows.'

'I don't suppose they'll hang him though, will they?' said von Papen, who did not sound entirely convinced of the matter. 'I mean, after all he *is* Swiss and a newspaperman. I don't think Berlin would like it. Last time I was there I found people, influential people in government, far more conscious of our image. All this Allied propaganda – Hun barbarians bouncing Belgian babies off their bayonets and the rest – it's half the reason the Americans are in the war, you know.'

'It may not be entirely a question of what Berlin likes,' said Krag. 'We may also have to consider, however much it pains us, what the Turks would like – and they are not famous for the quality of their mercy. We might have to take Vienna's feelings into account as well. That's where he was born. Technically, at least, he's still a citizen of the Austro-Hungarian Empire. That would make him a traitor. And they put the same price on treason as we do.'

'So he'll hang?'

'Probably. His only chance now is to agree to co-operate with us. Use his codes to send back false information and I don't think he'll agree to do that. It's a dirty business isn't it, Major?'

For once von Papen looked impressed.

29

Suddenly there was enough light for Maeltzer to see his hands clearly. Then the words that proclaimed there was but one God and Allah was His name echoed down from a nearby minaret. Again he wondered how the dawn could ambush him like this. Surely he hadn't been asleep? As far as he could make out the last time he had slept was in his room at the Grand New Hotel, content in the knowledge that a good day's work had been done and a despatch was on its way to his newspaper. That had been six days ago.

Since then Maeltzer had often found himself re-living his last conscious hour or so of freedom: the way he had put away his clothes, then washed himself in the warm water the night porter always sent up before cleaning his teeth in the drop he had saved at the bottom of the jug.

Then the nightly twenty minutes with his diary, until the need to sleep drove him from his desk before he had finished everything he wanted to say. He had left the notebook open on the desk top, promising himself, as he always did, that he would finish the entry in the morning. A last piss into his pot, his night shirt twisted up into his right hand while he aimed well with his left; when he pulled back the bed covers he remembered how pleased he was to see that the maid had put on an extra blanket, for the nights were getting colder now. At last came that gentle glide into the untroubled sleep that lasted until the soldiers came crashing in.

Since then fear had kept him awake. Dry-mouthed, clammy-palmed, heart-thumping fear that seemed to banish both hunger and fatigue and left him craving only for water and tobacco. His head

226

buzzed. His mind never seemed to stop working, but he seemed incapable of concentrating on any one thing for more than a few seconds at a time.

Maeltzer supposed he must have had the odd cat-nap. There were occasions at night when he was conscious that he had allowed his guard to slip and permitted a visit from the two-headed man or, worse still, the shadow figures who whispered that he would only make it worse for himself if he struggled. But he was always awake and shivering to hear the same reedy-voiced muezzin deliver *fajr*, the pre-dawn prayer that at this time of the year came at about four o'clock.

Duha, the dawn prayer he had just heard, was two hours later. Gradually his cell became as light as it ever would, for the places for the condemned were in fact mostly below ground, with their high windows just above the level of a paved courtyard. Maeltzer was sitting on a palliasse, with his hands around his knees and a grey blanket drawn around his shoulders. The stone turned bitterly cold at night. He was wearing cord breeches and a now grubby white shirt that Krag had had delivered to him from his belongings.

His shoes lay besides the palliasse. His feet were badly swollen from his latest interrogation at the hands of an Albanian major from the staff of Djemal Pasha in Damascus, who wanted to know the names of all his informants. On one wall was an iron ring, from which hung two lengths of chain with manacles on the end. He was attached to these when the Albanian beat the soles of his feet with his riding crop while demanding to know which Ottoman officers had given him information. Each blow was worse than the last. But the Albanian was not to be fooled by the journalist's inability to even make up a name. He was unable to do this because all his contacts, apart from the long-departed officer with whom he had traded his Colt for the *laissez-passer*, were among the German-speaking. In the opposite corner was a galvanised bucket, which did not stink as much as it might have done because it was emptied most days and, in any case, by eating little he had managed to induce a merciful constipation.

Soon after he judged it to be fully light outside there was the noisy rattle of keys and the drawing back of bolts. For Maeltzer the uncertainty of what would happen next always made these few seconds the worst of the day. No date had been set for his execution. Would they trick him like this on that last morning? Give him no warning, no time to compose himself? Simply turn up with the hangman and his shadows with their soothing words and binding ropes and that anti-Semitic Austrian bumpkin Liebermann who called himself a priest? The man had spent most of his visits questioning him closely about the sincerity of his conversion. There had even been trick questions about the New Testament.

When Maeltzer asked the priest if he would take a message to Weidinger for him he became even more pompous than usual. 'Haven't you got that young man into enough trouble?'

'Father, I want you to tell him I'm innocent.'

But he simply shook his fat, Tyrolean head, manifestly determined that the cunning of the race would not pierce the guard of Father Adolf Liebermann. 'He heard you tell the tribunal that.'

So now Maeltzer had to rely on Ibrahim, whom he thought a particularly loathsome specimen. His only worth was that he had been incarcerated long enough to have discovered ways of getting messages out.

It was Ibrahim, not the hangman, who entered now.

'Food,' he said.

As usual his painted eye lids were lowered as he came into Maeltzer's cell. He was no more than fifteen, and one of a clan of partly settled Bedouin from around Hebron. A guard had told Maeltzer the boy was in jail over a death in some tribal vendetta; only his age had saved him from the gallows. Now he was the plaything of the NCOs in the Citadel while his family tried to raise the money to pay the blood debt. Otherwise, even if the Turks had chosen to release him, he probably wouldn't have survived a week. Meanwhile, Maeltzer was alarmed to see how well the boy had adjusted to the role of captive catamite.

The journalist nodded towards the camp table they had brought him, along with a stool, a few hours after the court had announced that he was sentenced to death. For some maddening reason Ibrahim always feigned not to notice it. It was presumably one of the luxuries thought more befitting for a doomed European. Maeltzer had found his warders to be quite decent on the whole, brutal only when it was expected of them.

'Is it all there?' he now asked.

In fact, Maeltzer could not have cared less whether it was all there or not. He just wanted to give Ibrahim the chance to mumble any messages he might have for him before the guard standing at the door felt protocol demanded an end to this fraternisation. The best possible message he could hope for was that Weidinger had relented and would see him.

But the boy merely gave an almost imperceptible nod and fled. The guard shrugged. 'He thinks you want to make music with him,' he grinned.

'Then he has a mind like that bucket,' said Maeltzer.

'Wait until you've been here a year,' said the guard – not unkindly, for he thought that any hint of a future, however bleak, was bound to cheer. 'Your friends the English started their bombardment off Gaza this morning. Their attack is coming and we shall throw them back as we did before. We'll chase them all the way to Cairo.'

'I hope you do,' said Maeltzer. 'They're not my friends.' Even as he said it he thought he was no longer sure who his friends were.

The journalist sat on his bed for a while staring at the bread and goat's cheese Ibrahim had delivered on a metal plate. A tin mug was lying next to it. He hobbled over and saw that it contained milk.

He tasted it and shuddered: cow's milk, practically unobtainable outside military circles, and hardly diluted at that. He feared these little treats for he was never certain what they were leading up to. Was he, for instance, being given the best wartime Jerusalem could manage by way of the condemned man's hearty breakfast?

Maeltzer sat back on the bed and found himself caught up in a spasm of yawns. The last thing he wanted was to sleep in the day and spend another night awake. He quickly got up and began shuffling around the cell. He made himself eat some of the bread, regretting that he had finished the milk because his mouth was so dry and he found swallowing difficult. He also attempted a little of the goat's cheese but it was much older than the bread, and he had always been deterred by its faintly uric aroma.

Maeltzer yawned again. He tried to concentrate on Weidinger and what he would say to him if he came. If he could convince the young Uhlan that his old friend was innocent there might be hope yet. Maeltzer tried to think of the kind of message that would most entice him to visit him. Perhaps the Swiss consul would persuade Weidinger to come, but first it would be necessary to have some sort of communication with the consul, and as yet none had been forthcoming.

Maeltzer had expected to see him at the military court which sentenced him, but had been told by the young and unknown officer ordered to play defence counsel that he was away in Beirut. He had told himself so often that the Turks would never dare execute a neutral Swiss that it had become a kind of litany, but now he began to give in to a nagging fear that the Germans would persuade their allies that he was not a neutral at all but a treacherous citizen of the Austro-Hungarian Empire, and that by the time the diplomat returned his fellow-citizen would be beyond mortal assistance.

Yet there was some evidence that the Turks resented the way the Germans had taken over something they felt by rights was theirs. One of the people tending to confirm this was the major from

Damascus who, in between the beatings he so scrupulously administered, was fond of saying things like 'By the time this is finished you'll wish I had allowed the Germans to hang you straight away.'

The major from Damascus had arrived the day after the trial, which had lasted a day and a half. It took place in the headquarters rooms at Fast's where Maeltzer had been brought, manacled, from the Citadel.

Three officers had presided – Kress, and two others he was not familiar with. One was an Austro-Hungarian hussar with a Slav-sounding name and the other was a Turk. Maeltzer had started out well, looked them in the eye, spoke with the mocking indignation of a man who could still hardly believe that things had gone as far as they had.

'As for this unfortunate habit of mine of leaving large spaces between paragraphs,' he had told them. 'This dates from my early days in journalism, when sub-editors used to demand these gaps so they could write in printing instructions and the occasional cross-head. Nowadays, of course, it would be typed by a secretary at head office before being sent to the printers.'

'And would this secretary have kindly passed on the original copy to a gentleman who called from the British consulate in Zürich?' Krag wanted to know.

Maeltzer had even had managed a kind of chuckle at that, trying to visualise the plump little Calvinist lady who attended to these tasks at head office having any assignations at all. Of his three judges only the Turkish officer admired his display, thinking such insouciance in the face of death rather admirable.

The reality was that Maeltzer was still quite sure that he was within minutes, if not seconds, of convincing Krag that it had all been a dreadful mistake: that he would soon be given a slap on the back and be walking back towards his hotel with their profuse apologies ringing in his ears and an invitation for dinner. All those hopes collapsed when the dam burst, the truth came flooding in and he heard his own shrill, lunatic-sounding protests.

From the start the tribunal had been dominated by Krag, who seemed to have taken on the roles of both prosecuter and chief witness. Maeltzer could still hear the intelligence officer's sneer when he denied that he had written the secret message between the paragraphs of his article. Every now and then Krag would get up and wave the offending page like some bloody dagger. Even to himself his denials, delivered in a weak and uncertain-sounding voice over which he apparently had no control, sounded feeble.

'This message, this secret writing, is not mine,' he insisted. 'It's either a fake or the real Daniel has somehow managed to intercept my despatch, knowing that this would be picked up by a contact in Switzerland.'

'And how could that be, Herr Maeltzer?' Kress had asked in a gentle voice. 'Have you not said yourself that you send your work back by a different courier on almost every occasion? Surely it would be impossible to intercept these despatches on a regular basis?'

Maeltzer had had nothing to say as he knew he would have nothing to say, for he had asked himself that same question a thousand times and never received a satisfactory reply. He had been asking it ever since Krag had first waved his wretched proof before him and the guards had held him back as the intelligence officer, in that obdurate, thin-lipped way of his, declined to believe that he knew nothing of it.

He began to ask it again the moment he sat down beside his aloof young 'defence counsel' while Krag was allowed to continue with his calumnies. How could it be, when he didn't even know who was going to carry them back to Constantinople or Vienna until he let it be known that he was looking for somebody who was boarding the next train?

He had to conclude that it was only this particular despatch that had been doctored. And in whose hands had it been apart from his own? The nursing sister's and Krag's. Why would either of them want to harm him? It was inconceivable that the sister would have heard of Daniel and lost British documents, let alone produce a phial of concentrated lemon juice and scratch away exactly the words guaranteed to do most damage.

Krag, of course, would know exactly what to write. And there and then, in the first hour of his trial, the enormity of what was being done to him had burst in on Maeltzer. It was Krag. It had to be. The misanthropic bastard had incriminated him, was willing to murder him even, for the kudos of being the man who had unmasked a British spy. As far as Krag was concerned he was expendable. He was happy to see him to the gallows, and in the process not only eclipse Weidinger's little moment of glory but expose him as a garrulous young fool.

'This tribunal will see,' Krag had said, 'that the accused has lied about almost everything of importance. He is a citizen of the Austro-Hungarian Empire, not a Swiss; he is a Jew, not a Christian; he eavesdrops on the conversation of senior officers but denied it until confronted by the irrefutable evidence. Then he admits that he has taken the trouble to acquire a pass by which he can enter a restricted area – where he just happened to be strolling one evening and brought his ear to a handy opening "out of curiosity".'

Maeltzer had been up on his feet then. 'Damn you, Krag! It's you! I know it's you. I'm no more Daniel than you are.'

Several Anatolian infantrymen had pulled him back to his seat and managed to give him a few jabs around his kidneys as they did so. 'A novel defence,' Krag had said. 'If the tribunal wishes me to stand down while they question the accused on this matter . . .'

But, of course, they did not. Then Krag had brought Weidinger before the court and the Oberleutnant had testified, shame-faced, that it was true that he had shown the journalist the captured British documents, and that Maeltzer had indeed examined them at length during the train ride they shared back to Jerusalem from Beersheba. Maeltzer had tried to catch his eye but when at last he did was rewarded with the kind of look the Uhlan normally reserved for people who disliked horses. That had been the last time Maeltzer had seen Weidinger.

He sat on his bed, trying to stifle his yawns again. His mind went back to that last night in his room at the Grand New. How he had put the jug and bowl with its used water outside his door as he always did, so that the morning chambermaid could refill it with fresh water. Then came a few minutes with his diary before bed. When he had finished with the day's entry he usually flicked through the previous pages. He had written almost three pages on his trip to the Beersheba sector and had intended to finish it in the morning.

He savoured these memories for a few seconds, rolling them about his mind for taste like a child might suck on a sweet. After a little while he put his hands behind his head, spread the blanket over the length of him, and allowed himself to stretch out. The early morning sunlight was filtering through the bars in three dust-specked shafts. It was much warmer now. Perhaps he could permit himself half an hour's sleep? He started to stretch, screwing up his eyes as he did so in an effort to wring the mind blank.

Then suddenly Maeltzer sat bolt upright on the bed, the straw beneath him crackling like fire. The diary. Of course, that was it. The diary. Where was it? Did the soldiers steal it when they went through his possessions after his arrest? He had witnessed the beginning of the looting, seen the sergeant in charge casually pocket his watch and fob from the bedside table, then the squabbling that ensued over his clothes as he sat there waiting to be led away, bruised and dazed with the handcuffs already chafing his wrists.

He couldn't believe that the soldiers had taken it. It was hardly the sort of keepsake that would catch the eye of the average illiterate Anatolian private. So it must either still be in his room or Krag had it. And the more he thought about it the more the latter seemed

232

sure to be the case. How else had he been able to fabricate such circumstantial evidence? How else would he have been so positive that Weidinger told him about his captured documents on the train back from Beersheba, for instance? If he could retrieve the diary he could surely prove his innocence. That notebook was full of names, places, what people had told him, thoughts, impressions. No spy ever kept a journal like that. Maeltzer levered himself up off the palliasse and did his best to pace the cell on his crippled feet. After a while, this became too painful and he went back to his bed.

———————

'There is a German officer coming to see you,' whispered Ibrahim when he woke him at midday bearing bread and a grey-coloured soup with an archipelago of yellow fat floating in it.

'How do you know?' asked Maeltzer, already trying to resign himself to the fact that the boy had probably got muddled. Hope was hard to bear.

'He telephoned the office when I was bringing them coffee. I heard them talk about it afterwards.'

'When?'

'Soon – perhaps one hour.'

An hour was too small a unit to measure by his ration of sunlight at that time of day. He dunked some of the bread into the soup and tried to eat it, counting the number of chews it took to render it digestible. Twenty-three. He could not manage a second mouthful.

Maeltzer began his shuffle across the cell again, telling himself that he always knew that Weidinger would come in the end. When he had done this three times he agreed that well over an hour had passed and he had been quite right in thinking that the stupid little pervert had been muddled or simply made something up to please him. Weidinger was not coming. It was obvious.

In order to encourage a decent fatalism he lay down on the palliasse. Hardly had he done so when he began to consider the notion that, in fact, barely ten minutes had elapsed since Ibrahim gave him the news. He got up and started to pace again.

No, how wrong could it be? If anything the cell was gloomier, the sun a sight less powerful. There was even a faint chill. He was a fool if he thought any less than an hour had passed. Then he noticed the soup on the table. He walked over and stuck his fingers in the bowl. The liquid was still quite warm. It was possible that it had left the kitchen no more than thirty minutes before. Unless, that was, it had been scalding hot when it was brought in. He was debating this while licking his fingers dry when he heard the footsteps and voices coming down the corridor and then the rattle of keys outside.

But when the door opened it was not Weidinger whom the guard ushered in but von Papen. The major introduced himself.

'Yes, I know who you are,' said Maeltzer, breathing hard, hardly able to conceal his disappointment.

'I wish to ask some questions,' said von Papen, stiffly.

'I doubt whether you'll believe the answers. Won't you sit down?' Maeltzer motioned towards the table. 'I'll ask the guard to take the bucket away.'

The guard carried the bucket as far as the corridor and called for Ibrahim. A chair was brought in for von Papen and Maeltzer took the stool.

'Well, Major?'

'I thought perhaps you might care to clear some things up,' he said.

'Oh, I would care to very much,' said Maeltzer. 'But I don't think I know what you think I know.'

30

'There's a woman who wishes to see you,' whispered Ibrahim. 'She give them big baksheesh, I think.'

'What sort of woman?'

'Syrian.' The Bedu spat out the word in a way that made it plainly synonymous with whore.

'I don't know any Syrian women,' said Maeltzer and he wondered whether this was some trick of von Papen's or the Albanian major's or whether, to Ibrahim's warped gaze, Mrs Vester might look Syrian. Mrs Vester was just the sort of person who would come and visit a condemned English spy – as if she didn't have enough troubles.

But, of course, he did know a Syrian woman. It was just that he had always regarded the Widow Shemsi as Turkish.

She came into his cell wearing a tight, olive green hobble skirt with a white blouse, silk stockings and shoes with little straps and buckles, and carrying a furled green parasol in a gloved hand. A guard held the door open for her. The width of her felt hat made her entry through the narrow frame the kind of careful triumph achieved by a deep-sea liner negotiating its way into a humble and unaccustomed port.

As soon as she was inside she drew a white handkerchief from a glove and held it just under her nose. For a moment Maeltzer thought he might be hallucinating but then he realised he could smell the *eau de cologne* from six feet away. A guard pulled up a stool and sat on the corridor side of the open door, smoking cigarettes and half asleep.

'Good afternoon, Madame,' said Maeltzer, levering himself off his

235

palliasse. 'This is an unexpected honour. I'm sorry if the air down here is not as fragrant as it might be.'

'Oh, Herr Maeltzer,' she said. 'It's distressing to see you like this. I brought you some oranges but they said they would give them to you later. I'm afraid they've opened them up. I really don't know why.'

'In case you somehow concealed poison in them so that I could cheat the hangman. Well, just as long as it wasn't lemons.'

'I see you haven't lost your sense of humour – may I sit down?'

Maeltzer nodded towards the table and then, to his horror, saw that his awful bucket was next to the chair she was about to sit on. He managed to shuffle over and move it to a position by the door while at the same time holding her chair back for her.

'Have you hurt your feet?' she asked, noticing for the first time the unshod and swollen lumps of mottled flesh he walked on.

'The bastinado,' he said simply.

'Oh my God! How barbaric.' She wondered whether her brother's feet had looked like that before Major Shemsi got him out of jail.

'They're not quite as bad as they look,' he said. 'Not quite.'

'Herr Maeltzer,' she said, composing herself by fiddling with a dagger-sized hatpin, 'I felt I had to come and see you before I leave Jerusalem.'

'Leaving? Where are you going?'

'I'm going to Jaffa for a few weeks. I have rooms at Hardegg's.' This was the hotel where almost every wealthy European or American pilgrim used to spend their first night in the Holy Land. ('Good sanitation. Cook's coupons.') 'Von Kressenstein has moved his headquarters down to Etline you see and – but I shouldn't be telling you military secrets!'

She sat with her hand at her mouth as if she might somehow force the words back in.

'Rest assured, Madame,' said Maeltzer with great gravity, 'your secret is safe with me.'

'Herr Maeltzer, you must not make fun of me. You know I shouldn't have told you. Why, if Major Krag found out –'

'My dear Madame Shemsi,' sighed Maeltzer. 'Even if I was the dangerous spy people say I am how would I communicate this startling information?

'Herr Maeltzer, I have something to tell you,' she said, playing with the hatpin again. 'I have a confession to make.'

'Ah confessions, Madame,' said Maeltzer. 'They're all the rage around here. Unfortunately I am unable to oblige although my feet would wish it otherwise. But they persevere. They seem to want to be able to hang me with a clear conscience. But what's this confession?'

236

'Herr Maeltzer, I feel responsible for ... your present predicament. You see, I was the one ... well, as you know, I have a certain friendship. I was the one who drew Major Krag's attention to your lemons. Not out of malice I assure you, Herr Maeltzer, but because I was amused by your juggling with your expensive fruit. Of course, now I know why you were prepared to pay so much for them. Not that I bear any moral judgement. I'm sure you did it out of conviction and not for money.'

'Were I ever to be a spy, which I most certainly am not,' said Maeltzer, 'I would only do it for a great deal of money. But are you saying that your friend showed no interest in my activities until you mentioned my little circus trick?'

'I don't know. How would I? The major would not discuss his work with a lady.'

'Even so, you seem to think that it was this that sparked him off?'

'Not quite that. But perhaps it was as if he at last had the missing link, the answer to something which had been puzzling him for a long time. I'm sorry. I am truly sorry, even if we are in opposite camps.'

'My dear lady,' groaned Maeltzer. 'We are not in opposite camps, I assure you. Why on earth would I bother to lie at this stage of the proceedings? It's hardly likely to save my neck. I really am an innocent man. As a young reporter, I often covered murder trials, and watched as some poor devil was dragged from the dock screaming his innocence. And, I suppose, I found their denials about as credible as you seem to find mine. Now I begin to wonder just how many of those poor wretches really didn't poison their husbands or cut a throat for that particular purse.'

Maeltzer looked away, rubbing an anguished hand over his face and through his hair – and was then astonished to feel a gloved hand briefly touch the one he had left on the table. He looked up to see his visitor gazing at him with an expression which seemed to contain an element of genuine affection towards him as well as pity.

'Dear Herr Maeltzer,' she said. 'I would like to believe you, really I would, but from what I heard the evidence was – well, it was very convincing.'

'You mean the writing – the lemon juice between the paragraphs?' She nodded.

'You heard correctly. It was very damning. It was also fabricated. My lemons were for exactly what you thought they were for – for making drinks with.'

'Then if you didn't write this message who did? I heard that at your trial you accused Major Krag of writing it. Is that true?'

'Yes, it is.'

'But that's a ridiculous idea! Why should Major Krag, an honourable man, wish to incriminate you in this way?' She sat up straighter in her chair, her hands clasped firmly together just beneath her chin, as though she was frightened about where they might stray if left to their own devices.

'Why indeed? I know it's hard to imagine, but I can't see who else would be responsible. According to Krag's own evidence my report never left his sight during the period it was with him for censorship. So there wasn't much chance of anybody else doing it.'

'I don't see how, even in your present position, you can make these wild accusations.' She was not looking directly at him, and one hand was fiddling with the hatpin again. For the first time he sensed that her indignation was a front. She genuinely wanted to know.

Maeltzer permitted himself another long sigh. 'Madame Shemsi, I don't know how much you know about my case. I assume you know what most of Jerusalem must know by now: which is that I'm supposed to be the British spy who calls himself Daniel and has amazingly easy access to von Kressenstein's headquarters?' She nodded, her lips compressed and her chin leaning on her hands.

'I fear that what I'm about to say you will find offensive,' Maeltzer went on. 'But since I'm very flattered that you've come and because you may well turn out to be the last friendly face I see before I meet my Maker I would like you to promise me to hear me out. Will you do this?'

'Say your piece. I won't walk out.'

'Madame, I'm sure that there is a side to Major Krag's character that is admirable, otherwise a lady of your undoubted quality would not have him as a friend.'

She blushed a bit at this and nibbled at her lower lip.

'However, the major has never been, during my time in Jerusalem, a particularly well-regarded figure among his colleagues, although they would concede that he did his duties well enough. As far as working with the Turks was concerned, he is the most experienced member of his staff. Nevertheless, it can't have escaped your notice that, despite his undoubted qualities, Major Krag has remained Major Krag. By which I mean he is old for a major, older than Kress I should think, and this in a war where boys of twenty-five are carrying his rank on other fronts.'

'As a matter of fact I never thought about it,' she said, honestly enough. 'I suppose I'm used to the Turkish army, where people remain majors for a long time.'

'Well, there it is,' said Maeltzer. 'By the standards of the modern

German army Major Krag is underpromoted. As you know, he is not from the traditional officer class. He comes from a fairly humble background, he's had to make his own way and all credit to him for that. But his lack of progress after a certain point appears to have made him a bitter man. His rank does not bear out his considerable talents.

'This inner demon makes him an acerbic character. He appears to have no friends, at least no male friends. Recently he has been on the receiving end of one humiliation after another. First of all von Papen, von Falkenhayn's poodle – who is everything Major Krag is not – is put in charge of the investigation into the Daniel Affair. Then young Weidinger goes off on a routine patrol in the Beersheba sector and by an incredible stroke of luck comes back with the crown jewels – one of the biggest intelligence scoops of the campaign. No wonder your friend feels eclipsed.

'But what if it is Krag and not von Papen who catches Daniel? Now there's something. Major Krag is in possession of a certain piece of information. Weidinger, young puppy, always anxious to please, has reported to him that one of our licensed religious maniacs, Magnus the tall Swede, has been changing gold sovereigns. Much to Major Krag's annoyance – this was one of the things that came out at my so-called trial –Weidinger has even hired a man to follow the Swede about the place and report on his movements. Krag orders Weidinger to call his man off and puts his own agent onto the case.

'Before long this poor prophet is trailed to the hovel of the elderly Jew Smolenskin, who is now quartered not far from here and may shortly achieve his life's ambition to die in Jerusalem. He pays Smolenskin in gold to place those written prayers the Jews call *kvitals* in the cracks in the Wailing Wall. Smolenskin swears that the prayers were written in the same kind of gibberish which the Swede ranted all the time – his pentecostal tongues.

'Your friend says that this was merely a cunning ruse, that these were not prayers but coded messages from Daniel, and that Magnus was part of a chain of go-betweens that got them back to the British through the Aaronsohn network, the Nili group as they called themselves. You may have noticed the reward posters up for one Joseph Lishansky, who was Sarah Aaronsohn's beau – at least that is what she seemed to want people to believe. He was the one who collected Daniel's droppings when he went to pray at the wall.

'What a brilliant piece of detection work by Major Krag! The only trouble is he is still no nearer to Daniel, who has skilfully ensured that there are two people, Smolenskin and Magnus, between him and his messages getting to the Wall. Of these only Magnus may have actually met the spy, and even then it is possible that Daniel avoided contact by leaving his prayers for the Swede to collect from various hiding-places, or even from a third person. For this Daniel takes endless precautions to cut himself off from the other British agents in the Nili group. He is like one of those Chinese puzzle boxes. You remove one box only to be confronted by another. At the very bottom of the pile (or is it at the top?) is a secret place called Daniel.

'So if Krag is correct Magnus would have provided the missing link, but poor Magnus is murdered. By a common thief? Another religious maniac? By Daniel himself? We will probably never know. Certainly, it was very convenient for Daniel, wasn't it?

'Now let's say your friend, unable to interrogate Magnus, starts to think over the people around headquarters who had anything to do with him. I mean, everybody knew him. He was always there with his ridiculous staff, gibbering at the sentries at the main entrance. And as the major puts his not inconsiderable brain power to work it occurs to him that the journalist Carl Maeltzer has often been seen slipping the Swede the odd coin, patting him on the back, that sort of thing. Could it be that he is slipping him more than a coin? Perhaps, sub-consciously, he has always resented Maeltzer for his access and a certain intimacy with Kress, who used to give him the odd titbit just to remind the German press that the Kaiser does have soldiers in Palestine.

'Suddenly it all seems to fit. The more he thinks about it the more convinced he is that Maeltzer is Daniel. For what other reason would Maeltzer be the *only* correspondent – foreign, German, Austrian or Turkish – to be permanently based in Jerusalem? A couple of other newspapers have correspondents in Damascus who divide their time between there and here and sometimes Mesopotamia. But why is it that Maeltzer has apparently persuaded his employers that Jerusalem is the *only* place to be when his colleagues seem to think that it is not worth more than an occasional visit? Why does Maeltzer put up with the heat, the dust, the malaria, the bad food, for month after month, very often not getting more than a few paragraphs a week in his newspaper? I think the major, being a thorough man, would have checked that sort of thing, don't you?'

'Yes, he is a most meticulous man,' she said, remembering the way his uniform hung at the end of her bed on the dumb valet he had had delivered to her room at the Grand New Hotel. 'Please go on.'

'As I said, it all fits. But the only trouble is there is precious little material evidence. His father would have told him that. Funny, I didn't know that he was a policeman. That fits as well.

'Let's look what he's got. If you will accept for the moment that the secret message discovered between the paragraphs of my despatch was not written by me, Major Krag has one exhibit: the message from Daniel which the Turks intercepted when one of the Nili group's pigeons went astray. Smolenskin gave evidence at my tribunal that it looked like one of the prayers Magnus used to give him.

'Apart from that, there is nothing but conjecture. I am a journalist. I have certain access. I may know more than I write. I have a friendship with a young staff officer who is known to be a bit garrulous. And yet Major Krag is *certain* that I am the British spy. All his instincts tell him this. How intolerable for him! How frustrating! Nor is it simply a matter of his own ambition. Lives are at stake. The Fatherland must be protected. In war the rules have to be broken from time to time. Even in peacetime policemen have been known to manufacture evidence in order to secure the conviction of a cunning and vicious criminal. And then, in the midst of all this you, dear lady, happen to mention the business of the lemons. Can he afford to wait until more harm is done? Isn't it his duty to act now?'

The Widow Shemsi held up a gloved hand. 'I'm sorry. I really can't hear any more of this,' she said, playing with her hatpin again. 'You don't have a single shred of evidence to back your theory. To me it just sounds like a fanciful web concocted to smear an honourable and clever man. There *is* evidence and it is against you and all you can do is cry forgery. I don't blame you for trying to save yourself, Herr Maeltzer, but surely this is pathetic? It has so little chance of success that you would have done better to have preserved your dignity by not starting it at all. I think I'd better –'

'No, wait. Please. There is not much more, but there is something I really do want you to know.'

'Just a few more minutes. Major Krag would not be best pleased if he knew I was here.'

The tone was almost conspiratorial. Once again he saw that her indignation was an act, something she considered propriety demanded. And there is nothing, thought Maeltzer, more proper than a lady in her position. She had no intention of leaving.

'At my trial young Weidinger testified that he let me see the British papers he had captured and thus proved that I was privy to the information discovered in the invisible writing on my despatch. Now I've never denied that Weidinger showed me those papers. How could I? I've written an account of it all in my diary which was lying on my desk when I was arrested. And yet, it's an odd thing, your friend never mentioned that diary, either to me when he was questioning me or later to the tribunal. Was it simply because there were some

241

unflattering references to himself? Surely the major is not such a sensitive soul? Or could it possibly have been because master-spies are unlikely to keep journals giving detailed accounts of who told them what and when as well as much else? Doesn't quite fit that sort of thing, does it? But it's a handy primer for manufacturing "evidence", isn't it? Perhaps you could ask him, Madame, whatever became of my diary?'

'But why didn't you raise it at the tribunal?'

'Why indeed. It just didn't occur to me. Like everybody else my mind was entirely concentrated on the words between the paragraphs. I couldn't believe that something so monstrous was happening to me.'

'Well, I suppose it is a strange thing,' she conceded.

'Will you mention it?'

'To Major Krag?'

'Yes. When you see him at Etline.'

'Oh Herr Maeltzer, that would be very difficult. He would want to know how I knew about it and that would mean telling him I had visited you.'

To his surprise Maeltzer saw that she looked quite frightened, even tearful. She dabbed at her eyes with her handkerchief, which was carefully replaced in her glove. 'Would it be of real assistance to you?' In her agitation she had removed the hatpin and was tapping it on the table.

'I don't know,' said Maeltzer. 'Probably not. It's always possible that it was picked up by a soldier as a souvenir, though it seems unlikely. It wasn't bound in Moroccan leather or anything like that. It was a perfectly ordinary child's school exercise book with a green cardboard cover. It may well have been destroyed. I'm sorry to impugn the honour of your friend again, but if I were him that's what I would have done. I'm sorry, it was wrong of me to ask you to inquire about it. Please don't do it. In fact, it was not only wrong but also foolish.'

'Foolish?'

'Well, if Major Krag does have my journal he might be tempted to destroy it. Besides, I've asked somebody else to look into the matter.'

'Tell me, Herr Maeltzer, since the tribunal I've heard people say that you are a Jew. Is it true?'

'I'm afraid I can't give you a straight answer on this. It depends on your point of view. It comes down to the age-old question: is being a Jew to be a member of a race as well as a religion?'

'Is it a fact that Yiddisher-speaking Ashkenazim, Ladino-speaking

242

Sephardim, the descendants of the lost Caucasus kingdom of the Khazars, the black Falashas of Abyssinia, the Chinese Jews of Kaifeng, Russians, Lithuanians, Galicians, red, blond, brown and crinkly-haired people, brown-, blue-, and grey-eyed people, white-, olive-, black-, and yellow-skinned people, some with noses as hooked as America's Red Indians who, as far as I'm aware, make no claim to be Jewish, are somehow all the children of Abraham? Surely the blood must have got a bit diluted by now?

'I can plead guilty to being born of Jewish parents, but I converted to Catholicism as a young man, largely at the urging of a female friend. She did not in the end marry me but I have remained a Catholic – more or less.'

'And hide your Jewishness?'

'No, I don't hide it. As far as I'm concerned, my racial background, if that's what it is, is irrelevant. I just don't make a point of telling people. There is a difference, you know.'

'How did they discover it?'

'They found my father's yarmoulka when they went through the contents of my trunk. I have kept it since he died – for purely sentimental reasons. I was very close to my father, a remarkable man.

'Like my mother he was the child of Galician Jews. My grandparents must have come to Vienna about one hundred years ago. They were very kosher, very observant. They probably looked rather like some of the religious ones who live here. They had some weird customs. I mean the small things that get in the way of ordinary day-to-day social intercourse. Those acorns of misunderstanding which become the great oaks of prejudice.

'For instance, they would enrage the Viennese, whose own manners as you probably know are as delicate as Dresden china, by doing things like asking for directions and then, once they had received them, walking away without a word of thanks. The Austrians didn't understand that these Orthodox Jews weren't being arrogant. It was simply that they considered that by taking the trouble to give them directions a man had already won favour in the eyes of God. To thank him might somehow rob him of the divine credit that was due from the Almighty.

'But they were ambitious, these Polish refugees. My grandfather was a rabbi and scholar who lived on the charity of his community. My father was allowed to escape the Talmud for medicine and eventually became a skin specialist. He did a lot of research on the relationship between some skin complaints and various nervous disorders. It came to the notice of quite a distinguished Swiss specialist in the same field. He invited him to bring his family and come and work in his sanatorium near Zürich. I was four years old at the time, the youngest of three sisters and a brother. I don't know when we officially became Swiss citizens. I think it was sometime in my teens.

'My father gave up the appearance of being an observant Jew. He had cut off his sidelocks just before he went to the university to study medicine. But he did expect my mother to keep a kosher kitchen, and the candles were lit on Shabat, when his yarmoulka came out and he would walk to the synagogue and decline wheeled transport for the rest of the day.

'I, of course, went one stage further, in fact several stages further, though the habits of my mother's kitchen die hard: I couldn't care less whether something is kosher-slaughtered, but I still find it hard to mix meat with dairy.'

'Aren't some of the Zionists like that?' asked the Widow Shemsi, who was adjusting her hat again.

'I believe so, but I'm not a Zionist – though if I were I would support the Germans because they're the people who'll make sure that the Turks aren't too hard on the Jews here despite this Aaron-sohn business.'

'The way they did with the Armenians, you mean?' She quite shocked herself with this. It was the sort of thing Krag would have said.

'That was different,' said Maeltzer. 'In the last month German influence has become much stronger. They have to do what they tell them. No, the Zionists will be all right as long as the British don't win. I think Jabotinsky and the others are fools to trust the British. They probably won't even let them be a self-governing colony. It might give some of their older imperial subjects ideas. Personally, I hope the Germans don't put too much pressure on the Turks to give the Jews a homeland. I don't subscribe to this *Altneueland* nonsense.

'But the reason that I don't advertise my Jewishness is not because I am ashamed of what I was born, although I'll admit that it is more convenient to be a Catholic. It is still amazing the prejudice one encounters in even the most enlightened and convivial circles. No, it is because I regard myself as a fully assimilated European. I'm a German-speaking Swiss and I wish to live out my days there. I don't want to be told that there is only one country for a Jew and that is Uganda or Palestine or whatever other pestilential spot some European power has decided it might be convenient to plant us.

'I'm sorry. I'm making speeches at you. I've been here for too long on my own. Too much time to think.'

She brushed the back of his hand again. Just the lightest of touches. It could almost have been accidental.

'Herr Maeltzer,' she said, and he fancied that her moist eyes sparkled. 'I like your speeches. I'm not sure I believe everything you say, but I hope they don't hang you.'

'Ah well,' said Maeltzer. 'At least that's something we have in common.'

She rose then and kissed him gently on the forehead, like a sister or a daughter. Before he could get properly to his feet she had gone, leaving a faint scent of *eau de cologne* behind. And something else.

After the guard had locked the door Maeltzer noticed it gleaming on the floor near the chair she had been sitting on. He picked it up, pricking his finger in the process. It was the hatpin. At least six inches long, with an imitation pearl top, it was the kind of hatpin that ladies had been known to preserve their honour with.

Maeltzer wondered whether it had been left there by accident or design. Surely she didn't intend it to be his last resort before the hangman? He decided it had to be an accident. By her lights she had risked enough already by visiting him.

He looked around his cell for a hiding-place. After a moment's hesitation, he plunged it into the side of his palliasse near the spot where he rested his head. Maeltzer lay there for a second or two, exploring the straw with his fingers until he discovered the pin's rounded top. After a couple of tries, he found he could do it quite easily.

31

'Have you seen Maeltzer since the tribunal?' von Papen asked Weidinger.

'Sir, two rats have ruined my career. One I shot, and I wish to God I could shoot the other. As I can't, the only place I want to see him again is on the gallows.'

'Two rats?' Von Papen's curiosity was aroused. This ruined young man . . . how could anyone have behaved so foolishly?

'The first one bit me in the arm. This arm.' Weidinger slapped his empty sleeve. 'It was in the Champagne sector. My regiment were serving as infantry. It wasn't ideal, but we had hardly seen any action after the first month of the war and most of us welcomed it. At least we would be doing something better than trying to protect our horses from air raids.

'We were expecting a French attack. They were trying to take the pressure off Verdun. Two nights before it happened I was bitten by a rat while sleeping. You probably know, it happens all the time in France. They feed on the dead and in latrines, and they're in every dugout. We had just taken over and the previous unit, Bavarians I think, had been a bit slack over sanitation. Anyway, I found the damn thing with a flashlight and shot it with my Luger.

'I thought nothing of it. But the next morning the bite had begun to fester and the arm to swell. I swabbed it with brandy and put a wound dressing on it. The following day it was really getting painful and was obviously badly infected. I suppose it had taken quite a bite. You see, it wasn't attacking me. It was trying to eat me, mistaking

246

me for a corpse. It must have been a very old and stupid rat. Not like Maeltzer at all.'

Von Papen grimaced. He found himself wondering how Weidinger could have gone through all this and still remain so in love with his chosen profession.

'I showed it to our medical officer who put a dressing on but told me I should go to the divisional field hospital and get it properly treated. But, of course, I didn't go. We were expecting an attack and I wanted to be with my men. I got one of our own stretcher-bearers to drain and dress it as best he could.

'The next day the attack came. The French took part of our line. Our regiment was virtually cut off for eight days. We had to bring everything up at night.

'By the time we were relieved I was lying among the wounded. I had hardly received a scratch from the poilus; some grenade splinters in the leg, that's all. But I had an extremely high temperature and was almost crazy with pain from the rat bite, which was throbbing like a thousand toothaches. I was practically delirious. One of the orderlies thought I might even have rabies. The field hospital was in a church. Lines of us were waiting outside on stretchers for the surgeon. It was raining – drizzle at first but then suddenly it got heavy, almost as if I was lying under a waterfall. I looked up and saw the water gushing out of the mouth of this corner gargoyle right onto the end of my stretcher which was soon full of water. I just lay there looking at it until some orderlies spotted what was happening and moved me. I remember that very clearly out of my delirium.

'When my turn came it was night. I vaguely recall the smell of the oil lamps in the operating theatre before the chloroform knocked me out. They told me afterwards that it had turned gangrenous. A doctor friend of my father's told him that he thought the arm could probably have been saved had it been properly drained, but it was late and the sawbones had had a very hard day. A decision had to be made. I'm not bitter. At least, I used not to be bitter. It could have been a shell. It happened to be a rat. And rats don't rate Iron Crosses.

'Maeltzer was the other rat in my life, the biggest and the cleverest. Perhaps I was a little indiscreet with him at times, but nothing stupid – and there were things Kress wanted to get into a neutral newspaper. I always had complete confidence in Maeltzer because he was so whole-heartedly on our side. None of your neutral observer there. What an actor, what a chameleon our Jew turned out to be! I had no idea. Now I know it I can see it. But on my oath, I never suspected for one moment that he was Jewish. It just didn't cross my mind. It should have done because half those socialist swine on the Berlin press before the war were Jews. But somehow Maeltzer, I don't know. . . .

'The strange thing is I've always regarded myself as a good judge of character. When I commanded my first troop in '13, my squadron commander congratulated me about the way I handled my men – the way I could tell a good 'un from a bad 'un. Not that we get many bad 'uns in my regiment. But I couldn't tell this bad 'un. I think I must have been under a spell. Perhaps I'm only a good judge of German character?'

Weidinger shrugged, slumped in his chair before von Papen's desk at Fast's, the picture of defeat. He was indifferent to the other's seniority, for he already felt a civilian.

'Being a Jew doesn't necessarily make him a spy,' said von Papen. Weidinger found his tone irritating; it reminded him of a schoolmaster.

'The Aaronsohns are only one faction of the Zionists,' the ADC went on. 'The headquarters of the movement is still in Copenhagen even if the Rothschilds do try to call the tune.'

'Yes, that may well be,' said Weidinger, refusing to be mollified. 'The point is he always made such a damned secret of his Jewishness.'

Von Papen gave him a quizzical look. 'Tell me something, would you have been so friendly if you had known he was Jewish?'

'Of course not!'

'Then why should he tell you?'

'It was all part of his lies,' insisted Weidinger.

'Was it? Did he ever tell you he was not Jewish?'

'No. One just assumed.'

'He still denies he is Daniel? Says Krag wrote the secret message on his despatch?'

'Yes, he does.'

'Extraordinary.'

'He also told me about his diary. Do you remember him keeping a diary?'

'Oh yes. A green-covered exercise book. He was always scribbling away in it. He used to say it was for his memoirs.'

'He claims that everything he ever did of importance was in that journal. People, places. . . .'

'Well, that was my impression. Every fart and sneeze he ever made lovingly recorded. Also some mention of the soldiers he encountered in these parts.'

248

'Wouldn't that be an odd thing for a spy to do though?' asked von Papen. 'Surely, if it was a true account, it would be a very odd thing to do?'

'Perhaps it was intended to be camouflage? A lot left out and a lot of lies put in?' suggested Weidinger. But he was beginning to perk up a bit, sit straighter in his chair.

'It could be. To my mind the odd thing is that it was not produced at the tribunal.'

'I suppose the Turks could have taken it?'

'I've asked them and they say they didn't. I think you would probably agree that doesn't mean much, but apparently there was no officer on that raid. I can't imagine some Turkish sergeant or one of his men bothering to pick up a book.'

'So where is it?'

'Good question. Major Krag might know, but he's no longer here. He went down to the new headquarters at Etline with Kress and the others the day before yesterday.'

'But surely if he had it he would have produced it at the tribunal?'

'Ye-es – unless he didn't find anything of interest in it.'

'There *must* have been something of interest in it.'

'Well, one would have thought so,' said von Papen in a puzzled voice. 'Then again, perhaps it *was*, as you said, all farts and sneezes.'

'In this context I should have thought even those could be of interest.'

'Yes, but Major Krag is an experienced intelligence officer. He knows what's important. Wouldn't you agree?'

'Oh yes, he knows what's important,' said Weidinger bleakly. 'And, of course, he was very pleased with – well, everybody was very pleased with him. Kress in particular. He was delighted that he had cleared up the Daniel Affair.'

'Quite so,' said von Papen, shuffling some papers on his desk and avoiding the other's gaze.

Weidinger sat there, waiting for the other to continue, his posture beginning to return to its former slouch. The pause was in danger of becoming indecent, a yawning punctuation, when the younger man, suddenly upright again, a little bead of sweat forming on his brow, said: 'You think Maeltzer's innocent, don't you? You don't believe he's Daniel?'

The words echoed around the room like a drum.

'I believe there is room for doubt,' said von Papen, in a prim, rank-pulling tone.

There were limits, frontiers of behaviour he was not prepared to cross. It was his calculation, his almost total lack of impulse, that made von Papen so much cleverer than people like Weidinger whose emotions were already hitched to the ever-widening pendulum of the incipient manic-depressive.

The ADC detected some of this and was alarmed to find the old jaunty exterior already so visibly fissured. He wondered whether a man who felt his star had run its course would even be able to accomplish the small thing he now had in mind. He had the look of a young man whose pistol might soon be reaching for his temple. God knows he had seen it often enough before the war with Weidinger's sort. They were fine with the wind behind them, capable of great physical bravery and endurance. But when it came to more subtle wounds they had little resilience. Humiliation was the worst blow of all.

'And does he still insist that he didn't murder his holy friend?'

'Yes, he does. He appears to be quite upset about it. He said there was no harm in the man.'

'But if not Maeltzer – who?'

'Well, the motive could have been exactly what we would have assumed it was had Krag – thanks to you, of course – not discovered his involvement with Daniel and the Aaronsohns. Robbery. His empty purse was found some metres away from the body, tossed onto a grave.'

'That could have been anybody – a passing Turk.'

'Do Turks pass through the Jewish cemetery?'

'If they're looking for a grave to rob they do. Arabs and Turks.'

Von Papen found himself becoming increasingly irritated by the other's truculence. He longed to say something like: 'Pull yourself together and sit up straight, man!' But what if he didn't? In any case, he was saving something that would probably correct his posture.

'Well that may be, Oberleutnant. But to get back to the matter at hand, I find this business of the missing diary puzzling. What I want you to do is go down to Etline and deliver Major Krag a note from me asking if he has any idea of its whereabouts. I should tell you that I have already sent him two encoded telegrams but have not yet received any reply. Of course, everybody down at Eighth Army Corps is very busy at the moment and I hesitate to involve Colonel von Kressenstein himself. As you may have heard, since six o'clock this morning he has had the British offensive on his hands.'

'Sir? I heard the bombardment had started at Gaza but –'

'No, not at Gaza. It looks as though you may have been intended to pick up those documents, Weidinger. The bombardment started at Gaza all right but it was the Englishmen's last trick. Allenby has attacked at Beersheba.'

PART 4
The Plain of Philistia

32

*P*onting's throat was parched, his eyes burned, and his ears felt as though half the Sinai had been poured into them and somebody had rammed in a cork. He had tried to unblock them by squeezing his nose and blowing but it didn't seem to work. From the hills above him came a series of hollow clanging sounds, as if great sheets of corrugated iron were falling on concrete. The British artillery had been keeping up a steady harassing fire for almost twelve hours now, ever since Allenby had launched the second stage of his offensive at five o'clock that morning, about three days behind schedule. In between the salvoes could be heard the crump of incoming rounds. The Turks might be on the verge of a general retreat, but they did not appear to be short of ammunition.

The intelligence officer took another guilty swig from his water-bottle, holding down the map it was helping to keep in place as he did so. He was seated at a desk that, exactly a week before, had been used by Ismet Bey's *aide de camp* and still bore several traces of that gentleman's occupation, including a bottle of scent somehow left undrunk by the victorious Australian Light Horse.

A *khamsin* wind, that clinging fog of mobile desert dust, had smothered the town ever since the Australians captured it. Apart from reducing visibility and forcing itself into every orifice of the Egyptian Expeditionary Force, it had considerably added to Allenby's water problem and hence to Ponting's guilt. Every man on the British right flank now seemed to be drinking almost twice the allocated ration of four pints a day.

Aaronsohn's ancient wells at Abasan el Kebir and Khalasa, the ones corroborated by no less than Josephus Flavius in the agronomist's original report to Ponting, had been there all right. Ponting had been present at Abasan el Kebir when Aaronsohn ordered some mystified Royal Engineers to start drilling near a pile of rocks alongside an old camel track.

At one stage the soldiers had wanted to call it off – and would have done so if Aaronsohn had not begged them to continue, and Ponting had not outranked the officer in charge. And suddenly there it was, yellow and brackish at first because of the amount of topsoil they had dislodged but then, after they had pumped out the first few gallons, marvellously sweet and refreshing: water that had not seen daylight in two thousand years.

'A bleedin' miracle!' one of the sweating Sappers had declared. And Aaronsohn had smiled, which Ponting had observed to be a rare thing since his sister's death – an event which, with Allenby's blessing, he had taken to retelling to assembled battalions in order to disabuse them of any lingering notions that, unlike the Hun, Johnny Turk was a bit of a gent.

On the British side of the line the water problem had been solved. It started again once they captured Beersheba. For although the fantastic charge by the Australian Light Horse had resulted in most of the wells in the town being seized before the demolition charges could be fired, they had not lived up to expectations. They simply did not pump enough water. Some of the Australians had had to ride back to Karm to water their horses – a round trip of almost thirty miles.

Ponting went back to his map. He had before him a deciphered wireless message from GHQ, to Lieutenant-Generals Sir Harry Chauvel and Sir Philip Chetwode, Bart, who were, respectively, commanders of the sector's cavalry and infantry – in all about 40,000 men. Partly, Ponting was pleased to say, through his own recommendations, based on analysis of interrogation reports of officer prisoners and their revelations about water supplies, Allenby had now modified his plans.

He had intended to send his cavalry up to a place called Tel En Nejile, which was on the main railway line south from Junction Station. It was to have been an ambitious outflanking movement designed to net von Kressenstein's Eighth Army Corps and some of the Turkish Seventh before they had time to get back to their well-prepared concentric defences in the hills around Jerusalem. Now the *khamsin* had obliged him to reduce the size of the net. Instead of Tel En Nejile, the cavalry were going to try to advance in a more north-westerly direction and capture Jemmameh and Huj.

Ponting had himself confirmed that there was adequate water there in a ludicrously simple way. Among the prisoners was a proud young Damascene captain of the 27th Division who had been knocked senseless by a flying hoof when the Light Horse cantered over his trench. He had regained consciousness well after dark when he woke up to find himself pinned down by the bodies of those of his men who had not fled or surrendered in time. Trying to extricate himself he drew the attention of some passing Diggers who, magnanimous in victory, had elected not to kill him but pulled him out and gave him water in exchange for his watch and silver cigarette case.

By the time he came to Ponting's attention the Syrian had spent twenty-four hours in the EEF's field hospital and was probably in better shape than the intelligence officer, who had hardly slept for forty-eight hours. But fortunately for Ponting the Arab, who had finished his education at a Protestant school in Beirut, was anxious to show off his knowledge of English.

'Aren't you worried, Major,' he had asked politely, a large grin on his bruised and handsome face, 'that since you have so many men here in Palestine the Germans will soon be able to march to London?'

'And aren't you worried,' Ponting had snapped back, 'that your army has no decent water supply between here and El Dhaheriye?'

'That is not true,' the Arab had beamed. 'The wells at Huj and Jemmameh are bigger than the fountains of paradise.'

'Really? How very interesting. Have a cigarette, Captain.'

And Ponting had left the crestfallen young officer sucking deeply on one of a specially rolled brand sent to officers in the field in plywood boxes of one thousand by a Mayfair tobacconist.

Ponting worked solidly over his interrogation reports and maps for another three hours, as all the Corps commanders and GHQ would want copies by dawn in time for their first conference of the day. It was a pity, he mused, that the chances of Daniel confirming any of his theories appeared to be practically nil, unless he somehow found another means of communication.

At about nine Ponting broke off to take dinner in a room pock-marked by grenade shrapnel, which had been designated the officers' mess. Dinner was what Ponting called *Boeuf à la Fellaheen* – bully beef mashed into a stew, to which had been added the beans and onions that were the staple diet of the Egyptian peasant. Hard-tack biscuits were also available. A piece of sacking had been nailed across the broken window and they ate at a long trestle table by the light of candles and hurricane lamps, waited on by two old soldiers, both lance-corporals, who were officially designated clerks.

'There'll be a mutiny if they serve too much of this slop to the lads,' said a major in the Black Watch with a patch over an eye that had been sightless since his last visit to Ypres. His name was Archie Wavell. He was on Allenby's personal staff and reputed to be close to him.

It was well known that the men always loathed heated bully, much preferring it cold. However, authority had decreed that a fighting man must, whenever possible, be given at least one hot meal a day whether he wanted it that way or not. Bully contained a good deal of fat and boiling it made a greasy dish, guaranteed to sort out the hungry from the merely social eaters.

Ponting was in fact ravenous although one would not have thought so to watch the controlled mastication before he raised the next forkful. The only indication of his hunger was the way he mopped up some of the remains of the stew on one of the hard-tack biscuits.

'No complaints from you anyway,' observed Wavell.

'Well, it's not the Ritz,' said Ponting. 'As a matter of fact it's not even Shepheard's, but I get so damn hungry I could eat a horse.'

'You probably just have,' grinned Wavell.

'Shush!' said Ponting. And then in a stage whisper, 'There might be a cavalryman about.'

In fact, there was almost nobody but cavalrymen about. Most of the other diners belonged to the staff of Harry Chauvel's Desert Mounted Corps or were visiting line officers who had dropped in on the off-chance of a meal. They looked like men who had spent the best part of a week locked in a desert trying to prevent 27,000 horses from dying of thirst. 'It couldn't have been one of ours. They're so bloody dry they'd choke you,' said a New Zealand captain with black rings of weariness round his eyes.

'I'm told the Fifth aren't much better off, and they're in the van tomorrow,' said Wavell. Ponting looked slightly alarmed at all this talking shop in the mess, even if they were within range of the enemy's guns.

'About time somebody else had a chance!' exclaimed another captain seated at the far end of the table. Ponting looked up and saw a square-jawed fox-hunter well into the nursery slopes of middle age, as was typical of the Yeomanry. 'About time somebody else had a chance. The Light Horse are the only ones who've had a decent charge, and we'll have the rains soon.'

'And we're not even cavalry, Mr Valintine,' said an Australian voice. 'Just poor bloody mounted infantry. Some of my boys got bloody backache they had to lean so far over to get at those Turks with their bayonets.'

'We feel for you,' laughed Wavell. 'We'll have to get you some proper prongs just like the Fifth Mounted Brigade. Nice long ones.'

'Not too soon,' said the master of foxhounds in a captain's uniform. There was a smudge of campaign ribbons from the South African war on his tunic. 'Give somebody else a chance first. It's only fair.'

'It could be too late,' said the Australian, lighting up a cigarette – which would have been unthinkable behaviour at table in most British regimental messes even if the 'meal' was finished. 'They seem to be on the run.'

At that moment there was a particularly loud wheee-crump of an incoming shell, which probably landed on the nearest British positions north along the Hebron road, about a mile away. Everybody laughed.

'Perhaps not all of them,' said Ponting and, always willing to adapt, lit up one of his own.

Later he slept fitfully on a camp-bed his batman had made up alongside his desk – the man had only put on one blanket, and the temperature dropped enough at night to warrant two. Once he was woken by a telephone call from Meinertzhagen, who urged him to pick up any information he could from captured officers about persecution of the Jewish colonists since Balfour's declaration promising a homeland. 'It's not gone down too well with Djemal Pasha,' Meinertzhagen had said. Ponting wondered how well it had gone down with the Palestinian Arabs.

At about one he came shivering into consciousness again, with the blanket on the floor. He had been drawn out of his dreams by a persistent humming, almost a dirge. Then he caught the clip-clop of horses and realised he was listening to the Yeomanry moving out, singing words that some wag, amused at yet another night ride, had probably started up out of a sense of irony. But they caught the mood and were taken up along the length of the column – which was hardly surprising since they belonged, after all, to one of the most popular songs of the war.

> There's a long, long trail a-winding,
> Into the land of my dreams,
> Where the nightingale is singing,
> And the white moon beams

259

There's a long, long night of waiting,
Until my dreams all come true,
Till the day when I'll be going down,
That long, long, trail with you.

33

Morning conference in the map-room at the Turkish Eighth Army's new headquarters was interrupted by an air raid – the second in twenty-four hours.

The day before when, because of some oversight, no air raid look-outs had been posted, the Royal Flying Corps had taken them by surprise. Bristol Fighters had come in with the rising sun shortly after dawn just in time to catch the headquarters platoon paraded around the flagstaff for the raising of the Imperial Eagle. Casualties had included a recently-arrived Oberleutnant who was supposed to replace Weidinger.

'Where the hell are our aeroplanes?' Kress von Kressenstein asked Krag. They were among the last of the German and Turkish officers to find a friendly dugout. Krag landed almost on top of a portly clerk, while outside the first of the Royal Flying Corps' bombs exploded, followed by long bursts of machine-gun fire.

'Berlin thinks we can manage without them like we manage without everything else,' said Krag glumly. He had just returned from a trip to the Gaza sector to find von Papen's telegrams waiting, and his mood would have been morose enough without the RFC's intervention.

'If we had had a couple of squadrons of Fokkers,' said Kress quietly, 'we might have discovered that Allenby had moved his cavalry to the Beersheba flank.'

On this fifth day of the battle it was already quite plain to Kress that they were not going to be able to hold the British. All they could do now was launch a limited counter-attack and hope it would knock them off balance enough to organise that most difficult of all military manoeuvres, a general retreat. The loss of Beersheba to General Grant's Australian Light Horse on the first day had been crucial. It had knocked a hole in their line which they had not been able to plug.

The Australians in their plumed slouch hats, which always reminded Kress of the chevaliers' costumes Bavarians donned during autumn pageants, had captured the town on Day One. They came at dusk in a mad charge, swinging low in the saddle and slashing at the Syrian 27th Division with their seventeen-inch bayonets, the nearest thing these mounted infantry had to the swords of the Yeomanry.

The 27th had watched them approach and had expected them to dismount once they were within rifle range and to come skirmishing in, one platoon giving covering fire while the other advanced. These were normal tactics for mounted infantry.

Even when they kept on coming, entrenched riflemen should have murdered the Australians. Instead, they had been so transfixed by the great cloud of dust bearing down on them that they failed to adjust the sights on their Mausers. They were still firing with rifles set for 800 metres when the colonials were only half that distance away and about to let out a baying 'Hurrah' that the surviving infantry would remember until their dying days.

The noise of an aircraft intensified, and then Krag felt the friendly tug that a nearby explosion gives to clothes in that half second before the sound catches up. When the bang did come it had them all crouched on the floor of the dugout with their hands on their heads, while great curtains of sand fell from between the roof beams. It powdered their hair, mingled with the sweat down the necks of tunics, and started a dust storm. Someone began a bronchial coughing. Krag fancied the entrance to their hole darkened with the shadow of the aircraft as it pulled out of its dive. Beside him the fat clerk murmured, 'No, no,' almost as if he was trying to reason with a child.

An anti-aircraft pom-pom opened up. It had been set up on the flat roof of a building the signals section had requisitioned as their wireless and telegraph station, and was crewed by some of the reinforcements von Falkenhayn had squeezed out of the High Command for his now defunct Yilderim scheme.

'They took their time,' grumbled Kress, who nonetheless started back up the rough stairs of the dugout, ashamed to be taking cover while some of his command faced the enemy, however irrelevant his own presence. Nobody followed him. Only when the explosions stopped and the engine noises had subsided to distant and discordant hummings did Krag and the others emerge, dusting themselves down, to find Kress handing out cigars to the anti-aircraft crew.

They soon saw why. About a mile to the south a tall column of dirty black smoke was rising from a spot near the railway tracks. 'That's one Englishman who won't be following the lines home,' said Kress while the victorious Feldwebel in charge of the anti-aircraft gun carefully held a lucifer to the cigar the colonel had saved for himself.

They all walked over towards a brick-built bungalow. Substantial by Etline standards, it was the station-master's residence. This official now lived in a tent pitched behind his home, and his family had evacuated to Jaffa. Just outside the front door some Syrian soldiers were prodding gingerly with their bayonets at a small unexploded bomb, its yellow fins protruding jauntily out of the red earth. Krag ordered them to stop and sent a runner for the well-boring engineer, the only person he could think of who was in any way qualified to deal with it. They would have to dig it out before they could defuse it.

The officers went inside to resume the briefing. A couple of Turkish stretcher-bearers went by carrying a dark, quivering bundle which even the veterans – especially the veterans – contrived not to see. From the horse lines, near a grove of dusty-leaved olives, came the sound of pistol and carbine shots: some cavalrymen were finishing off five remounts.

Otherwise, the casualties appeared to have been light, thought Krag. Most of the bombs had landed wide of the headquarters buildings, although not a single pane of its glass remained intact and just below the anti-aircraft gun three feet of the wall had been neatly embroidered by the Bristol's .303 machine-guns.

Some bell-tents in the German lines had also suffered the effects of a near miss. Krag's tent had been toppled by blast, and books, papers, maps and bits of uniform were scattered over a wide area. His batman was going around picking them up. He had got within two metres of Maeltzer's diary when Weidinger and the Widow Shemsi turned up.

They had met on a night train down from Jerusalem. Night trains were a recent innovation because of the increase in air raids on the railways, and neither side flew at night in Palestine. Their particular train had been crammed with a German-trained Turkish shock-troop battalion – military athletes in coal-scuttle helmets.

The train took hours longer than it should have done to grumble down the gradient to Junction Station. Normally, the journey could be done in less than three hours but now there were frequent stops while a platoon, accommodated in a cattle truck immediately behind the locomotive's coal tender, went forward with swinging hurricane lamps to check the line for tulip mines. Ever since Allenby's offensive had started Palestine was supposed to be brimming over with British agents and saboteurs, and rifle shots were becoming the norm after dark in places miles away from the front. Lishansky was still at large. Reward posters for him were everywhere.

They came into Junction Station with the first faint streaks of dawn. Stretcher cases were being unloaded from an ambulance train which had then been shunted into a siding. As they approached they could sense the urgency in the firefly bobbing of the lamps carried by the doctors and orderlies moving among an array of dark bundles on the platform. Afterwards, it seemed to the Widow Shemsi that she had heard the groaning long before their locomotive hissed to a halt.

There were about two hundred wounded from the Gaza sector. Most had been hit by shellfire, victims of the diversionary barrage that had included a demonstration of Anglo-French naval power. Some of them had been on the ambulance train since the previous afternoon when they were jolted up to the south-western terminus at Deir Sineid in the back of horse-drawn ambulances. They had then waited for over eight hours while all the carriages were filled before the train rattled its way up the thirty kilometres of permanent way to Junction Station. Some had already succumbed to their wounds, and others were dying. There had not been enough orderlies to tend them. There had not been enough water. Many of them lay in their own filth, and some were in so much pain that even the natural stoicism of the Anatolian had broken down.

Weidinger helped the Widow Shemsi down with her Gladstone bag and two hat-boxes. She alighted wearing a straw concoction with a green plume, its front brim pushed back and up in a manner which reminded Weidinger of a Mexican bandit. Shemsi was due to change here for the northbound train through Lod to Ras el Ain where horse buggies were said to be available to take passengers to Jaffa.

'My God!' she said when she was on the platform. 'This is horrible. Why doesn't somebody do something?'

'I think we'd better get you out of here,' said Weidinger, who realised that they had landed in the middle of a charnel house.

Shemsi had turned to go when her skirt seemed to catch on something. She looked down and saw that a hand had attached itself to the hem. At her feet lay a teenaged Turk, asking for water. 'Please, sister,' he was saying. 'Could I have some water? Please, sister.'

An orderly, a Syrian, came up and snatched his hand away. 'Wait.

264

There are others!' he snapped in what Shemsi recognised as Beiruti-accented Turkish. The soldier lay back without a word.

'Come on, this way,' said Weidinger, pointing to a well-lit brick building which he imagined must be where Authority dwelt. He spoke in a rougher tone than he intended, convinced that his train would pull out and leave him stranded if he failed to galvanise the woman sufficiently.

'Not until I've got this boy some water,' said the Widow Shemsi firmly.

'Madame,' pleaded Weidinger. 'They all want water.'

But she had already turned back towards their train, going to the overcrowded trucks and broken-down carriages behind the officers' car, where the heads of the storm troopers clustered at doors and windows like bunches of grapes. Some of them were throwing cigarettes to the less badly injured.

She came back with a full water-bottle and knelt besides the private who had clutched her skirt. He drank greedily.

'Not too much,' urged Weidinger. 'He may have a stomach wound.'

'No. It's his leg,' she said without looking up and for the first time Weidinger noticed the right trouser-leg cut off at the thigh, the blood-soaked bandages and the bare toes.

The occupants of nearby stretchers realised what was going on and called out to her. The Widow Shemsi moved from man to man. When the water bottle was empty she went back to the troopers for another. Weidinger was beginning to resent her. What the hell was Krag up to letting her run loose like this? The woman was a menace.

'Madame, please,' he begged, as he followed her about with her bag. 'I'm going to miss my train.'

'Then go back.'

She was cradling the head of a man whom Weidinger thought was dying. His eyes were going back and he appeared to be having difficulty in swallowing. 'Oh for God's sake,' thought Weidinger. 'This is ridiculous.'

The Oberleutnant was debating whether to dump her bag and go when a lamp lit up the stretcher.

'What do we have here? An angel of mercy?' asked a voice in German. It was a queer accent. Almost Viennese but not quite. Behind the beam Weidinger could make out a figure wearing a white overall coat over a tunic with a stethoscope around his neck.

'Ah Herr Doktor,' said Weidinger, visibly relieved. 'The lady here is waiting for the Jaffa train. Could you possibly –'

'I'm afraid you'll be waiting a long time then,' said the doctor who turned towards Shemsi. 'The English bombed the Ramleh bridge yesterday and cut the line.'

She stood up. Weidinger made the introductions.

'Dr Neumann.'

Weidinger understood the accent now. He was one of the Zionist Jews the Turks had conscripted.

'There must be some other form of transport,' insisted Shemsi. 'A buggy?'

'I'm afraid everything's been requisitioned down to the last camel and bullock cart,' said Dr Neumann. 'And even if there is anything available civilians now need a special pass signed by a major or above to travel by road.'

'Surely there's someone here who could help me?'

'Well, there are some Turkish officers . . .'

Neumann's voice trailed off. Everybody knew that a Turkish officer might well put a high price on his signature for a Syrian woman travelling alone.

'You'd better come on to Etline. I'm sure Major Krag would give you the necessary authorisation,' said Weidinger, pleased with his tact.

'Yes, you're probably right,' she said.

'I hope the rest of your journey won't be too uncomfortable,' said Neumann. 'Your train looks as though it's carrying half the Jerusalem garrison.'

'A battalion of storm troopers actually,' said the Widow Shemsi.

'Really?' said the Herr Doktor. 'One of those German-trained units I suppose?'

'Yes.'

'Almost as good as the real thing.'

'Almost,' said Weidinger. As usual, he warmed to a person who appreciated the innate superiority of the German military. For the moment the lesson of Maeltzer was quite forgotten.

It was almost fully daylight now. Weidinger need not have had any fear about missing his train, for its departure was further delayed while a flat-bedded wagon carrying a heavy machine-gun fitted with an armoured shield was hitched between the tender and the officers' carriage. The hold-ups en route meant that the storm troopers' last leg down to Deir Sineid would all be in daylight, which was not what had been intended.

As their train pulled out Dr Neumann counted the carriages. When he had a moment to himself he would jot down the number and the time and the type of troops they carried in the kind of arcane scribble a person might expect to find in a doctor's notebook. It was force of habit really. Since Sarah Aaronsohn had gone he did not know how to get his figures back to the British. He suspected there must be at least a dozen Nili orphans like himself scattered about Palestine.

Although the sun was streaming in and the officers' carriage beginning to warm up, most of the windows remained firmly closed against dust and the soot from the locomotive. Because of this neither Weidinger or Shemsi heard the machine-gun fire and the crump of the bombs from the RFC's raid on Kress's headquarters until they were almost at the Etline signals halt and the locomotive was again hissing to an unexpected halt. Apart from the anti-aircraft crew and a few riflemen who had apparently been travelling on the roof of the train ever since Junction Station, everybody scrambled down the embankment and took cover in some cactus shrub by the side of the track.

As he helped the Widow Shemsi down Weidinger thought that she seemed to grip his hand just that little bit longer and tighter than was strictly necessary. She had to hold her hat on while stumbling down to the cactus in her hobble skirt. He noticed how tight her breasts were against her blouse, the way her buttocks and thighs were clearly outlined by the skirt. Weidinger was not quite sure whether what he felt was lust, affection or the notion of an exquisite revenge against Krag. Perhaps it was all three.

'I've never been in an air raid,' she gasped. To his surprise he thought she sounded quite excited by the prospect.

In fact they were not in the air raid, which was taking place almost two kilometres away from them. However, they did see the smoking biplane on which Kress's gunners had won their colonel's cigars. Everybody cheered, including Weidinger and the other officers. Only the Widow Shemsi spared a thought for the man at the controls.

Their stop at Etline, which was no more than a signal halt ten minutes down the line from Junction Station, was just long enough for Weidinger and the Widow Shemsi to disembark. The troopers watched them go with indifferent faces as they stepped down. Shemsi detected no envy in their gaze, not even from the officers and NCOs who were all veterans and knew what they would shortly be going into.

Weidinger recognised their look. They were *Frontkampfers*, members of that exclusive club who habitually visited the sharp end. One-armed staff officers and their lady companions lived on another and grossly inferior planet. As their train pulled out Weidinger, despite his contempt for most things Turkish, saluted them. His behaviour did not surprise Shemsi. That's what these Germans were like. She had seen them wet-eyed at the words of a marching-song.

It did not take them long to locate Krag's toppled tent. At first they feared the worst, but the servant assured them that all the officers had been at conference at the time of the attack. They began to help him pick up the various papers.

It was Shemsi who spotted Maeltzer's diary, its cover too green to camouflage it in the dusty cactus it had been blown into. As soon as she picked it up she could see what it was, for the journalist had written his name across the top in bold Gothic script. She had put Maeltzer out of her mind. Now this confirmation that the diary was exactly where the journalist had told her it would be made her feel quite cold, even though the day was already warming up with the beginning of a *khamsin* wind.

Shemsi opened it at random on the entry for 17 May 1917, her lips moving with the words, for German was a language with which she had a much larger oral than written acquaintance. 'Sarah Aaron-sohn is a foolish lady,' she read.

She acts as if her brother Aaron was still around and a favourite of Djemal Pasha with his schemes to find some lost strain of wheat and turn Palestine back into a granary. But now there are also rumours that the Jew was always a British spy and has been seen wearing an English officer's uniform in the cafés of Cairo. If this wasn't bad enough she is always accompanied by this strange Lishansky boy trying to play the fop with his ridiculous monocle.

I fear for her. Today I found her dawdling by an open carriage door, on the north bound platform, practically willing to miss her train back to Haifa because Lishansky had not turned up. Doesn't she realise how sensitive the Turks and the Germans are about civilians hanging about rail terminals, people who might be trying to count how many soldiers get on and how many get off? I quite surprised myself with how forceful I was with her, practically ordering her onto the train. Of course, that young fool Lishansky arrived at the last minute.

So absorbed was Shemsi by this that she was quite startled when a voice behind her inquired, 'Interesting?'

Weidinger was peering over her shoulder, reading the words.

'I think it's Herr Maeltzer's diary,' she said, closing the book and handing it to him.

'So do I,' said Weidinger, who began to leaf through it.

30 May 1917. Weidinger in good spirits over the impending arrival of von Falkenhayn as commander in chief for this theatre. Seems to think this is bound to lead to more German reinforcements. They could certainly do with them. They appear to be short of almost everything – particularly artillery and aeroplanes. But even if they get them something will have to be done about Turkish logistics or they will never get

through. Kress is always grumbling at the state of their railways. It is really quite amazing that the British have been held on the Gaza–Beersheba line for as long as they have considering the size and equipment of the Turkish forces. Sir Archibald Murray must be one of the most incompetent commanders of the war. If the Turks had Christian de Wet and a kommando of two thousand Boers they would probably be in Cairo by now.

He turned to one of the last entries.

12 October 1917. After a briefing from Ismet Bey, the Turkish garrison commander, was told nobody was available to escort me to the Gaza sector as planned so returned to Jerusalem by train in the company of Weidinger. The boy has done very well! He went on patrol with some Turkish lancers and very nearly collared an English colonel who they wounded and appears to have got away by the skin of his teeth. Much more important was that in the process the brave colonel dropped a haversack containing papers that quite clearly show that Allenby does not intend to attack at Beersheba. W. got me to check them out for him because his English is not that good. On the strength of what I told him he sent Kress a short coded wireless signal about the situation and is now hurrying back with his prize. Of course, I won't be able to write a word of it – not yet.

Weidinger closed the book again with some emphasis, embarrassed to have shown an undue interest in it in front of her. He was also aware that Krag's servant was eyeing them both with some curiosity.

'Did you know about it?' asked Shemsi.

'Know about it?'

'Yes. Did you know Maeltzer kept a journal?'

'I was sent here to collect it,' said Weidinger with one of those bursts of candour that had so endeared him to Maeltzer in the first place.

'I see,' she said, not seeing at all.

After some hesitation Weidinger handed the book to the servant. It was, after all, in the possession of a senior officer. He could hardly seize it just because he had happened to stumble upon it while that officer was away from his bivouac.

'Do you want to stay here?' he asked. 'I think I'd better find Major Krag.'

'If you don't mind, I'll come with you.'

'As I was saying before the Englishmen dropped in,' said Kress who was standing by a map pinned to an easel. 'If we cannot recapture Beersheba we must at least see to it that Allenby does not cut us off. We must keep a door open so that, if need be, Eighth Army Corps can slip back to the hills of Judaea and Jerusalem.'

Most of Kress's audience were glum-looking Turkish majors and colonels seated on the old waiting-room benches. The rearguards were holding well and inflicting heavy casualties even when, as was frequently the case, the enemy were up on both flanks and threatening to surround them. Yet there was more than a whiff of defeat in the air. It was inconceivable that von Kressenstein would be talking about the importance of keeping doors open unless the situation was very grave indeed.

Krag knew what was coming next because Kress had already told him. Von Falkenhayn had ordered a counter-attack, start time 0600 hours tomorrow. It was not going to be launched by them but by Seventh Army Corps, which had just established its headquarters in Hebron, that malarial slum south of Bethlehem with its ancient community of observant non-Zionist Jews living among the Muslim majority. The Seventh were now under Fevsi Pasha because the irascible Mustafa Kemal had resigned his command on the 27th.

For the purpose of the counter-attack the Seventh was to be reinforced with the 19th Division, Kress's Corps reserve and not a bad outfit with some good Turkish battalions. They and the Third Cavalry, part of the 24th Infantry and what was left of the 27th were going to strike out towards a hamlet called El Dhaheriye on the main Beersheba–Hebron road. The important thing was to hold on to Tel el Khuweilfeh, a hill which commanded the entire area including its water supply, for as long as possible.

Krag watched him as he went into his spiel, using one of the captured British bayonets some of the staff had picked up after the Easter victories at Gaza. The bayonet hovered over the map until its point found the hatching that marked Khuweilfeh. 'Here, gentlemen. Any questions?'

Somebody wanted to know about the Jewish settlements. Surely they should implement Djemal Pasha's instructions at once and move them out of Palestine? Hadn't these places turned out to be nests of spies? And hadn't the British Foreign Secretary just announced their reward by telling them that they would be allowed to set up their own state in Palestine?

This was the kind of non-tactical question, totally inconceivable at a German headquarters meeting, that Kress dreaded. But it would

270

only exacerbate things if he refused to talk about it because there was a growing lobby among the Turkish officer corps who would have it that the Germans were soft on Jews and Armenians.

'It's true,' he said. 'Three days ago Lord Balfour, the British Foreign Secretary, made some sort of declaration promising he would support something he called "a Jewish homeland". But at the same time he said that the rights of what he called "the indigenous peoples" should be respected. I don't know about you, gentlemen, but I would consider these two propositions to be mutually exclusive. I don't think for a moment it will fool the Jews either. The majority of the Zionist settlers here are not only pro-Turkish but pro-German – always have been. And those that aren't had better watch out!' he concluded to a certain amount of laughter.

What Kress did not tell them about was the copy of Foreign Minister Zimmermann's telegram to von Falkenhayn's headquarters which he had received the previous evening. In the light of what it had called 'certain recent British promises to world Jewry', it had urged the German Military Mission to Turkey to do everything possible to foster good relations with the Jewish community in Palestine – and let there be no repetition of what it was pleased to call 'the Armenian calamity'. Von Falkenhayn had appended his own message saying that he believed the Kaiser himself was concerned that the Turks were driving the Jews into the arms of the English. No mention there of mutually exclusive propositions.

But did the colonel know that the Seventh Army had already started to move some Jewish settlements around Hebron?

'No, I didn't know,' snapped Kress. 'That's Seventh Army business. But by God I hope when you're speaking on the wireless to your friends in Hebron you're discreet. The English are very good at listening in.'

He looked at Krag for confirmation. Krag nodded but kept his mouth shut. Let him deal with the uppity bastards, he thought. He liked to see Kress getting rattled. The von was having a bad start to the day.

'Now let's forget this trivia,' said Kress. 'We may be in retreat but we are making Allenby pay a heavy price for every metre of Ottoman soil he occupies. Let us give him a hollow victory.'

But now the questions started in earnest.

How had the British been able to mass their cavalry before Beersheba undetected and how had they found enough water for their animals?

We don't know.

Were the wells destroyed at Beersheba?

We're not sure. According to some reports charges were laid but it is not known whether they were fired.

There were said to be reinforcements at Aleppo, several regiments of infantry, waiting to get down: what was holding up these reinforcements?

The shortage of rolling stock and the English air raids. A locomotive had been destroyed in Sheria station.

Where was the German flying corps?

'They're either dead or on the Western Front,' said Kress with unexpected bitterness.

He would have liked to call the conference to an end then and thrown the lot of them out, but he still had to lay down detailed instructions for the stonewalling tactics required of the Eighth Army Corps while the Seventh attacked. Reluctantly, he returned to his map.

The bayonet went to a hamlet called Huj which lay roughly between the two main railway lines and about five miles behind what was presently the central sector of his Corps' front. The engineers had completed laying a rail track to Huj – narrow-gauge admittedly, but they were already building up a fair-sized ammunition and supply dump there.

From outside came the sound of picks and shovels. Krag saw that the German well-boring engineer was supervising the digging out of the British bomb, which was now covered by a pyramid of sandbags. It seemed to Krag that the pick-axes were being wielded with unwarranted abandon but the engineer, a red-headed fellow with a face burned almost the same colour by the sun, did not appear to be concerned by it.

'Of course, what this campaign is really all about is men, not territory,' Kress was saying. 'Our 35,000 or so tying down Allenby's 400,000.'

Krag thought the imbalance a bit exaggerated, but judging from the reports that went across his desk it was a fact that Allenby had something like a ten-to-one advantage over them.

'There is no disgrace in making a strategic withdrawal from the Gaza–Beersheba line. You gentlemen all know that we are sorely outnumbered. And there is no way Allenby is going to get his forces through the Judaean hills in winter. They defeated Richard Coeur de Lion and they'll defeat him as long as we have the troops to man our defences there. Meanwhile we must at all costs prevent Allenby from cutting off Eighth and Seventh Army Corps, trapping us on the plain between the hills and the sea.'

Krag noted that the Turks began to look concerned again.

Kress paused to let what he had just said sink in and then suddenly dismissed them. 'Well, that'll be all, gentlemen,' he said.

Krag watched them file out past the well-borer and his party, who continued to swing their tools like men accustomed to more bluntly agricultural pursuits.

Kress was also looking at the stiff, retreating backs. 'I don't think the gallant allies were very happy this morning, Krag,' he said.

'Yes, sir. They want you to save a piece of their empire for them but pretend you didn't do it.'

'I know,' sighed Kress. 'They would also like the Kaiser to lend them all his aeroplanes for a month or so. Mind you, we probably wouldn't have been caught on the wrong foot at Beersheba if we had had a few more, however many staff officer's haversacks the British delivered us.'

'You believe the documents Weidinger's patrol found were fake?'

'I do now. Don't you?'

'Perhaps it was a bit too easy,' said Krag, after a moment's hesitation.

'It's possible it's some sort of double bluff, I suppose.' Kress had turned and was staring once again at his map on the easel. 'All the briefings I have received from Berlin informed me that this man Allenby was a heavyweight cavalryman of the English fox-hunting school. Brave, and perhaps capable of displaying a little dash in minor tactical matters, but hardly a Clausewitz. You know the breed I'm talking about, Major?'

'Ah yes,' said Krag. 'The English gentleman.' He did too. As a young officer with Liman von Sanders's military mission in Constantinople Krag had frequently socialised with the English. The French and Russians too. Even the Americans. It was all part of the business of spying on each other.

'Well, he obviously has somebody on his staff with a brain. Somebody who likes tricks,' mused Kress. 'I know I've just told the Turks what von Falkenhayn thinks and where his counter-attack is going to go, but I'm still not certain the field marshal is right about Beersheba. If another of our divisions is transferred to Seventh Army it could well be that Allenby will make his main thrust along the coast after all.

'The point is the English have so many men at their disposal. I don't suppose Allenby has even begun to commit his reserves yet. It could even be his intention to hammer away at both flanks and then put his reserves at whichever door shows the most signs of breaking down.

'But we don't have that many men, so we will have to be prepared

273

to move in either direction. That's why Sheria and Huj are important. In fact, what I would like you to do is have a good look at the central sector. You could start at Sheria. Get the first train down there you can. If there isn't one take one of the staff cars.

'Once you've had a look around there move over to Huj and see if those ammunition stockpiles I was talking about are building up properly. I don't know about Huj but there is definitely a wireless and telegraph at Sheria and Deir Sineid. If you get moving you should be able to send a cyphered situation report back to me tonight. Use telegraph rather than wireless if you can. I don't trust the wireless. It wouldn't surprise me if they've got our codes. If not from Maeltzer, from somebody else. Try not to take too long. Couple of days should do it. I need you back here.'

'Yes, sir,' said Krag who clicked his heels with an enthusiasm associated with a much more junior officer before striding out.

Kress watched him go and thought, he's a good man but he doesn't like me – which doesn't matter all that much, though it would have been pleasant to have more rapport with my chief intelligence officer. He found himself comparing Krag with von Papen, who would have departed with a little less abuse of his footwear. Then Kress von Kressenstein frowned, annoyed with himself. It was, after all, unworthy thoughts such as these that had made Krag the way he was.

Krag had not quite left the station-master's bungalow when the unexploded English bomb went off – as he had always known it would do. He was blown through the doorway and lay on his back across the threshold for a few seconds listening to the sound of bodies falling all round him. One landed with a terrible thump at the bottom of the porch steps. He looked down to see a headless trunk covered in scraps of uniform, its innards oozing out like sand. Then he realised it *was* sand and that it was one of the sandbags with which the well-borer had covered the bomb.

As he was getting to his feet, Kress arrived. 'Are you hurt?' he asked.

'Thank you – I'm all right sir,' said Krag. 'Those damn fools with the pick-axes – the vibration must have set it off.'

They both squinted at the spot where the bomb had been but an ochre-coloured cloud had settled over the place like a smoke-screen and visibility was down to a few feet. Gradually, they made out more split sandbags and figures getting shakily to their feet. Both Kress and Krag recognised the bearded drill-borer among them. There was no screaming or moaning. It seemed that by some miracle casualties had been confined to sandbags.

The yellowish fog prevented them from seeing Weidinger and the Widow Shemsi, who had been at the periphery of the blast and were now dusting themselves off. They were still about four hundred metres away when Krag began to return to his tent to throw what he needed into a grip for his journey down to Huj. He went by a different and more direct route than the one his pursuers had meandered along to the commandeered station-master's bungalow.

In the few seconds it took Shemsi and Weidinger to complete their journey Kress had also departed, bound for a nearby airfield. He was hoping that the personal touch might squeeze some more reconnaissance missions out of a bone-weary squadron commander. While Weidinger tried to find Krag, the Widow Shemsi flopped into a cane chair on the bungalow's porch, grateful to be spared the kind of butcher-shop scenes for which she had been steeling herself.

When they got back to Krag's tent, which was now upright again, his servant informed them that he had just left for Huj in a staff car.

'Did you tell the major we had called?'

'No, sir. I thought you must have met up with him after you left here.' The servant looked a bit sheepish.

'Did Major Krag take any papers with him?'

'A few, sir. Maps and suchlike.'

The tent's front flaps were open. Weidinger glanced inside to see if he could see the diary, but even if it had been lying on the camp table or the low canvas bed with its neatly refolded blankets and mosquito net – which it was not – he would have been as constrained about taking it as he was when he first saw it. For that he needed Krag's permission, and to get it he could either wait for him to return or go and find him.

As far as Weidinger was concerned there could only be one possible course of action. Huj was nearer the front and a battle was on. Somehow he might yet be able to redeem himself. The diary was not important. What was important was getting closer to the sound of guns. Perhaps he could even get involved with some cavalry. Once again he gave up heartfelt thanks that von Papen disliked Krag as much as the rest of them – which was what this obsession with Maeltzer's diary was really all about.

Before he left he went to the headquarters' signals office and wrote out a message for von Papen which he passed to one of the telegraphists there. It read: 'MAJOR KRAG NOW AT HUJ WITH DIARY. AM FOLLOWING.'

275

34

Maeltzer heard the *fajr* prayer as usual and then, just before dawn, he dreamed. They were sudden, small dreams that dissolved into each other so quickly that he quite forgot what linked them. First he dreamed he was a boy again in Switzerland living in the little red-gabled house with the pointed roof that went with the position his father held at the clinic. There was snow and he was lying on his stomach on a small green toboggan which his father was pushing down a slight slope that spring would reveal to be the meadow where the cow grazed.

Maeltzer had on a woollen hat and scarf and mittens attached to a string around his neck so that he wouldn't lose them. His father sported a check peaked cap of the kind English gentlemen wore, although he knew beneath it would be the maroon yarmoulka.

It was cold. He could feel how cold it was by touching his nose with the back of his wrist where there was a space between his mitten and his fur-lined jacket. As the sledge gathered speed he looked behind him and saw that his father's breath was coming out in great white clouds. 'You're breathing like a train, Papa!' he said. And he could see that the parent was delighted with the metaphor. Such precocity! The boy would go far! In his exuberance the man gave the sledge an extra hard shove so that it went so fast he was unable to keep up with it. It went careering off towards the snow-covered wooden fence at the bottom of the meadow, which had now grown steeper.

At first the child Maeltzer was thrilled by the way the toboggan's runners sprayed the loose snow into his face. He looked back for his

276

father but all he saw was the rushing whiteness. Then he was going faster and faster like the way his father had told him the mad English milords went down their ice tunnel at Cresta. He heard himself squealing in terror. The little green toboggan swayed from side to side and he knew that his only hope was to throw himself into the soft snow before he hit the fence. Yet he seemed to be paralysed with fear and gripped the wooden sides of the machine harder than ever. He could no longer even squeal. Instead, a soundless shriek rose from his throat as he approached his nemesis. At any moment he would have to pay for the cowardice which kept him glued firmly to the sledge.

Then, at the last second, in one stomach-turning transition, almost a metamorphosis, he escaped certain death by becoming airborne. Still on the toboggan he began to soar above the red-gabled house, saw his father waving to him as if he had intended this levitation all along. The flight continued and now he was floating over a valley which contained a quiltwork of green and yellow fields, so clear of snow they must have been in another country. He hovered like a hawk over this valley for some time, felt the friendly warmth of the sun on his back, and was beginning to fall into a gentle doze when the sky darkened and he heard the beating of the wings before he felt their draught in his face.

They appeared to be some sort of huge seabirds, albatrosses perhaps, and they swooped flapping and cawing, their filthy yellow beaks jabbing towards his eyes. At first he tried to beat them off with his fists, large fists for he had grown back into the adult Maeltzer. But their bills were razor-sharp and gashed his knuckles, so that in the end all he could do was put his head down and his hands over his face. He felt the grip of the talons on his shoulder and was wrenched off the toboggan. He fell with the bird, watched the ground come up. It was dark green; the tops of trees.

He was in a wood with Ilse, the daughter of his German teacher from school, a man he still feared and respected although he had now left the gymnasium and was studying modern history and philosophy at Zürich University. They were having a picnic in a small, grassy clearing. Ilse was eighteen and attending a nearby finishing school. She had high Slavic-looking cheekbones and rather thick pouting lips, a bit like the Widow Shemsi. There was an auburn glint in her dark hair which she had put up into a bun. She said, 'That chocolate gâteau, Carl – it was delicious.'

Her brown eyes flashed and as she turned towards him he caught the glint of the silver crucifix she wore at her throat. He offered her some more of the cake and refilled her glass of wine. They were lying on their sides facing each other on a tartan rug together with some plates and glasses that had stealthily been placed towards the edges, so that there was increasingly less space between them. His excitement at having this unchaperoned meeting with his darling Ilse was immense. The lies she must have told to arrange it! They were now practically hip to hip.

The top two buttons of her blouse were undone; somehow the crucifix had slipped down and planted itself in her cleavage. He picked it up and put it to his lips. When he looked up he saw that she was looking at him in a tender, quizzical way. They kissed, gently at first and gazing into each other's eyes, but these soon became great passionate tonguings that glued them together in unseeing bliss. He became aware of the monstrous swelling between his legs. He moved slightly forward so that the painful bulge was touching Ilse. Had she noticed? He pushed a little harder. To his amazement she pushed back, ambiguously at first but soon with a quite definite pelvic certainty.

Still joined by their lips his right hand went to her hair as he began to search for the pins that kept her bun in place. To his astonishment he found the entire device was held together by a single large hatpin. He pulled it out and as her hair came down felt her arms enfold him. He pushed her down onto the tartan rug and moved on top. His left hand was under her skirt now, under her skirt and under her other clothing and up on her thigh and then to the warm, moist place. He felt her legs begin to part. The grip on his shoulders became stronger, more urgent, talon-like. Then he became aware of movement above him and knew that the great bird was back on his shoulders pulling him away from Ilse. She tried to hold onto him but the bird proved too powerful. He saw the look of horror come over her face as he was pulled away – except that it was not Ilse's girlish beauty he was looking at, but the mature features of the Widow Shemsi.

Maeltzer woke up then, the hand on his shoulder becoming more persistent. His own right hand was still on the Widow Shemsi's hatpin where he had hidden it in the palliasse. He let it go and turned over onto his back. Above him somebody was holding an oil lantern. He squinted into the light and saw that it was the portly Austrian prelate, Liebermann. Behind him were some Turkish soldiers, one of them an officer. 'I'm sorry,' said Liebermann. 'It's time.'

'What?' said Maeltzer. He was still with Ilse or Shemsi.

'It's time – I'm sorry.' The priest looked embarrassed.

For a moment Maeltzer thought he might still be dreaming. Then he took stock of the waiting soldiers and some other shadowy figures behind the cleric and realised what he was trying to tell him.

'Now?' he asked. Fear was beginning to flood through him. 'Why no warning? I don't understand.' He made it sound as if it would be all right if he understood but as he didn't it was truly unthinkable. 'Why now?'

'Orders from Damascus, I think.'

'At night? They're going to do it at night? In the dark?'

'It's almost dawn.'

'Of course, I heard the *fajr* prayer. I always do.'

'At least you had sleep,' said Liebermann, who was secretly relieved that the Turks had not allowed him some agonising death watch in which he would have been obliged to have tried to save Maeltzer's soul for eternity. Normally, he would have been outraged by any authority which failed to give a condemned man at least twenty-four hours to prepare himself for his Maker. As it was, he was still convinced that this spy would be more comforted by having a rabbi on his last walk along the battlement to the noose that awaited him above the Damascus Gate.

However, Liebermann knew his duty. 'Wouldn't it be better,' he inquired gently, sitting himself down at the edge of the palliasse, 'if you met your God repentant and cleansed of your sins? If you are the spy Daniel then surely now is the time to confess it?'

'Oh my God!' cried Maeltzer, burying his face in his hands and then turning back onto his stomach.

Liebermann put his hand on his shoulder. Maeltzer was reminded of the dream bird. He plunged his fists into both sides of the palliasse and hung on the way he had clung to his flying toboggan.

'Death comes to us all,' said the Austrian. 'Be brave. You will only make it worse for yourself.'

But Maeltzer seemed to sink deeper into the palliasse.

Behind the priest the officer in charge of the escort, an elderly and befezzed major who had spent a good part of his career hanging men before breakfast on behalf of his Sultan, was beginning to get impatient.

'We cannot wait for ever, Father,' he said, in passable German, fingering the guard of the short sabre he was wearing. 'If the prisoner is unable to get to his feet I shall instruct my men to assist him. He will not be the first man to be carried to the gallows.'

There was a brief flurry of movement. Liebermann screamed, stood up and then began to stagger back across the cell, clutching his right bicep. 'Good God!' he shrieked. 'He's stabbed me.'

Maeltzer was on his feet, his right fist balled, and in the half light the major did not see the Widow Shemsi's hatpin contained in it although he felt it quickly enough. Its tip just pierced his colon and

279

would have done more damage had the organ not been protected by the waist lard of middle age. The Swiss left it there and removed the major's sabre from its scabbard while its owner was pulling incredulously at the excruciating slither of steel that now grew from his navel.

Once he had the weapon in his hand, Maeltzer's first action was to deliver a slashing blow at the officer's neck. The Turk saw it coming and tried to fend it off with his arm, which was almost severed below the elbow as a result.

Maeltzer then made a dash for the door, elated by his own courage. He had jumped from the toboggan after all. He was practically through when the soldiers, initially stunned by the speed of events, came to their senses. They went for the big man with their rifle butts and, once he was down, with their feet. An NCO finished it with a blow from a brass-ended butt to the head that could well have deprived the hangman of his morning's work.

Both Liebermann and the major, the latter bleeding profusely from his hacked forearm, had been carried away to the infirmary and the Turks were trying to revive Maeltzer with bucket of cold water when a breathless von Papen entered waving a piece of paper. He had arrived at the Citadel with the dawn, a good ten minutes after the hour fixed for execution, and feared he was too late. When he saw Maeltzer lying on the stone floor his first thought was that the hanging had taken place, and that the Turks had brought the body back to the cell for some macabre rite. It took a while to convince the Turks that the piece of paper in his hand was a telegram from Damascus ordering a stay of execution. Von Papen had secured it after Weidinger had confirmed the existence of the diary in his telegram from Etline. A reprieve would take a little longer – if Maeltzer survived a broken skull.

35

'*B*eautiful, isn't it?' said Weidinger. 'Better than a sunset.'

It was almost three in the morning. A cloud obscured the moon but in the cabin of the truck the Oberleutnant could see the Widow Shemsi's face clearly, lit up by the fire which had been started when the stores and ammunition were torched at Tel esh Sheria station. There was also a certain amount of British artillery fire. Weidinger estimated that one round had landed no more than half a kilometre from where they were parked.

'It's not my idea of beauty, Herr Weidinger,' she said, stifling a yawn.

'Madame,' intoned Weidinger, 'when a soldier is retreating he must learn to appreciate the beauty of the scorched earth.'

'Clausewitz, I suppose?'

'No. Weidinger.'

They both laughed, and not for the first time he marvelled at her ability to do so, though it was true that she did not always understand the danger she was in unless immediate and dramatic proof was provided. What he had not told her now, for instance, was that it was hoped that the blaze would deprive the English of enough cover to deter them from launching a night attack. This would give the rearguard a chance to escape. Or it would as long as they weren't outflanked.

Everybody dreaded Allenby's cavalry might come around the rear-guard to descend on soft targets like wolves on the fold – shooting up, for instance, a stationary lorry, which was protected by an amputee armed with a captured revolver and a sleepy overweight driver with a carbine stuffed under his seat. Ahead of them, already on the road to Huj, was an even juicier target: horse artillery on the move, unprotected by either an infantry or a cavalry screen.

They were waiting for Pichler, the Austrian artillery officer who had done so well against the British tanks outside Gaza at Easter. The lorry was the baggage wagon for his gun battery, whose horse-drawn limbers were about half an hour ahead of them.

'Do you think Hauptmann Pichler has forgotten us?' she asked.

'He's busy,' said Weidinger.

Pichler was no more than fifty metres away in the dugout of the Turkish commander of the infantry rearguard. They were poring over a map and trying to work out where to put his Skoda guns when they got to Huj. A ridge just outside the oasis seemed the best bet. By first light he was supposed to have his battery in a position where it could cover the latest phase of the withdrawal.

'Do you mind if I smoke?' asked Weidinger.

'Not as long as you give me one.'

It was the answer he had been expecting. In the last twenty-four hours the Widow Shemsi had abandoned all modesty as far as smoking was concerned. This had quite shocked Weidinger at first. The only females he had ever witnessed using tobacco in public had been common prostitutes. Even so, there had been enough reason for anybody to seek the solace of tobacco since they left Kress's headquarters at Etline.

She had insisted on accompanying him south despite his objections that it was much too close to the front line and no place for a woman.

'What am I going to do?' she had demanded. 'I can't get to Jaffa and I can't stay here.'

'Madame, I understand your anxiety to see Major Krag but –'

'No you don't. You don't understand at all,' she had screeched, and the rise in decibel level had greatly added to Weidinger's discomfort. 'Don't you see? I'm responsible. I'm the one who told the major about the lemons. I'm sure that if I hadn't told him about them – and I can tell you now I wish to God I hadn't – he would never have suspected Herr Maeltzer.'

'I see,' Weidinger had said, although he did not see at all.

'You know I saw him?'

'Who?'

'Herr Maeltzer. I visited him in prison, in the Citadel. He still swears he is innocent.'

'Condemned men usually do.'

282

But Weidinger had been impressed. Not with Maeltzer's continued protestations but her determination. It must have taken a lot of baksheesh to get in there.

'And now there is this business of his diary. Why wasn't it produced at the tribunal? Do you suppose it was because it would have shown where Major Krag got –'

Weidinger had interrupted her then. 'I really don't think we should speculate on these matters,' he had said, and said it so sternly that she almost believed him.

'Surely somebody must think that diary is very important to bother to send you to collect it.'

'Perhaps,' Weidinger had conceded in a more conciliatory tone, 'I don't know. What I do know is that the evidence against Maeltzer was overwhelming. It wasn't just your lemons, you know.'

'Wasn't he a friend of yours?'

'I thought he was.'

'Do you want to see him hang?'

'If he's guilty – yes. I would do the job myself.'

'But you're saying, "if he's guilty". It sounds as if you think there might be some doubt in the matter. Suppose he isn't? What would you do then?'

But all Weidinger had said was, 'I think you're being very foolish. It will not be a comfortable journey.'

He was right. For a start they had been unable to find motor transport. Almost everything powered by an internal combustion engine seemed to be coming the other way, as rear echelons began to anticipate the general retreat. It had to be the train down to Tel esh Sheria, unless one wanted to spend a day in one of the mule-drawn sutlers' wagons which were doing something that should have been attended to months ago: taking tenting down to the front-line troops, so that they might have dry billets when the rains started and their ranks would not be even further depleted by bronchitis and pneumonia.

British air raids had become so frequent that only the most urgent troop movements took place before dusk. Even so, there were still enough soldiers heading towards the front – some of them rounded up from convalescent centres to reinforce depleted formations – that non-priority passengers such as Weidinger and Shemsi were advised to claim a place hours before departure.

The train they had eventually boarded made their journey from Jerusalem seem like the Berlin–Vienna express. There were three horse boxes, two flat-bedded wagons carrying anti-aircraft guns in case they were caught on an open track in daylight, and a dozen open freight wagons, some with their sides down, crammed with troops.

The officers had been even more crowded because privilege of rank demanded that they travel in the covered guard's van in the rear, which was much smaller than any of the wagons. There were seats for no more than six people. After a certain amount of glaring on the part of Weidinger a young artillery captain, the most junior of the seated officers, had reluctantly surrendered his place to the Widow Shemsi, having first made it plain that unveiled women travelling with German officers could hardly be expected to be taken seriously.

In theory it should have taken no more than ninety minutes to cover the forty or so kilometres to Tel esh Sheria. But all their malnourished locomotive could manage on its dismal diet of olive wood and camel dung was a ten kilometres an hour crawl. They had been further delayed by the fact that the nearer they got to their destination the more frequently they stopped while fresh inquiries were made as to the whereabouts of the enemy.

By the time they had climbed the gradient up to Tel en Nejile the sound of the artillery fire from the battle raging around Tel el Khuweilfeh was distinctly audible. Weidinger had suspected the Widow Shemsi of being made a little nervous by this although she did her best to hide it. Every time he had caught her eye and raised his eyebrows slightly in a gesture that was meant to say, 'I told you so', she had smiled back at him with what he considered uncharacteristic sweetness.

Among the officers was a teenaged Austrian ensign from Pichler's battery who claimed, despite an alarmingly flavescent appearance, to have got over the attack of jaundice that had found him in hospital in Jerusalem when Allenby started his attack. As they bounced down towards the front like a bunch of city commuters, sometimes obliged to cling onto each other to remain upright despite the train's slow speed, the ensign told him that he expected to be part of a rearguard action intended to keep the English cavalry at bay until the rain started and flooded wadis did the job for them.

'Flooded wadis won't just give the British problems,' Weidinger had said, suddenly the wise old *Frontkampfer* before this madly optimistic youth.

It had not been long before the ensign had his eyes opened. When their train pulled into Ameidat station, about eight kilometres from Tel esh Sheria, the wounded were lying all over the platform as they had been at Junction Station. But there the similarity ended. For at Ameidat the stretchers were outnumbered by panic-stricken stragglers from the 27th Division, the routed defenders of Beersheba who had been allowed to hang about the rear areas for almost a week. They were ragged, they were hungry and they had convinced themselves that the British, and particularly the Australians, did not take prisoners. A few of them were still armed. Even before the train came to a halt they were trying to get aboard.

They came hammering on the door of the guard's van too, but the officers were prepared because some of them had been obliged to travel on the open balconies at both ends of the vehicle and they had seen what was coming. When the doors were opened the stragglers, who were mostly Syrian conscripts, had found themselves facing a line of drawn pistols, Weidinger's Webley .455 among them. They had begun to back off, until a big man at the rear of the crowd had levelled a Mauser rifle and put a round clean through the torso of a handsome Turkish major standing next to Weidinger which lodged in the right shoulder of a cavalry Muzalim-i-sani standing behind him.

The major, ashen-faced and blood beginning to pour from the exit wound in his back, had sat rather than fallen. Before collapsing onto his back, dead or very nearly so, he had squeezed off a shot that went through the van's wooden floor.

The sound of his shot had been lost in the return fire, in which Weidinger got off three rounds in so many seconds. The result of this fusillade was two dead Syrians, one of them the major's murderer, and three wounded badly enough to be unable to move. The survivors fled, telling each other the Prussians were murdering them.

Inside the van the Widow Shemsi had hovered uselessly over the wounded cavalry subaltern. 'I think we had better leave,' Weidinger had said, taking her, not all that gently, by the arm. His hand and face had smelt of the burned powder from the big .455 rounds.

Outside, after he had helped her down the steps, she had made her first request for a cigarette.

It was not until then that he had noticed how she was trembling.

That was at Ameidat. Now, seven hours later, he was out of cigarettes and felt obliged to offer one of his precious cheroots. He had discovered that she was just as fond of his dwindling supply of the stock Maeltzer had got his sister to send him from Zürich – a strictly business transaction, he was glad to say, although it had never occurred to him how few Swiss francs the Kaiser's money bought nowadays.

Weidinger supplied a light by gripping the matchbox in the right corner of his mouth and then extracting a match and striking it outwards on the projecting part of the box. When drunk he had been known to strike them inwards with painful results. He was slightly drunk now. They had both been drinking arak. He moved slightly towards her with the flame and she caught his wrist and brought her head close to his to get to the match so that he caught her scent – some French perfume supplied by Krag, he supposed. No doubt she had felt obliged to be unusually generous with it as their distance between Jerusalem and her last bath increased.

Ameidat had proved to be the terminus. The train did not go any further because the British had managed to bring their big 4.8s, siege artillery, across the Wadi Imleih and were shelling the line south of the station all the way down to Tel esh Sheria. It was the sound of this harassing fire that had panicked the remnants of the 27th Division. But Pichler had sent the baggage lorry to collect his ensign and, since his battery was last reported to be just outside Sheria station, Weidinger decided that they might as well go with it.

When they got to the battery Pichler, apparently his normal cheerful self, confirmed that Krag had left for Huj that afternoon. 'We're heading for the same place first thing tomorrow morning – a couple of hours before dawn, I should think,' he said. 'I advise you to get some sleep and come along with us. I'm afraid we weren't expecting any lady visitors just at the moment but I'm sure we can work something out after dinner.'

The Widow Shemsi thought he sounded exactly like somebody coping with an unexpected house guest and was duly impressed. Weidinger could not believe that he was still stuck with this woman.

'You'll have to go back,' he had said.

'We're all going back, aren't we?' she had inquired innocently. 'We're going to Huj, and that's back.'

He could not argue with this, but he did resolve that if Krag turned out to have left Huj – and with the start he had on them he was fairly certain that this would turn out to be the case – he would send her back to Etline on her own. He was in no hurry to return himself, not while there was a chance of attaching himself to a fighting unit even if it was artillery.

Dinner had been a surprisingly tasty goulash manufactured by a corporal cook from Budapest, a dark-skinned man with long eyelashes whom Pichler called 'Gypsy'. The only one who didn't eat was the ensign who excused himself and lay shivering under a greatcoat, apparently unable to get to sleep.

'Poor boy,' Shemsi had whispered. 'He shouldn't be here.'

'He doesn't know what's good for him.' Never having had hepatitis Weidinger was quite unable to imagine the nausea and lack of appetite that goes with it.

The officers and Madame Shemsi had dined off metal plates on a table made up from the wooden ammunition boxes that had contained shells. 'It is very good,' agreed Shemsi. Like Weidinger she was ravenous. 'What is it?'

'Camel,' grinned Pichler. 'That riff-raff in the 27th left a lot of their transport animals loose so we shot and butchered a couple for the pot.'

The Widow Shemsi put down her spoon, suddenly full. She had heard that the Bedouin and the Egyptians ate camel but she had no more expected ever to have to eat one herself than to consume another human being. And here were these Europeans acting as though they were weaned on it.

'I think I've got something that will help you digest your dinner,' Pichler had announced. A bottle of Mount Hermon arak, the best grain spirit of the region, had been produced, together with three tin mugs, and generous tots poured. 'We saved a wagon-load of this stuff from falling into enemy hands,' the Austrian had confided.

'Where was it?'

'Sheria station. We were ordered to burn it but I thought a case or two might keep the lads' morale up. And as you may have noticed, it gets cold at night.'

'In my army you'd get shot,' Weidinger had said, only half joking, and raised his glass. '*Prosit!*'

The men drank and so, only slightly more slowly, did the Widow Shemsi. After a while they began to drink toasts: to the Kaiser – may God protect him! To His Imperial Highness Charles, Emperor of Austria and King of Hungary – but not a patch on dear old Franz Josef, God bless him! To the Sultan! No, not to the Sultan. To the Fourteenth Army! Yes, to the glorious Fourteenth Army!

'The Fourteenth Army?' inquired the Widow Shemsi.

'The German Fourteenth Army has gone to fight alongside the Austrians in Italy,' said Weidinger. 'Seven very experienced divisions. That's 70,000 men, some of the best troops we have.'

'That's where we should be, my old friend,' drawled Pichler who was beginning to sound a little drunk. 'On the banks of the Isonzo. At Caporetto, hammering the Italians – who, I've heard, run even faster than the dear old Twenty-Seventh. We shouldn't be wasting our time on this sideshow, bleeding for a handful of sand.'

'I disagree,' said Weidinger. 'The Fourteenth Army should be here. If it was we would be in Cairo by now.'

'No, not Cairo, Calcutta. With the Fourteenth at our side we'd be in Calcutta. Don't you agree, Madame Shemsi?'

'At least,' she said, entering in to the spirit of things. 'Even New York.'

'Wrong direction,' said Pichler.

'Not if you go all the way round,' Weidinger had said quickly. After all, a woman wasn't supposed to have a sense of geography.

'That's what I meant,' she said, flashing him a grateful smile.

'To the conquest of America!' said Weidinger, draining his glass.

An orderly came up and announced that Pichler was wanted on the field telephone. He excused himself and disappeared into the gloom, which was broken every now and then by the embers from the small fire the men had started to try to keep warm. Weidinger had an idea that these fires were also against standing orders. Even though most of them had been built in the shallow foxholes scraped out near the guns, they would be a real giveaway if an English patrol did manage to slip through. No wonder the Austrians tended to get on better with the Turks. They were so much like them. Slack.

When Pichler came back he no longer appeared in the least drunk. 'I may be called on to give some support fire in a couple of hours,' he had explained. 'So it'll be a bit noisy. I should get some sleep while you can.'

The Austrian gave them blankets, choosing the least verminous for the Widow Shemsi, who tried to find sleep propped in the cab of a truck, which Pichler had indicated was the only proper place for a lady. Weidinger had stretched out, much more comfortably – and only a little colder, as it happened – in the open back of the vehicle, lying amidst cardboard boxes which contained the battery's supply of canned food. Some of it was stolen British bully beef the Bedouin had sold them.

A great twinkling canopy of stars was overhead, so closely clustered that only the most dedicated astronomer could pick out the pattern of the Bear or the Plough. It was, Weidinger had thought, so much more intense than the well-ordered night skies of the Fatherland. Then so was almost everything else about this land.

In Jerusalem he had never felt the slightest religious awe. He regarded himself as a good Christian, a good German Lutheran who would remain so as long as God stayed on the right side. Yet when he stepped into the Holy Sepulchre, even when he approached the spot which was supposed to be the site of Calvary itself, he was conscious only of the nauseating stench of the Orthodox tapers and the fawning greed of the importuning monks who tended the place. It seemed to Weidinger that the only people who could derive any sense of sanctity from Jerusalem were poor fools like that murdered Swede Magnus. But here in the Sinai, with its day heat and night cold, it was different. Here a man could believe in miracles, that great things had once happened. Might happen still.

He had hoped, prayed in a way, that this trip would provide a miracle of sorts, the kind of miracle that would save his military career, something a little more daunting than shooting panic-stricken deserters, shepherding other men's mistresses or retrieving the diary of an alleged spy. He still thought von Papen attached far too much importance to the latter. What if Krag had omitted to mention it when he gave his evidence at the tribunal? He had done it to make himself look cleverer – that was all. The intelligence officer wanted to be the man who had broken the spy by confronting him with his own brilliant deductions. No matter. There was still the journalist's secret messages in his despatches, his writing between the lines as Krag had so wittily put it. Nothing could be more damning than that. Unless – surely that was not what Shemsi meant by 'I can ask him things that you can't'? Did she suspect that Krag himself, so jealous of von Papen, so anxious to be the man who exposed Daniel, had made up those messages?

The idea became so powerful that for half a minute or so Weidinger seriously debated getting into the cab and confronting Shemsi with it. But what if he was mistaken? What if she said that she had never thought any such thing? How would he look suggesting to a brother officer's mistress that she might be toying with the idea that her lover was prepared to send an innocent man to the gallows as fuel for his own ambition? Nor would it detract from his own sins, also primed by ambition. For what other reason had he shown the captured British despatches to Maeltzer on the train other than his desire to know if they were important enough to risk bypassing Krag and delivering them directly to Kress? Beneath his blankets Weidinger squirmed like a drunk recalling the indiscretions of the night before.

Weidinger had wrapped the blankets more tightly about him but despite the arak and his general fatigue, sleep did not come as easily as he would have wished. In the distance the British guns sounded every two or three minutes. They made a barking noise. *Ba-grumph. Grumph! Grumph!* It was nothing compared to the Western Front, but by Palestine standards it was quite a heavy barrage. His mind raced on. What would happen to him once he returned to Jerusalem with the wretched diary? Would von Papen find him other work, other errands, however humble? Or would he think it not worth risking Kress's displeasure if he discovered that his sacked staff officer was still in the country? If that was the case it would be the next train for Berlin and the medical board that would finally declare that his services were no longer required. *Ba-grumph. Grumph! Grumph!* He found it rather soothing. Almost a lullaby. At least he was near where he should be.

Pichler's guns had started just before two o'clock. Weidinger, snoozing by then, had been half aware of the activity that preceded the first explosion: the crunch of boots, whispers, muffled orders, the turning of well-oiled machinery, the clang of metal against metal as a round was sealed in the breach.

Shemsi had appeared to have been in a deep sleep when the sound of the first salvo made her cry out. Weidinger had got up and jumped down to the side of the cab, to find her crouching there with her hands over her ears. 'Don't worry,' he said. 'They're ours.'

But she had seemed quite unaware of his presence until he gently pulled her left hand away and told her again. In doing so he had held her by the wrist for several seconds, and when he had finished telling her she had not immediately removed it but said, 'Of course. I had quite forgotten. You must think me a very silly woman.'

'I don't think you're silly at all. I think you're very brave.'

'For a woman?'

'For anybody,' he had said, suddenly conscious of the truth of his words. 'I've known men do far worse than cover their ears when they're close to the guns for the first time.'

'Yes,' Shemsi had said, recovering her poise a little. 'I suppose the first time at anything is always difficult.'

And in the dark she had not seen him blush when he let go her wrist, for Weidinger was still a virgin, his terror of syphilis keeping him out of the brothels. He had persuaded her out of the cab then, and together they had walked over to the nearest gun – where she had taken an intelligent interest in the proceedings although she still flinched every time a lanyard was pulled.

Brass cases glinted in the darkness. Men mumbled curses or roared orders. A man crouched over a shell holding in his right hand something that looked like a key, which he slotted into a groove at the business end of the round.

'What's he doing?' Shemsi had asked.

'He's setting the fuse,' Weidinger had said, suddenly as delighted to inform as any fresh-faced ensign at a field day. 'There are basically two types of shells you see. There are those that explode on impact. They're packed with high explosives and the sort of thing you want for getting into trenches or dugouts. The other kind you can set to explode in the air and scatter shrapnel over a wide area. That thing he's got in his hand is called a fusing tool. You can't see it from here but at the top of the shell there is a coloured cone. It's really a series of rings like one of those children's toys built around a central stick. Each contains a trail of powder around its rim. Once that's burned through it releases a firing pin and the shell explodes. You can usually set them from between zero and twenty-five seconds.'

'Zero? Why would you want to set them to zero? Wouldn't they explode in your face?'

'Well, almost. A couple of metres off the muzzle of your gun I should imagine. The spread would be incredible. Like the old grape-shot the Russian gunners used on the English Light Brigade at Bala-clava.' They had watched two of the newly-fused shells being fired. Then, much to Weidinger's embarrassment, the driver strolled up and, quite oblivious of Shemsi's presence, amused himself by pissing into an empty case, still warm enough to cause a visible column of steam to rise.

'I think we'd better go,' he had said, hastily taking her arm.

'Ah, the horrors of war!' Shemsi had giggled as they went back to the lorry.

That had been an hour ago. Now the guns had moved off and Pichler had just emerged from the dugout, where it had been finally agreed that the new position for his battery would be the ridge over-looking Huj.

'Let's catch up the guns,' he said as he joined them in the cab. The driver, suddenly awake, went out front with the starting-handle and the engine came to life at his third crank. As they moved away, Tel esh Sheria station was still burning fiercely behind them to the south-east.

'Like dawn, a false dawn,' Shemsi thought.

They passed the gun limbers, the horses sweating despite the night cold. Weidinger cast a professional eye over them and guessed that they had not been watered properly for days. The real dawn began to come up as they first sighted Huj, which seemed to consist of half-a-dozen single-storey wooden buildings and about twenty tents, all clustered round a clump of palms. As they got closer they could see by the number of people milling around that the camp was already awake.

It had been crowded with the four of them in the cab. Pichler sat by the driver, so that he could give him orders, and next to him was Weidinger. Shemsi sat at the end of the bench seat, occasionally hanging on to the door frame when they hit a bump. On the smoother stretches she would nod off, her head sometimes coming to rest on Weidinger's shoulder.

Weidinger enjoyed these moments. He liked the weight of her against him, the smell of her hair in his nostrils. There was something about these olive-skinned Levantines that both attracted and repelled him.

He always fantasised about German girls in scenes of operatic distress, perhaps beset and half ravished – though never fully, of course – by bandits in some dark forest. Once he had disposed of the girl's assailants with his sabre she surrendered to him what she had denied the others. Sometimes a storm blew up, a tempest as mad as King Lear's, and they had to shelter under his cloak on a bed of leaves . . . .

He thought differently about those females, like Shemsi, whom he categorised as Europeanised orientals, wild and haughty beings at war with themselves. He imagined them as odalisques in diaphanous pantaloons, offering whips for their chastisement, willing to undergo any carnal indignity to arouse their lords' jaded appetites, or as loud in their own desires, straddling a man as a girl would a pony. But he also saw them, whether Christians, Muslims or Jews, as cunning Semites, cosmopolitan and incomplete characters whose souls were not big enough to absorb notions as large as love of Fatherland, capable only of loving themselves or, at most, their immediate families.

For such people, Weidinger had long ago decided, no action was as spontaneous as it seemed; the poison phial was always hidden in the navel jewellery. He thought of how Shemsi had crouched by him and allowed him to hold her wrist when the battery started firing. He estimated that she had at least seven years on his twenty-three, and yet he had felt so protective towards her. What on earth, he asked himself, did Shemsi see in Krag? A man consumed by such venomous envy that he might even have manufactured all the evidence against Maeltzer for his own benefit. Once again he longed to have Shemsi confirm that this was what she really suspected; but this would have been hard enough when they were alone, impossible in front of Pichler, even though he was a friend.

As they drove into Huj they could see that the camp was being prepared for evacuation. Soldiers were slackening guy ropes or slinging haversacks and other boxes into the backs of carts and the few available lorries. When Weidinger and Pichler emerged from their cab they saw two German engineers running a line of electric cable from a clump of palms from which the sound of a pump engine could be heard, and guessed that the wells there were being prepared for demolition.

'Another tactical withdrawal,' muttered Pichler.

'At least we're not poisoning the water,' said Weidinger, whose mind had not yet totally disengaged from its recent anti-Semitic reverie.

They walked towards a building with heavily sandbagged walls and a wireless aerial on its roof, which they judged to be head-quarters. Shemsi trailed a couple of paces behind them, trying to ignore the incredulous stares of the soldiery. They were a few metres away when Krag emerged, saluted the Turkish sentry who had shuffled to attention and then descended the four steps that led from the narrow veranda to the street.

'Major Krag!' called Weidinger. He could hardly believe his eyes. He had never really expected to catch up with his quarry.

Krag wheeled and walked towards them. Shemsi and Pichler hung back as Weidinger went forward a few paces and saluted.

'Good morning, sir.'

'Shouldn't you be in more northerly climes by now?' asked Krag, scarcely bothering to return the oberleutnant's salute and showing not the slightest awareness of Shemsi's presence.

'Sir, Major von Papen sent me. He would like you to return Maeltzer's diary. He sent you several telegrams asking for it, but it appears you didn't receive them.'

'Of course I received them,' snapped Krag. 'Unfortunately, we've got an offensive on our hands and for some unfathomable reason the English appear to have attacked us from the wrong direction. We have been rather busy and some things have had to take priority over others. I must write to Major von Papen and apologise for my discourtesy some time.'

He turned to Shemsi. 'And to what do I owe this pleasure, Madame?'

'Bureaucracy,' she replied, with a coolness that quite startled Weidinger. 'I need your signature to travel to Jaffa.'

'Good heavens, you have come a long way for it. Couldn't you have waited at Etline?'

'Not really. It was difficult. I would have needed an escort, and Oberleutnant Weidinger was anxious to come down here.'

'Ah yes. Still the young firebrand desperate for the sound of guns. Well, I'm sorry to disappoint you, Weidinger, but yours has been a wasted journey – though I'm sure you've enjoyed some of the sights and sounds in your inimitable fashion. I have never seen any diary of Maeltzer's. I can't think what gave Major von Papen the impression that I had. I would have thought keeping a journal an odd occupation for a spy, even one posing as a journalist, although I suppose it could have been part of his camouflage. Kindly give Major von Papen my regards and tell him that if he finds any such diary I would be most interested to read it.'

Weidinger was trying to decide on a formula that would somehow convey to Krag that the diary's existence and his possession of it

293

were known facts without actually calling the man a liar, when he became aware of a kind of roaring sound behind him.

'Liar! Liar! We've seen it, you idiot. You damn fool, we've seen it,' shrieked a voice Weidinger had never heard before. 'We saw it when your tent was blown over by the bombs at Etline. I picked it up. We both looked at it. We know it exists. Tell him, Weidinger, for God's sake tell him. You have Maeltzer's diary. Why don't you admit it? What are you hiding?'

Weidinger turned to see that the Widow Shemsi had undergone a startling metamorphosis. Her face was contorted and she was streaming tears, her body visibly trembling. Behind her stood an embarrassed-looking Pichler, his hands resting lightly on her shoulders as if he expected at any second to have to restrain her from flying at Krag's throat.

For a moment it seemed as if the intelligence officer was going to answer her question. 'Nadia,' he said – and to Weidinger this revelation of her given name, pronounced in a tone he had never heard Krag use before, spoke canyons of intimacy.

But then he seemed to rein himself in: 'You go too far,' he said, and abruptly turned away. For once he was white rather than yellow and Shemsi detected a tremor in his voice she did not altogether associate with anger.

She went as if to pursue him but Pichler held her back. 'Let him go,' said Weidinger. 'Let him go and think about it. Perhaps he'll talk to you later. I must send a message to Jerusalem.'

In the wireless room Weidinger found a German signaller as unshaven as himself bent over a morse key, a forgotten cigarette slowly incinerating itself in a full ashtray beside him. A pile of messages waiting to be sent lay in a wooden tray. There were code books on the desk and a metal spike on which those despatches already sent were impaled.

As he entered the signaller was tapping out a message. He looked up and went on with what he was doing. Weidinger felt a flush of annoyance and for a moment was tempted to put the man's cigarette out, although he knew it was nonsense to interrupt a morse message or to expect the man to stand to attention for a visiting officer. Even when there wasn't a flap on, telegraphists tended to be a breed apart.

When he had finished the signaller began to rise reluctantly to his feet but Weidinger waved him down.

'I have an urgent message for Major von Papen in Jerusalem. He's on the staff of General von Falkenhayn,' he said, hurling the last name at him.

The man looked deeply unimpressed. 'With respect, sir,' he said, 'they're all urgent, every single one of them. I couldn't give yours priority. And they all have to be sent by 11.00 hours, which is when we destroy the wireless – providing the English don't arrive before then. I'm on my own here. The other telegraphist was wounded in an air raid a week ago and the cypher clerk has been evacuated with dysentery. I have to do all the coding myself.'

'What if you didn't have to code it?'

'Sir?'

'What if you sent it in plain language?'

'But, sir, I thought you said it was priority,' said the telegraphist, his impudence rising to Weidinger's desperation.

'So it is,' he said, somehow controlling his temper. 'A man's life might depend on it. But it's a judicial rather than a military matter and if the English do pick it up just imagine the time they're going to waste trying to decode it.'

The telegraphist sighed and slid over a message pad and a pencil. 'It would help if you could keep it under ten words, sir,' he said.

'Certainly,' grinned Weidinger, making large block capitals on the paper.

It was six: 'MAJOR KRAG HAS DESTROYED MAELTZER'S DIARY.'

Ponting had just got back from breakfast – hard tack and sardines washed down with weak tea – when Meinertzhagen came over the field telephone.

'It looks like Daniel's in trouble,' he said.

'Was he able to get a message out?'

'No. Wireless intercept an hour ago. They weren't using his code name either.'

Ponting thought, 'So they've told you who he is at last.' But all he said was, 'That was quick work.'

'What was?'

'On the cypher, sir.'

'Ah, that's the funny thing. It was plain language. All we had to do was translate it. Mind you, if I hadn't recognised a name the brains would still be working on it now.'

'Perhaps we were meant to pick it up?'

'Hmm. Doubt it somehow. If it was a present they would have wrapped it up nicely with plenty of string to unravel. It might have been because of pressure of traffic from a wireless transmitter they're about to pack in.'

'How much trouble do you think Daniel is in?'

'I'm not certain. It could be big trouble.'

'Is there anything we can do to help?'

'I don't think so. Not at the moment. But I think I'm going to move over your way.'

36

A *ridge almost two miles from Huj: shortly after midday, 8 November 1917*

The ideal exploitation by mounted troops is not a pursuit but an interception. It aims to strike, not the rear of the retreating columns, where the sting is, but the less protected flanks or head to cut in on the line of retirement at the most favourable time and place – a defile for choice – to head off as large a portion as possible of the withdrawing force and to hold it till the infantry can come up and complete its destruction.

Wavell in *The Palestine Campaign*

*P*rivate Calderwell, lying on his back, looked up to see a sun the size of a shilling slide behind the one small dark cloud that marred an otherwise blue and white sky. If we were home, he thought, if we were in Coventry that cloud would definitely be a rain cloud and very shortly it would do what it was supposed to do. But we're not at home, we're in bloody Palestine where nothing works quite the way it should do. And there have been clouds like that around for days and nothing has happened although Isaiah Mace assured me that by this time last year they were well into the winter rains. After a few days, Mace had explained, the land turned into the kind of nice thick glue that persuaded generals to give their cavalry a rest unless you were unlucky enough to be used as infantry. But this year it wasn't going to happen. This year the land would stay baked and they would go on chasing the Turks until the poor fuckin' horses dropped dead or they did.

Shells from an enemy battery ahead of them were landing among the 60th Division, Shea's Cockney infantry, whose dust could be seen on the plain below. Some of them passed close enough for the Yeomanry, who were behind the lee side of a shallow ridge, to hear the whiz and zip of them overhead. Only the horses paid any heed. Calderwell noticed that every passing shell caused Villa to pin her ears back and paw the ground on which she was trying, mostly unsuccessfully, to find some nourishment.

The whizzing overhead may have worried the horses, but their riders were so exhausted that some had fallen asleep almost the minute they had dismounted and stretched out on the bank. Others had not yet learned that the ability to cat-nap was an essential military virtue and found their dread of being wakened kept them awake.

Through lowered lids Calderwell watched a small cloud of dust detach itself from one of the larger clouds on the plain and weave towards them through the black and white shell bursts. Dully, he registered the fact that this must be a motor vehicle, but apart from that he viewed the events below with complete detachment. His mind barely registered what his eye took in. It never occurred to him that he was witnessing Allenby's advance grind to a halt for the first time in forty-eight hours as the artillery fire maimed and murdered the infantry on ground almost devoid of cover. They were in their war and he was in his. And he was very tired.

It was two nights now since any of them had slept properly. They had started out fresh enough shortly after midnight the day before, having rested themselves and the horses at Beersheba for a couple of days after fighting as mounted infantry around El Khuweilfeh. Calderwell had emerged from this baptism at ease with himself. He had been under fire and had not disgraced himself in front of his mates. He felt his newness was wearing off. Certainly, he would no longer be the automatic choice to return stray pigeons to their rightful owners while everybody else went racing.

They had all set off from Beersheba in cheerful mood, singing their heads off, sad songs and glad songs, as they said at the music halls. After the elegiac, 'Long, long trail a-windin'' that had woken Ponting from his slumbers they had gone straight into:

'Oh the moon shines bright on Charlie Chaplin
His boots need blackin', his bag needs packin',
And his old baggy trousers they want mendin'
Before they send 'im, to the Dardanelles.'

Between songs someone would inquire in a loud voice: 'Are we down-hearted?' And everybody would yell back, 'Nooooohhhh!!!'

Which was true enough. On the first day of the battle one man had been killed and Captain Valintine slightly wounded by shrapnel in an air attack when they were lying in reserve behind the Australians. Valintine had declined to relinquish command of B Squadron, declaring that he'd done a damn sight worse to himself hunting than the Hun had ever achieved. Another man had been killed and nineteen wounded during the hill fighting around Tel el Khuweilfeh. But these casualties were far lighter than expected. For the moment they were winning, and they knew it.

Calderwell had an additional reason not to be down-hearted. In the left breast pocket of his tunic, next to his now slowly beating heart, lay a coloured Bamforth postcard from his beloved Ethel. On it she had written: 'I trust this reeches you as it leaves me. All My thoughts are with you in your dangerous duty in the Holy Land. Me and your sis went out for a little drink the other night and we both had a good cry and I hope it will not be long before your safe return so until then we are all praying for you. God Bless. Your friend, Ethel Parkinson.' All this was in pen and ink in a careful, sloping hand, with loops on the 'f's and little curls on the capital 'm's.

It may have been a bit more formal than even *The Complete Letter-Writer for Ladies and Gentlemen* laid down for correspondence of a romantic nature and there was that breathtaking leap from the general to the particular between the second and third sentences. But as far as Calderwell was concerned it was the most exciting thing he had ever possessed. Just gazing at the picture on the cover with the four lines of verse underneath made his throat go dry.

It showed a good-looking girl about Ethel's age – as good-looking as Ethel almost, in a different kind of way – seated in a well-kept garden with what looked like a lake behind her, beyond which the sun was setting. She was seated on a stool, staring thoughtfully at what appeared to be a row of pink busy lizzies growing up bamboo poles. Just in case anybody had any doubts about them, her thoughts were spelled out in the top right-hand corner of the card, where the clouds had opened to reveal her, in a different dress Calderwell noticed, falling into the arms of a tall, dark young soldier whom he had to admit looked a lot like himself had his hair been dark and his nose a different shape. Beneath the picture were four lines from a song which Calderwell vaguely remembered, though he could not properly recall the tune. Tired as he was he got the card out and tried to hum along as he read them, like the message on the back, for the umpteenth time.

'Sometimes you'll remember, tho' the skies are blue,
Someone's sadly pining all the time for you;
Somewhere we shall meet, dear, when the years have
   flown,
Someday you will tell me you are mine alone.'

This sort of concentration proved too much, and he suddenly fell asleep with the card still clutched in his hand. It had come in the last batch of mail they had received, which had caught up with them at Beersheba on the afternoon of the sixth, the day before their first night ride.

In the early hours of that first morning they had ridden in a north-westerly direction to Abu Irgeig, which was about six miles from Beersheba and yet still behind the vanguard of the EEF. They had cooked breakfast there as the sun came up – fried eggs that had been carried in a sackful of straw, and plum jam smeared on hard-tack biscuits, all washed down with very black and very sweet tea. They had also fed the horses some of the hard barley they were carrying, nineteen pounds of it in the two nosebags that were on every horse. By nine o'clock they were back in the saddle and heading towards Abu Hareira, which was still believed to be in Turkish hands and was being pounded by British guns as was the station at Tel esh Sheria.

That was the day they had expected to tangle with the Turkish rear-guard but it hadn't happened. At one point they had been quite heavily shelled but had escaped casualties by an extremely rapid withdrawal, which Calderwell had found himself leading because he had virtually lost control of his terrified horse – though he had to admit afterwards it was a toss-up who was more scared or farting more.

'Oi'll tell yow wun thing, yow're a good man in retrait, Caldy,' was Isaiah Mace's only comment when he caught up with him.

They had re-formed, lunched on hard tack and bully and then resumed the advance at a gentle walk, with frequent rests for the horses. That evening the Yeomanry had crossed the Wadi Sharia and wandered about for a couple of hours with drawn swords looking for the enemy or the Australian Light Horse, who were supposed to be somewhere on their right. They had failed to find either party, which Mace had said was just as well since both were liable to be equally trigger-happy after dark. Calderwell was relieved. He had found the whole business quite nerve-racking, wondering whether every second shadow was a Turkish rifleman or lancer with a some-what longer reach than the thirty-eight inches of cold steel in his own right hand. They had turned back, stopping to water the horses at a well near Tel esh Sheria – where, like Weidinger, they were impressed by the way the night sky was lit up by the stores the Turks had torched there – and were back in their bivouacs shortly before midnight.

Like the others, Calderwell's last bed had been a dent he had scraped into the ground with his bayonet and his boots – none of them had entrenching tools, which were thought an unnecessary encumbrance in an attack. (As it was, even the horses with the lightest men on board were not carrying less than two hundred and fifty pounds.) Into this shallow grave he had laid his rubber groundsheet; he had used his saddle for a pillow and, after removing his boots and tunic, lay fully clad under a single blanket which stank of horse.

It had been a bitterly cold Sinai night, and sleep was surprisingly hard to come by. When it did come it had not lasted very long, and Calderwell woke shivering to find that his blanket was soaked with a heavy dew. He did not possess a watch – his mother was saving from her housekeeping to give him one for his twenty-first – and had no idea what time it was. Eventually he had groped in his tunic pocket for a packet of Woodbines and lay there for almost an hour chain-smoking for warmth, until a corporal came round to get them up shortly before five.

A rum ration was issued from one of the barrels kept in the general service wagons that followed them about the place with their rations. They did not get it neat but poured into the black tea the cooks had brewed. Old sweats like Mace had groused about their drink being diluted but Calderwell, who had hardly ever had spirits in his life, thought it was just the thing although he pretended to agree. After a second mug he could almost feel his feet, which were housed in boots as sodden as his blanket.

They had set off at six o'clock across an undulating countryside that became increasingly less of a desert until they were eventually riding through fields of newly threshed corn, though the Arabic-speaking peasants who owned it had disappeared. They were joined by two squadrons of the Worcesters, and together they found the Turkish rearguard well before ten – and kept finding it, for they had practically fought them from ridge to ridge after that. But it had been distant stuff. Twice they had dismounted to open rapid fire with their rifles at small figures on a far skyline, and on one occasion the machine-gun troop came up and joined in with their Hotchkiss guns.

As he lay in the prone position and worked the bolt of his Lee-Enfield, the sights up and set at one thousand yards, Calderwell had had very little sense that he was firing at people. It was not until he had heard the distinct zizz of bullets passing close overhead that he paused to think what his own bullets might have been doing.

'The boggers are firing back,' he had said, genuinely surprised.

'Try not to take it personally,' the corporal alongside him had said. He was a man in his mid-thirties from Birmingham, who had stopped Mauser lead when he was about Calderwell's age in the South African War.

Then the order had come to mount and they were up and galloping towards some mud ruins which turned out to be an Arab village called Kauwukah. They were slightly behind – in echelon, as the staff officers said – the Worcesters, whose dust obscured their view. And for the first time in Palestine Calderwell had heard a sound which made his blood chill: ahead of them somebody was playing 'Gone Away' on a hunting horn, the doubling note a huntsman makes when a fox is sprung from the covert.

When they got into Kauwukah the only Turks left were the dead and the wounded, whom they had helped the Worcesters to make as comfortable as they could while they waited for the ambulance wagon to catch up with them.

'Did you 'ear it?' Mace had asked. 'Did you 'ear old Toby Albright blowin' 'is horn?'

They were both crouched over a young Turk who appeared to have caught a burst through the back from one of the Hotchkiss guns. Mace had an arm around him. They had given him water but it had reappeared on his lips as a blood-tinged froth, which the flies were trying to feast on.

'November, you see,' Mace had gone on. 'Start of the 'untin' season. If we were 'ome now our Val would be polishin' his topper with Guinness stout and gettin' his ridin' boots polished with champagne and apricot jam.'

'Oh yeah,' Calderwell had said, fanning the dying Turk. The boy had looked even younger than he was, not a day over seventeen, and he had hoped it was the Hotchkiss and not one of his bullets. 'I could think of better things to do with that lot than cleanin' my fuckin' kit. I could think of a lot better things to do with it.'

'He's gone,' Mace had said, and Calderwell had looked down to see that the boy's eyes had disappeared into the top of his head.

The Turks had started shelling Kauwukah shortly after that and they had moved forward again, leaving the medics to sort out the dead and wounded, who now included three British. Within an hour they had chased some Turkish stragglers through another field of freshly threshed corn and reached the ridge where Calderwell was now dozing, oblivious of the shellfire. Ethel's postcard was still loosely attached to his right hand – though she did not feature in his dream, which was of a bicycle ride to a South Wales beach that he and his mates had always intended to do but somehow never got organised.

He was arguing with Ron Ash – which was odd because Ron had gone missing in France the year before – about whether a patch of blue ahead was sea or sky, for Ron always took a contrary view, when some terrible unseen marine creature began roaring at them. When he woke, Calderwell realised he was listening to the agonised sound of an internal combustion engine tearing its guts out as the wheels it served fought for purchase on the slope.

He sat up just as one of the strangest vehicles he had ever seen came to a halt about a hundred yards below him. It was a Model T Ford to which a few sheets of steel had been bolted, turning it into an armoured car. Somebody stepped out of the passenger door. From where he was sitting Calderwell could just make out the back of a pith helmet, but he guessed it must have been a senior officer by the sharp salute the visitor got from Hugh Gray-Cheape, the Warwicks' colonel.

Calderwell watched as Gray-Cheape listened intently to what was being said. Twice the colonel turned to follow a blackthorn stick his visitor was pointing, first in the direction of the exploding shells he had just driven through and then the other way, vaguely towards the guns that were firing them. Then Gray-Cheape said a few words and saluted again, and the visitor departed towards the incoming artillery fire in his strange conveyance – which rapidly became once more the fast-moving dust cloud which Calderwell had noticed before he fell asleep. Shortly afterwards they got the order to mount.

'You know who that was?' said Mace, who was riding alongside him. 'That were fookin' General Shea himself. I reckon we're gooin' after those guns hammerin' the Sixtieth down there.'

'Why are we takin' the horses?'

'So we won't have so far to walk, I suppose,' said Mace.

'Thank Christ for that,' said Calderwell. 'For a moment I thought you were going to say we were goin' to have at them like the bloody charge of the light brigade. Half a league, half a league, half a league bloody onwards.'

'Not while we've got these,' said Mace, tapping the Lee-Enfield in his saddle boot. 'Besides, those lazy sods in the machine-gun squadron and the 'orse artillery ain't caught up with us yet. We'd never charge without cover from them.'

'I'm sure that mad bogger in the Worcesters with the huntin' 'orn wouldn't mind going in with his sausage-sticker.'

'Not before we've got them runnin',' said Mace. 'I think them Diggers were bloody lucky at Beersheba.'

'Well, just as long as your huntin' friends remember that. They might have brought the rations up first. Moi belly tells me it's time for me dinner.'

'It's twenty past wun,' said Mace, extracting his fob watch from the top pocket of his tunic.

Calderwell no longer felt in the least tired. He might have slept for ten hours instead of ten minutes.

Because they were riding along the ridge they could not spread out as they usually did but rode in columns of half squadrons, with each squadron of about eighty men divided into two lines. Calderwell was riding to the right of Mace, who was that much nearer to the enemy. There was a gap of about two hundred yards between the squadrons, and the Worcesters were in the van. Their CO had ridden back to Kofkah just before Shea's arrival to ask the Third Australian Light Horse if they would come up and cover their right flank. With the colonials he found it politic to do this sort of thing himself rather than send a messenger.

When they got to the crest of the ridge the two lines of horsemen automatically speeded from a walk to a trot and then a canter, because for the first time they could see the enemy. To their left there was movement about three-quarters of a mile away on another dusty ridge which curved around so that one end was facing them. The Turks had a battery of small mountain guns here, which the leading Yeomanry officers could just about make out through their field glasses. The enemy's main batteries, the big guns that were still booming away at the infantry, were in a hollow to the enemy's right.

A shallow little valley of hard-baked earth and tufted grass lay between the small inverted boomerang-shaped ridge the Yeomanry were on and the enemy ground. At its narrowest point the valley was about six hundred yards across. Some shells started to come their way from the mountain guns ahead. Calderwell found himself hunching forward against Villa's neck, as if he was leaning into a heavy wind, but the rounds fell with a series of sharp cracks well behind them – the gunners were having trouble adjusting to the speed of their advance.

To the right of the column Calderwell noticed that four or five officers including Gray-Cheape and his regimental headquarters staff were bunched up, obviously holding a conference on the march. As he watched them the colonel removed the ash walking-stick he always carried tucked under his saddle and handed it to one of the headquarters' signallers – who were easy to pick out because they carried the tripods for their heliographs where the rest of them had their sword scabbards. The signaller gave a sort of half salute with it and rode back to his position in the column.

The conference broke up and people started shouting orders. 'Halt. Left wheel. I said left wheel!' The sergeants and corporals were going up and down the line yelling, 'Don't bunch. Spread out! Come on now, we know you're all in love with each other but spread out!'

Calderwell, dressing off to the left, noticed that the NCOs were not swearing and found it oddly worrying. He looked to his right and saw the Worcesters' squadron moving off at a canter towards the mountain guns. He caught the gleam of sword steel in their dust.

Then came the formal, parade ground voice of the squadron sergeant-major. 'B Squadron, drawaah swords.'

Calderwell leant to his left side, felt his right hand sticky against the bone hilt, and realised that he could have told Mace even before he saw what the Worcesters were up to that they were about to charge. He could have told him that he was wrong about everything. He could have told them that the officers were all bloody madmen, and that they were going to do it without the machine-guns and the horse artillery. They were going to do it because the general had come up in person to ask them to do something about those guns and they were all too well brought up to say no. They were going to do it because it was even better than hunting. Half a league, half a league. . . . Funny thing, it was the only scrap of poetry he could ever remember.

On the opposite ridge the mirror glass of a heliograph started flashing.

'He's tellin' 'is Mam we're comin' for 'im,' said Mace and Calderwell shortened his reins and joined in the laughter. It was good to be with your mates.

'Any more movement?' asked Pichler. 'I've just sent a message on the magic mirror saying it looks like cavalry massing on our front but there was no reply. I think they may have all cleared out of Huj.'

'It's cavalry sure enough,' said Weidinger.

He was lying belly down on the nearest point of the ridge to the Tommies examining the enemy dust through field glasses. Behind him, beautifully hidden in a broad shallow gulley that fissured the ridge at that point, were Pichler's four guns. Behind them, below the main body of the ridge, was a battery of Turkish manned

5.9 howitzers, and at the end of the ridge, was another Turkish battery, the little mountain guns whose first shots had given Calderwell a bit of a turn.

Pichler's .75mms and the howitzers were still laying down a brisk barrage on the British infantry, who had gone to ground in the scrub land about two kilometres to their right. Eight shells in the air every thirty seconds.

'Cavalry or mounted infantry,' said Pichler. 'Not that it makes much difference. The Australians who charged at Beersheba were mounted infantry.'

'They aren't going to charge – not yet anyway.'

'How can you be so sure?'

'They haven't started shelling us. The positions at Beersheba had been shelled all day before the Australians charged – that's what I heard in Jerusalem anyway. The last time the English cavalry attacked a position like this without artillery cover was in the Crimean War. And you know what happened then. They got massacred.'

'Perhaps they don't know their history as well as you do,' said Pichler, lying down alongside him. 'Perhaps Beersheba has given them the appetite to take bigger chances.'

'Well if it has, their officers should be shot,' said Weidinger. 'No cavalry officer worth his salt would send his men at a position like this without doing something to keep those fellows' heads down for a start.'

He leant back on the stump of his left arm and gestured with his binoculars to a line of three stone piles, each about fifty metres apart, beyond the gulley where the guns were. Each stone pile had a hole in the middle. Behind each of these sangers were three brand-new belt-fed Krupp machine-guns, the sort with a little square of armoured plate around the breach to protect the firer.

'That's if they know we've got 'em,' said Pichler. 'The other thing that worries me is that they're *behind* my guns. Bit unusual for infantry to be behind the artillery, don't you think? The way things stand it looks like my battery is the next obstacle in the path of the Egyptian Expeditionary Force. At least our friends with the mountain guns over there have the infantry mixed in with them.'

'They may be behind but they're *above* you,' said Weidinger. 'They won't let anybody get anywhere near your guns. Besides, you really can't compare those boys to Turkish infantry.'

Much to Weidinger's delight, the machine-guns were manned by two-man German crews who had arrived in Huj shortly before noon from the coastal railhead at Deir Sineid. They were part of the unit which von Falkenhayn had extracted from the High Command for Yilderim. They had spent most of the last month being shunted about the remains of the Turkish railway system and had now been broken up and scattered about the rearguard. More Corset Staves, Weidinger had thought, wondering what had happened to those splendid-looking storm troopers he and Shemsi had travelled down from Etline with. He suspected they were all dead or captured, sacrificed in the hill fighting around Tel el Khuweilfeh.

It was true the machine-gunners were tired. Who wasn't? But at least they were still discernible soldiers, which was more than could be said for the battalion of Turkish infantry digging in around them. Among them were men emaciated by dysentery and so exhausted they could hardly summon the energy to dig a slit trench, not even for their own protection. A few of Tommy's shells would soon sort that out one way or the other.

'You know, for men who are going to settle down and take pot shots at us until their artillery comes up they're making a lot of dust,' said Pichler thoughtfully. 'And I thought I caught the flash of steel. Don't some of the English cavalry carry sabres?'

'Their mounted Yeomanry regiments have a sword – they call it a thrusting sword,' said Weidinger.

'I think I'd better get back to the battery.'

Weidinger got up with him. He hated following Pichler around like a stray dog, but there was little point in remaining where he was, directly in front of their own infantry. If anything did happen he would be shot to pieces.

They walked down to the guns. The lorry was still there. So was Krag. So was the Widow Shemsi, who had extracted a pink parasol from her Gladstone and was twirling it over her right shoulder as if she was at some sporting event. All of them should have gone at least ten minutes before, and Pichler gave an audible little groan when he saw them. Weidinger's feelings on the matter were more confused, at least as far as one of the parties was concerned.

'It seems we have a mechanical problem, gentlemen,' said the intelligence officer. The bonnet was up and the most visible part of the driver was his large backside.

'It might not be your only problem,' said Pichler, who walked past the vehicle and started bellowing orders at his gun crews to turn two of the field pieces so that they faced the end of the inverted boomerang-shaped ridge where the English cavalry was now gathered.

'He thinks we're about to be attacked by cavalry,' Weidinger explained, a bit startled by the other's brusqueness.

'And what do you think?' said Krag.

'Not yet. Not until they have artillery support.'

'Do you mean we are about to be bombarded?' asked the Widow Shemsi.

'I do,' said Weidinger. He wanted to frighten her but he could see that he was not succeeding. Her tone reminded him of the way she had announced 'I've never been in an air raid' when their train almost ran into the bombs hitting Etline. That seemed a thousand years ago now.

Sometime during the morning Shemsi had changed into a clean beige dress with a little lace collar. The dress went tolerably well with her straw hat, though perhaps not with the parasol. In fact, thought Weidinger, considering the heat and the lack of sleep, Shemsi was looking remarkably fresh, poised and smiling at Krag in a way she had not the last time he saw them together. He still couldn't get over the transformation, the cynicism, the downright fickleness of this female.

———————————

When he had emerged from the wireless room after sending his message to von Papen, she had been standing alone under one of the palms with her back to him, her Gladstone at her feet. Pichler had gone off to see that all was well with his battery.

Weidinger had walked over to her, scraping his boots on the hard earth to let her know that he was coming, for he could see by the way her shoulders were heaving that she was still crying. He had contemplated putting an arm around her but at the last moment she had turned, red-eyed, tucking a handkerchief up her sleeve. 'Why?' was all she had said.

'Why what?' Weidinger had replied, because he wanted her to spell it out.

'Why did he forge those things in Herr Maeltzer's despatch?'

'We can't be certain –' Weidinger had started to say, but only for form's sake.

'Why else would he deny all existence of the journal?'

Weidinger had merely shrugged.

'Where do you think it is now?'

'I have the feeling it's been destroyed.'

'So do I, and I know why he did it.'

'You do?' He had wanted to hear her call Krag more than a liar. He wanted to hear her call him an unscrupulous bastard, rotten with ambition, who wasn't worthy to wear the Kaiser's uniform. But she hadn't obliged, not even when he had prompted her with, 'So why do you think he did it?'

'I can't tell you – not now.'

'Why not?'

'I don't know – it might be dangerous.'

'For who – yourself?'

'Perhaps.'

'What are you going to do now?'

'I'm going to do what I came here to do, Herr Oberleutnant. I'm going to find Major Krag and get the written permission I need to proceed overland from Etline to Jaffa.'

'And when you're safely ensconced in your new hotel, will you spare a thought for Maeltzer?'

She had looked quite angry with him then. 'You have sent a wireless message to Jerusalem about Herr Maeltzer's journal?'

'Yes.'

'Then nothing I could add would save him. I have no proof. Only . . .'

'Only what?'

'I don't know,' and suddenly her face had broken into one of her, rare mischievous smiles. 'It's called female intuition, isn't it? I don't think it would carry much weight at a military tribunal.'

'But you believe your feelings?'

'Yes, I believe my feelings.'

She had gone off then and the next time he saw her was almost five hours later when he had just emerged from the wireless office again, disappointed to find it already abandoned, the valves and condensers smashed, and no sign of any reply from von Papen. Krag was with her, and although they were not exactly arm-in-arm, Weidinger thought they might as well have been.

By then the confusion which had greeted them when they first arrived in Huj had turned to chaos. This was partly because the engineers had dynamited the wells without warning and most of the available transport, whether horse-drawn or motorised, had stampeded away in a northerly direction in the belief that the British were upon them.

'We seem to have a problem,' Krag had announced. 'My car has gone with the rest.'

He had not sounded particularly upset about it. In fact, for Krag he sounded quite cheerful. Weidinger had wondered whether this insouciance was for Shemsi's benefit or his – the cool head at the front.

'The lorry with Pichler's battery is going on ahead of them with their baggage and rations,' Weidinger had said. 'I suppose you could ride in that.'

Up to then Weidinger had been determined to stay on with Pichler and leave with him on the gun limbers, but now he found himself looking at Shemsi, hoping she would ask for him to go with her. Surely it was inconceivable that she would wish to travel alone with Krag after all that had transpired? The realisation of how anxious he was that she should want him to be with her had come as something of a shock.

'Where is it now?' asked Krag.

'The driver and one of the other men are looking for ammunition for the guns. There is supposed to be a dump here somewhere. They'll be back to pick me up.'

'You didn't want to go with them?'

'I was checking the wireless room for messages but I was too late.'

'Ah yes. I helped the operator destroy the set half an hour ago. It's a sad business, wrecking such fine machinery. I'm sorry if you wanted to send another telegram. I have just burned all the copies of the last outgoing and incoming telegrams I could find. I think there was even one for you, Herr Oberleutnant – something about a stay of execution?'

And Weidinger had nodded, stunned by both his nonchalance and the metamorphosis that had come over Shemsi – as indeed he was intended to be.

A cart with what looked like an entire regiment of Syrian Arab soldiers clinging to it staggered by, the men staring balefully at these German officers and the woman standing with them. Krag said, 'Excuse me a moment,' and walked off towards one of the abandoned buildings, presumably in search of a privy the engineers had not yet booby-trapped with a stick grenade.

'Why did you change?' he had asked Shemsi as soon as he was out of earshot.

'I have not changed, Oberleutnant Weidinger, but other things have. The first thing is that Herr Maeltzer is no longer going to hang. Major Krag tells me that he now doubts whether he will ever hang, although he still believes he should, because Maeltzer is Jewish and since this British declaration about a homeland for the Jews it is now German policy to encourage the Turks to show kindness to them. The second thing is that Major Krag has asked me to marry him. I have accepted.'

She talked about her second thing as dispassionately as the first, as though it had always been part of the agenda, something he should have been aware of.

It winded him. He had to hear it again, slowly.

'Major Krag has asked you to marry him?'

'Yes.'

'And you have accepted?'

'Yes.'

'But how could you, knowing what you do?'

'How could I not? I'm not of an age to turn down too many proposals of marriage.'

'But what about your feelings? That intuition of yours?'

'As I said, Herr Maeltzer is no longer going to hang – Major Krag showed me your telegram.'

'Did you ask him about the diary? Did he tell you about that?'

'He said that there was – what do you call it, rivalry? a feud? – a feud between him and von Papen, and that the diary is of no importance, but he doesn't want to give von Papen the satisfaction of handing it over to him.'

'And you believe this? You believe this story?'

'I believe that Maeltzer won't hang. That he will be released and sent back to Switzerland where he belongs.'

'And what will happen when you are asked to testify in front of a new tribunal about that diary – as you will be?'

'I am going to stay with my family in Beirut for a while. Besides, I shall be married.'

'God, if marriage is so much to you I would marry you myself if I were a whole man!' The words had come gushing out, spontaneous, almost out of control. He was quite exhilarated by them.

'Good heavens!' said Shemsi. 'Two proposals in one day! I like being at the front. But you wouldn't marry me although it's nice of you to think you would. And you are a whole man and you know it.'

And then she had kissed him on the forehead.

Now here she was, leaning against the lorry, twirling her parasol while the fat driver grunted over his engine with a spanner. Even Krag, his cap set at an almost rakish angle, was looking more relaxed than he usually did, which in Weidinger's eyes made him more odious than ever. As he walked the three hundred metres back to the guns he wondered why the intelligence officer had allowed himself to get into this predicament in the first place. Basically, he gloated, it was his reliance on mechanical transport.

No horse ever got dust in his carburettor or snapped a magneto. All the same, surely he could have departed with the signals personnel from the wireless hut?

At the battery the Austrians, great continents of sweat stencilled on the back of their shirts, were still manhandling two of their pieces around to meet the cavalry threat. Only the 5.9 howitzers behind them continued to fire at the English infantry. The gunners strained at the base plates while others fetched rope-handled ammunition boxes from the pile that had been unloaded from the stricken vehicle. The ensign, his eyes like poached eggs now with infectious hepatitis, was staggering from gun to gun distributing extra bullets for the crew's carbines and pistols.

Pichler was giving orders about the shell fusing to his Feldwebel, a giant of a young Tyrolean who had tried to disguise his youth with the kind of moustache small children hang on. 'Each gun to have five shrapnel rounds set to ten seconds, five to five, and five to zero.'

When the NCO had gone off to see about this Weidinger said, 'Zero settings? Expecting them to get that close?'

'I'm not taking any chances,' replied Pichler. 'I'm a conventional kind of soldier, I suppose. I know those machine-guns behind us won't let us down. I know they won't jam. I know they have the best field of fire where they are and that they will keep those nasty Tommy toothpicks away from us. But just between you and me and my grandmother's favourite saint I would feel a whole lot happier if we had some people out in front.

'And there's another thing. As you may have noticed, we may be hidden from them, but they are also hidden from us. There's at least four hundred metres of dead ground out there behind the spur which we can't cover over open sights. You must agree it's worrying. I'm going to have to send my young gentleman back to where we were lying, with a man on the field telephone to act as a spotter. At least he can lie down and pretend he's in bed which is where he should be if you ask me.'

Weidinger nodded. It was true enough. The boy looked as weak as a kitten. But he was still convinced that it wasn't going to happen.

'Don't forget you've got those mountain guns covering your left flank,' he said. 'If the Tommies come at you head on they'd have to face enfilade fire from over there. They'd be slaughtered.'

'Yes,' said Pichler, 'I suppose you're right – providing they can get the range.'

At that moment one of the most unearthly sounds either officer had ever heard floated across the little valley that separated them from the enemy. Others who were with the guns that day recalled that it was like something between an off-key bugle call and a canine's lunar howl. At the same time a large cloud of dust began to roll towards the mountain, which began booming away at a furious rate. They were soon accompanied by the rattle of rifle fire, and then the machine-guns behind Weidinger joined in. At first they fired short bursts and then longer ones as they appeared to get on target. Weidinger estimated the range at just over one thousand metres, and wondered if they would curb the tendency to shoot high at that distance.

'They're charging,' said Pichler. 'Perhaps it's the Australians again.'

Weidinger was looking at the dust cloud through his field glasses. It had now almost reached the Turkish position, and he could see the flashing of steel.

'No, I don't think so,' he said. 'Not this time.'

Then came that strange doubling note again, slightly closer now.

———————

Calderwell felt himself go cold.

'There goes old Toby tootin' his 'orn,' said Mace to no one in particular. To their right two troops from C Squadron, five officers and twenty-nine men, including Colonel Gray-Cheape, seemed to move off after the Worcesters. That left B Squadron and two troops of the Worcesters who had not gone with Albright on the ridge.

'All right, s'arnt-major,' said Captain Valintine.

'Squadron will advance in half squadrons.'

It was almost 1.30 p.m. Overhead a late flock of cranes flew south on their winter migration to the Great Rift Valley.

'Squadron advaaance.'

B Squadron of the Warwickshire Yeomanry, four officers and thirty-eight men, trotted their horses about twenty yards. They were still just below the crest, only their dust showing. The two remaining troops of the Worcesters, about thirty men under a lieutenant called Edwards, came with them, positioning themselves slightly in echelon to the right. Valintine was about a length ahead of everybody else on a grey. He turned in the saddle, his face flushed with excitement, and said, 'It's the guns we're after, lads. Good huntin' and keep spread out! Chaaaarrrrge!'

313

As Valintine's sword arm went down and his spurs went in so the pair of Skoda guns facing them opened fire on the Yeomanry for the first time.

———————

'High,' said Pichler. 'Down two degrees.'

The brass elevation wheels were turned.

'Fire! That's better.'

Weidinger, peering through his Zeiss alongside him, thought he saw at least three horses go down.

'Bloody ignorant, these Tommies,' growled Pichler. 'Don't read their own history books.'

But they were not coming in the way Weidinger had always imagined a cavalry charge, a great glorious mass of men and horseflesh advancing on the enemy stirrup to stirrup, as the Uhlans had at Mars La Tour. These horsemen were hardly in formation at all: they were riding in twos and threes, even singly, with as much as ten metres between groups in places. They looked more like Cossacks than regular cavalry, and every few seconds they would vanish into their own dust.

———————

When the first whizz-bangs from the Austrian battery came at them, just a little too late to do any harm, Calderwell's reaction had been the same as most of the other Yeomanry: the sooner they got past those guns the safer they would be. He raked Villa's sides with his spurs and even began to use his sword like a whip on her rump. At one point he was almost level with Mace, who grinned and shouted something that was carried away by the sound of the next explosion, which seemed directly above them. It was a Derby. Everybody had decided on speed, and the best riders and the best horses, who almost invariably went together, edged into the lead, so that soon Calderwell was squinting into the dust of at least four mounts immediately ahead.

There was a noise like a hailstorm on an iron-roofed building and for a moment Calderwell wondered whether their own Hotchkiss teams had come up and were giving them cover. Then he had to swerve around an animal that was down in front of him and for a moment he felt Villa falter and break her stride as her hooves caught something. There was a scream, whether from horse or man he could not tell. The hailstorm intensified as the Turkish infantry joined in

314

with their Mausers. 'Bloody charge of the light brigade,' muttered Calderwell. 'Right, you bastards.'

Weidinger was standing by one of the .75s trying to make out what effect their fire was having. He had seen some horses go down and others appeared to be riderless, but the dust shrouded most of what was happening. Long bursts of automatic fire went overhead. He looked behind him and saw that the Feldwebel in charge of the machine-gun detachment was now directing two of his weapons at this new threat, while the third continued to cover the attack on the mountain guns on their left flank.

'Five-second fuses,' Pichler was shouting, his hand over the mouth-piece of the field telephone. Apart from about thirty horsemen who had started after the others, the English were out of sight now. His commands came after the ensign manning the observation post had recorded the distances through his Goertz range-finder and then reeled them off to the gunner operating the telephone set. The nearest horses were now at four hundred and fifty metres.

'C'est magnifique mais ce n'est pas la guerre,' murmured Weidinger who, like Calderwell, could not get the Crimea out of his head. What sort of a fool sent cavalry to attack a position like this without artillery support? Another hundred metres and the machine-gunners would really start to cut them to pieces.

He suddenly became aware that somebody else was standing alongside him. He turned and there was Shemsi, leaning on her rolled parasol and peering into the dust as if she was at the race track. 'What's happening?' she said, flinching slightly every time a gun went off. 'Where have they all gone?'

'They're just behind that little ridge in front of us, that spur,' said Weidinger, trying to conceal his astonishment. For the last few minutes he had completely forgotten her existence. 'I think it might be better if you went back to the lorry. Where's Major Krag?'

'He's trying to help get it started.'

Weidinger looked and saw that the driver was still tinkering with the engine while Krag stood stooped at the front gripping the starting handle with both hands.

'They almost got it going a few minutes ago,' she said.

'I think you ought to forget about trying to start it now,' said Weidinger. 'Please tell Major Krag that there is a possibility that a few of these English might break through. You must take cover until we've dealt with them.'

'But where?'

'Go under the lorry,' said Pichler, who had been listening to some of their conversation. 'And go now. They're three hundred metres away.' He started to shout down the telephone, 'You've done a good job. I'll try and get you a medal for it. Now get out of there. Come on! Come back and keep your heads down or you'll get them blown off by those excellent machine-guns behind us.'

The Widow Shemsi lifted her skirts and ran back to the lorry. The machine-gun fire intensified.

They had almost crossed the valley now and were approaching the slight incline that seemed to conceal the place where the guns that had been tormenting them lay. A riderless horse, a chestnut like Villa, came alongside Calderwell. He glanced across at it and failed to recognise whose it was but saw that the horse had got caught up in some sort of blueish tubing that was clinging to its left flank. Then he realised he was looking at the animal's intestines, which had sprung from a gaping wound in its side and were now easing themselves a little more into the daylight with every stride it took. To Calderwell's amazement, despite its impending evisceration, the horse easily overtook Villa and other laden stable-mates. When they reached the crest the hailstorm on the iron roof became noisier, though Calderwell was concentrating so hard on avoiding falling horses that he hardly noticed. He glimpsed a dismounted Yeoman pulling his Lee-Enfield out of his saddle boot, and then he was at the top and his sword arm went down.

'Just point your weapon,' the instructor had said. 'Thumb in the groove, and the speed of your horse will do the rest.'

But what do I point at, sergeant? What do I point at when the dust is so thick I can hardly see the end of my sword? Then the dust cloud parted and he saw the guns for the first time. At almost the same moment the machine-gun fire stopped.

'Zero fuses,' Pichler was shouting. 'Zero fuses. For God's sake, where's that boy?'

'Here they come now,' said Weidinger.

They were following the field telephone line down. The Hungarian gunner they called Gypsy was in the lead, winding the cable onto the apparatus as he went. Behind him came the ensign, who had the

316

gunner's carbine slung over his right shoulder and the range-finder in his left hand. He kept looking back. They were about four hundred metres from the guns.

'Come on, come on,' said Pichler.

The first horse appeared. It was riderless, and was almost instantly felled by a burst of machine-gun fire.

'Run, man. Come on, run,' pleaded Pichler, though there was absolutely no chance they could hear him above the din of exploding ordnance. The ensign would run for half-a-dozen strides before he had to pause for breath. Another riderless horse crested the ridge to meet the same fate.

'Oh for God's sake drop that phone,' whispered Pichler, 'I won't have you court-martialled for losing it.'

Horsemen were visible now, a man on a grey in the front. Almost as if he had heard him Gypsy dropped the phone and sprinted towards the guns. Weidinger estimated that the nearest Tommy was about thirty metres away from the ensign. For a few seconds the sick teenager looked as if he might keep up a sustained sprint too. But then he stopped again, put the range-finder down, and began to unsling his carbine. Almost at the same moment the machine-gun fire became suddenly much reduced, and for the second time that afternoon the gunners heard that strange double-noted horn.

Weidinger looked up at the sangers behind him. The Feldwebel in charge was desperately trying to turn his two remaining Maxims to meet a score or so cavalry galloping towards him along the ridge from the left. They had broken through the Turkish infantry protecting the pack howitzers, and outflanked his machine-guns.

'Open sights,' Pichler was saying. 'Wait for 'em.' He did not think the Yeomanry were quite close enough yet for the instantaneous fuse shrapnel.

Weidinger tapped him on the shoulder and pointed to what was happening to their rear. Pichler looked, shrugged and then went back to the task at hand. 'We'll have to look after ourselves,' he shouted above the din. 'The Russkies didn't have machine-guns at Balaclava, did they? Oh for sweet Jesus's sake hurry, boy.'

Gypsy was almost at the guns but the ensign, having unslung the carbine as if he might take a pot shot at his pursuers, had now changed his mind and was running again with the weapon in his right hand. He had abandoned the Goertz. The nearest Yeoman was now about ten metres from him and Weidinger could see the tip of the Englishman's thrusting sword. Pichler unholstered his Steyr automatic and began to shoot up the hillside, though the range was extreme for a pistol. At least three hundred metres, Weidinger thought. Nonetheless, he produced his Webley and aimed a shot at the horses, but was reluctant to fire more in case he needed the other five rounds for closer work. A one-armed man has to think ahead when it comes to reloading a revolver.

In any case, it was already too late for the cadet officer. Weidinger caught a momentary glimpse of him standing, it seemed, with his back to the guns and his hands going up as if he was trying to surrender, though this may have been because he had been knocked and turned by a horse. There was a brief equine scrum around the spot where he had last been seen and then the English came on yelling like banshees.

On the guns the soldiers manning the elevation wheel sweated to bring the barrels near parallel with the ground. The crews from the other two pieces now abandoned shelling the infantry and took cover behind the wheels or under the guns and limbers, their carbines and pistols at the ready.

'Fire!' yelled Pichler, and for the first time his guns facing the cavalry used the instantaneous fuse shrapnel. In less than a second the two rounds travelled fifty metres from the muzzles of the Skodas before exploding about ten metres in front of the first rank of the advancing English and a metre above them. The effect was devastating. A great tangle of shrieking men and horses went down in front of them. Out of it emerged a horse without forelegs which was trying to gallop, and a terrified mare which bolted past the guns dragging a dead or dying Yeoman by his stirrup.

'This is sheer bloody murder,' murmured Weidinger to himself. They had not yet had a shot fired at them and their only casualty was the poor boy too sick to run fast enough. Even without the machine-gun cover it seemed inconceivable that they could lose as long as the infantry continued to beat off the few horsemen who reached the ground above. The next wave was upon them and the next rounds were in the breech, only some of the English veered a bit left this time towards the guns that had been firing on Shea's infantry.

Lying beneath the lorry Shemsi had such a restricted view of things that she had decided she could stand it no longer and had to come out. The noise sounded like the end of the world. Yet all she could see through her small window on the proceedings was one of the gun crews, labouring so calmly that they might have been engaged in some methodical industrial process.

She announced her intention to Krag, who had given up the starting handle and was now leaning against the side of the vehicle taking a cigarette out of the case that had been presented to Second Lieutenant Anthony Buchan by his loving parents. The driver continued to tighten nuts and clean things with a bit of oily rag. When Krag didn't hear her the first time, Shemsi rapped the side of his boots with her parasol. This brought the sharp retort that she should stay exactly where she was. The English, he said, were behind them on the ridge above. Shortly after that she heard a horse gallop close by, and then the driver squeezed his bulk under the vehicle and explained that even if he did get the thing going they couldn't go anywhere for the moment because their road out was cut.

'What's happening?' asked Shemsi.

'We're killing a lot of them,' he grunted and worked a round into the breach of his carbine.

Shemsi thought he sounded scared.

———————

Calderwell was not aware that the machine-gun fire had stopped. He was not aware of anything other than a flash which had destroyed the three men and horses in front of him and left him seeing nothing but the colour orange.

Villa had shied off to the left. He shook his head and his vision began to return. He saw that he was galloping down into the hollow where the guns lay on a course that would take him straight through the middle of the battery. The two guns on his left were slightly forward of the other pair. He saw their crews crouched behind the wheels and under the gun barrels firing their pistols, and then a Yeomanry officer he failed to recognise rode up on his inside and shot back from the saddle with his Webley.

Calderwell nudged Villa away from him towards the other guns, the pair the blinding flash had come from, thinking that the sooner he was past them the safer he would be. He almost immediately regretted this, for standing just inside the wheel of the first gun was a red-cheeked Austrian officer pointing an automatic pistol. The Austrian fired and he felt Villa give a little lurch.

'*Just point your weapon and the speed of your horse will do the rest.*' Calderwell did not feel the thrusting sword enter Pichler's neck. He was only aware of the awful ripping sound it made as his rigid right arm went back and the blade was pulled clear by Villa's momentum.

He rode on up the rear of the hollow away from the guns until he was on the high ground where the enemy infantry and their machine-gunners were. Here Calderwell, by now as excited by what he was doing as he had been when the horse bolted on him at Warwick Castle, expected to collide with Turkish infantry armed with saw bayonets. Instead, he was amazed to see that the ridge was already full of Yeomanry, some dismounted, whom he identified as Albright's Worcesters because they didn't have the Warwicks' black diamond flash on their topees. He now understood why he hadn't recognised the officer alongside him at the guns. He must have been a Worcester who had gone in on their right flank with Albright, galloped along the ridge, somehow lost his troop in the mêlée, come down around the guns and then gone back up again. He looked at his sword, which he was holding upwards. Some of Pichler's blood had run down the central groove and come to rest against the basket hilt.

'Get down! Get down!' Weidinger was shouting. 'They can't get at you if you're under the gun.'

Weidinger was not in fact under the gun himself but crouched behind the wheel besides which his friend Pichler had collapsed, his head almost severed from his body, those apple cheeks already drained to a marble white. The eyes still stared in dull surprise, quite oblivious to the flies feeding on the gore at his neck.

It had all happened so quickly. Weidinger had been standing about a foot to Pichler's left when the Tommy, the first one to get that close to them alive, was on them. Pichler had fired one shot, made a faint gasping sound and then sat rather than fallen against the gun wheel, his head at a ghastly angle. His cap had fallen into the dust. Weidinger had ducked to one knee and fired two shots at the rider coming behind the man who had killed Pichler and thought he had at least winged him, for he seemed to veer off.

Those gunners who had not already done so now followed his example – some had even squeezed themselves beneath the axles of the guns, where they could be reasonably certain that mounted men with swords could not reach. In any case, apart from the inherent dangers of standing up, it was pointless to continue manning the guns because there was nothing left to fire at. All the English cavalry that had survived were now the other side of their muzzles. Weidinger was not alone in thinking that the best thing was to make themselves as inaccessible and as prickly as possible until the infantry pushed the Tommies back.

The ground around the guns was burnished with spent shell cases, and there were at least a dozen dead or dying horses in the immediate vicinity. It seemed certain that no more than a handful of the English who had charged them were left alive. Weidinger looked up at the ridge where the machine-guns were, but there was so much dust it was impossible to be certain what was happening. He had to admit that there might be more horses up there than he had at first imagined. Even so, it had been a very ragged charge. Hardly a cohesive mass at all. It was inconceivable that there was anything like enough cavalry to take on a regiment of infantry. Even cavalry as willing to die as these English boys had been.

Weidinger found Pichler's cap on the ground near him and put it over the Austrian's face. He could do nothing about the flies. He suddenly felt very lonely and longed to hear those machine-guns start up again. For the first time it occurred to him that if they didn't it would mean that the English had won. He began to wonder if these cavalrymen would take prisoners after all they had had done to them.

As he approached the high ground after killing Pichler, the first thing Calderwell was aware of was the shouting. It was the kind of noise you might hear outside a crowded football stadium, and it was the sound of the Yeomanry colliding with the Turkish infantry. Only when he got closer did he realise that men were not only screaming at each other but screaming for other reasons.

He glimpsed Mace, hatless, blood running down his face, put his sword through the shoulder of a Turk who had lunged at him with a fixed bayonet. Nearby one of Fifth Mounted Brigade's most popular NCOs, a stocky little Worcesters sergeant called Allen, was engaged in a furious duel with a large German machine-gunner who had picked up a rifle with fixed bayonet. The Yeomanry were now all over the machine-guns and there was no chance of the Germans using them.

Calderwell went to help Allen but was distracted by a broad-shouldered figure with his back to him and a rifle in his hands who popped up a few feet to his front. He pointed his sword and kicked some speed into Villa, only to pull up in horror at the last moment when he realised the man was wearing a British rifle bandoleer. Up until then he had not noticed that there were a number of dismounted Yeomanry about who had removed their rifles from their saddle buckets.

For a moment it looked as though the charge might have lost its momentum, but then another fifty horsemen crashed into the scrum.

These were the two troops from the Worcesters who had charged at the Austrian battery slightly behind the Warwicks, plus the men Colonel Gray-Cheape had led behind Toby Albright's squadron and then around the ridge to capture the 5.9 howitzers. Gray-Cheape's men were the last to arrive. They had come at the infantry who had been covering Pichler's guns from what the Turks still considered to be the friendly side of the ridge, and it had been too much for them. They began to fall back – in ones and twos at first, then by sections, then by platoons, then whole companies that were no longer firing and retiring but simply running madly downhill.

Those among the Yeomanry who had not already killed now made up for it. Men on foot, some still burdened by rifle and pack, were trying to outrun baying men on horseback who were both hounds and huntsmen combined in this most exciting sport of all. It was a downhill race in which the majority of the quarry were, in fact, overtaken unhurt because there were simply too many to kill.

Those who had, for some capricious reason, caught the eye of a horseman – perhaps because they were bigger built or had made themselves a more tempting target by becoming detached from the mob – were collected like litter at the end of the Baden-Powell swords. It was the work of a moment to impale a man and then let the onward rush of the horse pull the thirty-six-inch blade free of bone and gristle. Here and there a Turk brave enough to have retained his weapon turned and fired, and sometimes a horse would go down or a Yeoman's grip slacken on his sword.

Calderwell spotted one man throw himself to the ground and pretend to be dead. He dealt with this by leaning low out of the saddle like a pig-sticker and piercing him as he lay there gasping in terror. This produced a shriek so ghastly that for the first time it began to occur to him exactly what he was doing. It was shortly after this that Villa's forelegs suddenly buckled and he somersaulted over her head to land heavily on his back. As the horse went down Calderwell's pack came off the saddle and burst open, scattering the contents – among them his copy of *The Complete Letter-Writer*.

Krag at last joined them under the lorry, squeezing in between Shemsi and the fat driver. 'I'm afraid it does not go well,' he announced. 'It looks like we're surrounded.'

'Does that mean we might be captured?' asked Shemsi.

'It's possible,' conceded Krag.

'My God!' said Shemsi, whose thoughts immediately turned to rape.

Krag divined her fears. 'Don't worry,' he said. 'I'm sure the English will treat you with respect.'

Shemsi thought she detected a certain irony in this but said nothing.

'I'm going to the guns,' said the driver.

'I don't think that's a good idea,' advised Krag. 'A man with a long sword is quite likely to reach you before you reach them. What's more, you would draw attention to the fact that we're under here. If we have to surrender it's better to do so when the fighting's over and people are calmer. Their blood's up now.'

'No, I'm going,' the driver insisted. If the worst came to the worst he wanted to be with his mates, not stuck with this desiccated Prussian and his tart.

'You'll do as you're told,' snapped Krag, who was not going to tolerate insubordination from the ranks of the Imperial Austro-Hungarian army any more than he would his own.

'You're not my officer,' said the Austrian, who was very frightened. Suddenly it was more important than ever to get back with his friends. He rolled onto his back and got his head and shoulders out from under the lorry, still gripping his carbine in both hands.

Krag pulled him back, grabbing him by his tunic, just under the armpits. The fat man, frantic now, began kicking. Krag went onto his left side and began to reach for his pistol holster.

'Oh let him go if he's that desperate,' said Shemsi.

There was a shot, deafening under the lorry. Shemsi turned her head away. From the moment it had started she had known Krag would end up doing this.

The wriggling had stopped. Krag was breathing heavily. She sensed it was him.

'There was no need,' she said. 'No need for that.'

'He's gone,' said Krag in a hoarse voice.

She turned to face him. Krag was lying on his back, his mouth slightly open, both hands pressed tightly against his lower right side. His pistol was still in its holster. There was no sign of the driver.

'You're quite right,' he said. 'No need for that at all.' And he opened his hands to reveal the bubbling red underneath. 'The fat swine shot me with his carbine. I think it hit the cigarette case.'

From outside came two single rifle shots, then the machine-gun fire started up again. They were short, almost hesitant bursts at

323

first, but after a few seconds they became longer, more confident-sounding.

———————

A metre or so above Weidinger's head a rifle round pinged off the breech-block of the gun.

The Oberleutnant was lying on his stomach, his face pressed in the dirt against his field-glasses and more or less in line with Pichler's knees. He had been there ever since the Tommies had shot the fat driver when he tried to make a dash from the lorry, a movement that had encouraged them to start peppering the guns as well. It would be suicide to attempt to man them again, and Weidinger very much regretted he had not joined the rest of the crew under the axle while he was still able to move.

When the machine-guns started up again Weidinger had felt a momentary spurt of hope. He had even forced himself to use his Zeiss to examine the top of the ridge four hundred metres away, though he had half expected the glass to attract the bullet which had just ricocheted off the breech-block. It had not been worth the risk. As he had feared, there was nothing but khaki moving up there. Whatever else that machine-gun fire meant, it was not the remains of the English cavalry being beaten back.

Pichler seemed to twitch back into life as some part of his body was hit by a .303 bullet from above. Besides him, Weidinger tried to lie more still than his lifeless friend.

———————

'Look at the boggers run, Caldy,' said Mace, who was squatting behind the German machine-gun they had just turned round while Calderwell fed the belt in from the ammunition box. Those Turks who were not dead or prisoners were off the ridge and running north along the dirt road, where the two troops Colonel Cheape had taken around the right flank had intercepted the 5.9 howitzer battery as its gunners tried to pull it away. They could see the four guns spaced along the road in a ragged single file, with some dead horses lying next to them.

Theirs was the last of the three captured machine-guns to be brought into action against the Turks. This was because it had so many bodies around it that had to be moved, the strangest being those of Sergeant Allen, the little veteran from the Worcesters, and the large Feldwebel who had taken him on with rifle and bayonet.

In death the two were literally pinned together, for Allen's hand still gripped the sword which had disappeared up to its hilt into the man who had killed him.

'I reckon the old sarge 'ere wanted to make bloody sure,' Mace had gasped as he gently prised Allen's hand off his sword and they moved him aside.

Calderwell had said nothing. Just as he said nothing now as they watched the Turks below them try to run all the way back to Etline. His main concern was Villa. The mare was lying down a few feet behind him making strange rasping sounds of a kind he had never heard from a horse before.

As soon as he had got his breath back he retrieved his sword and walked over to Villa. She had struggled to her feet as he knelt besides her and asked, 'What's up with yow, old girl?'

He had walked her back to the top of the ridge, passing some small scattered groups of Turks who put their hands up as soon as they saw him and walked in front of him. After a while he had about thirty Turks in front of him like this and he thought he had captured them single-handed until he realised that Mace and another man were walking alongside him with their rifles at the ready. Of the three of them he was the only man who still had his horse.

When they got to the summit a couple of men, including the signaller who had borrowed the colonel's ash walking-stick for the charge, were firing at the Austrian .75s they had galloped through. 'Some of them fuckers are still movin',' the signaller explained, extracting another five-round clip from his bandoleer. He was lying in the approved prone position as if he was on the range, and Calderwell noticed the crossed rifles of a marksman on his sleeve.

It was then that he had examined Villa carefully and found a small hole in her neck which he guessed was caused by a bullet from the pistol of the Austrian officer he had killed. Shortly after that she had gone down for the second time. He had looked over the bodies and found a half-full water-bottle on the belt of one of the German machine-gunners, and then picked up a helmet, because he had lost his own, and walked over to the mare and poured all but a swallow for himself into it. Villa had barely had time to drink it before he was ordered to lend a hand with the machine-guns.

'Keep the fuckers on the run,' a wild-eyed corporal had urged. 'If they find out how many of us are left they'll be back at us like a fuckin' ferret up a sick bunny.'

Calderwell had stared at him in amazement. The NCO's left sleeve was all red rags, with something terrible hanging inside. Yet he was holding a Lee-Enfield in his right hand and seemed quite oblivious of his mutilation.

Luckily for the Turks, Mace fired the Krupp gun with more enthusiasm than skill. Of the three captured guns his had been fired for the longest bursts with the result that the barrel had become too hot and its rifling almost reduced to smooth-bore accuracy. Inevitably it jammed when a slightly misshapen cartridge case refused to eject.

At this point, when almost all the captured guns were out of ammunition, some brave Turks attempted to save the most northerly of the abandoned howitzers on the dirt road by hitching a team to it. Calderwell thought they might have succeeded – and in a way he would have been glad of it, for he was tired of killing – had not the Yeomanry's own Hotchkiss gun teams at last caught up with them, finicky men equipped with the latest in Barr and Stroud range-finders. This last piece of mayhem, which took place barely an hour after General Shea had so politely asked the Yeomanry to charge the guns, marked the end of this particular skirmish, though it took a while for most of its participants to realise that this was the case.

On the ridge some of the Yeomanry started to collect the wounded of both sides in readiness for the ambulance wagons. Calderwell found some more water and went back to Villa. Mace wandered off in search of cigarettes. On his return he announced that Toby Albright was dead and that, by the look of him, Captain Valintine was dying.

'Oh ar,' said Calderwell, accepting the proffered Woodbine. He had taken Villa's saddle off and extracted his .303 from the rifle boot, and was squatting by the mare, who was still on her side, drawing finger patterns in the dust between the clumps of tussock grass.

Mace had knelt briefly beside him and put an arm around his shoulder before walking away with a party who were going to take what prisoners were left of the Austrians before Sixtieth Division or, even worse, the Australians arrived and claimed them for themselves.

———————

Weidinger looked at his watch. The hands told him it was five minutes to two. He found this incredible, and put his right ear over the watch to see if it was still going. It was. The whole action had taken just less than half an hour.

It was several minutes at least since the English snipers had last fired at them. Then they had obviously been laying down covering fire for something that came rattling by at a great pace, either horse artillery or a Hotchkiss squadron. Shortly afterwards the machine-gun fire intensified, and he guessed it was the latter.

He raised his head a centimetre or two off the ground, conscious that this might be all a good sniper was waiting for: the moment when curiosity or cramp overcame fear. Above the drone of the flies feeding on Pichler he thought he heard a footfall, perhaps several footfalls. He managed to push aside sufficiently thoughts of telescopic crosshairs on his cranium to raise his head slightly more, just enough to look over the upper part of Pichler's thighs and through the wooden spokes of the gun wheel. He could see the wheel of one of the other two guns, the pair that had been manhandled around to face the cavalry, and that was all.

There were voices. Loud, confident voices. Weidinger could not understand what they were saying at first. Then he caught the words 'Hande hoche!' Even then they were only comprehensible because they were repeated several times, along with English exhortations he did not understand at all such as 'C'mon, Fritz. C'mon out of it, you silly buggers. Game's over. Kamerad? You savvy? Kamerad?'

Weidinger took a deep breath and almost sprang to his feet. A crowd of Tommies, young men in cord breeches and cloth puttees from knee to ankle, were around the other two Skodas, where those gunners who were capable of it were standing with their hands raised. He noticed that the young Feldwebel with the moustache had had to be helped to his feet by one of his men. The Tommies began to walk towards him and he was relieved to see that they were carrying rifles rather than swords. He raised his own hand thinking, as he did so, that at least as a prisoner-of-war he would remain on the active list. He wondered what Kress and von Papen would have to say.

Mace was the first to reach him. He assumed that the German officer who could only manage to raise one hand was wounded, and was a bit taken aback when he realised that most of his left sleeve was empty. He took Weidinger's Zeiss binoculars, almost knocking his cap off with the strap as he brought it over his head, before he bothered to remove the holstered Webley, which he tucked in his belt. The Uhlan hardly noticed. For the first time he had the opportunity to look at almost all the battlefield, apart from the dead ground above which the ensign had died arranging air bursts. There was a trail of dead horses and men which started just before the guns and led up to the ridge, at the base of which he could see two riderless horses.

327

It had never occurred to him that a successful charge would look so much like a defeat.

'Perhaps I'd better get help,' she said.

It had become strangely quiet. Shemsi suddenly realised that there had not been any machine-gun fire for several minutes. For a short while there was an occasional rifle shot, but now that had stopped as well. Somewhere quite close a horse whinnied once. Then there was nothing, no sound at all apart from the droning of insects.

'No, don't go,' said Krag, who was lying on his back. 'I think all that can be done has been done for the moment. Thank you.'

The thanks unnerved her slightly – so out of character. She thought he looked white enough to be dying, though he appeared in no immediate danger of losing consciousness. Shemsi did not want to be alone with him if he died. She wished Weidinger was there.

'How are you feeling?'

'Wonderful,' said Krag. That was also out of character. It re-minded her of Maeltzer's little ironies in the death cell. She decided it was the kind of pose a certain type of man considered obligatory before a woman, and warmed to him for it.

At first there had been an awful lot of blood. It was all over her. On her dress, her hands, her face where she had wiped away the sweat. She had torn his tunic and shirt open, ripped great strips from her petticoat, folded the swabs of yellow cotton against the wounds, watched them turn a soggy red, torn some more and repeated the process. The last ones still showed traces of yellow.

She was still uncertain how badly hurt Krag was. He was right about the bullet hitting the cigarette case. She had removed it from the upper right pocket of his tunic and the silver-plated alloy was holed right through. 'So now it's a silver and tobacco bullet,' he had gasped when she showed it him. 'At least it must have slowed it down a bit. Look after it. It'll make an interesting keepsake.'

One of the reasons it had taken her so long to slow the bleeding was that she had not immediately discovered that there were two wounds, about ten centimetres apart. The main wound was just below the right rib cage and there was a second one on the hip where she assumed the bullet must have come out. Now she had bandages on both, and the bleeding seemed to have subsided a little.

'Do you enjoy playing nurse?' he asked. Shemsi thought that sounded much more like the Krag she knew and was prepared to marry.

328

'Am I playing?'

'Oh please. I didn't mean to be unkind. But we all play roles when we have to don't we? Soldier, nurse, journalist, spy – even a poor widow is obliged to make certain accommodations.'

Shemsi chose to ignore that, which disappointed him – though it was what he had expected. 'And do you play roles?' she asked.

'I suppose I do sometimes. Why not? Everybody else does.'

'And what role are you playing now?'

'I should have thought that was obvious. The wounded, perhaps dying, officer being a little philosophical in the presence of his lady love. A disciple of Stoic, I should say. I wish it were a more honourable wound. Does it count being shot by your own side?'

'Will you tell me something?'

'If I can.'

'Why did you forge those messages in Maeltzer's articles to his newspapers? Why didn't you give Weidinger his journal? Have you destroyed it?'

'All these questions, nurse. You mustn't excite the patient, you know. Anyway, you know the answers to all of them, don't you?'

'Then why would I bother asking them?'

'Because you have to be certain, you have to know.'

'Then tell me.'

'Let me ask you a question first. When I left you alone with Weidinger after it was plain we had become reconciled, what did you tell him?'

'I told him that you had offered to marry me and that Maeltzer was no longer a problem between us because we had seen von Papen's telegram to him and knew he was not going to hang.'

'And what did you tell him about the diary?'

She looked briefly away from him as if she thought she had heard some movement outside. 'I told him there was rivalry between you and von Papen and you didn't want him to get his hands on it. It would have shown that you had not been quite as clever as the tribunal believed you had been.'

'How clever of you. I'm sure he believed you.'

'He did. Now tell me why you forged that evidence against Maeltzer?'

'Weidinger believes that I did it solely to further my own career doesn't he? The little popinjay thought that I was so jealous of his success with Kress, so determined to be the man who unmasked Daniel, that I would be willing to send an innocent man to the gallows, didn't he? No spy keeps a diary. Isn't that what he told you?'

329

'Yes, that's what he believes,' she said softly.

'And do you believe it?'

'No. No, I don't. Not for those reasons.'

'Then why do you think I did it?'

'I want you to tell me. Please.'

'You know damn well why I did it. I did it to protect you.'

There was a long pause, the longest yet. Then she said, 'To protect me?'

If Shemsi sounded astonished Krag chose to ignore it. He sat up slightly, leaning on his right hand. He was beginning to feel as if the whole of his torso had been kicked by a horse.

'Yes,' he sighed. 'And myself, I suppose. A staff officer should not bring his problems back to his lady's rooms or leave his papers in places which an intelligent and curious eye might find too tempting. Why did you do it? Was it revenge for having to marry Major Shemsi to save your little brother's neck? But you have always given me the impression you admired the man. Or did you compromise yourself with somebody in Beirut while your husband was away, perhaps one of those young English blades on leave from Cyprus, there to pick up a little Arabic and taste the wine? The English excel at blackmail.'

'Erwin Krag,' she said, a small, furious smile on her lips. 'I don't think you did it to protect me at all. I think you know very well that such protection is unnecessary in my case. I think you did it to protect yourself. If the English really do excel at blackmail you must have been a very good target. There you were in Constantinople for all those years and the more you got to know the Turks the more you loathed them. Their vanities and corruption, their spectacular incompetence, their brutality. Above all their brutality. Weren't you disgusted by the way the Kaiser's favourite Muslims were treating the Armenians? Perhaps you had an Armenian sweetheart?'

'As a matter of fact I did have an Armenian friend,' he said. 'But she died of diphtheria, which was probably better than the death she might have suffered had she lived.'

Shemsi gave a sort of understanding nod, as if this had merely confirmed all that she had been saying. 'And then time after time you were unfairly passed over for promotion,' she went on. 'And all the time you were attending diplomatic functions where you would rub shoulders with the French, the British, the Russians — even the Americans. And sooner or later, of course, you found a sympathetic ear, a shoulder to cry on, somebody who knew your true worth. And the more you talked, the more they wanted to listen. I should think it was very flattering. And then one day they asked you something and you said you couldn't tell them because it was a secret and although you hated the Turks you would never betray your country. And they said, "But what if General Liman von Sanders found out about all the other things you've been telling us?" As you say, the English excel at blackmail. So you went on doing it.'

'I must say,' said Krag, 'I shall always admire you. But sometimes you can be too clever. Don't you think, Nadia, that you have just revealed a remarkable familiarity with the techniques of espionage?' He was smiling, eyebrows raised, pressing the petticoat cloth on his wounds.

Before she could make any answer a shot was fired and an English voice said, 'Come on out of it, Fritz.'

Krag slid out from beneath the trailer on his back and his captors immediately took in the blood and the makeshift bandages and helped him to his feet. Shemsi emerged on her stomach clutching the holed cigarette case and then stood blinking down the strong afternoon light, brushing the dust off her dress, quite unaware of how strange she looked in her blood-soaked clothing. 'I told yow I could hear a bint talkin',' said Mace, who held in his left hand the pineapple grenade he had decided not to roll under the vehicle.

On page 143 of *The Warwickshire Yeomanry in the Great War* it is mentioned that among the captives at Huj was a Syrian woman, who is described as the wife of a captured officer. What the regimental historian failed to record are the words of one of the wounded captives to a perplexed young subaltern of the Gloucesters, the third Yeomanry regiment of Fifth Mounted Brigade who were relieving the ninety intact survivors of the charge. Thirty-six of the Warwickshire and Worcestershire yeomen were dead or dying and fifty-seven wounded.

Stretcher-bearers treated the casualties as they found them, regardless of nationality. Krag was lying with British shell dressings on his wounds, waiting for a place in one of the horse ambulances. Shemsi hovered over him, occasionally fanning flies from his face.

Krag turned to the second lieutenant who had been landed with the problem of what to do about Shemsi. 'I wish you to do something for me,' he said in his workmanlike English.

The Gloucester nodded, thinking it might be something to do with the woman.

'You must get a message to the senior intelligence officer at General Allenby's headquarters,' he ordered. 'Tell him you have rescued Daniel.'

'Oh yes. And who might Daniel be?' inquired the subaltern who couldn't make out whether he was dealing with natural Prussian arrogance or gross delirium.

'They will understand,' said Krag. 'They will understand what I'm talking about, won't they, Madame Shemsi?'

She didn't say anything. She was staring at Meinertzhagen and Ponting, their red staff tabs easily visible, looking down on them from a spot where a young soldier had just persuaded a brown horse without a saddle to its feet.

37

The Adjutant General, a lean Scot who had spent the last two years of the war as head of Military Intelligence at the War Office, paused for the water glass. He was thinking of the night train to Folkestone and the comforts of Martello House and his Finnish wife, Aline.

His audience stirred slightly, sensing that he was getting to the end of his speech, and there was a final outbreak of coughing. One of the worst offenders was Ponting, who was seated in the third row next to his old boss. He looked at his watch. He had been looking forward to dinner with Meinertzhagen at the Army and Navy but he had this perfectly awful bloody cold coming on, a real ear, nose and throat job, and the old boy had gone on a bit longer than expected.

'The truth is,' said Lieutenant-General Sir George MacDonough as he put down his glass. 'It is impossible to anticipate victory in war without being ready to take risks.'

He paused to inspect his audience, and here and there his gaze forced a nod of assent. A few of them were in uniform because they had come straight off duty at the War Office or, in a couple of cases, from regimental soldiering at Chelsea Barracks. Most, including the general and even some of the newspaper reporters, wore the kind of brogues and pinstripes or hairy tweeds that were the undress uniform of the British officer corps.

'But all risks have to be logical,' went on Sir George. 'Someone looking from the sidelines, lacking knowledge about the situation, is likely to think that Allenby took unwarranted risks.' ('And so might you, if you'd been in Beersheba when we expected the cavalry to die of thirst,' thought Ponting, who was sitting with his arms folded. He was shortly to leave the army for a job with a merchant bank with interests in the Middle East.)

'That is not true,' continued the general, who was now looking directly at Ponting and Meinertzhagen with what appeared to be a slight smile on his face. 'Allenby knew with certainty from his Intelligence of all the preparations and all the movements of his enemy. All the enemy's cards were revealed to him, and he could play his own hand with complete confidence.'

MacDonough paused just long enough to drop his voice to what was almost a conspiratorial whisper. 'Gentlemen,' he confided. 'Under these conditions victory was certain before we ever began.'

Outside, strolling past the Guildhall in search of a cab, the cold air did wonders for Ponting's tubes and supper no longer seemed such a bad idea. Besides, there were some questions he wanted to ask Meinertzhagen, questions it would have been quite improper to ask four years ago.

They were still improper now, but he was on the verge of a new career and this post-war world was such a different place. Secrets dating from before 11 November 1918 seemed to belong to another century. The Bolsheviks had shot, bayoneted and bludgeoned the Imperial Russian family out of existence in a cellar in Ekaterinburg and now their relatives among the remaining thrones of Europe all lived in terror of constitutional regicide. The Austro-Hungarian and Turkish empires had disintegrated and a batch of unlikely republics had been hatched from the ruins. In Turkey itself Mustafa Kemal, the hero of Gallipoli and the man who had relinquished command of the Seventh Army on the eve of Allenby's offensive, had emerged as Commander-in-Chief and was preparing to smite the Greek occupiers and establish a nationalist government that would ensure the Sultan never returned.

Even in Britain it looked as if the Irish rebels were going to get their Free State if they were prepared to let Lloyd George save face by allowing the Crown to retain some nominal hold over it. The Kaiser was in exile in Holland, and Germany was in danger of either breaking up into its pre-Bismarckian parts at the mercy of wandering Freikorps, or of turning Communist. Allied troops occupied the Rhineland where the French were actively encouraging separatist tendencies among the natives. Meanwhile, Palestine had its first

Jewish ruler since the Romans had overthrown the last of the Macca-
bees almost two thousand years before.

He was Sir Herbert Samuel, first High Commissioner of the new
British Mandate. Sir Herbert was a Zionist but he had been obliged
to suspend the emigration of his co-religionists, mostly Russians and
Polish Jews, to their promised land because in Jaffa there had been
serious riots. The British army was trying to get Balfour's famous
declaration promising the Jews a homeland torn up, or at least
rewritten. People like Allenby, who was now High Commissioner
for Egypt and Sudan, felt it failed to live up to its second part. This
was to respect the rights of the indigenous people, who were no
longer called Syrians by the British but Palestinian Arabs in order to
distinguish them from their brethren who lived in the new French
Mandate of Syria, which included Damascus and Shemsi's home
town of Beirut.

Meinertzhagen was among the very few quite senior British officers
to be pro-Zionist, and for this reason he had fallen out with the
administration early on and was no longer serving in Palestine.
Ponting, who did not share his views, suspected that they were part
of his habitual contrariness, tinged with the genuine admiration they
all felt for people like the Aaronsohns, whom Ponting regarded as in
no way typical of the Jewish settlers. Meinertzhagen particularly
enjoyed it when people assumed that his support stemmed from the
fact that he was Jewish and delighted in giving sharp little lectures
on his Viking ancestry.

Ponting waited until after the meal, when they had both been
loosened up by one of the last bottles of '08 claret on the premises
and the prospect of a vintage port was looming. He lit up one of the
cigarettes he still bought in batches of a thousand from the Mayfair
tobacconist.

'Well, you're not going to tell me Daniel was a woman,' he began.
'Not after what his nibs said tonight.' Ponting was a bit drunk, his
normal tolerance for alcohol eroded by his cold perhaps. It made
him willing enough to play the buffoon a bit, always a good ploy
with his old boss because he could rarely resist showing off.

'Why not?' said Meinertzhagen, resisting the temptation to add
that he might not necessarily tell him anything. 'Sarah Aaronsohn
was a woman. Nurse Cavell was a woman. So, for that matter, was
Mata Hari.'

'Yes, but the quality of Daniel's stuff. That sort of thing could
only have come from somebody very close.'

'Or somebody close to somebody very close,' smiled Meinertzhagen, who was thoroughly enjoying himself.

'Are you saying Daniel was that Syrian woman – Shemsi? I find that difficult to believe. Why would she do it? How on earth did we get hold of her?'

'I didn't say anything of the sort, but you shouldn't exclude her just because she's a woman. She had the opportunity and she had the motive. You remember the things she told us about herself once our learned friends from the Arab Bureau had tired of her.'

'Do you mean that tale about being forced to marry an elderly Turkish officer in order to save her little brother's neck? I never knew what to make of that.'

'It was true. I got a French friend to make some inquiries in Beirut after the Armistice,' said Meinertzhagen. 'It all seemed to have happened the way she told it. The same with that journalist – what was his name? Maeltzer! He confirmed that she did leave him the hatpin just as she told us she did. And that saved his life, didn't it? That and the fact that he was at least nominally a Swiss. My God, only the Turks would want to hang a Swiss in the middle of a world war. Even the Germans made sure he was released and safely hidden away just in case Djemal Pasha decided to have a final necktie party before we came in. Anyway, she certainly did him a favour. Did you know, by the way, that he has become a Zionist and is living in Haifa?'

'No, I didn't,' said Ponting who hadn't the faintest interest in this late rallier to the Herzl doctrine. 'But if Shemsi was Daniel, surely our smart friends in the Arab Bureau wouldn't have thrown her back as if we had just netted a dead sprat? They'd have looked after her themselves. Besides, I don't believe she was a killer. When we got to Jerusalem and discovered Maeltzer he told us all about that Swedish Holy Joe who was murdered. What was his name?'

'Magnus.'

'Yes, Magnus. Well, it seems to me that Magnus was definitely the link between Daniel and Nili, the cut-out through the old Jew Smolenskin between our best placed spy and the courier network –'

'Smolenskin was almost as lucky as Maeltzer,' interrupted Meinertzhagen. 'He's still going strong, you know, forever ranting on about the trouble that Swedish madman had got him into. He was trying to get a pension out of us just before I left on the grounds that he had been an unwitting servant of the Crown.'

'We're probably lucky the Swede's relatives aren't demanding some sort of compensation too,' said Ponting, determined to stick to the main issue. 'I've no doubt that he was bumped off by Daniel when things got too hot.'

'You're surely not suggesting that agents of the Crown go around

336

murdering neutral civilians, are you?' It was difficult to tell whether Meinertzhagen was teasing or not.

'Oh, only in the direst cases,' grinned Ponting. 'Anyway, I don't believe she was capable of it. Not with a bayonet. And apparently he was a big chap.'

'You may have a point there,' conceded Meinertzhagen, which only added to Ponting's frustration. He didn't want to be told he had a point. He wanted it confirmed that Krag was Daniel and this Shemsi nonsense was a smokescreen, a last attempt to give their agent some cover probably concocted by Meinertzhagen himself. It certainly had his touch.

Yet it was true enough. At first the Bureau could not get enough of Shemsi. They had hardly got her back to their field headquarters at Deir el Belah before GHQ was screaming for her to be sent to them. Meinertzhagen had escorted her personally. Then three weeks later, just before they captured Jerusalem, Ponting had been called back to Cairo from a rain-swept advance intelligence HQ in the Wadi Surar, specifically to show Shemsi Krag's grave in Alexandria.

It had been an odd affair and one that still irritated Ponting. What really rankled with him was that he might have been the dupe for another one of Meinertzhagen's grand deceptions. He might raise that strange encounter with the nurse.

Most of the wounded had been taken to Alexandria by hospital ship from Gaza because it was thought preferable to a long road journey across the desert to Cairo. For reasons that remained a mystery as far as Ponting was concerned, Shemsi had not been allowed to visit Krag there. In fact, her last sighting of the German officer had been, like his own, as he was loaded into the ambulance at Huj. Even worse, a few days before she had been told that Krag was mending well, so the news of his death – apparently there had been a devastating nocturnal haemorrhage – must have come as an even greater blow.

Ponting had picked her up at a hotel in Zamalek where she had been moved from the padre's quarters at Kasr-el-Nil barracks, having evidently convinced people that she had been genuinely trapped with Kress's rearguard and was not some daring stay-behind agent. The hotel was probably cleaner than the Grand New, but the Greek management was less obliging for a lady who had been billeted on them at a rate decided by the British army. It was the kind of place that, before the war, had been favoured by less successful Levantine commercials, who drank arak and left small but frequent tips.

'I would prefer Kasr-el-Nil with cold porridge and prayers for breakfast to this place' was how she had greeted his cautious 'Bonjour Madame' when he had helped her into the back of the car that was to take them to the Alexandria train.

'Something wrong?'

'This morning there was no coffee – only that muddy Indian tea you English like so much.'

Ponting had feared that she would go on in this vein throughout the journey, but after that she was silent unless he spoke to her and then responded with great economy. They had a first-class compartment to themselves on the train to Alex and spent their journey staring out at a flat, monotonous vista, broken only by glimpses of the fellaheen and their oxen. Once the line ran alongside a canal where a few grey-haired workmen, too old for the Labour Corps, were loading lumps of gold-coloured stone onto a barge.

She had on new clothes, a lace-trimmed blue dress which was perhaps a little on the tight side, and another broad-brimmed straw hat. Over this she wore a white scarf which she had tied under her chin as if she had expected to motor all the way to Alex. The hat and scarf had made Ponting sad because it had reminded him of Sarah Aaronsohn being brought out to the monitor by the Arab fishermen at Athlit.

'Of course, after the Bureau had finished with her you took her to see Krag's grave, didn't you?' said Meinertzhagen – a rhetorical question, since he was the one who had sent him.

'Yes,' said Ponting. 'At least I think I did.'

'Think! Don't tell me you're having trouble with the old memory box. I remember signing the rail warrants.'

'I've never been totally certain in my own mind whether that was a grave or not.'

Ponting remembered a fresh mound of reddish earth and a rough wooden cross on which was written in black paint 'Major Erwin Krag – German forces – died of wounds, 2 December 1917.' It lay next to the graves of two Kriegsmarine who had been washed ashore from their rammed U-boat.

'What makes you say that?'

'Why was she never allowed to visit him in hospital?'

'As I recall it, that was due to a combination of things. Firstly she was being interrogated; secondly he was very ill; and thirdly – well thirdly, he didn't want to see her anyway.'

'He told you that?'

'Myself and other people.'

'But why? She told us he had proposed marriage to her just a few hours before they were captured.'

'I dunno,' chirped Meinertzhagen. 'Perhaps he felt he no longer needed her. I don't ever remember him speaking of her with what one might have perceived as love. It was more a kind of cynical affection – almost the sort of feelings you might have for an old enemy, really.'

Ponting thought about the way Shemsi had stood at the grave, dry-eyed, not displaying any grief. All she had said was, 'He was a strange man. I never really knew him.'

It was not long afterwards that the Australian nurse, plump and bouncy, had wandered by in her overall. She had stopped alongside them, obviously assuming they could have no reason to be drawn to that particular spot other than idle curiosity. 'Do you think Fritz does the same for our boys, sir?' she had asked conversationally.

'Oh I should think so.'

'Funny thing about this last bloke, you know. None of us saw it happen.'

'Saw what happen?'

'Saw the burial. I mean one day there were two Jerries here and the next there were three. They must have done it in the middle of the night if you ask me. With the other two there was a navy chaplain and some sailors to lower the coffins. We were quite surprised. We thought they would have thrown U-boaters back to the crabs.'

Shemsi had not appeared to understand a word of this exchange. Ponting himself, thoroughly irritated by the nurse's intervention and anxious to be rid of her, had not attached much importance to it at the time. It was not until they were on the train heading back to Cairo, with the warm night air blowing in through the window and his charge feigning sleep opposite him, her hat alongside her, that it came back to him. Then, as his mind ranged over the whole strange business of this woman and the man she had slept with but couldn't weep for, the nurse's words sowed the doubts that had remained with him for over four years. 'None of us saw it happen.' Perhaps they didn't see it happen because it hadn't happened.

'He's alive, isn't he?' Ponting asked, sipping his second glass of port. He was getting too fond of port. Have to watch it.

'Who?'

'Daniel – Krag.'

'You know, you really are full of wild stories tonight, old chap,' beamed Meinertzhagen. 'It must be because you're almost a civilian. You saw his grave. It *was* his grave.'

'I've also heard about a note from one staff officer to another complaining about Allenby's stupidity because he insisted that the next offensive should be at Gaza again.'

'Ah well, I see there's no convincing you,' grinned Meinertzhagen, who did not in the least mind being reminded of his greatest coup. 'Where's your Christian charity? Give a chap a bad name and you never believe a word he says again. I don't know what we can do to put your mind at rest. I suppose you could always write to the Bull and ask him if you could exhume the poor fellow. Might be worth a try.'

Ponting knew when he was beaten. Once Meinertzhagen got into one of these bantering moods he could keep it up all night. He lit another cigarette.

'Personally, I've always thought Daniel was a bit over-rated,' his tormentor went on, apparently quite forgetting that he had once told Ponting the spy was worth three divisions. 'If Kress had had a bigger army that was likely to take the offensive it might have been different. As it was, all they could do was sit and wait for us to attack. Our general was very flattering just now, but I think Allenby's biggest help, as far as the Beersheba battle was concerned, came from Aaron Aaronsohn. He told us where we could find the old wells that would enable us to move the cavalry over to the right. Everybody else said it was impossible. Well, most people did. He's a great loss to the Yishuv, that chap.'

Aaronsohn had disappeared two winters ago when the Handley Page taking him to the peace conference at Versailles had crashed into the Channel. Through Lawrence he had grown friendly with Faisal, who thought the Zionists would contribute ideas and money to the newly independent Arab lands.

'Yes,' said Ponting, who was beginning to feel his cough coming on again and was desperately trying to signal a waiter for a carafe of water. 'Rotten luck. Rotten luck for the whole family, especially after what happened to Sarah. But the Nili group did bring us some good stuff from Daniel. It certainly didn't hurt us to know about what they were planning even if they never did get the wherewithal to bring it off. And if we hadn't known how weak they were they could have bluffed us more easily.'

'Oh yes, Daniel was useful, very useful. I'm not denying it. But all this stuff about Allenby knowing every card the enemy had in his hands is ridiculous. If that had been the case we should have been in Jerusalem six days after Beersheba instead of six weeks. Cigar?'

'No thanks,' gasped Ponting who had just put out his fifth cigarette since dinner. He began this terrible dry cough which went on for almost a minute.

'My dear fellow!' said Meinertzhagen, 'You really ought to watch that.'

EPILOGUE

*L*ife is not a tidy business, and one of the reasons for its loose ends is that people are unpredictable, even to themselves. The good and the bad are usually the same people at different times. Meek men murder. Cruel men are kind. Honourable men act dishonourably. And courage is often proved a finite thing. A man may be brave as a lion one day and yet fail to summon even that minimum of nerve that might ensure his own survival the next.

On 26 May 1918 Private Walter Calderwell was aboard the trooper *Leasowe Castle* which was taking the Warwickshire Yeomanry to France where, to their almost unanimous disgust, they were to serve in an infantry role as machine-gunners. There were over one thousand soldiers aboard for, besides the heroes of Huj, there was another dismounted Yeomanry unit, the South Nottinghamshire Hussars. Twenty-five minutes past midnight and about one hundred miles out of Alexandria the trooper was torpedoed on her starboard side, a little forward of amidships.

There were few initial casualties, mainly because the soldiers had been ordered to sleep on deck in those submarine-infested waters. Nor was there much panic, although Calderwell was by no means the only Midlander aboard who had never learned to swim, despite the beach camp days before Beersheba.

It was a warm, moonlit night and the *Leasowe Castle* took ninety-five minutes to sink. The remaining five transports in the convoy steamed on but a Japanese destroyer circled the stricken vessel in

343

case the U-boat should be tempted to return and put an end to this orderly abandoning of ship.

Most of the Yeomanry escaped in the lifeboats wearing cork lifejackets. The majority still carried their rifles although they were ordered to dump their packs because they took up too much room. There were not quite enough boats to go round. Some, perhaps two or three hundred, were expected to jump in after life rafts that had been tossed into the water. Calderwell and Mace found themselves in this group, and stood at the handrail for some time contemplating the dappled surface almost thirty feet below them. Dark shadows indicated occupied rafts and beyond them loitered the long boats. Neither of them fancied it much.

A second lieutenant of about the same age as Calderwell, who had come out a couple of months before to replace one of the Huj casualties, assured them that they would 'pop up like corks'. To prove the point he removed his riding boots, climbed over the hand-rail and, holding his nose with his right hand, jumped in with all the elan of a small boy determined to make the biggest splash. They looked over but a cloud had temporarily struck out most of the moon, and although the splash was impressive they could not be certain whether he had popped or not.

Shortly after this they saw a signal lamp flickering in the darkness and watched the sailors who were still on the bridge make a reply. Much to their relief they were told that there was to be no more jumping over because the Royal Navy was coming alongside to pick them up. Mace wanted to take the young officer's riding-boots but they were much too small. Disgusted, he threw them overboard together with his own footwear.

His Majesty's sloop *Lilly* came up alongside the starboard bow of the *Leasowe Castle*, and by 1.45 a.m. had thrown up a line and made fast. A sailor stood at the end of the rope with an axe ready to cut it if the *Leasowe Castle* should suddenly go down. She was settling gently by the stern with a list to port that was getting more pronounced by the minute. On the bridge Captain Holt told Colonel Gray-Cheape and his adjutant, Captain Drake, that they would best think about leaving. The officers assured him that they would not leave until the last of their men were off.

The remaining soldiers began to jump down onto the deck of the sloop, some of them delivering kitbags laden with the treasures of the Cairo souk first. It was a bit tricky because the port side of the stern was now completely under water and as the list became more pronounced so the trooper's bows rose. The *Lilly* was at least fifteen feet below them and bobbing on the slight swell that had come up.

Every few seconds, despite the line linking it to the bigger ship, the gap between the two vessels widened.

Mace went before Calderwell, sliding across the wooden deck on his back as his bare feet failed to find the purchase that would have been provided by seventeen studs on each boot. A couple of sailors helped him to his feet and he looked back up to the big ship where his mate was standing by the rail.

Calderwell had already thrown his kitbag and rifle down onto the *Lilly*. Now he gripped the handrail and stared down after them. The ship lurched a little more to port and the bow rose by another foot. He tightened his grip.

'C'mon, lad,' said a sergeant from the South Notts. 'You're holding everybody up.'

Calderwell put one leg over and looked down. For a moment the moon once again slid behind a cloud and he could hardly make out the sloop – which, according to practice, was not showing any lights in U-boat waters. Then it came into view again – the drop now was almost the height of a Coventry terrace. He started to bring his other leg over the rail but at that moment the *Leasowe Castle* gave a sudden lurch and he tightened his grip on the rail, terrified that he might be cast into that darkness before he was ready for it.

'C'mon, Caldy,' shouted Mace, who was still standing among the sloop's reception committee. Calderwell looked down and saw the white faces looking up at him. His legs felt like jelly. The idea of launching himself into that space was horrific.

'C'mon, man!' This time it was an officer's voice, stern and a trifle impatient.

'If you can't shit get off the pot,' muttered the sergeant.

'C'mon, Caldy – jump!' said Mace.

'I can't,' said Calderwell. Somehow the admission gave him an enormous sense of relief. He climbed back across the rail, careful not to let go until both feet were safely the other side.

The sergeant put a fatherly arm around his shoulders although he was probably less than ten years older. 'Have another go in a minute,' he said.

Calderwell nodded – but he knew he wouldn't.

There was a kind of muffled explosion from somewhere below them.

'Bulkhead's gone,' said the sailor who had attached the line the Royal Navy had thrown up. Without more ado he jumped onto the deck of the sloop, just as the leading seaman with the axe severed *Lilly*'s link with the sinking trooper.

The *Leasowe Castle* gave the kind of shudder she had made when the torpedo first struck her and then slid gracefully, stern first, into the soup-warm Mediterranean, beginning to capsize as she did so.

Calderwell, lying full-length on the deck, gripped the rail with both hands. He was certain – almost certain – that this was a temporary state of affairs and that the ship would soon right herself. He supposed ships were like horses – you just had to be patient with the buggers, outlast 'em. Even as the warm waters welcomed him he promised himself that next time he would jump. He really couldn't go on making a bloody fool of himself in front of Mace.

———————

Joseph Lishansky, Sarah Aaronsohn's monocled friend and possibly her lover, was captured by the Turks and died bravely in an execution gown on a tripod and chair gallows in Damascus on 8 December 1917. A photograph of him hanging there is on display at the Nili group museum in the Aaronsohn's old house at Zichron Jacob, which is now a middle-class ghetto occupied by the kind of liberal-minded professionals who seem increasingly at odds with the contemporary Israeli ethos.

It is not certain how many other secret admirers Sarah Aaronsohn had other than the boy who grew up with the Druse. Lawrence dedicated *The Seven Pillars of Wisdom*, his account of the desert war, to 'SA', above four verses of his only published poetry. The second verse reads:

> Death seemed my servant on the road, till we were near
> and saw you waiting:
> When you smiled, and in sorrowful envy he outran me
> and took you apart: Into his quietness.

Lawrence experts have been arguing for years about the identity of 'SA', and the Sarah Aaronsohn theory has been put up and shot down on the grounds that Lawrence was either totally homosexual or a masochistic celibate who hired a young Scot to birch desire out of his bare backside. One theory is that 'SA' was a teenaged Arab boy called Dahoum, nicknamed 'Sheik Ahmed', with whom Lawrence lived in 1913 when he was part of the British Museum's archaeological team working on the excavation at Carchemish, some sixty miles north of Aleppo. The expedition is thought to have provided cover for British Intelligence to observe the progress of the Berlin-Baghdad railway at the point of its greatest vulnerability, the bridge across the Euphrates.

But Lawrence is known to have had affectionate relationships with women; as a young man he had even proposed marriage to a family friend called Janet Laurie who laughed it off. Perhaps, like many young homosexuals in a far less tolerant age, he hoped that the right female might one day come along who would 'put him right'.

He went to Cairo several times between June and September 1917 and Sarah Aaronsohn is known to have made a visit to Cairo that July and returned to Palestine. Sarah Aaronsohn did shoot herself with a pistol that was small enough to be concealed from her Turkish captors, but it has never been recovered since they took it with them. Nor was Lawrence the 'anti-Zionist' of popular imagination. Like many of his Arab friends he thought the Jews' money, energy and cleverness would help develop the new Arab nations. In 1919 only the Palestinian Arabs, whose land the Jews were moving into, were beginning to demur. Lawrence died in the spring of 1935 as a result of a motorcycle crash without ever revealing the identity of 'SA'.

Before the Turks kicked the chair away Lishansky's last words are reputed to have been, 'Long live the English Redeemers'. He was executed the day before General Shea and his Cockney territorials accepted the surrender of Jerusalem from the mayor, who approached the British waving a white bed-sheet he had borrowed from Mrs Vester at the American Colony. This official had previously tried to persuade two foraging cooks to accept the keys to the city but they had declined on the grounds that they were merely searching for eggs for their officers.

———————

The Bavarian aristocrat Kress von Kressenstein survived the war and wrote a boring book about the Palestine campaign, devoted to complaints about Turkish logistics, particularly the railways. A much better book was written by Archie Wavell, the same Wavell whom Ponting had sat next to at the makeshift officers' mess at Beersheba the night before the charge at Huj. In *The Palestine Campaign* Wavell, who ended his career as a field marshal and Viceroy of India, mentions the effectiveness of the Entente's Intelligence services.

To his great disgust, and mainly due to a clerical error, Weidinger, the incipient Nazi and disciple of the *arme blanche*, was released from British internment in the late summer of 1918. He was part of a Red Cross-sponsored exchange of officer prisoners considered so badly crippled they were unlikely to be of any further military use. In fact, in the confusion of the last three months of the war, when the dizzy hopes raised by Ludendorff's spring offensive were dashed

347

and followed by a terrible autumn of humiliating retreat, he managed to wangle a job as a horse procurement officer. This was a thankless task, because the British naval blockade had made horsemeat a highly-valued substitute for Argentinian beef. But it did keep Weidinger on the active list, and to him that was all that mattered.

After the armistice he returned to his parents' home in Berlin. Along with some other young ex-officers in threadbare uniforms he learned that the greatest army the world had ever known had been stabbed in the back by the Jews and the Bolsheviks. Weidinger sometimes told his new friends about the Jewish journalist who had betrayed them – for he preferred this story to revelations of misconduct on the part of a brother-officer, however much he detested him. After all, Krag had died of wounds incurred fighting Allenby's cavalry. He often wondered what had become of Shemsi, and was thinking of writing to the management of Fast's Hotel to see whether they had heard anything of her when he died in the great influenza epidemic of 1919.

Franz von Papen went on to hold high office. After the war he entered the Reichstag as a member of a centre Roman Catholic party and for six chaotic months he was the last Chancellor of Germany before Hitler was elected in January 1933. Von Papen, the great trimmer, then agreed to become Vice Chancellor, telling people that he would be a moderating influence.

Most of his friends were murdered by the Nazis, but for some reason the Führer spared him and he was sent abroad. He spent four years as ambassador to Austria, becoming redundant when, to the unbounded joy of most Austrians, the Nazis subsumed their country into the Reich in the Anschluss of 1938. For most of the Second World War he was ambassador to Turkey, where he was able to renew his acquaintance with its ruler, Mustafa Kemal, who had decreed that Turks should adopt the Christian European system of surnames and declared his own to be Ataturk.

Towards the end of the war von Papen put out some peace feelers to the Allies, which would have cost him his life had Hitler discovered it. In 1945, to his utter astonishment, a denazification court sentenced him to eight years in a labour camp, but he was released after three. In 1952 he published his memoirs. Like Kress, he made no mention of the Daniel Affair and his large part in saving the life of an innocent man.

This was probably out of sheer embarrassment. For Maeltzer, whose wartime experiences had converted him from a confidently assimilated Jew to a raging Zionist and resident of Haifa, chose in later life to be quite ambiguous about whether or not he had been involved with the Nili group. Indeed, shortly before his death at the age of eighty in 1954 he gave an interview to a Hebrew newspaper which glossed over the question of whether he had been rightly or wrongly accused, but concentrated instead on his extraordinary escape from the noose with the help of a hatpin left by a woman friend, whom he declined to name. The reporter put this down to some sort of old-world regard for a lady's reputation. The truth of the matter was that Maeltzer could never be certain in his own mind whether Shemsi had dropped the pin intentionally.

More important from von Papen's point of view was that, for a brief period in the late Thirties, Maeltzer was not unknown to the Nazis. The journalist discovered that there was at this time a tremendous appetite in the National Socialist press for articles extolling Palestine as a solution to the Jewish question, the soil where a new breed of muscular Jew had taken root. They were even better received if they also attacked the British for betraying their promise to International Jewry by imposing immigration restrictions. In this respect Maeltzer made a trip to Zichron Jacob which, from a journalistic point of view, was particularly rewarding. He often started feature pieces with his visit to Sarah Aaronsohn's grave, which was shaded by a young oak in the settlement's well-kept cemetery there. Later a large stone was placed nearby to commemorate her brother Aaron, whose remains were in the English Channel.

Maeltzer married late, at the age of fifty-two, a fortyish widow. She was a Greek Jewess from Salonika called Sarah who was staying with friends in Haifa with her two small daughters and son. A slim, high cheek-boned woman, who looked a little like Shemsi, she bore him a son. His mother wanted to call him Benjamin, which was appropriate, but Maeltzer insisted on Jacob after his father.

Jacob grew up to fight in the Israeli-Arab wars of 1948, 1956 and 1967. During the 1973 conflict, which the Israelis called the Yom Kippur, he was among a group of reserve officers, all of them captains or above, based at Beersheba. Because of their language abilities (Jacob speaks fluent German and Greek and passable English) they were given the thankless task of escorting visiting foreign war correspondents around the Sinai front.

On one trip the journalists included a young British photographer called Mace, who said that an uncle of his had fought in the area during the First World War, whom he described as a 'horse soldier'. It was only then that Jacob himself remembered that this latest blood-letting was being played out on the forgotten battlefields his own father had once reported on.

As they drove south towards the sound of guns, past incinerated tanks crewed by stick-men made of brittle charcoal, and under a sky vandalised by the doodles of vapour trails, Mace had his travelling companions rocking with laughter when he told them that he thought somewhere close by his uncle had chased Turks with a sword. They examined their maps but nobody could find Huj in a land where Arab place names have often been changed to Hebrew ones. The actual site of the Yeomanry charge probably lies somewhere between the Jewish settlements of Nir'am and Gevim in the citrus-growing area just north of the Gaza strip, about ten miles south-east of the resort town of Ashqelon.

Between his military engagements Jacob trained as an architect, married twice, fathered three sons, established a successful practice in Tel Aviv and moved into a large house near the beach at Herzliya with bougainvillea vines on the walls and a grape trellis in the back yard. His youngest son served as a sergeant in a mobile artillery unit during the Israeli siege of West Beirut in 1982. He was among a number of young soldiers who disapproved of the war, and when Israel's Christian Lebanese allies massacred Palestinian civilians in the slum shanties of Sabra and Chatilla he participated in the huge 'Peace Now' demonstration in Tel Aviv which demanded withdrawal from Lebanon and a settlement with the Palestinians. Once he had completed his military service he left Israel and joined the growing colony of Israelis living in New York. When last heard of, Maeltzer's grandson was trying to make a living as a freelance journalist.

Among the Beirutis who were shelled in the summer of 1982 was Shemsi. She was dying at the age of ninety-six, on a bed in a corner of the basement car park of an apartment block near the Corniche. She was surrounded by neighbours, friends and relatives, including several nephews and nieces and their offspring, who had also taken shelter there. After the First World War Shemsi went to live with her brother in California, but in 1931 she returned to Beirut, then part of the French Mandate of Syria, to look after her sick mother. She never married again or ever, as far as can be ascertained, talked about Krag.

Despite the nationalist traditions in her family she became a firm francophile, and after the collapse of France in 1940 she seemed to be a staunch supporter of the pro-Axis Vichy government which Petain established in the Lebanon. Over the years her dress sense improved and she remained a slim, elegant woman well into late middle age. She became on intimate terms with several middle-ranking French officers and is reputed to have had her last affair at the age of fifty-five with a tubby little colonel of ordnance who had risen from the ranks.

Friends and relatives were therefore quite amazed when, in 1941, within weeks of the British victory over the Vichy forces and the occupation of Beirut, she should have found a job as an interpreter in the occupiers' headquarters. She shrugged this off with the explanation that times were hard and it was a pity to waste the English she had acquired in California.

During the Lebanese civil war she remained, like many other Christians, in the predominantly Muslim western half of the city. On her deathbed the sound of the Israeli guns might have taken her mind back to Huj, for she spoke some words in German, but nobody could understand what she was saying. When one of her nieces ventured upstairs to her apartment to go through her things she found an old cigarette case with a hole in the middle. Its contents, when she could eventually get it open, were green with mould. She could not think what had possessed her aunt to keep such tat and threw it away.

The success of Allenby's cavalry in Palestine – the charges at Beersheba and Huj being its high points – eventually did the British army a grave disservice. It gave weight to the reactionaries who, between the wars, argued against total mechanisation and insisted there would always be a place for horses. Imagine the astonishment of Isaiah Mace therefore – once again a private, but this time in the newly-raised Home Guard – when he opened his newspaper in Henley-in-Arden one morning in 1941. Among the reports of the latest carnage wreaked by the Luftwaffe and of tank battles in the Western Desert was a photograph of his old regiment back in Palestine, and still on horseback. Later that year the Warwickshire Yeomanry, sent there to replace regular troops used for internal security, were one of the last regiments in the British army to give up their horses. They finished their war manning Sherman tanks in Italy.

Meinertzhagen's military career never recovered from his uncritical support of the Zionist cause. Allenby sacked him from his postwar job as Political Officer in Palestine, and he left the army altogether in 1925, having married four years previously. In the Second World War he served, like Mace, in the Home Guard.

In his published diaries he claims to have fired his last shots in anger on behalf of the fledgling Jewish state, when the British were withdrawing from Palestine in 1948. According to Meinertzhagen, who would then have been aged seventy, he bribed a British soldier into lending him his uniform and rifle and fought with a British rearguard that had become embroiled with the Arabs around Jaffa.

However, some of his diary entries probably need to be treated with caution. For instance, he writes that when he returned to England from Palestine in 1921 he had with him a large stock of the opium-laced cigarettes Allenby forbade him to use. These, he claims, he used to offer to loquacious and unsuspecting fellow-passengers on the railways, with the result that they invariably fell asleep. It is a good story, but it is unlikely, to say the least, that the amount of opium which could be introduced undetected into a single cigarette could achieve this. Meinertzhagen died on 17 June 1967, a few days after the Israelis had occupied the West Bank of the Jordan and all of the Sinai following their stupendous victory in the Six-Day War. It was also before the nature of the Jewish state had changed to the point where many of the old Zionists would not recognise it.

Ponting's job with his first merchant bank did not last long. Nor did the one after that, or the one after that. Sooner or later Ponting would always turn up at that crucial meeting just a little slurred, a little loud, often quite funny at first, and then he would say the wrong thing or, on one memorable occasion, nothing at all, having collapsed on arrival. Each time he would swear it was the last, hurl the offending bottle from desk drawer to waste-paper basket, and dictate a solemn letter of resignation to the membership secretary of his club. Some employers were more patient than others. All, in the end, reached the same decision.

In 1936, after a messy divorce for which he was not entirely to blame, an old army chum who also knew Meinertzhagen offered him a job in Johannesburg selling insurance. He pointed out that the pay would not be marvellous but that the climate would help what was left of his lungs. He didn't mention the drink. The friend knew Ponting's problem and he made his offer with his eyes open. Besides, he drank himself. It worked out. Ponting still went on benders but as he got older his dry spells got longer. And if his health didn't improve, at least it didn't get worse.

Twice a year he was required to visit Windhoek, the capital of what, until 1918, had been Germany's colony in South West Africa, and later became a League of Nations territory mandated to the Union of South Africa. It was here, some forty years before, that the German army had all but wiped out the Herero tribe in a campaign that had caught the imagination of young officer cadets like Krag.

Windhoek was still, despite a growing Afrikaaner population, a very German place. German was the native tongue of most of the white community. Its newspapers were in German, with stirring Gothic mastheads. Bronze memorials commemorated the deeds of the Imperial Army. The best hotel in town was called the Kaiser Wilhelm. The streets had German names. In 1938 there was a strong Nazi element, and its blond youth were full of blood and iron.

Ponting had mixed feelings about the place. It was true there was this dark, worrying side. There were troops of 'boy scouts' who rambled in step, and even whistled the 'Horst Wessel Lied' when they thought they could get away with it. There were newspaper editorials that obliquely equated the case for the Sudetenland with other 'lost territories'. There were shopkeepers who somehow never heard English.

Yet in some ways it was a refreshing change from Johannesburg. It was about a tenth the size but more prosperous looking. The beer was sharper, the streets cleaner. Jolly Bavarian bands played outside open-air cafés. Its Lutheran churches were much more solid-looking than the shacks of the Dutch Reformed Church and even made Anglican Gothic appear whimsical. The whites were generally better-looking and there was a nicer class of whore, most of them mixed-race Afrikaans-speaking Coloureds from a little dorp called Rehoboth, who called themselves the Basters. And because it was so far away from Johannesburg, once the small amount of business on hand had been dealt with it was a bender town as far as Ponting was concerned.

He usually ended his night having a few cleansing beers in one of the mud-walled bars behind the railway station where there was no electricity and the candles and the oil lamps lit up the faces of the Baster whores, so they looked as though they might have been painted by Rembrandt. In the autumn of 1938, at about the time of the Munich crisis, when the bands seemed to be playing louder than ever before, Ponting entered such a bar and saw Krag standing alone at the end of it. He recognised him instantly despite the white hair, the features creased by time and sun, the civilian linen jacket and the open-neck shirt over a frame that was as lean as ever.

As far as Ponting was concerned the immediate effect was to sober him up. He sipped his drink, lit a cigarette, coughed, and ignored the young woman who came up and mechanically asked for 'Just-one-beer, man.' The girl went away. Krag had a bottle of brandy by him and was drinking it from a whisky glass. After a while, he became conscious of Ponting's stare, gave him a brief glance and then looked away.

'Don't we know each other?' asked Ponting.

By way of reply Krag poured himself another drink.

'In Palestine?'

The German turned. 'You were in Palestine?' he said in English.

'Yes. I was in Palestine. I was at Huj. You remember Huj? You were wounded.' Ponting had this urge to pull his shirt away and reveal the purple scar he knew would be there.

'Huj?'

'Yes, Huj. I was a staff officer with Meinertzhagen.'

'A staff officer with Meinertzhagen.' Krag scratched his head, drank his drink, poured another. 'One of the English Redeemers? The Redeemers of Zion?'

'My name's Ponting, Major Ponting. And you're Major Krag, Erwin Krag.'

'Er-win Krag,' the man repeated. 'Er-win Krag.' He sounded as though he was trying it out for size.

'That's right.'

'Excuse me a moment.' He nodded towards the Afrikaner barman who nodded back. The brandy bottle was almost empty.

Ponting lit another cigarette and ordered another beer. A different girl came up. 'Just-one-beer, baas.' He told her he was busy, perhaps later. He noticed his own beer was almost finished and asked for another one. When the barman came back he said, 'He's a long time.'

'Who?'

'The gentleman I was talking to.'

'I don't think he's coming back,' he said. 'Not tonight.'

'Why not?'

He shrugged. 'I don't think he likes talking. Not the sociable sort.'

'But he hasn't paid for his drink yet.'

'He has. He always buys a full bottle at the beginning of the evening.' The barman put the top back on the brandy and placed it on the shelf behind him. 'He'll finish it next time.'

'How often do you see him?'

'About once a month.'

'And he always drinks alone.'

'Not always.' He nodded towards the girls.

Ponting waited another hour, perhaps two, but Krag did not return. The barman said that the German managed a farm a hundred kilometres or so out of town, and he had heard he was soft on his kaffirs. He said he didn't know his name. The girls called him 'Baas'. They called all white men 'Baas'.

It was almost dawn when Ponting left the bar and by then all the young ladies had given up on him and were asleep, head down, at their tables. Back in his hotel an African woke him with coffee at 11 a.m., sent for the barber to shave him (for Ponting was still careful about his appearance) and helped get his things together. It was

354

something they had done before, and the tip was always generous. Ponting had to get the noon express to Johannesburg. An air service had started but he liked aircraft no more than he had liked those wallowing monitors off Athlit.

He sat in the restaurant car, drenched in sweat, trying to drown his hangover with more beer. It was Krag. It had to be. If it wasn't Krag why did he run away? Could he have been mistaken? How long was it? Twenty-one years in a couple of months. And he had only seen him once. Couldn't it just have been some Hans Nobody who didn't much feel like a conversation with a drunken English stranger about Palestine?

But what had he said? 'One of the English Redeemers? The Redeemers of Zion?' That's what the Nili group and the other Zionists had called the British. Not many people knew that. But then the campaign had been written about from time to time. And a lot of Germans knew about Palestine. It was all part of this thing they had about the Jews.

It would be at least six months before he could get back to Windhoek. In the meantime he wrote a light-hearted note to Meinertzhagen asking him to confirm that he had been seeing things. His old boss was away on one of his ornithological expeditions when it arrived and it was two months before he telegraphed a reply. It read: ALL THAT GLITTERS IS NOT GOLD.

Ponting was quite pleased with it. He was right, of course. It probably wasn't Krag, just some deeply perplexed German who had dredged up that bit about 'English Redeemers' from the depths of his own drunkenness. He really had to watch it. It wouldn't do to go on bothering complete strangers in bars like this. And, to his own and everybody else's amazement, he never took an alcoholic drink from that day forth.

However, the tobacco habit was harder to kick. Ponting died in 1953 aged sixty-eight of lung cancer in Port Elizabeth, where he had made enough money to retire three years earlier.

Four years later Meinertzhagen was made a Commander of the British Empire, an honour often given to retiring desk officers of the Secret Intelligence Service (MI6), although he does not appear to have done anything on behalf of his country since the Home Guard was stood down. Most of his latter years were spent writing various volumes of memoirs, usually in journal form. He never mentioned Daniel.